YOUNGER DRYAS

Cover photo by Sean Thoman (@sthomanns)

Younger Dryas

THE SPIRITED QUEST OF A PERUVIAN HUNTER-GATHERER

Michael McKay

Based on real events documented by Graham Hancock in his books: Fingerprints of the Gods, Magicians of the Gods and America Before.

1

SUMMER. 10,817 BC.

GANUNG PADANG. INDONESIA.

Before I met Jung, the hero of this story, I worked as a one stripe Uzman for the Viracocha.

The door squeaked as it opened. The buzz of cicadas heightened to a roar. I smelled cookfires and heard distant voices—the Fects laughing and joking from down on the shore.

I stepped out of the yurt into the milky starlight. Earth's Rock sat high in the sky, round and full like the belly of a pregnant woman. In front of me was a forested hill. Above the tangle of vegetation was the pyramid, standing more than 50 men high. The white faces appeared to levitate above the ground.

Suddenly crunching sounds came from the brush, followed by snorting.

Two elephants appeared from the thick. They were heavily armored—wooden plates with one-foot spikes were fastened to their front legs and heads. The creatures had crossbows hanging from each of their sides. It was said the weapons were so powerful, one arrow could kill five men standing in a line. The bows were controlled from the passenger cabs tied to the backs of the elephants. The cabs were made from the same bamboo posts that secured the crossbows. Sheets of spider web fibre were stretched between the posts to create walls. The material was said to be impenetrable to any weapon.

The elephants walked up to me and stopped. They stared at me with black eyes, their ears twitching in the breeze like fat meaty sails.

I smelled dung and honey.

A flap on one of the cabs opened and a man with skin as fair as mine climbed out and dropped onto the sand. He wore a grubby sleeveless garment, which seemed oversized in every way. He was clearly a combat man. It wasn't just his enormous size and spear that gave away his role—it was the giant c-shape scar starting at his chest and ending at his stomach. *C* for *combat man.* The mark of the Fect.

"Can I help you?" I said.

"Where's the girl?" he said.

Like most combat men he approached with intention, shoulders drawn back, chest puffed out. He had a chiseled chin, brown eyes and blonde hair to his shoulders. He was handsome despite his crooked nose, which looked to have been broken at some point and left to mend on its own.

He aimed his fire torch at me. "Where is she?"

I felt the heat on my skin, even through the thickness of my beard. I shielded the light with my hand. "She's not here."

He pulled the torch away. "Where? If not here, where?"

"She's fetching water."

He took a step toward me and ripped my hood from my face.

I brushed my gray fringe from my forehead.

He craned his neck so his eyes were in line with mine. The skin beneath one of his eyes twitched.

He said, "In the middle of the night?"

I nodded. "Less people on the paths. Less chance of collusion."

An owl hooted from the darkness.

"Bosh! I'm coming in."

I shook my head. "No."

"Get out of the way, storyteller."

I didn't move.

He pushed against me.

I widened my stance.

"Get out of the way!"

"I told you, she's not here."

"I'm checking regardless."

"You can't, I'm an Uzman. I hold rank over you."

He glared at me, his nostrils flaring. Then in one action he lowered his body, drew back his shoulder and rammed it into my chest.

I felt the air rush from my lungs as I crashed through the doorway of the yurt and slid across the bed of reeds, tangled in the looseness of my robe. I tasted blood in my mouth.

I sat up as fast as I could. The round room was dimly lit by a crackling cookfire in the corner. There was a bed on one side and a desk covered in books on the other.

Crooked nose charged across the room and stood over me. He grabbed the back of my neck and squeezed so tight my lower back spasmed. "Where is she?"

"She's at the well," I said, short of breath, winded.

He bent down and stared at me with menacing eyes. "Don't lie to me!"

"You have no right to treat me like this. I'm with the school."

He grinned and stood up. He took a step back.

I felt his foot crunch against my ribs. I folded over and gasped for breath. One of my ribs felt cracked but I wasn't sure.

"It gets worse if you don't cooperate, storyteller."

I gritted my teeth. "You're nothing but scarred scum." I knew the words would anger him. The Fects hated their scars being mentioned.

Surprisingly he smiled, apparently knowing what I was trying to do.

He squatted next to me. "I know she's not out collecting water so let me put this to you simply: you have one more chance to tell me where she is or I break your pretty face."

"I told you. She's not here. I can't do anything about it until she returns."

"Your choice," he said. He stood and kicked me in the face.

I felt my nose explode beneath the force. Blood sprayed across the floor. My whole face felt numb and swollen. A high-pitched squeal rang out in my ears. I knew my nose was now broken just like his.

"Tell me now!" he said.

I spat blood on his deerskin boots.

He took a step back. "Not smart, storyteller."

I felt his foot crunch against my face again. I groaned in pain and buried my head in my hands. Warm blood poured from my swollen nose, everything was spinning.

He grabbed a fistful of my hair and pulled my head up. He held the sharp edge of his knife to my neck. "Last chance or I cut your throat."

A whimper came from the floor beneath us, an involuntary noise delivered by a scared child. *Was it my imagination?* I was only half-conscious.

Crooked nose dragged me to the other side of the yurt by my hair. He let me go and ripped the bed away from the center of the floor. He brushed the palm fronds away with his boot. Buried in the sand was a wooden door. He turned the latch and yanked it open, revealing a dark hole around one man in length and half-a-man in width. He disappeared into the blackness.

A moment later came childish screams.

Crooked nose climbed from the hole with the tiny dark skinned girl tucked beneath his arm. He gripped her so tight his arm was turning blue.

I tried to grab her leg.

Crooked nose lunged forward and kicked me in the ribs.

I heard a crack and felt the wind leave my body. I dropped flat on my stomach and buried my face in my hands.

He stepped over me holding the girl and disappeared out the door.

I listened to their movements and the girl's terrified cries. It sounded like he was trying to get her up into one of the cabs on an elephant. The creature sounded restless, its energy being wound up by the struggle.

I stood and stumbled for the door.

Suddenly a figure stepped into the doorway.

I froze. It was a Tæcan. A woman of average height and slender figure. She wore a robe like mine only hers was black. She had the hood up and wore a white clay mask concealing her identity entirely. The one difference in the robe design was how her hood was much bigger than mine to accommodate her larger skull. I saw the tall point of the head in the hood just as the book of knowledge had described. The book said the stretched-out elongated skull allowed the Tæcan's brain to grow larger so they could communicate better with the stars.

"Kon-Tiki?" she said.

I pulled my hood up over my face. "Yes."

"I'm here on behalf of the school. I have a message for you."

"What will happen to her?"

"The girl?"

I nodded.

"Never mind about her. Her work with us is done."

"What will you do with her? She has done nothing but help."

"She will go back to her people."

"The basin?"

She nodded. "And you will go with her."

"What?"

"You are ready for your mission. This is your opportunity to earn your second stripe on the path of the Tæcan."

"What mission?"

"You know the language of the Peru tribes now. You know the temperament of the people. You know what motivates them and what angers them, you know what makes them believe. The school believes you have what it takes to win their hearts and minds."

"Win their hearts and minds?"

"Yes, you will travel to Peru and prepare the tribes for the arrival of our stonemasons."

"What do you mean by *prepare the tribes?*"

"The Artery of Earth is ready. We must build the pyramids in Egypt, Angkor Wat and Nazca to complete the machine. Your responsibility will be Nazca in Peru. You will integrate with the natives and convince them to help us build the pyramid when the stonemasons arrive."

My heart was racing. "You want me to convince them?"

"Yes, have them ready to help us when the second fleet arrives. If they comply you will earn your second stripe."

"How many people do I need to get? And how long until the stonemasons would come across?"

"You will be taught everything you need to know on the trip across. You will be given so much knowledge, you alone will be able to preserve a great amount of what our people know."

"What type of knowledge? Like how the machine works?"

She nodded. "Yes, and much more."

"Like what?"

"You leave at dæġbreak," she said.

"Dæġbreak?"

"Yes, we're short on time. The arcs are ready. We have to move."

"Why so urgently?"

"Because the stars are coming," she said in an icy voice.

"What?"

"The Star from Taurai that entered Earth's orbit last rotation has broken apart just as the star watchers warned. And now, Earth is on track to hurdle right into the middle of it."

"What does that mean?"

"It means we're en-route to crash right into the middle of a gauntlet of stars. I'm sure you've noticed our skies have been thick with fire for some time?"

I had certainly noticed an increase in the number of shooting stars in the sky over the past season. The fiery balls were not only getting more frequent but they were getting bigger too. I had convinced myself to ignore it but now I saw the danger.

She slowed her speech and sensualized her tone to build up the heroic nature of the mission. "When it happens, we'll see firestorms, wildfires, earthquakes and floods. We could lose all of our people's knowledge in a single dæġ. We need your help to protect the school and all of the knowledge it contains. Your mission will be to settle with the natives and establish a new Viracochan settlement in Nazca, a school to preserve our knowledge and to keep us connected to the stars."

I bowed compliantly, "Ready. In service of the school." I was prepared to give my life for the opportunity to gain my second stripe as an Uzman. I was desperate to get my hands on the *book of the stars*.

She knew it too. "The school is grateful, Kon-Tiki. I see a second stripe in this for you. I take it you have read *Book 1 of the Tæcan, the book of knowledge?* You know it well?"

"Very well."

"Good. It's time to share what you have learned with others. Pack your things, the Fects are here to escort you." She bowed. "Path of the Tæcan."

I bowed again. "Path of the Tæcan."

The following dæġ, three arcs would leave the shores of Gunung Padang—one heading for Egypt, one for Angkor Wat, and the one I would board heading for Nazca. The journey would take one lunar cycle by sea and one lunar cycle on foot. I had no idea by the time I would reach the lake in the sky, I would be the only Uzman alive.

2

THE BASIN. PERU.

Jung had his hands on his head, struggling to breathe. He smelled the heavy scent of decaying wood and wet earth.

The boy was fifteen rotations in age, dark skinned and thin framed. Despite his wiry physique he was muscular for a boy of his age. He had big brown eyes, a round face and dark, shoulder-length hair covering his forehead. He wore only a loincloth made from the skin of a puma. He carried a large wooden bow almost as tall as him and wore a quiver on his back made from woven reeds. The chute encased ten good-working arrows, each meticulously crafted and tested by his father. On his back he had a similar designed bag made from woven reeds just big enough for a few personal items. The bag was made for him by his mother just before her death.

He walked behind his father, Hatun.

The man was thickly built, the muscles on his shoulders glistened orange in the light of Earth's Star. He carried a bow equal in size to Jung's and had an identical quiver and bag. He wore an identical loincloth to his son too—the skin had been cut from the same cat. Hanging from his waist was a large fang that had been taken from a jaguar.

They were deep in the jungle basin, following an animal track that skirted the river. Ahead green wrens with yellow bellies flew the trail. The jungle was alive with the sounds of woodpeckers, kingfishers and parrots. Enormous trees towered above their tiny figures, many standing more than fifty men tall, their roots crowding the jungle floor. Shafts of light pierced the canopy and danced across the brown earth that writhed with rhinoceros beetles, fire ants and centipedes. Butterflies of all colors hovered above the floor covered with fleshy ferns, bulbous mushrooms and ancient rocks coated in moss.

Suddenly Jung collided with his father. Their sticky skin momentarily touched then peeled free.

Hatun turned and held his finger to his meaty lips. Beads of sweat glued his dark fringe to his forehead. He had a round face and big brown eyes just like Jung. Wispy black hairs sprouted from his chin and cheeks. His wide nostrils flared to his quickened breaths. He pointed ahead.

Jung looked.

Upwind, in a clearing, three capybara stood together on the bank of the river. The rodents had brown fur, barreled bodies, stubby legs and large squared heads with small eyes. Each of them weighed around as much as Jung. They gnawed on tufts of grass that sprouted from the river bank.

The animals were just what Jung and his father had been looking for.

Hatun pointed to a fallen tree.

They nestled behind the tree and prepared for the wait.

Earth's Star had covered ten lengths of itself by the time the creature arrived.

They were alerted first by a kingfisher that let out a warning whistle. *Chuh, chuh... chuh, chuh... chuh, chuh.*

Jung sat up.

Hatun had his finger in the air.

Jung turned.

The three capybara looked uneasy. They were frozen, aside from their nostrils that flared and their eyes that darted one way then the other.

The kingfisher let out another warning. *Chuh, chuh... chuh, chuh... chuh, chuh.*

Several other birds began to chorus a response.

The jungle was alive.

"There," Hatun said. He pointed downwind to the other side of the river.

Jung saw a flicker of movement but had to blink twice before he made out the form of the jaguar. The dark markings on the cat's fur made it dissolve into the vegetation. The cat was down by the waters edge, moving silently through the tall grass, twenty lengths-of-man from the rodents. Its golden coat reflected the light from Earth's Star. The cat was even bigger than Jung had imagined. It was around the same size as his father with an impressively muscular head and powerful shoulders.

He looked at his father and smiled.

"Female," Hatun said. He grinned.

Jung watched the cat.

The jaguar moved a little closer and stopped.

Despite looking directly at the cat, the capybara hadn't seen the predator yet. The animals had terrible eyesight and the jaguar seemed to know it.

She lay down to wait.

Jung watched the nearest capybara's heart racing in its chest, the thumping organ stenciled in the veiny flesh. He looked at his father and shook his hand mimicking the pace of the capybara's heart.

Hatun smiled and nodded.

The capybara nearest to the cat whipped its head around and sniffed the air. Its whiskers twitched. It turned again and looked in the direction of the cat.

The jaguar was still, patient. It was as if she knew the longer she waited, the more the rodent's brain would quieten. It was a law of nature—fear was such a big part of a capybara's life that its tiny brain had evolved to move on quickly after becoming suspicious of a threat. It had to or else it could never get on with its life.

The jaguar waited calmly, even taking the time to lick the mud from her two front paws.

Eventually the capybara nearest to the cat relaxed and returned to grazing. The other two animals followed suit.

The moment all three rodents had eased, the cat advanced forward, her chest grazing the earth. She took a few paces and stopped.

Suddenly the wind turned and a rich sour smell wafted through the air. It was the smell of the capybara.

The wind turned toward the jaguar.

Jung held his breath.

The kingfisher let out another warning whistle, this time a higher alert. *Chah, chah, chah... chah, chah, chah... chah, chah, chah.*

The three capybaras gathered together nervously. Their eyes flickered faster, their nostrils flared larger. They looked directly at the jaguar who was less than five men from them.

She didn't flinch.

To the rodent's poor eyesight, she must have appeared like a mound of mud and grass.

Then the wind turned again, this time flowing from the cat to the rodents.

The capybara closest to the jaguar raised its snout and took in a waft of the threat. It threw back its head and turned.

"Now," Hatun whispered.

The jaguar leapt from the sand.

Seeing the flash of movement, the nearest rodent squealed in fear. It ran along the bank as fast as its stubby legs could carry it.

A second capybara who had wandered chest deep into the water was slower to realize what was happening. It found itself caught between the river and the advancing cat.

The jaguar switched targets and ploughed into the water after the second rodent. It landed square on top of the prey.

Both animals plunged beneath the surface. The water began to redden as silt was whirled up from the bed.

Hatun stood. He coaxed his son to do the same.

Jung stood just as the jaguar rose from the water.

The cat had the rodent's neck seized in its jaws.

The capybara's eyes were wide, fear-stricken.

Every muscle in the cat's body flexed as she dragged the prey, almost equal in size to herself, out of the water and onto the bank.

The other two capybaras were gone.

The prey was alive but only barely. With the cat's jaws locked onto its throat, it was suffocating fast. Its body sank onto the sand, limp. Only its eyes moved, rolling from one side to the other.

Jung's legs quivered to the animal's suffering.

The jaguar began to haul the rodent up the muddy bank toward the brush.

Hatun moved out from the cover of trees and onto the bank so only the narrow river separated him from the cat and its prey. He waved his hand, encouraging the boy to do the same.

Jung followed.

The cat turned and saw them, the limp rodent wedged between its jaws.

They were standing less than ten men from her.

Hatun pulled an arrow from his quiver and rested it against the tort string of his bow. He aimed it at the cat.

Jung did the same. He drew back the string on his bow.

The jaguar released the neck of the prey and hissed at them. Long lengths of saliva dangled from its enormous yellow fangs.

The rodent was still alive but only barely.

Jung was still, he was waiting for the command from his father.

The jaguar seized the prey again and used the last of her energy to shake the animal until its neck was broken. She dropped the dead rodent and panted.

Jung knew it was the right time to shoot. The cat was exhausted, making it an easy target. *Why hadn't his father called the command?* He decided he would shoot anyway. He squinted one eye closed, a drop of sweat trickled down his top lip. He licked away the moisture, tasting the saltiness. He exhaled slowly, and fired.

"No!" Hatun said, knocking Jung's bow up. The arrow went flying up into the canopy.

The jaguar plunged her jaws back into the rodent's neck and dragged the kill into the thick, this time disappearing for good.

"Why did you do that for?" Jung said. He was angry.

Hatun was serious. "This is not your kill, son. This kill is hers."

"But I need a kill to earn my tooth."

"No, to earn your tooth you must be alone."

"Then leave me alone!" Jung said. He heard distant crashing sounds from the cat making ground. He waded into the water after her. "Let me hunt from here alone. I'll meet you back at camp."

"No," Hatun said, sternly.

Jung stopped and turned. He was waist deep in the brown river. "What?"

"To earn your tooth you must set off alone from camp. No kills count on this trip."

Jung clenched his teeth. His face was red, enraged.

Hatun smiled. "Your time will come, son."

Jung turned and stormed towards the shore, sending a plume of brown silt swirling to the surface. "Let's go then. I want to go home." He marched up the bank.

"Stop!" Hatun said.

Jung froze. It was the way his father had delivered the words. It wasn't an order, it was an alarm.

"Be still."

Jung was still.

"Move back slowly and calmly."

"What is it?"

"Slowly."

Jung moved back. "What is it?"

"Pit viper."

The green snake was wrapped around a low-hanging branch, camouflage against the vegetation. It was the perfect height for Jung to walk face first into. The poisonous snake had its neck flared and coiled back, ready to attack.

When Jung was a safe distance from the snake, he turned to his father.

Hatun's face was pale.

"What is it? I'm okay."

Hatun shook his head. "We have to leave now."

"What do you mean?"

"It's a sign. We have to get back to The Cloud Forest now."

"Why?"

Hatun rushed past him. "I'll explain on the way."

3

THE SACRED VALLEY. PERU.

In the distance a snow-capped mountain towered above the surrounding peaks like a protective mother watching over her children. The sky was blue, not a cloud in sight. There was a chill in the air and the smell of ash from the smoldering campfire.

Jung was in a dreamy daze, riding the waves between wakefulness and sleep. He lay on his back next to Hatun, watching two condors circling overhead. The black shapes had wide flared wings with white tips on the underside. They craned above the valley, their heads sunk low, slowly spiraling up and down on the currents of air.

"Spirits of the sky," Hatun said.

Jung looked at his father and smiled.

"He is your grandfather."

"What is?"

Hatun looked to the sky and smiled. "The condor. The feeling. The plant."

The plant meant san pedro. Jung still tasted the bitterness in his mouth from the brew. His father had prepared the san pedro drink by boiling an arm of cactus the dæġ prior. They had collected it on the return from the basin. He had pointed out the plant to Jung the moment he had spotted it. It was the only cactus in the desert that didn't have spikes. It was the most obvious omen Jung had ever seen. It was as if Pachamama—Mother Nature—was giving man a leg up. *Pick this one*, she said.

Jung sat up. He heard the muffled sounds of churning rapids coming from down in the valley below.

Hatun sat up too.

They were on a flat stony ridge, high in the mountains in The Sacred Valley where only the most rugged of vegetation could survive. Below them, red earthy hills crumbled away—their wrinkled, folded passages bleeding streams of pea gravel. Covering the ridges were long blonde grasses and yellow flowers that bent to the wind.

Jung felt a whirl in his stomach. With the plant in his blood, everything seemed brighter, more layered, more complex—the flowers were more intensely yellow, the distant trees were more vibrantly teal, the skins of the endless cacti were more bulbous and fleshy. His body felt weak and his penis was shriveled. He hovered his hands in front of his face. The skin looked more translucent and the veins more pronounced.

One of the condors screeched from above.

"And your mother," Hatun said. He was still looking up. "They travel together."

Jung felt a jolt in his chest from the sound of the word *Mother*. He looked up and watched the birds circling above.

One of them appeared to wink.

Jung chuckled.

Hatun's cheeks pinched and tightened as he smiled.

Then the condors dived, one after the other, speeding down beyond the edge of the cliff toward the snaking river below.

Jung felt his stomach lift, light as a butterfly's wings. He raised his bum from the earth, preparing to stand, to chase.

Hatun squeezed his shoulder. "Leave them."

Jung paused. He felt a flurry of movement ascend from his chest to his throat.

"Do you remember the three stages to life?" Hatun said. "The spirits?"

Jung nodded. "Snake, jaguar, condor."

"That's right. Can you explain them to me?"

"The snake is the keeper of the underworld, the protector of wisdom and knowledge. It represents the beginning of all new life. The jaguar is the spirit of our earthly being. It represents the bulk of our life and the becoming of our full physical being. And the condor represents our connection to the higher realm, the divine. It is our passage through to the afterlife."

Hatun smiled proudly. "Yes, perfect."

"Is that it? The snake. Is that what you meant?" Jung said.

"Is *what* what I meant?"

"You said it was a bad omen."

"What is a bad omen?"

"In the basin. You saw the pit viper and said it was bad."

Hatun shook his head. "I didn't say it was bad. I said it was a sign. The three realms must be connected for us to have a healthy passage through life. When I saw the realms of the jaguar and the snake connect in such a short space of time, I knew we had to move. Such a sign is very rare. Pachamama was communicating with us. She was telling us that the passage is now open. Now, we have connected all three realms for you—the snake, the jaguar and the condor."

"What does it mean?"

"It means you are ready to journey alone. After you visit The Healer of course. She will ask the spirits for permission."

Jung's empty stomach growled. "Can I go to her now?"

"Not now. We must return to camp. You'll go at the end of the season."

"But she's on the way home."

"I know, but we have been gone for long enough. You will have your time, son."

"You always say that," Jung said.

The wrinkles around Hatun's eyes intensified as he pressed his lips together. "Because you will."

"When?"

"At the end of the season."

"It's been forever!"

"I know, Jung. But remember, it doesn't just take strength to be a man, it takes patience too. You will have your time. Sooner than you know."

Jung shook his head and stood, frustrated. He was about to rush off down the ridge when he spotted it. He looked back at Hatun, a look of horror on his face.

"What is it?"

Jung pointed. "Is that camp?"

Hatun turned to where Jung was pointing.

In the distance a narrow chute of gray smoke climbed into the sky. The thin stream was broken into sections—there were three small streams bundled close together followed by three long streams spaced out, then back to the same. Over and over.

Hatun stood. "Smoke signals."

"What do they mean?"

Hatun was already beginning to pack up their things.

"What is it?" Jung said.

"We have to get back to camp. Quick! Wrap up the tinder."

Jung snapped to attention and ran to the smoldering fire pit. He picked up the large clam-shaped tinder mushroom sliced in half and lay splayed open. The mushroom was used to keep an ember alight between camps. All you had to do was seal a hot coal in the fungus and tie it closed. The ember burned so slowly that it would still be hot up to a dæġ later.

Jung tied the fist-sized mushroom closed and placed it in his bag. That's when he spotted the second smoke stack. It was just beginning to climb into the sky in the opposite direction. It was the same pattern.

"There's another one there," he said.

Hatun looked.

"Isn't that the watchtower in Ollantaytambo?"

"Yes."

"What is it?" Jung said.

"I'm not sure."

"Are they getting attacked? We should help them."

Hatun was frozen, thinking. He licked his lips.

"We have to go to them," Jung said. "There are only two scouts at Ollantaytambo. Back at camp there are dozens of warriors."

Hatun looked back to the smoke coming from their people's camp then back to the watchtower.

Suddenly a shell horn blasted from the mountain passage. It was coming from their people's camp, The Cloud Forest.

"Ignore the watchtower," Hatun said. "We have to return to The Cloud Forest."

"What does it mean?" Jung said.

"They're preparing for war."

4

20 dægs to star impact.

THE BASIN. PERU.

I was being followed. I stumbled through the jungle in darkness, clutching the spear the Fects from the arc had given me. I was terrified to be on the move at night but even more terrified to be still.

I heard a banging sound, like someone hitting a rock against a tree.

The creature spoke, "Waah, duh, reh, huh, huh."

It sounded like a man with a deep voice although I was sure a human voice could never reach the low growl it reached when it angered.

"Hello, hello, hello," I said.

The creature howled, then spoke. "Duh ez eh furr... Waah, duh, reh."

I had no idea what the thing was but it had been toying with me for two dægs. It seemed to speak its own language and wanted me to communicate with it. When I talked back it communicated in gibberish and seemed calm. It was only when I didn't talk back that it would get angry. That's when it would come closer. It never let me see it in the whole. I caught only glimpses. The creature looked like a man who was ten foot tall and completely covered in hair, even his face had hair all over. It walked like a man too. It stood on two legs, its shoulders drawn back and its arms swinging by its sides. It even talked in a similar way to a man. Although it definitely wasn't a man. The creature's vocals could extend to a much wider frequency than any mans. Plus its eyes were much bigger and more yellow than a man's. Even despite these clues the biggest sign it wasn't human was the way it read me. It read me better than any man could. It knew when I was confident and strong, that's when it kept its distance. And it knew the moment I was frustrated or scared, that's when it would draw closer and taunt me.

I heard its crunching feet moving quickly. It used the ferns as cover.

"Yuuuguh. Eaaaghup. Ay ay ay ay ay," the creature said.

"Yeah. Eazy. Hello hello hello hello hello."

The creature screamed, "Ahhhhhhhhhhhhhhhhhhh!"

It was running towards me.

I ran, branches whipped my face. I tripped on my robe and hauled myself back onto my feet.

The creature changed octave, "Orrrrrrrrrrrrrrrrrrrrrrrrrr!"

It was making ground on me fast.

I stopped and turned. I aimed the spear in the direction of the attacking creature. I watched the dark vegetation, listening to the thrashing footsteps.

Two figures broke from the thick.

It was two women. They were short and broad with dark skin. They had identical hair—black and cut straight just above the shoulders and just above the eyes. They were naked aside from snake skins that were wrapped around their waists.

I smelled burning tobacco. Then I saw the drifting trails of smoke wafting up from behind the women.

On their backs, they wore woven baskets that must have been full of tobacco. Smoke poured out, blanketing the jungle in a white cloud.

Suddenly faces began to pop up from the vegetation all around me. The faces were all female. The women looked just like the girl they had given me back home, only much older. There were perhaps fifty of them, all with identical hair and dressed the same. They carried spears and axes.

"I mean your people no harm, I am lost," I said. I spoke fluently in the jungle tongue just as the girl had taught me.

The jungle women looked at one another seemingly impressed by my knowledge of their language.

"I have come from across the ocean, from the other side of Earth."

They were quiet, watching. They slowly approached me and surrounded me.

Although I stood a foot taller than them and my shoulders were twice the width of theirs, they weren't afraid of me. They poked me in the shoulders and tugged on my beard. I felt like some prized animal being inspected before trade.

I looked at their feet. They were wide and splayed with big toes that stuck out like fat wandering thumbs. The design was no doubt a gift from Pachamama to help them climb the trees and navigate the surface roots.

I felt one woman grab me between the legs from behind. She was gentle but her touch caused my entire body to arch tensely.

The women with the tobacco baskets had long disappeared in the direction of the creature that had been following me.

One woman stood directly in front of me. She was dressed the same as the others and had the same hair but her eyes were bigger and her eyelashes longer. She had a red stick pierced through her nose. She was around 20 rotations old with a healthy figure and toned arms and legs. She wore a necklace made up of dozens of teeth, bones and feathers. I recognize a few items: a jaguar tooth, a bear claw and a condor foot.

She pointed to her chest. "Killa."

"I'm Kon-Tiki," I said, pointing to my chest.

She pulled on my beard and nodded, apparently impressed by the thickness of it.

"Do you understand me? That I come from the other side of Earth," I said.

"Far away."

"Yes."

"Do you understand I come in peace. I am lost."

Killa smiled. "Yes, you are defenseless. It is apparent."

"Against that thing I was. Thank you for helping me."

"Not me, thank them."

"Who?" I said.

"The plants."

"The plants?" I said.

She nodded.

"The plants sent you to me?"

"Yes."

"How?"

"Mother Aya told us. Anyway you're safe now."

"Mother Aya?"

Killa looked to the ground. "Doesn't matter."

"Do you know what it was?" I said.

"What?"

"The creature following me."

She was serious. "No. You tell me?"

"You've never seen that before?"

She shook her head.

"That doesn't scare you?"

She laughed. "Every dæġ I see a new thing down here that I've never seen before and I've seen a lot of things scarier than that. But if you're trying to source where it came from you need to ask yourself because you brought that thing."

"I brought it?"

Killa nodded. "Yes."

"How?"

She pointed to her head. "You think bad thoughts. You let that thing in."

"I let it in?"

"Yes."

"Let it in from where?"

"We have to go. It's not safe here anymore," Killa said. She disappeared into the plants. "Follow me."

I followed, terrified of being left alone.

We were walking through the jungle in darkness. I heard buzzing cicadas, croaking frogs and the haunting screams from a loon. Spider monkeys followed us from above, they whispered in the trees.

Suddenly a crashing sound came from ahead.

Killa stopped and held her hand in the air.

The party of jungle women all stopped too.

I froze among them, my spear pointed forward.

An old woman staggered out of the vegetation naked. Her small wrinkled body was painted head-to-toe in geometric patterns that shined in every color of the rainbow.

She moved through the scattering of jungle women and stopped in front of me. Her pupils seemed to fill her entire eyes, there wasn't a slither of white. The black pools looked like portals to other realms.

I had the strangest feeling she could read my every intention.

She touched me on the shoulder then turned and disappeared back into the vegetation.

Killa laughed. "Ayahuasca."

"Mother Aya?"

Killa was serious.

We continued on.

Eventually we reached the jungle women's camp. We stumbled right into camp before I saw the outline of two dozen huts surrounding me in the darkness. The huts were made of mud and straw. In the center of camp was an enormous shelter, raised a foot above the ground, with a wooden floor and a thatch roof. There were bodies slumped all over the deck, perhaps three dozen people moving sluggishly and murmuring in the blackness. I couldn't make out their faces. I heard a woman being sick out in the jungle and one woman off on her own roaring like a cat.

The sounds made the hairs on my neck stand tall.

Killa stopped and pointed to the ground. *Stay here.*

She went to one of the huts and squatted near a large shadowed figure. She whispered in the ear of the stranger who nodded.

Suddenly I saw the base of the shadow the stranger was sitting on begin to stretch. The person Killa was talking to was lying on top of an enormous snake.

The anaconda began to unravel in the darkness and move down from the shelter. It slithered slowly towards me, its tongue licking the air. The creature was at least four men long and had a body as fat as a man.

"Is it friendly?" I said growing increasingly concerned.

"Oy!" a heavy woman's voice yelled. It was the same woman Killa was speaking to.

The anaconda froze.

The stranger stood and moved out from the shadows. She began to walk over to me.

The woman was middle-aged with plump cheeks and a wide nose. She had identical hair to the other jungle women and dressed the same but was enormous compared to the others, not just in height but width. She was not much shorter than me and a good amount rounder. She had large drooping breasts and a bulbous belly. There were decorative burn marks around her eyes. Her eyes were like the old woman's, nothing but black pupil.

She grinned. "Hello Kon-Tiki, I'm Yaku Mama. I've been expecting you."

5

I sat alone in one of the mud-straw huts with Yaku Mama. The room smelled of blood and tobacco. There was very little light but my eyes had adjusted well to the dark. I saw mosquitoes with bodies as big as fingernails buzzing around and the anaconda coiled up in the corner.

Yaku Mama drank from a wooden cup that stained her lips red. She puffed on a large roll of tobacco leaves and blew the smoke towards the mosquitoes.

There were two knocks at the door.

Through the smoke two women entered the hut with half a jaguar, cut from the waist down. The carcass looked fresh, the wound was bright and sticky. They dragged the slab of meat to the back corner of the hut and left.

The anaconda unraveled from Yaku Mama's waist and slithered over to the meal. It snapped at the flesh and dislocated its jaw so it could get to work consuming the meat whole.

The two women returned with the rest of the jaguar, the waist to the head. They lay it between Yaku Mama and I and handed her a knife.

She took the knife and handed me the rolled tobacco.

I inhaled a big lungful of smoke as I watched her slash open the stomach of the jaguar. The organs poured out onto the floor covering the space between us.

She cut out the heart and began to eat it.

"Where are all of your men?" I said.

She stared at me, eyes wide as a cat's, blood on her lips. "They went deeper into the basin."

"Further into the jungle?"

She nodded.

I handed the tobacco to her. "Why?"

"They have a lot to fear. The stars are against them."

"What do you mean?"

She nodded at the array of organs.

I picked up what looked like the liver and took a bite. It was a good choice because although it was chewy it had no odor or taste.

Yaku Mama nodded approvingly. "So, Kon-Tiki. What's your message?"

"I was followed in here by a creature," I said.

"I know."

"You saw it?"

"No, I saw you."

"You saw me?"

She nodded chewing. "In a vision."

"What did you see?"

"I saw you in the basin being hunted by a dark spirit."

"I'm being hunted by a dark spirit?"

She smiled, her teeth red with blood. "Who isn't?"

I noticed the anaconda watching me from the corner of the room. A bulge as big as half a jaguar protruded from the snake's neck.

"Where did you come from Kon-Tiki?" Yaku Mama said.

"I was sent by my people."

"From where?"

"The other side of Earth. I came by boat."

"Where exactly?"

"Indonesia, beyond Easter Island.

"Who did you travel with?"

"I came alone."

She paused. "Alone. Are you sure?"

"I've been sent by my people to tell you about a machine we are building. A machine that can take you to the stars."

She smirked. "You are here for The Artery of Earth."

"Yes, to protect us from the disaster. A big disaster that will strike any moment."

She smiled, her black eyes staring through me. "You think we don't know already?"

"You know a great disaster is coming?"

She nodded. "We were warned about Zep Tepi a long time ago."

"How?"

"Mother Aya."

I nodded at the cup to her side. "Is that it?"

She finished the liquid in the cup and placed the cup behind her. "Not for you. Mother Aya is for those who have first exposed their true intentions."

"I'm not here for the brew. I'm here to share a message from my people." I pulled out the book of knowledge from the inside pocket of my robe. "I'm here to share what's in here. To save us."

"Have you heard the story of greed?" Yaku Mama said.

"What?"

"The story of greed?"

I shook my head.

"Let me tell it to you, Kon-Tiki."

I placed the book down. "Sure."

"There was once a young hunter from the basin named Poma. He was the strongest and bravest of all the men in his tribe. Before he could even talk he wrestled pythons and capybara. By the time he was a man he was hunting and killing a new jaguar once every few dæġs. This made the other men in his tribe pleased because they knew if they fell short on their hunts they could rely on Poma to feed everyone. Everyone in the tribe respected Poma for the security he offered them.

"The problem was this admiration only fueled Poma's fire. He became so obsessed with pleasing his people that soon enough he was killing a new jaguar every dæġ. Over time Poma became so reliable that the other men stopped hunting altogether, there was simply no need. The women also stopped bringing in fruits and vegetables because there was such a surplus of meat. At first everyone in the tribe loved doing a little less work but over time they became bored and started to quarrel over trivial things like how hot the water should be when cooking or whether it was better to sleep on your side or your back.

"One dæġ, while out on a hunt, Poma came across the biggest jaguar he had ever seen, it was twice as large as any of his previous kills. *Wait until the tribe sees this one*, Poma thought. He raised his spear and was about to throw it when the jaguar spoke. 'Before you kill me, let me ask you a question about death,' the jaguar said.

"Poma was so taken back by the talking cat that he dropped his spear. The jaguar said, 'Every dæġ you kill a new jaguar. You think this is good for your tribe because you can feed everyone with ease but now you no longer kill for hunger. Your tribe already has more than enough to eat and yet you continue to kill. Have you not seen what happens to an animal a few dæġs after it dies?'

"Poma remembered the many rotten jaguar carcasses his tribe had thrown into the river after the flesh had become infested with maggots. The jaguar said, 'You have become so good at killing that your tribe now wastes more meat than they eat. You have become greedy and stopped respecting life. You don't know it now but in the end the hunter is always killed by the hunted. It's a law of nature. Sometimes the hunter dies of starvation because there are no animals left to eat, sometimes the hunter becomes sick because he loses variety in his diet, sometimes the hunter is killed at the hands of his own people because of greed. Whatever the cause the greedy hunter is always killed because nature is forced to rectify the imbalance.'

"Poma was so taken back by the talking jaguar that he fled back to camp where he told his tribe about his conversation with the cat. The tribe had been bickering all dæġ so when he turned up empty handed and told them his experience with the talking cat they became angry and said he must return to the jungle because they were running out of food. Poma refused, afraid of running into the enormous jaguar again. The tribe was so infuriated by Poma's response that they all banded together and speared him to death. They carried his body to the bank where they dumped all of the rotten jaguar carcasses and they threw his carcass among them."

Yaku Mama picked out the pancreas and took a bite. "That's the story of greed."

"What does it mean?" I said.

She grinned. "A good storyteller never tells you the moral of the story, do they?"

I swallowed.

She picked up a rock and cracked it against the jaguar's skull four or five times until there was a hole in the head. She wrenched out the brain.

I must have been staring because she stopped. "It's okay," she said. "We'll share."

I nodded.

She took a bite from the brain. "So tell me about your great discovery. Your machine." She handed the brain to me.

I took the slimy, bloody organ and bit into it. "Oh, yes. The Artery of Earth."

6

THE CLOUD FOREST. PERU.

It had just begun to drizzle when Jung and Hatun approached the bridge that led into their people's camp.

The bridge was a living thing and had a name, Anku. Anku had been created several generations earlier by training trees from both sides of the river to entwine together. The trees were now hundreds of rotations old and grafted solidly together as a shared being.

Jung climbed onto Anku and shuffled across the slimy wood. Below, the frothing whitewater was speckled with boulders that had fallen from the cliffs. He smelled cooking guinea pig wafting from the camp hidden in the forest blanketed in cloud. He barely made out the vertical stone cliffs that stood well over 100 men high and surrounded him in all directions. There was good reason their people's camp was called The Cloud Forest—four out of five dægs, clouds crept into camp by evening and it rained.

Jung stepped from Anku just as a flock of macaws erupted from high in the canopy. They screeched out of sync as they flew together, two flocks entwined. The first flock had red on their heads and shoulders and bands of yellow, green and blue from the shoulders to the tail. The second flock was teal and blue on top and yellow underneath. The two flocks broke apart and flew off in different directions.

Jung smiled. He loved the sounds of their chaotic squawks, he thought they were a welcome relief from the hum of the river.

Suddenly something caught his attention.

A flag was waving from high up in the canopy, twenty men high. It was attached to one of their people's pods. The pods were cone-shaped structures that slept around 10-15 people. There were 12 pods all up, each had the same design—taken from the shape of a closed flower just before bloom. The pods were built the same way as Anku, generations ago their people trained the trees to grow around frameworks they had made of bone. Now the people had large hollows to live inside that were high from the ground. Like Anku, every pod had a name because it was its own living being. Jung's family pod's name was Sisa, meaning flower.

Jung had noticed the flag flying because it was flying from Sisa. That meant his uncle or grandmother had sounded the alarm. The flag was painted red—the color of war.

Suddenly a cat appeared in a tree next to Jung. It was an ocelot, an exact replica of a jaguar if it was shrunken down and stretched out.

"Misi!" Jung said.

Misi jumped onto Jung's shoulders and wrapped around his neck. It nuzzled against his face and purred.

Jung's legs bent to the cat's weight. "Off Misi."

Misi bounced lightly to the ground.

Jung dropped to his knees and patted Misi with both hands.

The cat nuzzled her head into Jung's lap and flopped onto her back, her spine arched backward, her paws dangling in the air. She looked at him with big loving eyes.

Hatun laughed. "Misi, Misi, Misi."

Jung smiled.

Misi rolled onto her feet and leapt back into the tree.

Jung stood just as his uncle, Uma, appeared from the cloud.

The man looked opposite to his brother Hatun in every way. Uma was taller and thinner and his face was longer. He had dark voluminous hair and sparse threads of facial hair clustered on his upper lip and chin. He wore a loincloth made of alpaca fur and had a jaguar tooth hanging from his waist identical to his brothers. He chewed on coca leaves, an anxious look on his face.

Uma said, "They sent another messenger." He had to shout to clear the sound of the rushing water. He ushered them away from the river.

"Who?" Hatun said.

"People of the lake. They said we have until Earth's Rock turns blue to decide."

"Seven dægs?"

Uma nodded. "Yes and it will take five dægs to get to the lake to deliver the answer."

Jung trailed behind the men and looked at the ground. He knew his uncle got funny when he thought the boy was hearing too much.

"What are we going to do?" Uma said.

"We take council," Hatun said.

"The elders? Do we really need to consult the elders? We must go to war. You said that yourself."

Hatun stopped. "I said war was *an* option. I didn't say it was *the* option."

Uma frowned.

"We cannot act on impulse. We must take council. We must consider the good of the whole tribe."

Uma's face twitched, aggravated. He dipped his hand into his loincloth and plucked out a handful of coca leaves. He spat out the leaves in his mouth and replaced them with the fresh leaves. He nodded at Jung. "Can we at least talk, among men? Sort this out."

There it was.

Hatun nodded. He handed his bow and arrows to Jung. "Please put these in the hut." He smiled unconvincingly.

Jung nodded and took the items.

He watched his father and uncle head towards an orange glow in the distant clouds where secret men's business took place.

"What are you looking at?" a voice said.

Jung turned and saw Puma.

The man stood a foot taller than him. He had muscular arms and legs and an angular chin covered in fluffy hair. He had black hair tucked behind his ears that ran past his shoulders and he wore a puma skin loincloth. Puma was one of their tribes greatest assets, he was the biggest man in their tribe and one of their greatest hunters, second only to Hatun. He was also known to be a brute. He could be forceful and intimidating.

Puma had his thumb tucked into the waistband of his loincloth. In his palm he held his jaguar tooth. "Did you bring back a tooth?"

Jung shook his head.

"Get your eyes off the sacred site then. That's knowledge for ritualized men." Puma brushed past him. "Go on, off you go."

Jung lifted his father's bow and turned towards camp just as Little Puma, Puma's son, walked up to him.

The boy was of a similar age and look to Jung, only he had wider set eyes and a more angular chin. He was wrapped in a llama hide shawl that covered him from shoulder to toe. His black hair was wet and shiny, slicked back. He smelled of mineral salts from the springs. He stopped in front of Jung and held up the jaguar tooth that hung from his waist.

"Did you get a tooth?" Little Puma said.

Jung sneered.

"When are you going to get one?"

Jung mocked him. "You smell clean, Little Puma."

"What?"

"Like you've bathed."

"I have."

Jung scoffed. "I know. While I've been out hunting for a full lunar cycle, you've been bathing, getting soft." He nodded at Little Puma's wrinkled hands. "Look at your soft skin."

Little Puma balled his hands into fists and shook his head. "I don't have time for this. I've got men's council to get to."

He brushed past Jung, like his father had done.

"I could have got it this time," Jung said.

Little Puma stopped and turned. "No you couldn't. You have to leave camp on your own."

"I know."

"So why did you say you could have got it?"

"Oy!" a voice yelled from the distance.

It was Puma. He was stopped halfway to the foot of the mountain. He waved his hand through the air.

"Got to go!" Little Puma said, he grinned and ran off.

Jung clenched his teeth angrily. He looked up to the sky and was immediately softened by the drops on his skin. It was beginning to rain.

Suddenly there was a scream from Anku, the bridge.

Jung turned.

It was Inti, one of their tribe's scouts from Ollantaytambo, where Jung had spotted the second smoke signal. He was running across the bridge screaming.

Inti yelled, "She's dead! She's dead!"

7

The harpy eagle arrived first. Jung heard the wings whooshing in from the clouds.

The enormous bird caused a cloud of dust to lift from the ground when it landed in the clearing. The eagle stood as tall as Jung's waist. It was mostly gray with black on its wings and white on its legs and chest. It had a powerful shield-like face, flared at the sides, and a crest of feathers on its head. It's curved beak was as long as a man's fist.

"They killed her!" Inti said as he reached the eagle.

The man was rake thin with gaunt cheeks and a mop of brown hair. He was breathing heavily, his hair and face were soaked in sweat.

"Who?" Jung said.

Inti was bent over, trying to catch his breath.

Jung noticed his bow legs. It was a common condition among all the runners, their joints eventually wore down from the constant pounding against the stone paths. Just this morning Inti would have run more than 50,000 steps to make the distance from Ollantaytambo to camp. Over a lifetime, it took its toll.

Suddenly Hatun appeared through the cloud. He ran to them. "What's going on?"

"They killed her," Inti said.

"Who?"

"Wayra."

"She was posted at Ollantaytambo?" Hatun said.

Inti nodded.

"Who did it?" Hatun said.

"People from the lake," Inti said.

"Lake Titicaca?"

"Yes."

Uma appeared through the cloud and stood by Hatun's side. "They must have killed her on the way out."

Hatun turned to Uma. "But you told me they said we have time."

"They did," Uma said.

Hatun stared his brother in the eyes. "And what did you say?"

"Nothing much."

"What exactly?"

Uma looked to the ground.

A group of men including Puma and Little Puma arrived and gathered around. They were quiet, listening in.

Hatun looked at Uma. "What did you say?"

Uma looked up. "Just that we didn't want their conditions."

"You said what?"

"It was just a comment. It wasn't a decision."

"Did they know that or just you?" Hatun said.

"They knew that."

"Are you sure?"

Uma shrugged. "I think so."

"You fool!"

"It wasn't final," Uma said. "And anyway, this is an act of war."

Inti nodded. "Murder is murder."

"They have declared war on us," Uma said.

Hatun scowled at his brother and looked at Inti. "How many people?"

"Three. Two men and a woman."

Hatun turned to Uma. "How many people came here?"

Uma nodded. "The same."

"What will we do?" Inti said. "I saw them do it. They stabbed her thirty- maybe forty times. Uma's right, they have declared war."

Hatun frowned.

"We have to go to war," Uma said.

"No," Hatun said. "We consult the elders with this new knowledge."

Uma frowned. "Come on, do we really need the elder's say on this? They killed one of us."

"I have explained this already!" Hatun snarled. "We always take council before we blow the horn of war. And you don't have a say on this one because you caused the problem."

"I made a comment. *They* declared war."

"Your views are understood," Hatun said. "So you can sit this council out."

Jung watched his father and Inti disappear into the cloud. All of the other men followed aside from Uma.

Jung turned and ran toward Sisa before his uncle made eye contact.

It would be just before dawn when the elders adjourned council and the horn of war was sounded.

8

It was dark when Jung entered the hot springs that were surrounded by lush ferns and moss-covered rocks. The water was warm enough to make him sweat. He sank to eye level and watched the steam rise as the last strokes of Earth Star's light made everything yellow.

Misi was lying flat on her stomach in a tree above him. She had two legs hanging on either side of a branch. Her eyes were closed but her tail flickered playfully.

"There is a shift happening," Jung's grandmother, Wasi, said.

Jung was surprised to hear the woman's voice.

She was sitting in the hot springs but on a shelf further down the river. She wouldn't have known Jung was nearby. He imagined the tiny woman, barely four feet tall, nude beneath the water. Her squinted eyes and her gray mop of hair.

Jung heard another woman's voice. "You're telling me. I cannot handle another war. We have already lost too many people this rotation."

It was Kusi, a middle-aged woman who was pregnant and close to due.

"Something bigger than this battle though," Wasi said.

"What?"

"I don't know exactly," Wasi said.

"I have felt something strange too," Kusi said. "The water is getting warmer and the rain is coming more often and more furiously."

"I know," Wasi said.

"They will be safe though, the women are going too. They will protect them."

"It's not this war, Kusi. It's something bigger."

"What?"

"I don't know but I feel her moving. She's restless, uncomfortable," Wasi said. There was a pause then she said, "Pachamama, be kind to us."

"She will, she is kind," Kusi said.

"Please don't be foolish, Kusi."

"Wasi!"

"Don't *Wasi* me."

"What's the matter?"

"You didn't lose someone, I lost someone," Wasi said.

"She takes care of *all*, Wasi. Even those who have passed. Earth is uncomfortable, I have felt it too. But she will settle again."

"Of course she will settle again," Wasi said. "That's not the point. She will always settle again. The point is that first she will rouse. She is going to buck."

"You've seen it?" Kusi said.

"In the animals, yes. They have left my dreams. They left when Earth's Rock last turned blue. I walk all over Peru in my dreams and they are gone. It's like a mass extinction."

"You remember what Palla said in women's council?" Kusi said.

"Yes, that's what I'm worried about," Wasi said.

Suddenly Jung saw Hatun standing above him on the rocks.

The man was naked and painted head to toe in red paint. He was holding a single arrow. Soon he would hand it to Jung. It meant he was leaving on a dangerous journey. The idea was that the warrior would make sure they return so they can collect the item. In truth it often meant the warrior wasn't coming back.

Hatun waved the arrow, encouraging Jung to follow him.

Jung silently left the water.

9

Jung and Hatun sat together in the cave.

An unbroken sheet of water poured over the rocks in front of them.

Jung clutched the arrow in his fist. The sound of water thundered in his ears, the wet mist tickled his skin. Two fireflies hovered in the darkness.

Despite the cold and the wet, the cave was their favorite place to be together.

Jung studied the paint on his father's skin. The red color was produced by crushing cochineal insects, tiny bugs less than a freckle in size that fed on cacti in The Sacred Valley. It would have cost the lives of at least ten thousand creatures to cover his father's skin. His people believed wearing the bodies of past life gave the warriors strength.

"Do you understand this war?" Hatun said.

Jung shook his head.

"They have given us terms, terms that we cannot accept."

"Who?"

"The people of the lake."

"Lake Titicaca?"

Hatun nodded.

"What terms?"

"They want our eyes and ears. They want us to let them know if we see or hear anything strange in the mountains. In exchange they have said they will tell us if they see anything strange around the lake."

"We don't want this?" Jung said. "We could use their eyes and ears."

Hatun shook his head. "We won't get their eyes and ears. It always starts out this way, it never ends the same."

"What do you mean?"

"One tribe will eventually begin restricting knowledge, they will be selective about the information they hand over and the moment that happens it will be the most dishonest tribe who will have the advantage."

"What do you think they want?" Jung said.

"I think they want us to protect them. They know they have prized land. They are likely afraid that another tribe will try to take it from them. Maybe another tribe has already tried." Hatun shook his head. "It's their own fault. They chose to live by the water. We all know water leads to war."

"Do you think they found out about our springs?"

"No, they have lakes and rivers of their own, and our people have sworn to keep the springs secret."

"Do you really think they want us to help protect them? They have lived at the lake forever. Why do they need our help now?"

Hatun shook his head. "Honestly, I'm not sure."

"But we're going to war?"

He nodded.

"But why? Can't we just leave them alone and tell them to leave us alone?"

"It doesn't work like that."

"Why?"

"Because the moment we refuse their terms, war is declared. It's how it always goes—after a failed attempt of negotiation war always takes place. A natural hierarchy must be re-established. We have had the power for some time. Your grandfather worked hard to make it so. Now, I'm assuming young men are coming of age at the lake and challenging those old agreements."

"What agreements?"

"That we would stay away from one another and respect each other's borders."

A rainbow had appeared in the mist from the waterfall.

"You were always going to go to war weren't you?" Jung said.

"What do you mean?"

"You said you had to consult the elders but you were always going to go weren't you?"

Hatun nodded. "As soon as there was a body."

"Why did you have to go to the council then? You don't need their permission."

"Who said I asked them for permission?"

"Then why did you consult them?"

Hatun smiled. "Who do you think were the last warriors to fight the people of the lake?"

"Really?" Jung said. He struggled to see the elders as warriors.

"It was your grandfather who led our warriors. In fact his last battle was against the people of the lake. He actually died fighting them."

"He fell at the lake?"

Hatun nodded. "Our warriors fought back and killed many of their people. We lost a lot of people too but they lost more. We proved we were stronger and they agreed to a truce."

It wasn't a surprise to Jung to hear his people fought back and killed more people than they lost. It was common knowledge among all the tribes in Peru that his people were deadly rivals. While they were typically peaceful they were by far the most accomplished hunters which made them deadly warriors. They were also great craftsmen. They practiced bow hunting more often than any other tribe and they took more time to craft their weapons. They would fire arrows over and over, stripping a little wood from here and there until each arrow moved with perfect accuracy. They were so in touch with their weapons that the bow was like an extension of their body.

"Now the truce has been called off," Hatun said.

"I want to fight. Let me come," Jung said. He sat up on his knees.

"No."

"But they use axes and spears. I can keep my distance–"

"I'm sorry, Jung."

"But I'm ready."

"I'm sorry."

"I'm more of a man than him."

"Who?" Hatun said.

"Little Puma."

He smirked. "I know you are, but unfortunately it's protocol. You don't have The Healer's blessing. It's far too risky."

Jung stood. "I can get it now. You said the three realms are connected for me. I can go to her now and be back within a dæġ."

"I'm sorry, son. This is the last one you need to sit out." Hatun looked at the ground seemingly upset with himself.

Jung squatted and squeezed his father's shoulder. He had remembered the man was about to go to battle and needed every ounce of strength he could get. "It's okay, I understand. I can wait. When you come back, I'll leave."

Hatun hugged the boy tightly, a sheen of moisture on his eyes.

Suddenly a voice came from beyond the waterfall. Someone was shouting. "Hatun! Hatun!"

A shadow dived through the sheet of water. It was Uma. He had on the same red paint as Hatun.

"We have to go," Uma said. "They killed another scout, near Cuzco."

10

10 dægs to star impact.

THE BASIN. PERU.

Killa stopped in front of me and pointed to what appeared to be an ancient vine. The vine was so wide it would take three men holding hands to extend the circumference. Each thread on the rope of twisted vegetation was more than a man's arm in thickness.

"Ayahuasca," Killa said.

I nodded and smiled. I twisted my bag around my back and pulled out the book of knowledge. I sketched the plant quickly and noted my coordinates before putting the book back into my bag.

"And the other one?" I said.

"What other one?"

"The chacruna plant. The plant that supplies the spirit molecule."

Killa nodded. "This way."

11

THE CLOUD FOREST. PERU.

Jung sped through the maze of tree roots. He ran the same path he had run every dæġ since the warriors had left.

Potoo, a small gray owl with enormous yellow eyes, flew beside him.

Misi ran the trail behind.

The forest was alive with the screeches of screaming pihas, the squawks of mealy parrots and the throaty roars of howler monkeys.

Jung stopped.

Potoo landed on a branch on a tree next to him.

Misi skidded and shot up a different tree.

Jung said, "The song line from The Cloud Forest to Lake Titicaca."

Potoo nodded.

"From The Cloud Forest follow the dipping stars sǒro; Pass one volcano to the plain of many lakes; Round the lonely mountain reflected in the water; Continue to the ridge in the shape of a lizard's spine; Walk the speckled hills until they flatten; Cross seven snaking rivers; Walk the undulating hills until a second volcano appears nǒro; Continue through the rift valley shaped like a puma's tail; Cross the plains for one more dæġ and Lake Titicaca will appear."

As Jung recalled the verses he remembered the stories his father had told him to accompany the lines. These included the story of the girl who became lost and raised by dire wolves and the volcano created as a symbol of unity between dire wolf and man; the story of the giant beaver who dammed all the rivers and how the other animals fought back leading to the creation of seven rivers; and the story of the short-faced bear who dug a hole so deep when making a den that the mountains collapsed causing a rift valley.

Potoo squawked approvingly. "Birds," he hooted.

Jung smiled and stood. He flipped his bag around to his back and ran.

Misi shot down the tree and chased the boy.

Potoo flew to Jung's side.

Jung smiled as he ran. He loved watching Potoo maneuver through the trees so effortlessly.

He skidded to a stop. There were orange butterflies everywhere. The section of the forest was filled with them. They brushed every part of Jung's body.

Potoo landed on a branch and plucked a few out of the air.

Misi waved her paw through the air, trying to swat them.

Jung laughed.

Potoo croaked happily.

As quickly as the butterflies had arrived, they were gone like a wave, drifting off to another part of the forest.

Jung sniffed the air. He smelled a recent troupe of tamarin monkeys, the tang of their wet fur was still in the air.

He took a step forward and placed his palm on the trunk of an enormous pijio tree standing in front of him. The swollen column was twice his width and twenty times his height. He felt the subtle pulse from the being's breath. His tribe called this particular pijio tree the *tinamous tree*. The tinamous were a family of birds who had fat puffy bodies, thin necks and small round heads. His father had taught him 22 species from the tinamous family using the tree.

Jung nodded at Potoo then studied the nodules on the tree. The tune played in his head. *Hah dah mah, tee mah... fah mah tee mah... Hah dah mah, tee mah... fah mah tee mah.* He spoke out loud scanning his eyes from the base of the tree up. "Tawny breasted, highland, hooded, gray, black, great, white-throat, cinereous, little, brown, undulated, pale-browned, gray-legged, black-capped, variegated, small billed, barred, tataupa, red-winged, ornate, curve-billed, puna."

Potoo squawked praises.

Misi rolled on Jung's feet, seeking attention.

Jung closed his eyes and pictured the tree in his mind. He had done the exercise so many times over that the 22 nodules were impressed upon his memory. "Puna, curve-billed, ornate, red-winged, tataupa, barred, small billed, variegated, black-capped, gray-legged, pale-browned, undulated, brown, little, cinereous, white-throat, great, black, gray, hooded, highland, tawny breasted."

Potoo squawked twice as loud and jumped up and down on the branch.

Jung smiled.

The memory technique was called *location learning*. The idea was simple yet profoundly effective. The tribe cut a nodule into the trunk of the tree each time a new species of the tinamous family was discovered. Each nodule came to represent a different species from the family. When a small species was discovered a small nodule would be cut and when a large species was discovered a large nodule would be cut. The technique also allowed the tribe to record the shape and prevalence of each species. For instance regular shaped nodules were cut for more regular looking birds and irregular nodules were cut for more irregular looking birds. And nodules toward the top of the tree were cut when the species was typically found a long way from camp and nodules toward the base of the tree were cut when the species was abundant in the local area. It meant just by remembering the location and look of a nodule a hunter could recall an enormous amount of information about each species.

"Guans," Potoo hooted.

Jung nodded. This meant climbing higher up the peak to an old rustic tree where they listed the guans and curassows. Logic was always applied, even with altitude. Higher up the mountain was where the tribe had marked trees to represent those families of birds that dwelled higher in The Cloud Forest: the owls like Potoo, and the hummingbirds, woodpeckers, parrots, kingfishers, toucans, swallows and wrens. Higher up again, in the cliffs, was where they marked trees to represent the raptors: the falcons, hawks, ospreys, eagles and kites. The opposite way, back down the slope, was where they marked trees to list the water birds: the ducks, grebes, plovers, flamingos, ibises, spoonbills, geese and waterfowl. And further down again was where they marked trees to list the shoreline birds: the sandpipers, penguins, albatrosses, petrels, boobies, gannets, pelicans and herons.

And there weren't just trees for the birds, there were trees for every family of animal Jung's people had encountered.

Suddenly a crashing sound came from the thick.

There were rushing footsteps and the sound of something being dragged.

Jung turned and saw Uma appear through the trees. Then Puma appeared. Both men were sweating and breathing heavily.

Then Jung spotted it. The men were carrying something between them. A man lay unconscious with his arms drooped to the sides like a moth whose wings were soaked in water. He felt a whirling in his gut.

It was Hatun.

12

Jung skidded to his father's side and grabbed his hands.

Hatun was white and lifeless, his lips were blue and his eyes were rolled back in his head.

"I'm sorry," Uma said. His voice was choked and tears streamed down his face.

Other warriors began to appear from the thick, all painted in red. When they saw Jung they looked to the ground with shame.

Misi sniffed Hatun's legs.

Potoo sat in a branch nearby, a sad look on his face.

"What happened?" Jung said.

Uma broke into sobs. "He's dead."

Jung rested his head on his father's cold chest. Tears filled his eyes. It didn't feel real, it didn't feel like him.

Misi copied Jung and lay on the ground with her back against Hatun. She placed her chin across the dead man's legs and watched the boy.

Uma squatted and hugged Jung tightly.

Tears flowed freely from both their eyes.

Time seemed to disappear altogether as Jung's mind was thrust back and forth, from joyful memories of his father to imagined moments in the future when he and his siblings would come to full terms with losing both parents.

By the time Jung was back in his body, the other warriors had well and truly returned to camp. It was just him, Uma, Potoo and Misi left alone with the body.

"What happened?" Jung said. "Was it at the lake? In battle?"

"No."

"How then?"

"I'm not sure," Uma said.

Jung stared at his uncle. He sensed the man was holding back, not telling him everything. "Where did he die?"

"He saw an omen, a star. It appeared over the lake before we got to Lake Titicaca. He said it was a bad omen and that we needed to return to get a blessing from The Healer. We never made it to the lake."

"Did you see it too?"

Uma nodded.

"Where?"

"Sorð, beyond the lake."

"On the other side of the lake?"

"Yes, above the people of the lake's camp."

Jung locked eyes with his uncle. "I thought you said you never made it to the lake?"

Uma frowned. "We didn't. We saw it in the distance."

"And it was definitely a star?"

"Yes, it came very close. We felt its heat. It was a powerful omen."

Suddenly a white and black hummingbird appeared between the two of them. Around its beak was a fluorescent sequin patch that started purple and transitioned to yellow, green, orange and blue. At its tail were two long strands, each a hand in length.

It's wings buzzed as it hovered in the air. The appearance of the bird was eerily mesmerizing. Such a moment Jung's people called *lechero*. It referred to a moment so strikingly beautiful and so well-timed that it almost appeared like an abnormality, a glitch in the system.

Before the hummingbird had even really arrived, it was gone.

"Then what happened?" Jung said.

"We turned back."

"But when did he get sick? When did he die?"

"As soon as we left the lake he complained about stomach cramps," Uma said. "You know Hatun, he never complains about anything. Then he started throwing up and had diarrhea. He deteriorated from there."

Jung looked at his father's stiff body.

"We tried to get him back here but it's five dægs walk."

"You think the star poisoned him?"

Uma nodded then he seemed to change his mind and shake his head. "I don't know, maybe, or maybe it took his spirit. All I know is the star showed up and he deteriorated fast soon after."

"Like it took his life?"

"I don't know."

"You said it appeared above Lake Titicaca. From the norð shore looking sorð?"

Uma nodded.

Jung bent down and picked up his father's bow and quiver. He ran his thumb across the white marbled plate embedded into the wood at the front of the bow. The grooved surface helped aim an arrow while providing as little resistance as possible. His father had told him the plate had come from the remains of the largest animal he had ever killed. In fact his father's name Hatun Tujllaki meant 'Big Hunter' and had originated from this very story. Hatun said he traveled further norð than any other man in their tribe to make the kill. He had promised to one dæġ take Jung to the place where he said thousands of such animals roamed. It was a promise that now would never come true.

Jung threw his father's bow and quiver over his shoulder next to his bag.

"Where are you going?" Uma said.

"I'm going to look for the omen. To see if I can find out where he's gone."

"Where *who's* gone?"

Jung scowled. "Father!"

"What do you think you'll find?"

"I don't know, but he's gone somewhere. I need to look for him."

"Look for who? He's dead. He's here."

Jung looked at the body. "Wherever he is, he's not here." He looked at his uncle. "You always said, if you are supposed to see an omen, the omen will present itself to you. It showed up for all of you. Maybe it will show up for me too. I'm his son after all."

"But we need to bury him, Jung."

"We need to bury what? That's not him."

Uma looked pained. "We still need to bury him."

"Then bury him! I'm going to the lake. If the omen doesn't show after four sleeps I'll return."

Jung went to leave.

"You can't!"

Jung turned. "Why?"

The forest quietened of all bird chatter, only the drone of cicadas remained.

"If they see you, they'll kill you," Uma whispered.

"They won't see me."

"You don't know that."

"I'll take my chances."

Uma grabbed Jung's arm. "You don't understand. There is something different about their camp. It's why we didn't go in."

Jung ripped his arm free. "Get off me."

"You don't understand. They seem to have evolved."

"Evolved?"

Uma nodded. "Their boats are bigger and better designed and their houses are the same, bigger and more considered. And they are carving out the hills and building enormous stone walls. They seem like different people, like men possessed by gods."

"You're afraid of big boats and houses?"

Uma looked afraid. "It was just strange, it felt strange. We all felt something eerie out there. We were contemplating whether to turn back before the star even crossed the sky. Then the omen arrived and we knew it was a warning so we left."

Jung twisted his father's quiver around and pulled out an arrow. He handed it to Uma.

Uma shook his head as he took the arrow. He knew he had to agree to take the item. Nobody could turn down an arrow offered to them without jinxing the warrior's journey.

The moment the arrow was in Uma's hands, Jung turned and fled towards the trail that led to Ollyantambo. Misi and Potoo followed.

He had no idea that by dark, Earth would be cold and dead.

13

THE SACRED VALLEY. PERU.

Jung sat on a ledge, high in the mountains, above his people's camp. He smelled a dank earthy aroma, it would rain soon. All around him were steep granite cliffs bald on the sides and covered in thick forest at their tops. Below, he saw Sisa and the other pods and the snaking river.

Misi and Potoo sat next to Jung, they were battling the wind that whistled between the cracks in the rocks.

Jung knew he needed to make a decision fast, for the sake of the animals as much as himself. He had to decide whether he would try to get The Healer's blessing before leaving for Lake Titicaca or whether he would go without it. The dilemma was that if he asked permission she might say no. Whereas if he never asked he could never have his journey denied. However, this also meant he wouldn't be protected.

Suddenly he doubted his chances. How could The Healer possibly say yes to blessing his journey when his father's burial hadn't even taken place? Plus, if she knew what his uncle knew, that the people of Lake Titicaca had evolved in some way, she was guaranteed to reject his request, and of course she knew.

He had made a decision, he would go to the lake without her blessing.

"Let's go guys," Jung said to Misi and Potoo.

Suddenly Jung froze. He saw a figure appear on the side of the next peak over. It was The Healer. The tiny old woman wore a tan alpaca hide that covered everything from her neck to her ankles. She had long streaked gray hair with black and white condor feathers tucked into the wavy folds. She was hunched over carrying a large wooden pot. She carried the pot to the edge of the ravine and tipped the water over the edge.

She looked in Jung's direction.

He thrust his back against the shelf and cussed himself for possibly being seen. He knew he should have left earlier. He shuffled sideways down the ridge.

Suddenly an orb of white light appeared in the sky and there was a flash. A fiery orange ball appeared from nothingness and sped across the sky. It looked almost like a bird whose wings were made of fire and body made from smoke. The fiery condor caressed the sky, gaining speed.

It had to be his father's spirit, Jung thought. The Healer had looked at him and then the sky had changed. *Had she just sent Hatun to the third realm?* He knew she had the power to do so, she was the most powerful person in all of The Sacred Valley.

Suddenly the trail of smoke streaming out from behind the bird blackened and intensified. The bird's emblazoned tail dipped and fragments broke free from the creature, the crumbling pieces looked like giant men jumping from a burning boat.

Jung shielded his eyes feeling the heat. He watched the bird getting lower and lower until it disappeared beyond the mountains norð. Then came a flash of white so bright he went blind and could see only white. A wave of heat hit his body throwing him to the ground. He heard Misi squeal and Potoo flying.

Blind, Jung grabbed at the earth, squeezing two spiky shrubs in his fists. Then came a deafening explosion—a cracking sound. It was the loudest sound Jung had ever heard. It felt like his eardrums had burst as the bang gave way to a high-pitched whistle.

Now Jung was blind and deaf. He pressed his hands to his ears and squeezed his eyes shut. He could feel liquid pouring from his eardrums.

Then came a creaking sound from deep beneath Earth's crust. At first a thudding, grinding sound then a winding groan. The mountain began to shake building in intensity.

Jung crawled into a ball as the ground shook.

A faint voice just cleared the hiss whistling in Jung's ears.

"Boy! You need to get out of there," The Healer said.

Was it a dream? Jung thought. He opened his eyes. The white light was still there but slowly dissolving away. He saw vague shapes, everything over-saturated. He knew Misi and Potoo were gone. He felt their distance.

"Boy! Quick!"

Jung climbed to his feet, the mountain trembled beneath him. He felt a drop of rain on his cheek, then another and another. Suddenly everything turned from gray to black as thick storm clouds gathered overhead. The clouds were dark and murky, moisture enmeshed with ash and debris. It began to pour black rain.

"Now!" The Healer said.

Jung put his hands out and crawled as fast as he could toward the woman.

"Yes! Yes!"

"I can't see!" Jung said.

"Follow my voice, keep following my voice, keep following."

By the time Jung reached the entrance to the cave, the sky was black as night and forks of purple lightning filled every corner of the sky.

The Healer took Jung's hand and led him through the crack in the rocks.

He had no idea that as he sheltered, floods and earthquakes were pummeling the coasts while wildfires and hurricanes raged across the interiors.

14

0 dægs to star impact.

LAKE TITICACA. PERU.

I was with the people of the lake when the star hit.

We pushed the boats onto the choppy waters just as birds covered the sky in black droves, species after species, flying together. The birds were fleeing the orange beacon that throbbed beyond the mountains norð where the bulk of the star had hit. The fiery furnace billowed black smoke that clawed its way across the sky fast. The closer the cloud came, the more difficult it was to breathe. We were racing the cloud.

We aimed the boats at Pachamama Mountain, an island in Lake Titicaca where the natives said there were caves in the hills we could use to shelter. There were six sturdy-armed rowers to each vessel. Despite the men's small frames, they were impressively strong. They gritted their teeth when they rowed, their arms red and inflamed, veins popping from their necks.

They yelled in sync. "Stroke, Stroke, Stroke."

With each yell there was a splash as their oars thrust from the water, followed by a squeaking sound as they lifted from their seats.

I lay at the bottom of one of the boats, bent over, coughing and being sick—the ash irritating my lungs. I tapped my finger to the rowers' yells—it gave me something to concentrate on other than my own death.

One thing I could be proud of was the design of the boats worked perfectly. We had followed the instructions in the book of knowledge just as the Tæcans had described. The result was a pulpy craft that sat high on the water and sliced through the swirling waves with ease.

The problem was I knew the conditions were about to turn. Any moment the winds would turn to hurricanes and the waves to mountains. Any man with fishing knowledge would have felt it. I saw it in vibrations on the surface of the water. The buzz was being passed on from the buzz in the crust of Earth. Beneath the lake she was shivering from the impact. It added an extra rough edge to the already gnarly waves.

The earthquakes weren't my concern though. My concern was the wave of electrical storms flooding the sky. It was as though other realms had found a way to poke their way through the fabric of the sky. Forks of lightning burst from the blackness and struck the water around us. Enormous bangs erupted from the fiery impacts.

One explosion was so close even the boats were kicked back.

Children screamed to the popping sound.

I felt a sharp pain shoot through my ears. I ducked lower and hid my head in my hands. I smelled burnt wet, wildfires after rain.

"Stroke, Stroke, Stroke."

Then came the hail, blocks of ice as big as fists pelted us.

The natives yelled as the blocks caused instant welts.

I was grateful to be covered by my robe, which protected me from the brunt of the impacts.

Then Earth began to shake more intensely, doubling the waves in height, whirling the lake into a muddy shake. The storm was right overhead.

A few of the women screamed, seeing some big waves approaching.

Children from all directions crying in fear.

I tapped my hand harder and faster.

"Stroke, Stroke, Stroke."

We reached the shores of Pachamama Mountain just as the storm turned the lake into a swirling mess of tsunamis—a death sentence for even the most well-designed boat.

We jumped from the craft and dragged them high up the bank before running to the top of the mountain where we poured into the caves like flooding water.

I knew the natives would blame me for the disaster, the book of knowledge said they would.

I needed to get my story straight fast.

15

THE SACRED VALLEY. PERU.

Jung crawled across the cold granite stones in the dark. He coughed and listened to the echo, the space sounded enormous. He looked up and saw the roof five men high made of the same large stone blocks, cut at perfect right angles. The chamber was clearly made by man and designed for something enormous. He saw a flicker of light, a passage out. He crawled quickly towards it.

When Jung woke from his dream he was lying on the sand covered in a blanket made of condor feathers. The smell of the cave was familiar. He couldn't figure out exactly how but the muskiness reminded him of his mother. It wasn't the smell of her but it reminded him of an early time with her, perhaps the earliest time he could remember. Deep below, he felt the earth creaking and moaning. It caused the cave to buzz and shake with endless tremors. Dust poured from the roof. Outside it was raining heavily and the wind howled. He licked his cracked lips, his mouth was dry and tasted of ash. He rolled over.

Jung saw a cave around five men wide and ten men long. A small fire wavered in the center casting orange light across the stone walls. There were plants everywhere, the entire cave was full of them. They were of all sorts and sizes, each growing from its own wooden case packed with black soil. There were trays of mushrooms too, the most exotic mushrooms Jung had ever seen. There were dozens of types, including an orange species with a honeycomb structure; a purple species that looked like a clump of worms; a white species that had juicy red bubbles; and a yellow species that had a see-through lattice cover.

"You're awake," The Healer said.

The tiny woman emerged from behind a row of plants. She had wrinkled cheeks like wilting flower petals and her eyes were small and dark like compressed opals. She was still wearing the alpaca-skin shawl that covered most of her body. Her hair was tangled in a clump from where she had slept.

Jung sat up, slowly.

"You've been asleep for dæġs," she said. "You obviously needed the rest. Just be slow, you'll be weak."

"What are all the plants for?" Jung said. He still heard a faint whistling in his ears and his vision was a little blurred.

She looked at the plants. "My attempt to save a few."

"From the storms?"

She nodded.

"You knew the storm was coming?"

"Yes."

"How?"

She smiled. "We'll get to that."

Jung sat up straight. "Where is Misi and Potoo. Did you see them?"

"They are gone. They fled back to The Cloud Forest."

"I have to get after them."

The Healer shook her head. "You need to stay here for now. It's okay, they are safe. They are back in the protection of the forest. I've seen them."

"I have to get going."

Thunder rumbled in the distance.

Jung looked around, he was searching for his bow. He spotted it resting against one of the cave walls with his quiver and bag.

"You must stay here for 12 dægs," she said. "Well nine, now."

"What?"

"We are rounding the bend, switching energies. The feminine age is over. Pachamama is washing herself—being reborn. For 12 dægs she will rage with earthquakes, wildfires, floods and storms. Then we will start again in the masculine age. You must stay here until then."

"What do you mean masculine age?"

The Healer smiled. "Masculine doesn't mean male and feminine doesn't mean female. Masculine means structure and feminine means creativity. Our reality, what we see and experience, is determined by the interplay between these two things—structure and creativity. We have just completed the feminine age, a period of around 2,000 rotations where creativity was the dominant force in the creation of our reality. Now we're entering the masculine age, a period of around 2,000 rotations where structure will dominate those things we bring into being."

Jung went to stand. "This is all very interesting, maybe we can pick this up again another time. For now I have to go, I have somewhere to be."

"Unfortunately, you can't."

"What are you talking about?" Jung said.

Her voice was suddenly cold. "I've seen it."

"Seen what?"

"Your future."

She sat down and opened a small alpaca-skin pouch. She picked up a green coca leaf and held it up to the light of the fire. The leaf was heavily scarred and had a slight fold at the tip.

"What is that?" Jung said.

She put the leaf back into the pouch. "It's not good. But stay here for 12 dægs and you'll be safe."

"But what does it say?"

"Very little but nothing good. I would like to read your fortune properly. Would you allow me?"

There was a glint of moisture in the woman's eyes.

Seeing her teary eyes made Jung teary too. He nodded.

The Healer smiled and pointed to the sand on the opposite side of the fire. "Please come closer."

Jung shuffled closer.

"First let me cleanse the area," she said.

She went to the back of the cave to retrieve more wood which she added to the fire. She built the fire up and waited for it to take. All the while, it rained and thundered outside and the ground creaked and trembled.

Jung knew exactly what she was doing. When the smoke rose in a straight line, it meant the energy in the cave had been cleansed.

He watched her stack the wood and the smoke disappear through a crack in the roof. He smiled at the coincidence of finding a cave that had a built-in chiminea.

Soon enough the fire was ablaze and the smoke rose straight.

The Healer patted the ground next to her. "Can you come here please."

Jung stood and moved around the fire and sat next to her.

She twisted her body so they were facing one another. Between them she laid out the alpaca pouch. On top of the pouch were a set of objects: a pile of coca leaves, the claw of a condor, several sea shells and a shiny black stone.

She stared into Jung's eyes, the flames from the fire dancing across her pupils. She picked up the black stone and closed her eyes. She squeezed the stone in her fist and muttered something under her breath, then she opened her hand and gave the stone to Jung.

Jung took the cold rock, he was immediately astounded by the weight of the object. It was if the action of The Healer whispering to it had given the stone extra mass.

"This is your stone of power," she said.

She closed Jung's fingers around the rock. "It must be kept safe and never lost. Do you understand?"

Jung nodded. He felt the dimpled rock pulse in his palm.

She picked up the pile of coca leaves. She held them in the cup of her hands and hovered them near Jung's face. "Blow."

Jung blew onto the leaves until she closed her hands.

She raised her hands up and allowed the leaves to fall to the ground. The moment the leaves reached the sand, she leaned in and began to study them. After some time, she looked at Jung. "You are from The Cloud Forest. You are the son of Hatun and Tuta?"

She nodded at Jung, requesting confirmation.

Jung nodded, a knot in his stomach. *Was.*

She looked back at the leaves spread across the floor. "Your tribe is strong, connected. Your people are healthy. You are too." She paused, studying the leaves with greater intensity. "Although your shadow-self is heavy."

Jung felt the knot in his stomach tightening and beginning to rise.

"I can see you're caught between the realms of serpent and cat. I see you are caught in the shadow of another. The shadow of someone who is very strong."

Jung was silent. He felt the knot in his throat.

The Healer studied the leaves. "But I also see you are your own being. You see things others overlook. You have good intuition, good instinct. You understand that you exist in a world as conscious of you as you are of it."

Jung gasped for air. He hadn't even realized he was holding his breath.

The Healer paused for some time. Eventually she raised her head.

She said, "I see the death too."

A spark from the fire shot into the air.

Jung buried his face in his knees.

"I know it hurts," she said. "Death always hurts. But I want you to know that death isn't bad. It introduces us to a more intimate love, the love of our own being. In time you will see that the touch of death makes everything more precious, more sacred, more meaningful."

Jung kept his face buried in his knees.

"Your journey is long but she watches over you. She wants you to know that she wants you to succeed."

Jung raised his head. His eyes were red.

"She wants you to know that your growth is her growth and your strength is her strength. She will ground you until your wings are strong enough and you are ready to soar."

She reached for Jung's hands.

Jung put the power stone under the waist of his loincloth and took her hands.

He immediately felt heat in her small sweating palms. The energy pulsed from her body to his. He felt both electrified and overwhelmed by a deep sense of peace.

"Close your eyes," she said. She closed her eyes. "Trust more in your experiences than my words. Trust what you feel."

Jung closed his eyes. He felt a warm sensation swirling in his gut.

"I see a long journey ahead of you. A journey full of many dark spirits."

"Dark spirits?" Jung said.

"Shhhhhhhhh. No questions." She took some time to regain her focus. "Yes, many dark spirits but many light spirits too. I see an explorer, a man whose own desire for adventure will take you further than even he intends. And I see a sage, a man with great knowledge who will set you free." She paused. "But beware, I see a jester, someone who may deviate you from your goal." Her hands began to shake. Her voice quivered. "And I see magicians- many magicians. More magicians than one individual should ever encounter."

A spark zapped between their fingers. They released hands.

Jung was drenched in sweat. He felt the energy still circulating in his palms.

The Healer was looking at him. "You must go to the star norð, where the orange beacon pulses. That is your passage."

Jung shook his head. "I'm heading sorð, to Lake Titicaca."

"Your journey is norð, I have seen it."

"Too bad," Jung said shortly, tired of people telling him what to do.

He stood and walked around the fire to where his bow and quiver stood. "I have to get out of here. Do I have Pachamama's blessing to leave or not?"

"You can go another way Jung but you'll always eventually end up at the same place. What's for you won't miss you."

"Do I have the blessing or not?" Jung said.

"He calls for you from the star."

"Who?"

"Your father. Hatun."

16

120 dægs to stars return.

LAKE TITICACA. PERU.

I was sheltering in the caves in Pachamama Mountain with the people of the lake. The space was 10 men high and 20 men wide, comfortably housing us 150-ish people. The entire cavern had been excavated by hand, it must have taken the tribe dægs to remove all of the earth. How they knew to build the caves I was yet to find out. The space was a sanctuary compared to the inferno outside. Only small windows, built to allow airflow, provided hints of the devastation. The air was thick with smoke from distant wildfires and everything was covered in several feet of black ash. The sky was red from the debris in the air. It was like a different planet, the surface of Mars.

Light from Earth's Star hadn't reached us for several dægs causing the temperature to plummet. If it wasn't for the natives' persistence with starting a fire and going out into the storms to collect wood, we were sure to have died from the cold. My other fear was the floods. I wondered how many more dægs we had left before the lake filled so high that the cave was submerged.

The only thing that gave me comfort was pouring through the book of knowledge. I was doing the equation again to pinpoint the exact location the star had hit. I had noted the flash at the time of the impact and counted how long it took for the bang to arrive. Now it was just a matter of dropping in the numbers.

A woman began to cough hard. Her lungs sounded layered with ash.

I no doubt would have been the same if I hadn't cut the hood off my robe and used it as a face mask. The cloth covered my nose to my chin, keeping the bulk of the ash out of my breaths. Although my lungs still burned from the smoke.

"You brought this!" an accusatory voice said.

I knew the words were directed at me.

It was Kichka. He was around twenty-rotations and one of the larger males. Although he still only reached my shoulders in height. He had short dark hair and bushy eyebrows and was missing a good chunk of one ear—the result of a hunting accident.

He was sitting with a group of young males. They had spent the best part of the morning whispering to each other and throwing glances my way.

I closed the book and looked across the fire.

Kichka sat forward, glaring at me.

"I know it seems that way," I said.

"It doesn't *seem* that way, it *is* that way," Kichka said. "You arrive here and within a season everything dies."

Thunder cracked overhead and rippled across the sky.

I gripped my staff tightly and looked at the different faces of the tribe, sharing eye contact with as many of them as I could.

I said, "I certainly see how it looks but I didn't cause the disaster. The truth is it wasn't an accident that I arrived here and then the disaster occurred. My people foretold this dæġ. We knew it was coming. That's why I was sent here."

The faces looking back at me looked unenthused. We were all tired and hungry and running on limited air.

I held the book up. "But my people also showed me a way out. It's all in here. This book shows us how we can bring Earth back into balance and put an end to the destruction."

"What's all in there?" a timid voice said.

The thin woman had her knees bent and drawn close to her chest. She was young but she looked weak like she could collapse any moment.

"The steps to restore balance to Earth," I said.

"Enough!" Kichka said. "You've done enough damage."

"Leave him Kichka," a woman's voice said.

It was Quya, one of the elder women. She had a round face and plump red cheeks. She was wrapped in a llama-skin blanket and bounced a young boy, two rotations in age, up and down on her knee. The child had a piece of my robe covering his face. I had cut the strip and offered it to Quya one night when the boy wouldn't stop coughing.

Kichka was quiet, obeying.

Quya looked at me. "How?"

I tapped the cover of the book. "Like I said, it's all in here."

"But how, explain," she said.

"Through a machine my people have designed. I can show you." I lay the book back across my lap and began to thumb through the pages.

Suddenly the cave began to shake violently. The ground creaked and shook causing the sandy walls to vibrate and crack. Dirt poured from the roof. Children began to scream and cry.

I braced every muscle in my body, riding out the vicious shaking. I was expecting the roof to collapse and crush us to death any moment.

We sat in silence for some time after the rattling had faded away. We sat tense, anticipating aftershocks, aftershocks that never came.

Eventually Quya spoke. "What does it do?"

"The machine?" I said.

She nodded, rocking the boy back and forth on her chest.

"It will get us out of the way,"

"Out of the way of what?" Kichka said.

"The stars."

"But the stars have already hit us," Quya said.

"I know, but they're coming back," I said.

"They're coming back?" she said

I nodded. "Yes, we're right in the thick of the storm now. There is star debris all around us. There will be impacts every two seasons until we clear a path through the debris."

"How long will that take?" Quya said.

"Our star watchers predict three decades."

"Three decades!" she said. "Nothing will be left."

"I know," I said. "That's why we have to stop them."

"Why *twice* a rotation?" Kichka said.

"Because Earth wobbles as it moves around Earth's Star," I said. "Which means it moves up and down each rotation, like a wave on the ocean. This means we pass through the belt of star debris twice each lap around Earth's Star, once on the way up and once on the way down."

"We'll never survive that long," Quya said.

"Like I said, there is a way out," I said.

"How?" she said.

I held up the page so everyone in the tribe could see it. It showed three large circles side-by-side with a horizontal line running through the center of them. There were three dots marked on the line, one on each circle.

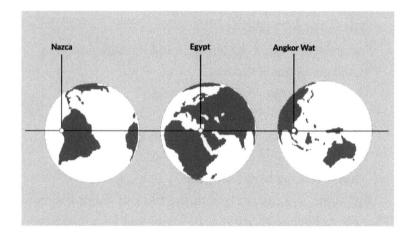

"We call the machine The Artery of Earth."

17

THE SACRED VALLEY. PERU.

Jung and The Healer sat on opposite sides of the fire.

The woman was mixing charcoal from the fire with a brown dirt she had in a pouch.

"What's that?" Jung said.

"Terra preta—dark earth."

"What does it do?"

"It helps plants grow in barren soil," she said.

She shuffled over to the plants and added a little of the mixture to the troughs at the base of their stems. The leaves on the plants were beginning to get droopy, it had been several dægs since they had seen light from Earth's Star.

"Do you think they'll survive?" Jung said.

She touched a particularly saggy branch. "I don't know, probably not."

"Why did you grab them all then?"

"Because 12 dægs is a long time. I'm sure I'll find a use for many of them before then, especially now that I have company." She returned to the fire. "You know, your father used to visit me a lot for the plants?"

"My father?"

"Yes, Hatun used to come up here a lot, especially after your mother passed."

"Why?"

"For dietas mainly."

"What's that?"

"A contract you make with a plant."

"A contract with a plant?" Jung said, excited. "What plant?"

"Many species, there are many master plants. Your father did several dietas with several different plants."

"What do they do?"

"They guide you so you can heal yourself and grow. It is all about opening a clear line of communication between the person and the plant. Often the plant is the one who will request that someone does a dieta so they can communicate with them. Whether the person is listening to the call is another story. Mapacho—tobacco—is most often the plant who will tell you if another plant wants to speak to you."

"What happens in a dieta?" Jung said.

"Well, that depends on the plant and the person. Typically a dieta lasts anywhere from eight dægs to several months. The person vows not to eat and to drink only very little. They also vow not to communicate or interact with other people, nor touch themselves sexually or fixate on sexual thoughts. Mapacho is used to facilitate all communication between the plant and the person."

"And the plant tells you things?"

The Healer nodded. "Yes and they show you things. And a protective bond can be created."

"How long does the plant protect the person?"

"If the person holds true to the contract made with the plant then the bond can last for many seasons. This is why your father was so strong and wise. He was protected and guided by many master plants."

Jung scrunched his face. "Protected? He's dead."

The Healer closed her eyes and shook her head. "He's not dead."

"What are you talking about? I saw his body."

"There is more going on than you think. Your father is still here."

"Here? At camp?"

She opened her eyes. "No, norð. Where the star hit. The orange beacon."

"That doesn't make any sense. He didn't even go there."

"How do you know? Maybe not recently."

"Okay, but not now. I saw him. He's dead."

She shrugged. "All I can say is that I feel his energy. I feel he is alive and well. He calls for you from the orange beacon."

18

108 dæġs to stars return.

LAKE TITICACA. PERU.

After 12 dæġs we exited the caves and trudged through feet of ash. The sky was black and thick with smoke that burned my eyes.

I immediately noticed the haunting silence. There was not an animal to be heard, not even a tweet from a bird or the buzz from an insect. I heard only the sound of Earth creaking from within. Far away the gray hills were covered in stalks of stubble and great gouges that bled into the bloated lake.

We pushed the canoes onto the black water and paddled for the shore.

An elder man who sat at the front of my boat hummed an eerie tune that only added to the heaviness of the scene.

It wasn't until we entered the shallows that we saw just how much damage had been done. The water was black and the once vibrant green reeds that had stood tall on the pristine blue waters now floated on their sides, turned to a soggy brown.

Then came the tangy smell of death. It arrived long before we saw the bodies of flamingos, ducks and guinea pigs. The animals looked poisoned, they floated on their backs, bloated and rotten.

The natives whimpered seeing the layers upon layers of bodies.

I found watching them mourn the destruction of their land just as difficult as seeing the destruction itself. It seemed to empty them of all life.

Without speaking, we all knew camp was one hundred feet below the surface of the water. Evidence of the people of the lake's long history in the area had been scrubbed clean from existence almost overnight.

Norð, the orange beacon pulsed beyond the mountains just above Cuzco. Above the beacon a dark vortex of circulating clouds painted an ominous scene. Flashes of lightning bleached the cloud in purple then white then blue.

I knew convincing one of the natives to make the journey to the crash site was going to be my most difficult task yet.

19

CUZCO. PERU.

Jung ran the mountain passage, heading sorð. He smelled mud and wet soot. Everything around him was caked in ash and cloaked in a low-hanging fog. It looked like a charcoal drawing smeared by hand—brown dry ferns, black soggy moss, gray bent-over trees.

Jung had his hand in his bag feeling through the items The Healer had given him. There was the power stone, a tinder fungus with a burning coal inside, two fists of coca leaves, a water bladder made from a bear's stomach, a knife carved from the leg bone of a llama, two dehydrated guinea pigs and an assortment of vegetables, including potatoes, corn and cucumber. For warmth he had a deerskin shawl The Healer had given him and for protection he had his father's bow and quiver.

Suddenly a shadow appeared sitting on the path ahead.

Jung's heart skipped a beat at the sight of the figure. He stopped and squatted.

It was a man sat cross-legged, wrapped in animal skins. He didn't appear to have any items with him, which meant he was most likely local. He was looking over the edge of the ravine, down at the river.

Fifty lengths-of-man below, the surging waters clawed at the walls of the canyon. Running ten men higher up the ridge than usual, the churning red slurry sucked and gurgled, breaking violently into giant twisting whirlpools. Jets of foam shot into the air like poison spat from a snake's fangs.

The man sat peacefully still.

Jung slowly slid his quiver around and pulled out an arrow. He placed it across his bow.

The man turned and looked at him.

Jung froze.

Then, as if never seeing the boy, the man returned his attention to the river.

Jung knew he had to have seen him—he had stared right at him. Yet somehow he was unfazed by the boy's presence. It was abnormal. An armed stranger on your land was a threat, especially to an unarmed man.

Jung aimed his bow at the man. "Hello."

The man nodded but didn't turn.

So he had seen him, Jung thought. He drew back the loaded arrow and walked a few steps closer. "What are you doing here?"

The man faced him.

In the darkness, Jung barely made out the old man's bald head and wrinkled face. He had a large arrow-shaped nose.

"What's your name, boy?" the man said.

Jung was silent, considering his move.

"I'm Apo."

"I'm Jung."

Apo smiled. "Jung. Nice to meet you, Jung. So Jung, who is your tribe?"

"The Cloud Forest," Jung said without a pause. He believed he would have the most chance of being protected if the man knew he was from The Cloud Forest.

"Ah, Sacred Valley. Good people cloud forest people." He patted the ground next to him. "Sit."

Jung took the arrow from his bow and slid it into his quiver. He sat, keeping a little distance from the man.

Apo turned to him and smiled.

It was the first time Jung had seen the old man's face up close. The pupils in his eyes were gone, they were clouded over in white. He was blind. It explained why he had looked right at Jung without seeing him.

Apo shook his head. "You may think so."

"What?" Jung said. *Had he spoken without realizing?*

"You may think I didn't feel your presence, but I did."

Jung nodded to himself, remembering what his grandmother Wasi had told him about losing a sense like sight. She said when one sense was lost the other senses were sharpened. The man must have heard him approaching.

"Actually, I smelt you," Apo said.

Shivers rolled down Jung's spine. He definitely didn't speak that time. The man seemed to be reading his thoughts.

"People always assume I hear them," Apo said. He shook his head and tapped the side of his nose. "No, I trust my nose more than my ears or any other sense. It goes right to the center of the head and links us with the very oldest parts of our being. For this reason it is the most trustworthy of all of the senses. Your eyes and your ears are likely to deceive you—to play tricks on you—but your nose never will."

Jung was captivated by the man. He seemed to have rhythm, speaking in beats.

Apo looked at him. "Have you ever smelt something that thrust you back to your childhood? Perhaps the sweet tang of a hide, the richness of a plant or the musk from a recently passed herd?"

Jung remembered the smell from The Healer's cave and how it had brought on a memory of his mother from when he was very young.

Apo smiled as if sensing the boy's realization. "A smell can send us back to the last time we were exposed to the same aroma, flooding us with memories." He paused and inhaled slowly through his nose, letting his chest fill with a big breath of air. He held the breath for a moment then slowly exhaled through his nose.

He said, "The difference between the nose and other senses like the eyes and the ears is that while the other senses have one purpose, the nose has three. The first function is to perceive the smell itself for guidance. For instance, a smell can warn us that a rotten carcass should be avoided, while a ripe fruit should be picked. This is obvious. The second function is to breathe. When we breathe through our nose we relax our baseline and can operate for longer. Always a fairly obvious one."

Apo paused and lowered his voice, as if telling a secret. "But beyond these two important functions the nose performs another function that connects us with our unconscious. You see our nose detects odorless scents released by others that alert us on their intentions. For instance, we can tell whether someone is searching for food or sex or dominance."

"Really?"

"Yes, you will not smell these things but your body will understand the message and your gut will warn you. If you are ever unsure what to trust, place all your focus on the nose and follow the breath in and out. It will guide you."

Jung rolled his eyes, maybe the man wasn't that interesting. He was starting to sound like just another kook who wanted to tell everyone else what to do.

Apo looked at him.

Jung froze.

The man stared at him for some time then turned back to the river.

"What are you doing out here anyway?" Jung said.

"Making peace with things. And you?"

"Passing through."

"From where to where? The Cloud Forest to?"

"I'm heading sorð," Jung said.

"Sorð? Where sorð?"

"La-" He cut the words. *Stupid.*

"Lake Titicaca?"

Jung was silent, kicking himself.

Apo looked suddenly concerned. "You can't go to the lake, boy."

A grinding sound came from down in the river. Several logs had become wedged between a pile of boulders and were beginning to bank up. The wood creaked and groaned until there was a giant snapping sound and the mass of logs tore off down the passage.

"I'm not going to the lake," Jung said.

"It's dangerous there. The people of the lake aren't who they once were."

"What do you mean?"

"They are not alone. The children of gods are with them now."

Jung felt butterflies stretching their wings in his stomach. He remembered The Healer's words, *I see magicians, many magicians.*

Apo scratched his head and clenched his teeth.

"What is it?" Jung said.

The man bit his lip and rocked back and forth slowly.

"Who are they?"

Apo looked at him. "The children of gods?"

Jung nodded.

"They are creatures from the other side of the ocean. Creatures who know every star in the sky and every island on Earth. Big hulking creatures who look much like sea foam, fair skin and thick beards. Creatures of great knowledge and power. But also creatures of great darkness."

Jung looked around, expecting to see the creatures appear from the darkness any moment. He looked at Apo. "Who are they?"

Apo swallowed hard. "You can't go to the lake, it's far too dangerous."

"I have to. I won't go to the people's camp."

Apo shook his head. "You will."

"No, I won't."

"You don't understand their powers, they will lure you in."

Jung smirked smugly. "I'm sure I can handle staying away."

"You won't, boy. You must turn around now."

Jung scowled and went to stand. He was frustrated at being told what to do by yet another adult.

Apo grabbed his arm.

The man's bony fingers sent a spark running through Jung's shoulder.

"Turn around now," Apo said.

Jung shook his arm free. "Get off me." He picked up his bow and quiver.

"Many rotations ago they came to the jungles," Apo said. He looked up at Jung. "They took many people from my tribe."

Jung stopped.

Apo nodded at the ground.

After a moment of consideration Jung sat.

Apo said, "I was returning from a hunt alone when I saw them rounding up the people in my tribe. I hid in the trees and watched them. There were several of them in blue robes. They were led by one creature who was in black. His robe had an enormous hood and he seemed to levitate in the air. They took the people from my tribe deep into the jungle. I followed them for a long time, until we were far into the basin. There the blue robed creatures pointed out two plants—the leaves of chacruna and the vines of ayahuasca. They made my people cut down the plants in mass quantities."

Jung looked around, spooked.

"Then, out of nowhere, came a strong breeze that pulled open the black robed creature's hood. No one else saw before he managed to flip his hood back on but I did. He had sickly white skin and black eyes like a serpent. Strangest of all, he had a long cone-shaped head, almost one and a half lengths taller than your head or mine. As soon as he had his hood back on he turned and looked where I was hiding. It was as if he sensed my gaze. He pointed to me and yelled. I ran as fast as I could, disappearing into the jungle. They didn't follow me but as I ran things began to get more and more blurry and I felt disoriented and weak. I hid under a large fallen tree and fell into a deep sleep."

"What happened?" Jung said.

"I woke several dæġs later without sight," Apo said, his voice choked. He shook his head in sadness. "I've never been able to see since. That creature took my sight."

"How?"

Apo's voice was shaky. "I don't know but I can feel them now. I can feel them whenever they come back. They have returned for the plants."

20

100 dægs to stars return.

LAKE TITICACA. PERU.

I first encountered Jung when he was dragged into camp by Kichka.

It was a bitterly cold night, a low mist sat above the lake. The smell of dew and wet wildfires lingered in the air, almost overpowering the scent of cooking meat.

I was sitting on a log by the fire with a group of elder males. From the darkness the reflection of the flames danced across the cream walls of the newly-built mud huts.

"Let me go!" Jung said. His hands were tied behind his back.

Kichka had Jung's bow and quiver over one shoulder and his reed bag over the other. He lifted the boy's wrists higher, forcing his head close to the ground.

Jung winced, tears in his eyes.

Hearing the commotion other people in camp approached the party who had appeared from the darkness.

"Drop to your knees," Kichka said.

Jung dropped to his knees in front of the fire.

"Who is he?" Quya said.

"He's from The Cloud Forest," Kichka said. "He was poking around on the shores."

"Do you think it's retribution?" she said.

Kichka stood over Jung. "Is it? You want revenge, boy?"

Jung was silent. He looked down at the ground.

Kichka clicked his fingers in front of his face. "Huh? Why are you here?"

That's when things escalated fast.

Kichka drew his knife from his waistband and held it in front of Jung's face.

"Leave him," Quya said.

Kichka turned. "You think he comes in peace? We killed his men."

"We don't know. He might come in peace," she said.

Kichka looked at Jung. "What do you think, boy? Are you here in peace?"

"I said leave him," Quya said. "Until we work out his intentions, we don't harm him."

Kichka turned and was about to protest when Jung reacted.

He leapt from the ground and ripped the knife from Kichka's grip. He had clearly been working on freeing himself while he was knelt on the ground, both his wrists were free. Before Kichka realized what was happening, Jung was on his back with one arm wrapped around his neck and the other holding the blade to his throat.

Jung's eyes were dark and menacing. "Give me my bow!"

A man in the crowd picked up the bow and threw it to him.

"And the quiver."

The same man threw the quiver over to near the bow.

Jung unhooked his arm from Kichka's neck but kept the blade close to the man's face.

"Lie on the ground, face down," Jung said.

Kichka lay down and put his face in the ash.

Jung held the knife to Kichka's spine as he used his foot to drag the bow closer.

As he did, one of the young males rushed forward.

Jung slashed the knife across Kichka's back.

Kichka delivered a murderous squeal.

The man rushing forward stepped back.

Jung dived toward his bow and rolled across the ground. In one motion he pulled an arrow from his quiver and loaded it across his bow. He stood and drew back the string. He moved the target from one face in the crowd to another.

Kichka climbed onto his feet, enraged.

There were now 20 or so people surrounding Jung. Others were making their way over.

"Get back!" Jung said. He pulled two more arrows from his quiver.

It didn't stop the mob. More and more people were attaching themselves to the edges of the crowd. A few with weapons were ushered to the front.

Jung whipped the aim of his bow from one person to another wildly.

The mob was slowly closing in.

"Get back!" Jung yelled.

Then someone pushed Jung from behind.

He turned but it was too late.

In a moment the mob was on top of him. They ripped the bow from his hands and kicked and punched him.

Before I even knew what I was doing, I advanced forward. "Get off him! Get off him!"

At first only some of the crowd pulled away.

I broke through the mob, ripping their bodies away from him. "Now! Get off him."

When I reached Jung he was curled up in a bloodied ball.

I looked around at the angry faces. "I need to talk to him. I need to find out what he's doing here. He has knowledge we can use."

"Let the boy be," Quya said.

The woman commanded the attention of the group. They all looked at her.

She said, "Let Kon-Tiki speak to him. Let's see what he has to say."

Slowly the mob broke away and returned to the fire.

Kichka was the last to leave. He scowled at Jung as he walked backwards, touching the gash on his back.

When everyone was gone, I nudged the boy with my boot. "Roll over, son."

Jung uncoiled and looked at me. He had a gash on his forehead and blood smeared across his nose and cheeks.

It was just the boy I was expecting to see.

21

I sat next to Jung in front of the campfire. Most of the tribe sat around the same fire—a few people sat on logs like Jung and I but most were spread across the ground.

Next to the fire lay the body of a giant sloth, cut into pieces and stacked in a pile. Before dissection the creature was twice the length of any man and covered in a thick mat of hair. It had two large hind legs and a massive meaty tail. All the parts were arranged neatly on top of one another. At the top of the pile was the animal's head—its eyes were black, its tongue dangled from its leathery lips.

A round-faced woman who was squatting by the fire fished out the sloth's two front arms. The charred limbs were small compared to the hind legs but could still feed 5 hungry men. Each arm bore 4 claws a foot in length. She cut the claws from the meat with a knife before cutting the meat into chunks.

I waited until Jung had the warm meat in his hand before I spoke.

"So what's your name?" I said.

He chewed on a large mouthful of meat. When he had finished the mouthful he took another bite.

"Where do you come from?"

He ignored me.

I nodded toward Kichka.

The man was sitting on the other side of the fire with several of the other young men. They were watching us as they ate.

I said, "I'm sorry but if you don't communicate with me I'll have to turn you over to them. That's not a threat but I went out on a limb to protect you. It's my head they'll take if you don't share your intentions."

Jung stopped chewing and swallowed. I saw the lump moving slowly down his neck.

"Who are you?" he said.

"I'm Kon-Tiki. What about you? What is your name?"

Jung looked at Kichka.

"Well, what should I call you?"

"I'm a hunter."

I smiled. "And where do you come from, hunter?"

Jung stared into the fire.

"Sacred Valley?"

His nostrils flared. *Yes.*

"Well, what brings you to the lake, hunter?"

Jung looked at me. "I was lost and saw the fires."

His pupils darted to one side. *Lie.*

He immediately knew I could tell he wasn't telling the truth. It wasn't just his eyes that gave him away, we both knew hunters didn't just get lost.

"I was separated from my tribe," he said.

"Well, you're safe now."

Thunder cracked overhead.

We both looked up. A dry storm was crossing the sky. The black clouds were wrapped in drifts of ash.

"And what are your intentions?" I said.

He placed the last piece of meat in his mouth. "I'll return to my people."

"You know, I think you came here for a reason."

His chewing slowed.

"Don't get me wrong, I don't think you mean us harm but I do think you came here for something in particular."

Jung shook his head. His nostrils flared again. *Yes.*

"I tell you what," I said. "If I tell you the story of how I came to arrive here, will you tell me the story of how *you* came to arrive here?"

Jung looked at me with curiosity.

I grinned. "It's a great story."

He looked briefly at Kichka who scowled at him. "Okay."

"Good," I said. I lowered my voice. "Although, I can't tell you here."

"Why not?"

I whispered. "Well, the truth is, I haven't been completely honest with these people."

"What do you mean?" Jung said.

I stood. "Come with me, I'll show you."

22

Jung and I were in my hut. A small fire burned in the center of the room soaking everything in orange. I was sitting on the chair next to my desk and Jung was sitting on my bed—a raised mud platform covered in reeds. The space smelled of damp rot. I had done my best to dry the waterlogged reeds before adding them to the mixture for the walls but the smell had stuck.

I had the book of knowledge open on my lap and was thumbing through the pages.

Jung was leaning in, staring at the book.

I found the page I was looking for and placed a finger inside before closing the book. I looked at Jung. "My people, the Viracocha, come from a place across the ocean, a place of many islands. There we have a large civilization which we call Gunung Padang, which means 'Mountain of Enlightenment'. At the center of this civilization is an enormous pyramid as big as a mountain. Inside its walls is a school of knowledge, a place where all of our people's sacred learnings are housed. Learnings accessible only to our most elite minds, those we call the Tæcans."

I opened the book a little and closed it again.

Jung stared at my hands.

"You see the pyramid at Gunung Padang is not just a stone building. It's a node, an anchor point. A room that can be ridden forward and back in time. A portal that connects the minds of our Tæcans to the stars and beyond."

Jung's mouth was open, he stared at the book.

I opened it just a little. "Our Tæcans knew that if we were to lose this channel to the stars, we would lose everything. This is why I'm here."

"Why?" Jung said.

"Well, many rotations ago our Tæcans arranged arcs to be sent to every corner of Earth. The goal was to find the perfect locations for the building of three new pyramids."

"Why three?"

I smiled. "We'll get to that." I opened the book fully. The page showed a white and gray sketch, a map of a peninsula with ocean on three sides. In the middle of the landmass was a small triangle.

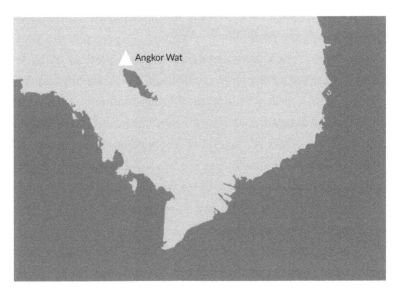

I pointed to the sketch. "The gray is ocean and the white is land. That triangle is the pyramid to be built in Angkor Wat. I know the pyramid looks close to the ocean but it's actually three dæġs walk inland so it will be well protected from floods." I pointed to a gray patch beneath the pyramid. "There is a lake nearby with fresh water and plenty of forest for food and wood. Plus it is near enough to Ganung Padang for our people to easily travel back and forth. That is site one, pyramid one—Angkor Wat."

I turned the page.

The next page showed a large landmass with ocean at the top and a channel of water running down through the center, dividing the land in two. A triangle sat next to the channel of water around a third of the way down.

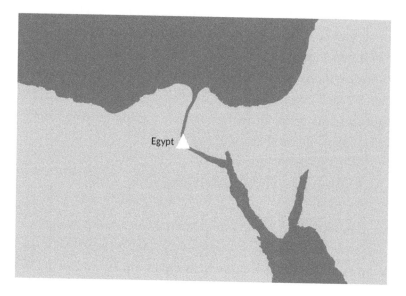

"The second site chosen was Egypt. It too is located three dægs walk from the ocean. It sits on the bank of a mighty river we call the Nile River, which floods once every rotation." I traced my finger down the gray crack in the image. "When the river floods, a shallow spill of water spreads across the plain, irrigating the land and bringing the entire savanna to life. During the floods you'll see everything from fish to frogs, flamingos to impala and elephants to lions, all sharing the land. Those who have been there say it is the most fertile savanna on all of Earth."

"Not anymore, no doubt," Jung said.

"What makes you say that?"

"Look around us. The entire Earth is dead. I'm sure it's the same there."

I shook my head. "Not by my calculation."

"Calculation?"

I winked. "We'll get to the calculations." I tapped the page. "You know what else is in Egypt? My people have built a giant stone cat there. A replica of a lion that is more than 50 men long and 10 men high. It is carved from a single block of stone, our stonemasons spent an entire rotation carving out the form so that it was a perfect replica of a resting lion."

"What's a lion?" Jung said.

"It's like a jaguar only much bigger."

"Bigger?"

I nodded. "Yes, quite a lot bigger. Almost twice as big. The lion is the greatest predator around Egypt. This is why it is such a powerful statue. All visitors to Egypt are in awe of it. We call the monument The Sphinx of Leo. And one dæg The Great Pyramid will sit directly behind The Sphinx. They will be connected by a long stone causeway. It means those arriving by boat on the Nile River will dock by the stone causeway and walk by The Sphinx on the way to The Great Pyramid."

"Why is it called the *great* pyramid?"

"I will get to that in a moment. For now all you need to know is that we are building a pyramid in Egypt too." I turned the page.

The next page showed a sketch, half ocean and half land, cut from top left to bottom right. A triangle was placed in the middle of the landmass.

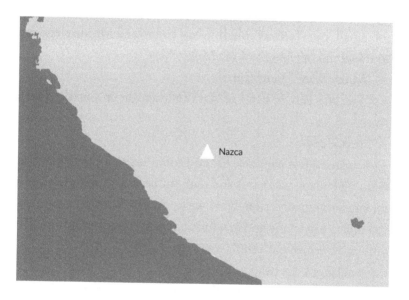

I said, "The third site is Nazca, close to here. I'm sure you're familiar with it?"

Jung nodded.

"Each site has been specifically chosen because of its location. You see the three sites will all be connected and together they will create a machine more powerful than any before."

"Machine? What's that?" Jung said.

"Well, in this case, the machine is a building that can take a man to the stars."

Jung looked confused.

"You see when my people first built the pyramid at Ganung Padang, we always intended to connect it with the stars. That's why we built it. And it worked, our Tæcans used it successfully to travel to the stars. The problem was they built the pyramid too small, our Tæcans couldn't stay connected for long enough to travel the full length of the Milky Way."

"Milky Way?" Jung said.

"Yes, the cloudy band of stars that appear in our sky like a river.

He nodded.

I turned a few pages back. "You could say that the pyramid at Ganung Padang was a test and that our architects have learned a lot since its construction. Now we know just how large we need to build the machine and in which pattern." I winked at him. "Do you know which pattern?"

Jung shook his head.

"Let me give you a clue: it's the pattern of an animal. In fact, more than one animal."

"What?"

I opened the book. "See for yourself."

23

It was raining outside, heavy drops thudded against the reed roof.

I twisted the book towards Jung. On the page were three white circles, side by side. Within each circle were blocks of gray representing the areas of land on a white ocean. A horizontal line ran through the center of the circles. There were three dots marked on the line.

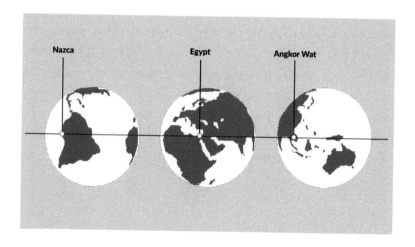

I pointed to the first circle. "You'll have to use your imagination here. Imagine you are sitting on Earth's Rock, looking down at Earth as it spins around beneath you. These are three different images you would see at different times over the course of a dæġ, three different snapshots of Earth as it rotates beneath you."

Jung pointed to the line. "What's the line?"

"*That* is The Artery of Earth—the machine."

"What's that?"

"A perfectly straight line that spans the entire length of Earth and connects the three sacred sites of Egypt, Angkor Wat and Nazca."

I pointed to the first large dot from the left, which sat on the first circle. "The first dot on The Artery of Earth is Nazca. As Earth spins you next see Egypt on The Artery of Earth. And next Angkor Wat."

I turned the page.

The next page showed a sketch of a spiral that looked like a snail's shell. The shell curved from left to right. There was a horizontal line running through the center of the shell with three dots marked on the line. The two outer dots were positioned at the edges of the shell and the middle dot was positioned where the center of the shell curled in.

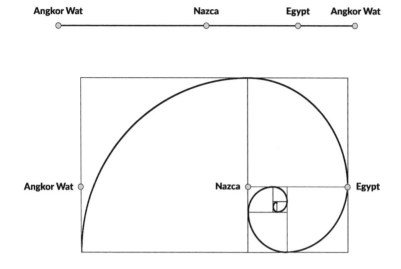

"What's that?" Jung said, pointing to the shell.

I smiled. "Remember I asked you to guess the shape of the animal we were imitating with the layout of the pyramids."

"It was a snail?"

I nodded. "A snail or a ram's horn or a pinecone from above. It's a lot of things, it's the golden ratio."

"What's that?"

I grinned. "The golden ratio is a ratio of 1.618. It is a miraculous number that appears repeatedly in nature, a spiral shape that shows up in a snail's shell, a mammoth's tusk, the branches of a tree, even the proportions of our face. The closer the ratio our temple to our eyes and our eyes to our chin is to the golden ratio, the more beautiful we consider a person. It is a quintessential component of all beauty—balance."

Jung stared at the shell, transfixed.

I lowered my voice. "But the golden ratio is more than just an element of beauty, it is a law of nature. The ratio is programmed to appear out of nothingness. It is what allows a creature to grow as quickly as possible, while keeping its center of gravity in balance. It's what allows a creature like a snail to grow a shell or a deer to grow antlers as quickly as possible without becoming lopsided and crushing itself. The same pattern shows up in spinning whirlpools, swirling hurricanes and the rotating arms of galaxies too. It is a quintessential pattern of life, birth, creation. It is a whisper from the voice of the cosmos herself."

Jung stared at the page, lost in thought.

"This is the pattern we are using to connect the three sites along The Artery of Earth. You see The Great Architect, one of our people's greatest minds. He recognized the limitations of our pyramid in Ganung Padang. He saw a bigger vision. He saw that operating on its own the pyramid in Ganung Padang would never produce enough energy to carry a man across the full length of the Milky Way. He saw that it needed to mimic the pattern of nature herself in order to produce enough energy to make the full distance."

I pointed to each of the dots spread across the spiral. "The pyramids to be built in Egypt, Nazca and Angkor Wat are not just positioned in a perfectly straight line, they also follow the golden ratio. Remember I said the golden ratio is 1.618?"

Jung nodded.

"Well, if you multiply the distance from Egypt to Angkor Wat by 1.618 you will get the distance from Egypt to Nazca and if you multiply the distance from Egypt to Nazca by 1.618 you will get the distance from Angkor Wat to Nazca. It means from anywhere on The Artery of Earth, when you measure the distance between the three sites, you get the golden ratio."

"But why?" Jung said.

"Like I said, so our Tæcans can make the full journey along the Milky Way."

"But what for?"

I said. "To reach the door to the grid, of course."

24

It was raining hard outside, the wind was howling. An icy draft funneled through the crack at the base of the door. There were shouts from outside and the sounds of splashing feet. It sounded like one of the huts had been damaged by the storm and men were trying to fix it.

I twisted the book towards Jung. On the page was a beautifully detailed sketch of a pyramid, it was a cross-section showing the internal rooms and passageways.

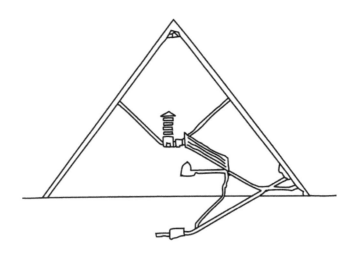

"You asked earlier about The Great Pyramid in Egypt and what makes it different to the other pyramids. The biggest difference is the sophistication of the structure. You can think of it as the heart of The Artery of Earth. It is where the energy is first extracted from Earth's crust and transferred along to the rest of the machine. The Great Pyramid in Egypt will stand more than 80 men high and will weigh more than 80 million people."

Jung scrunched his face. "Million?"

I smiled. "Never mind. It's a lot, let's put it that way."

"How big is the pyramid in Ganung Padang?" Jung said.

"It's around two thirds the size. It's still enormous, but like I said, it's not just the size that makes The Great Pyramid so special, it's the sophistication. The Great Pyramid will be built to a much higher standard than the pyramid in Gunung Padang. Every block used in The Great Pyramid will be cut to perfection and the location will be perfectly selected so we can extract just the right amount of energy from the ground."

"What do you mean?"

I pointed to the page. "Inside The Great Pyramid there will be two chambers, the main chamber near the center and a second chamber near the base. There will also be a third chamber, the sub-chamber, which sits underground beneath the pyramid." I pointed to the area beneath the pyramid. "You see under the ground in Egypt there is an enormous limestone aquifer. An aquifer is like a giant sea sponge. It is a series of tunnels that fill with water when the Nile River floods and drain when the river falls."

I looked at Jung. "Although these tunnels already exist, our people will excavate them further to make them even bigger."

I pointed to the sub-chamber. "The rising and falling of water from the river above creates pressure in these tunnels. This pressure is absorbed by the chamber that is connected to the pyramid. The chamber will be filled with water and encased with granite, a very hard stone that can carry even the most minor current."

I traced my finger from the sub-chamber up along an angled passageway to the second chamber that sat in the base of the pyramid. "This minor charge pulled from the ground is first amplified in the sub-chamber before being transferred up this angled passageway to the base chamber."

Jung stared at the page.

"The walls of this passageway will also be encased in granite so the frequency is not lost as it travels up. In fact, as the energy travels, it builds in amplitude because it reverberates in the space between the blocks. This is also why the blocks in the base of the pyramid will be so big—many will weigh more than 100 men—so they can hold the note of the ascending energy." I traced my finger from the second chamber up to the main chamber. "The pulse will build and build until it reaches this main chamber that sits close to the center of the pyramid. In this room, the energy will be tuned to perfect pitch using layers of granite blocks that sit in the ceiling. These blocks will be free to resonate at will, tuning the energy to just the right frequency."

Jung stared at the page, his mouth open.

I pointed to the very top of the pyramid. "The cap of the pyramid will be plated in gold, a material we call a *superconductor*."

"Superconductor. What's that?" Jung said.

"Remember I said granite blocks will be used because they can hold the building current? Well, gold too can hold a current."

"Gold. The dust of the stars?"

I smiled. "Yes, that's right, all gold comes from the stars. It is one of the most conductive materials on Earth." I traced my finger from the main chamber up to the cap of the pyramid. "The reason why the main chamber is a little off-center from the middle of the pyramid is so that when the energy is pulled to the cap of the pyramid, it is concentrated on one side, creating an imbalance of energy."

Jung looked confused.

"Think about it like a whirlpool in a river, the energy on one side of the whirlpool is always mimicked on the other side because the flow of energy has to be equally dispersed. This is why a whirlpool forms in the first place—to balance out the energy in the water."

"In the golden ratio?" Jung said.

I laughed. "Yes, exactly. The same will happen at the cap of the pyramid. The energy will flow up through one side of the cap, causing an imbalance of energy on the other side. Naturally the energy in the sky will attempt to neutralist this imbalance. This means while on one side of the cap, energy is being pulled from the pyramid on the other side energy is being pulled from the sky."

Jung looked lost.

I smiled. "Don't worry too much. The main thing to know is that one stream of energy is released from the cap of the pyramid, while another stream is channeled back into the pyramid.

This energy coming into the pyramid travels through the gold cap with ease and enters the walls of the building. The walls themselves are also very special. They will be made from a limestone render created by our stonemasons. You see, even though the ground in Egypt is full of limestone, our stonemasons will make their own limestone render where they remove all of the impurities and inject the substrate with pockets of air."

"Why?" Jung said.

I pointed to the outer walls of the pyramid. "To store the energy in the building, in the walls. You see, unlike the granite blocks and the gold cap, which are excellent at carrying a charge, the limestone render is the opposite. The substrate holds the charge rather than transferring it. This is exactly what we want, to trap the energy in the rendered layer so it builds and builds."

Jung looked at me. "Why though?"

"To create a field of energy that grows and grows so large that it's enough to power the other pyramids."

"How?"

I smiled. "Through the golden ratio."

I flipped through several pages until I found what I was looking for. On the page were three squares: a large square at the top right, a medium-sized square in the middle and a small square at the bottom left.

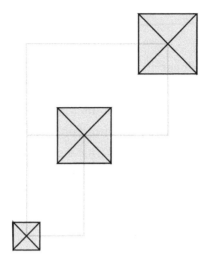

I twisted the book towards Jung. "You see there won't just be one pyramid in Egypt, there will be three. The Great Pyramid, of course, which is the biggest of the structures, but there will also be one medium-sized pyramid and one small pyramid. These three buildings will be aligned in guess what shape?"

"The snail's shell," Jung said.

I nodded. "Exactly." I traced my finger through the center of each pyramid, mimicking the spiral of a snail's shell. "The energy is first generated by The Great Pyramid before being directed and amplified further by the golden coil of the three pyramids in Egypt. This field of energy then builds and builds again until it reaches the other pyramids in Angkor Wat and Nazca-"

"And then the energy is amplified again by the coil of The Artery of Earth?" Jung said.

"Exactly!"

"And this is a portal to the stars?"

I nodded.

"How?"

I moved my finger around and around as I moved it up. "It's a spiraling track that leads to the stars. A track our Tæcans can use to travel to the other side of the Milky Way."

Jung frowned. "But a person couldn't travel on that."

"Not a person. A molecule. What we call the spirit molecule."

"What's that?"

"It's your consciousness without your body."

"My consciousness?"

I nodded. "Your mind, your thoughts."

"What happens when the spirit molecule gets to the stars?"

"Well, if everything goes perfectly, the spirit molecule will travel the full length of the Milky Way and reach the door to the grid."

"You said that before. What's the grid?"

I smiled. "Oh, that's the most exciting part. I'll tell you what the grid is."

Jung grinned.

"But first I want to know a little about you. That was the deal, right? I told you what brings me to the lake, now it's time for you to tell me what brought you to the lake."

Jung paused.

"That was the deal, right?"

25

Jung picked at the reeds on the bed.

I put the book on the desk and twisted my chair towards him. "So, tell me, what brings you to Lake Titicaca? But first, what do I call you?"

"Jung."

I smiled. "Nice to meet you, Jung. I'm Kon-Tiki. And what brings you here?"

"I- I was looking for an omen."

"An omen? What kind of omen?"

"A star."

"A star? What does such an omen mean?"

Jung shook his head. "I'm not sure."

"But it was definitely a star?"

He nodded.

"Interesting. Perhaps it's something to do with the grid."

"How?"

I grinned. "Oh, I don't know, you're being very vague. Did *you* see the omen or did someone else?"

"Someone else."

"From your tribe?"

He nodded.

"Okay, so you came here because you were following an omen?"

He nodded.

"An omen you knew about before coming here, *obviously.*"

"Yes."

"An omen seen by someone close to you. A blood bond?"

"Y-yes."

"Did you find it?" I said.

"I don't know. I'm here I guess."

I grinned. "True."

"You said that you lied to the people of the lake. What did you lie to them about?"

I paused. "Well, to be honest, I haven't told you the whole truth either."

Jung frowned. "What do you mean?"

"I have good news and bad news. I'll give you the good news first."

"Good news?"

I nodded. "Yes, about the grid. Let me explain what the grid is first." I lay the book across my lap and looked to the ceiling. "The grid is a place beyond Earth and even beyond the stars. It is a place invisible to the naked eye. Well, not one place but many places. It is the space between spaces, if you will. A place where you can access any channel you want.

"Channel?" Jung said.

"Yes. You see it's a common misconception that what we experience is all there is to existence. That's not true at all. Everything is happening right here right now. Change the channel and you'll see."

"What?"

"What we think becomes. Not the other way around."

"I don't understand?"

"What we see and feel physically, it comes from what we imagine. Our consciousness is not a bi-product of the physical world, it constructs the physical world."

"You're saying the physical world manifests from what we think?"

I nodded. "Yes, the laws of matter are built when we're all in agreement. The rules governing our reality come from the collective psyche of mankind. That means you can't just go running off the edge of a cliff pretending you live with your own laws of matter. You are a part of the human race and therefore your reality is controlled by the collective unconscious. But it is a fact that what we imagine is what comes to be."

"You're saying what the collective imagines comes to be?"

I smiled. "Yes. We live in an imagined nation. What we see in front of us is just one channel, one lens on reality. And there are infinite channels. Even the plants have channels. I'm sure you've experienced them?"

Jung of course remembered the san pedro he had had with his father not long ago and how it had seemed to draw out the layers of his reality, both visually and sensorily.

"There are even channels where the dead themselves participate," I said.

"The dead?"

I nodded.

"They exist in a different channel?"

"Yes, like I said, there is a channel for everything. Not just the living and the dead, but all the layers in between and all the layers beyond."

"Can you get into their channel?"

"The dead?"

Jung nodded.

"Yes, that's the good news. The Artery of Earth will permit us to travel to the grid and get in."

"But definitely the dead?"

"Yes, the dead, but also much more. Once you get into the grid, the control room, you can choose to go anywhere."

Jung's eyes widened. "Can you communicate with them?"

I smiled. "You can do a lot more than that. They become as real as you and I when the grid is opened."

"Opened. How do you open it?"

I looked up. "Well, first you have to travel to the other side of the stars. To the other side of the Milky Way. There you'll find a doorway, assuming you know where you're looking. Pass through this doorway and you can access a space inside the walls."

"A doorway?"

I nodded.

"What kind of door?"

I laughed. "Well, probably not a wooden one. I couldn't tell you exactly. Our Tæcans are the only ones who have passed through the doorway and they consider it sacred knowledge."

The latch on the door to the hut came loose. The wood banged against the frame in the savage throws of the wind. I stood and closed it then sat again.

"Have you been inside?" Jung said.

"The pyramid?"

He nodded.

"No, only our Tæcans have access to the inside."

"Will you ever use it?"

I bit the inside of my lip. "This is where the bad news comes in. To start the machine in Egypt, we need a shard of star. It is required for the ceremony that takes place in the main chamber. Without a star The Great Architect says we'll never accelerate the spirit molecule fast enough to make to distance from the pyramid to Orion's Belt."

"You don't have a star from another time?" Jung said.

I nodded. "Yes, we have stars from other times, but it has to be *this* star."

"Why?"

I held up the book. "The Great Architect, the designer of the pyramids and The Artery of Earth, created the plans in this book in anticipation for the arrival of the star. He knew the star was coming before anyone. He even planned the design of The Great Pyramid around using a fragment from the star. It is the key. He built everything in the design around it. He says without it transcendence cannot be achieved."

"Transcendence?"

I nodded. "Yes, that is what we call the process of converting consciousness from the body into the spirit molecule. Without a star The Artery of Earth cannot operate." I nodded to the door. "That is the lie I told them. I said we already had a star. I didn't think they would help me if they knew we didn't have a star. I just knew we had to get started."

"Help you? Help you with what?"

"Building the pyramid in Nazca. The project is far too big for us to do it on our own. I fear that if they know we don't yet have a star, they'll never agree to help. We have to get started though. They have already begun work building the pyramids in Egypt and Angkor Wat. We need to start the build here so the moment we have a star we can use the machine."

"Do you think someone will go and get the star?" Jung said.

"Yes, for sure. As soon as the weather gets better I imagine many will set off to look for it. Especially with the reward up for grabs."

Jung looked at me. "What reward?"

"The Great Architect has said that the person who finds the star will get a ride in the machine."

"A ride in the machine? What do you mean?"

"They will be permitted to use the machine like the Tæcans. They will have an opportunity to take the journey to the stars and to pass through the doorway to the grid."

"Can they come back?"

I smiled. "Of course, although when they do, they will never be the same. Once someone has crossed over they will forever have access to all of the channels."

"So when someone makes the journey once they forever have access to the grid?"

I nodded.

Jung picked at the reeds on his bag. "Will you go and look for it?"

I laughed. "No, I have a lot of work to do here. I need to prepare the site for the build. And like I said, there will be plenty of
others who will go. I'll wait for them."

"And whoever gets the star gets a ride in the machine?"

I nodded.

Jung bit the nail on one of his fingers. In his head it made a
lot of sense to get to the star before anyone else—The Healer had
said his father was calling for him from the crash site and now he
had met a man offering him an opportunity to not just go to the
star but to use a machine that could take him to the very channel
his father occupied. *He had to go.*

Then he remembered what the blind man Apo had said. He
said the Viracocha were evil and not to be trusted. But Jung had
seen my head, it wasn't strange like that Apo had described. And
my robe was white not blue or black. He remembered what The
Healer had said, that he would meet a sage—a man with great
knowledge who would set him free.

He would take the chance. "What was the deal you tried to
make with my tribe?" he said.

"What tribe?"

Jung shook his head, unwilling to say his tribe.

I shrugged. "I don't know then. I've spoken to many tribes."

"The Cloud Forest people. The people of the lake killed our
scouts because of a deal."

"They killed your people?"

Jung nodded.

"I had no idea, I'm sorry. They were never supposed to kill."

"What were they supposed to do though?"

"I just wanted all the tribes in The Sacred Valley to work together."

"Why though?"

"For the sake of the pyramid. We need the help of everyone to do it." I shook my head. "I'm so sorry they hurt your people."

Jung looked at the fire, thinking.

"There is something else you should know," I said.

He looked at me.

"The stars are coming back."

"What?"

"We're right in the middle of them now. In two seasons, actually one and a half, the stars will be back and they are likely to cause just as much damage. It's why we have to race to build the pyramids."

"Why?"

"To put an end to all of this."

"An end?"

I nodded. "Yes, change the channel just enough to prevent the stars from obliterating us."

"What do you mean?"

"We can use The Artery of Earth to bend our channel and adjust Earth's track through space, just enough to clear the gauntlet of stars we believe."

Jung looked concerned. "How long do we have?"

"Like I said, one and a half seasons until the next stars hit, but they will keep returning twice a rotation until we've cleared a track through the debris. It could take decades."

"But when we have the pyramids up the destruction will stop?"

I nodded. "When the pyramids are up and the machine is on."

"I'll go," Jung said.

"What?"

"I'll go get your star, for a ride in the machine."

"Really?"

He nodded. In his head nothing mattered more than getting to his father. Something told him that if he could just reach him then all of the destruction would end. And if it didn't, well maybe The Artery of Earth really would save the dæg. It was a long shot but it was better than sitting around waiting for Earth to die.

"That's great news! I believe I can help you on your journey."

"How?" he said.

"I have an arc and a party of men who can take you norð by sea. It will shave a lot of time off your journey."

"What men?"

"Men like me. Good men. Men who want nothing more than to help get the machine up and running. They will help you any way they can if your intention is to get the star and bring it back here."

Jung remembered The Healer's words, *you'll meet an explorer, a man whose own desire for adventure will take you further than even he intends.*

He looked at me. "How exactly does the spirit molecule travel from the pyramid to the stars?"

"Unfortunately, I can't tell you that. I would if I knew it but I don't. That's two stripe Uzman knowledge."

Jung looked confused.

I held up the book. "This is the book of knowledge. It is book one of three. There is the book of knowledge, the book of the stars and the book of death. I'm a one stripe Uzman so I know only what happens in book one. And I have shared most of what I know."

Jung looked disappointed.

I winked at him. "That said, there is a two stripe man on the arc I mentioned to you, the arc that can take you to the star. He is The Captain of the arc. He knows the story of the stars. He knows how the spirit molecule journeys along the Milky Way."

"Really?"

I nodded.

"Do you think he'll tell me?"

"I think so."

"Did he tell you?"

"No."

"Then why would he tell me?" Jung said.

"Because where we both come from there are strict rules about Uzmans sharing knowledge. To get caught sharing knowledge between Uzmans is a death sentence. However, sharing details with the natives is not deemed an offense so long as it helps us get the pyramids built. I guess you could say the Tæcans are desperate to get The Artery of Earth started. He could tell you the entire story without recourse. The only thing he has keeping the story from you is his own pride as a two stripe man. But every man has his price, right?"

"Where is he?"

"Nazca. Well, directly offshore anyway. His arc is there. His men can take you to the star by sea. What do you say?"

Jung nodded. *If it could get him to his father faster, he was in.*

26

NAZCA. PERU.

Jung was in the dark. He ran his palm across the stone wall next to him. It felt cool and smooth and was dimpled like the power stone The Healer had given him. He looked up at the long angled passageway around 50 men in length. The cubed shaft was made of perfectly cut slabs of granite that lined the chute on four sides. At the top a lantern dimly lit the space. He placed the flat side of his right foot in the groove between two stones and used his hands to feel around in the dark until he felt a lip he could hold onto. He began to pull himself up.

When Jung woke from his dream he smelled the salty air and heard the crashing waves of the ocean. It took him a moment to remember where he was. He rose and climbed up onto the limestone outcrop where he spotted the distant frothing foam. The white plumes in the break contrasted against the black sky and gray drifts of ash that covered the beach.

He had never seen the ocean this far in before. Usually it was another two dæġs walk to the sea. Usually there were also mud huts on the horizon—the camp of Nazca. Instead, there was only ocean, endless ocean. Those Nazcans who had been in camp when the floods had hit were almost certainly all dead. The camp was deep underwater now.

At the shore, there were enormous trenches in the sand. Channels from where the floods had dragged away the beach. They looked like claw marks from a creature as big as a mountain.

Suddenly a shape caught Jung's eye.

The black silhouette bobbed up and down on the silvered liquid. It looked like a beetle that had rolled onto its back and couldn't get onto its feet.

It was the arc.

Jung jumped from the ridge and jogged down the crumbly scarp.

He stood in the freezing shallows, water lapped against his legs. He stared at the arc, mesmerized by its size and shape. The steep bowed hull was well over 20 men high and 50 men across. It puffed out its chest proudly. He instantly recognized the shape of the rounded front. It had the same curve as a snail's shell, the golden ratio. The vessel looked perfectly designed to cut through the waves on the ocean.

Jung took off his shawl and tied it around his neck. He checked all of his items including the note I had given him before slipping into the water. His body spasmed and his breath quickened to the cold.

Reaching the creaking arc, he circled the vessel until he found a ladder that dangled from the side. He pulled himself free from the freezing water, his soaking shawl heavy on his neck.

Out of the water, he felt even colder. His teeth chattered as he rested his body against the warm wall of the arc, catching his breath. Close up, he saw the precision of the vessel's craftsmanship. The slats of teak had been interlocked with such perfection you could barely make out the seams. Stained in a clear resin, the wood looked pristine. It was as if the arc had been dropped onto the water only dæġs earlier.

Jung climbed to the top of the deck and peeked over the railing. A scratching sound caught his attention.

On the other side of the arc he barely made out the shape of one of the seafaring men. The man was tall with broad shoulders, long hair and fair skin. He was sitting against the railing with an animal skin wrapped around him. He appeared to be whittling something with a knife, perhaps a piece of driftwood.

Jung took his bow and quiver from over his shoulder and slowly placed them on the deck covered in a dusting of ash.

The Whittler didn't look up.

Jung placed his wet shawl down then his bag.

Suddenly there was a flash of lightning.

"Oy!" The Whittler yelled.

Jung scrambled over the railing and dropped onto the deck. He stood and held up his hands.

The Whittler yelled again. This time it sounded like he was saying words although they were gibberish to the boy.

"Capt-uh of thuh veer-uh-cosh!" Jung said, trying to recall the words I had told him.

The Whittler looked confused. He stood and held out his knife.

Jung waved his hands in the air, making it clear he was unarmed.

The Whittler stomped on the deck and yelled.

Jung said. "Duh capt-uhn of thuh cosh-uh!"

The Whittler stomped harder.

Then Jung remembered my words clearly. "The Captain of the Viracocha!"

The Whittler froze—he understood.

Suddenly a concealed door in the deck sprung open and two men leapt out. They had the same fair skin as the other man and were dressed similarly, only they weren't wrapped in shawls—the bare skin of their chests was exposed, revealing s-shaped scars burned into their skin. S for *seafaring men.*

The men exchanged words, gibberish to Jung.

He squatted and searched through his bag for the note I had given him. He cussed himself for not thinking to put it in his mouth before he swam. The contents of the bag were soaked.

The three seafaring men stared at the boy. There was a strangeness to the men, their cheeks were red and heavy, and they seemed somewhat blind and off-balance. They swayed on their feet, their pupils rolling from side to side.

Jung didn't trust their looks. Perhaps his nose was warning him.

The men began to advance forward.

Jung couldn't find the note so instead he grabbed his knife and began to carve a giant snail's shell into the deck.

The seafaring men jumped on top of him just as Jung slid away the knife.

27

The seafaring men let Jung go when the manhole was closed. The four of them stood crammed into the narrow stairwell lit by several fire-torches.

It smelled dank inside, like a hide left damp for dægs. Wooden slats were fastened to the walls, floor and roof. The surface was mucky, salt-spray mixed with ash. A muted drum roll came from the hull of the arc, creating the illusion they were underwater.

"This way," The Whittler said. He headed down the bouncy steps.

Jung followed, and the remaining two seafaring men came last.

He put his hand against the wall to steady himself as the arc rocked gently back-and-forth in the waves.

Suddenly a cackle of laughter erupted from the bottom of the stairs.

Jung froze.

The Whittler waved his hand.

Jung felt one of the men behind him poke him in the ribs. He kept moving.

The mess hall at the bottom of the stairs was enormous and lit up like dæglight from dozens of fire torches that were fastened to the walls and ceiling. Logs as thick as a man's chest were lined up along the walls. They were interlocked with logs just as large that made up the floor and ceiling. The joinery between the beams was so perfect that not even a sheet of papyrus could be slid into the gaps.

In the center, a dozen seafaring men were sat at an enormous table that ran two thirds the width of the arc. The table was made from a single piece of teak. The seafaring men were all dressed the same, their tattered garments were open at the chest, revealing the same s-shaped scar burned into their white skin. They were laughing and yelling and thumping their mugs on the table.

Jung hovered in the shadow of the stairwell and scanned the room. On one side of the hall were a dozen or so hammocks, fastened to the ceiling. Next to the hammocks was a kitchen packed with barrels and crates. At the other side of the hall was a corridor to three rooms. All of the rooms had their doors closed.

Jung felt one of the seafaring men poke him in the ribs again.

He walked out into the center of the hall and sat where The Whittler pointed, on a bench at the opposite end of the table to the seafaring men. He sat with his arms wrapped around himself, dripping wet and shivering. He instinctively angled his knees in the direction of the gap between the table and chair so he could run if he had to.

The seafaring men all stared at him. Each man had the same look: flush cheeks, bags beneath his eyes, rolling pupils.

The two men who had jumped Jung sat with their comrades. They placed his bag and his bow and quiver on the table.

One of the men at the table immediately picked up the bow and began to inspect it.

Jung squeezed his fists, angry.

The Whittler addressed the seated men. The words were gibberish to Jung. The only word he recognized was *Captain*. Then The Whittler disappeared down the hallway.

The seafaring men all stared at Jung.

He stared back.

Suddenly The Whittler appeared by Jung's side holding a gray and white dire wolf pelt. He wrapped the thick fur around Jung and disappeared back to the corridor of doors.

Jung nuzzled his face into the fur and sniffed. For its large size, it was softer than any hide he had ever felt in his life. It smelled sweeter too.

The seafaring men all watched the boy burying his face in the fur.

Jung pulled the fur from his nose when he saw them all watching.

Suddenly a chair screeched across the floor from the other side of the hall.

A burly man with a rounded gut stood and waddled over to a barrel. He plunged his mug inside and pulled it free, liquid dripped from the sides.

The man stood out from the others, not just because of his roundness but because he was the only man dressed in a robe. The rest of the men were seafaring Fects, while he was a one stripe Uzman.

The man made his way across the hall toward Jung. The wooden slats squeaked beneath his enormous legs.

He stood above Jung, clasping the table, shaky on his feet. He had a grubby beard and a pudgy face. His rosy cheeks looked stretched and blemished. His eyes were hollow, distant. He breathed heavily as he sat on the other side of the table and offered a sweaty hand.

"Ahm The Brewer here," he said as he pushed one of the mugs towards Jung. White foam spilled over the rim.

Jung was immediately taken aback by the man's comprehension of his language. For some reason it had been easy for him to digest me knowing his language but to hear such a grotesque man use the words of his people didn't sit right.

The Brewer frowned and withdrew his hand. "Suh name, boy?"

Jung was silent. He picked at a nodule on the underside of the table.

The Brewer looked at the mug in front of him, then at the mug in front of Jung. He nodded before picking up his mug. He hovered it in the air and raised his eyebrows, encouraging the boy to do the same.

Jung watched him without moving.

"Guh on," The Brewer said. He raised his mug a little higher and nodded his head.

Jung didn't move.

The Brewer slammed his mug down and yelled. "Pick up your drink!"

Shocked by the reaction, Jung picked up the mug.

The Brewer nodded appreciatively, although the anger was still there.

Jung hovered the mug in front of his nose. He smelled familiar earthy notes of grass and grain but something sour and off-putting too—a yeasty smell his people would certainly associate with decay.

The Brewer nodded at Jung and downed the liquid in his mug.

Jung smelled the liquid again, contemplating whether to take a sip. *A punch was better than a mouthful of rot,* he thought. He placed the mug down and twisted on his seat, preparing for the attack.

"Think yuh betuh than us, do yuh?" The Brewer said.

Jung shook his head.

"Yuh know, I used to have a native boy like yuh. Yuh. He was just luhk you. I had him fuh five rotations. Taught me yuh language und all about your people." He raised his mug and emptied the remaining liquid between his lips. "Then he died."

Jung's heart raced.

The Brewer's face broke into a sickly smile. He delivered a wheezy laugh that developed into a nasty cough. "Tragic really. He wuz a good boy but he had tuh go. Relly, he just ran out of value. Yuh nuh?"

Jung was frozen.

"Yuh nuh?"

Jung shook his head. "No."

The Brewer leaned in. "I got wuh I wanted from him und that wuhz it, ya know. He couldn't hulp any more. So, bye bye."

"Leave him alone," a voice said. It was one of the seafaring men who had jumped Jung.

The Brewer twisted on the creaking bench. "Sta- outta it!"

The man looked immediately nervous. He shook his head and returned to a conversation he was having with one of the other men.

The Brewer looked back at Jung. "Whuh uh ya doin here anywuh?"

Jung looked to the far end of the arc where The Whittler had disappeared to. *Where was he?*

"Oy!" The Brewer said. He slammed his empty mug on the table.

All the seafaring men turned. They looked concerned seeing The Brewer hovering over the small boy. Still they seemed un-inclined to act. Eventually they all returned to conversing with themselves.

"What do you want?" Jung said in the bravest voice he could muster.

The Brewer grinned. "He has a voice!" He burped.

"Yes, I do."

"So voice. Tell me, wuh yuh doin here?"

"I'm here to see The Captain."

"Oh, yuh? Why?"

Jung shook his head and looked away.

The Brewer slammed the mug on the table again.

The seafaring men all turned again. One stood. He was a big man with an enormous brown beard.

The Brewer turned and faced him, he pointed to the black stripe on the shoulder of his robe. "You ruhmumber, I have a stripe. I'm Uzman. I'm pruhtected. Yuh not."

The bearded man scowled and shook his head. He slowly sat.

The Brewer scoffed and turned back to Jung. "Do yuh have any plants?"

"What?" Jung said, remembering Apo's words: *they have returned for the plants.*

"Plants?"

"What plants?"

"The vine of the dead."

"I don't know what that is."

The Brewer scoffed. "Then what's your value?"

"My value?"

He nodded and belched.

"What do you mean?"

"Something you can offer us."

"I don't understand," Jung said.

The Brewer looked toward the corridor where The Whittler had disappeared to. "Well, I'd figure that out before he arrives. If he doesn't see value in yuh, yuh won't last long."

"What value?"

He smirked. "Yuh problem, boy."

Suddenly a door creaked at the far end of the corridor. A tall lean shadow appeared in the doorway.

"Too late," The Brewer said. He leaned on the table and stood as fast as he could. The wood bowed beneath his weight.

"Jung!" a voice said.

It was The Captain.

28

Jung stood in The Captain's quarters. The room was three men long and two men wide. In the middle was a hammock, fastened to the wall at one end and a post at the other. Above the hammock, mounted on the wall, was an enormous set of deer antlers. Attached to the ceiling in the center of the room was an ornate light-fitting made from curling sticks entwined with hemp vines. It's design seemed to mimic the antlers.

The Captain was at the far end of the room with his back to Jung. He was at a desk, sorting through a stack of papyrus. The man was tall and lean and had long white hair. He was wearing the same style of robe as The Brewer, only his was gray and there were two stripes on the shoulders.

He turned around, holding up the wet note. "Well, I've read this."

The man was older than the seafaring men, his face was stamped with shallow wrinkles. He had a thick white beard and a tidy mustache that looped at the ends. Cloudy caps in his eyes covered half his pupils.

"How is Kon-Tiki?" he said.

"He seems good," Jung said.

"Good, he's a good man. I'm glad he found safety with other good people. He certainly speaks favorably of you."

Jung was nervous. He had no idea what was on the note.

"How are the natives with him?"

"They seemed to like him," Jung said.

The sound of muffled laughter came from the mess hall outside.

The Captain locked eyes with Jung. The cloudy caps on his pupils seemed to swirl.

Jung felt suddenly foolish for entering the arc. Closed off in the room with the strange man, he was beginning to wonder if the deal he had made with me wasn't a deal at all but rather some elaborate trap.

The Captain seemed to read his thoughts. He turned to the desk and unrolled a large sheet of papyrus. He placed a stone on each corner of the curling sheet.

He turned back to Jung. "Would you say this is where the star hit?"

Jung approached the desk slowly and stood next to The Captain. He looked at the sheet that showed several dark shapes in a sea of white. An undulating line ran through the center of the sketch.

"The shaded patches are land and the white is ocean," The Captain said.

"What's that?" Jung said pointing to the undulating line.

"That is The Artery of Earth."

Jung looked confused. "Kon-Tiki said it was a straight line."

The Captain smiled. "Well observed. It is. It's just that this map is a flattened version of the spherical Earth. If we were to pin the corners of the map together and make a sphere, the line would flatten out."

Jung looked lost.

"Never mind about that. We know where the star hit," The Captain said. He made a small dent with his fingernail near the top of the map on the coast norð of Nazca. "This is where it hit. This entire area is an ice shelf well over 1,000 men in height. Well, at least, it was. We believe the star hit this shelf. This would explain the flooding—the heat from the explosion would have liquified the ice, triggering a flood of freshwater to tear across the land. An explosion of ice also explains the level of moisture in the air. It was this moisture that really sealed our fate. When it bonded with the debris thrown up from the explosion and ash from the wildfires, it never settled. This screen of debris is what's blocking the light from Earth's Star, which is the cause of these freezing temperatures."

"Will the star be findable?" Jung said.

The Captain pulled on one corner of his mustache. "Going up there would be particularly dangerous. If we're right and the star did hit the ice shelf then we would be sailing right into a wasteland of broken ice and rocks. I would be risking my arc and my men."

"You wouldn't have to get too close, just drop me nearby."

"Easier said than done, boy. The risk is the ocean itself." The Captain pulled the note out of his pocket and held it up. "I've read this and understand the importance of your journey but I just don't think it justifies the risk."

Jung pulled the wolf skin higher up on his shoulders. He felt a rash forming on his neck from the foreign fur. "But the machine can't get started without a star."

The Captain nodded. "Don't get me wrong, I see the mission is critical but if we sink to the bottom of the ocean we get no closer to your goal either."

"I can get you a piece too," Jung said. The words had left his lips before he even knew he had spoken them.

The Captain froze. "What do you mean?"

Seeing the change in the man, Jung dug in. "The star. I can get you a piece too. It must have split into fragments. I promise you the first piece I find."

The Captain smiled. "That's a big pledge, boy."

Jung nodded, swallowing the knot in his throat.

The Captain dipped his hand into the neck of his robe and pulled out a small wooden flask. He popped off the cap.

The pungent smell immediately irritated Jung's nostrils.

The Captain took a sip and puckered his lips before putting the flask back into his robe. He nodded. "You have a deal. I will take you norð. And in exchange you will get me a shard of the star. The first piece. We leave first thing."

Jung was suddenly afraid that the deal was too easy, but it was too late.

The Captain opened the door and yelled. "We leave at dægbreak!"

There was an enthusiastic roar from the seafaring men.

The Captain smiled to himself. He knew a man who would pay a lot for such a treasure.

29

LAKE TITICACA. PERU.

I was in my hut when the attack happened. I first heard shouts and screams then arrows whistling through the air. I crouched below the window and looked out.

There were around two dozen warriors entering camp. They were naked and painted head-to-toe in red. They shot arrows from their bows with almost perfect accuracy. The people of the lake's spears and clubs didn't stand a chance. It wasn't just their inferior weaponry that made the people of the lake easy pickings, it was also their lack of cohesiveness. While the people of the lake ran around frantically, the enemy warriors seemed to know exactly what the others in their group were going to do. It was as if they had trained the drill hundreds of times over. They knew who would go one way and who would go the other, who would advance first and who would hold back, who would grab the women and children and who would tackle the men. They attacked with such finesse and power it was like watching a hawk descend upon an ibis—two birds of equal size but only one was built to kill.

Kichka appeared just outside the window. He was holding a spear and yelling. There was a whooshing sound. He fell to the floor gurgling, an arrow wedged in his throat. Bright red blood pumped from the wound.

I felt warm urine drench my thighs. I crawled across the room as fast as I could and pulled the book of knowledge off the desk and tucked it into my robe.

Suddenly one of the enemy warriors entered my hut.

I raised my hands.

"In here!" he yelled.

Within a moment two more warriors arrived—a man and a woman. The three of them grabbed me and dragged me outside.

I was placed on my knees in the middle of camp.

Other men who had been captured were dropped onto their knees beside me, while the women and children were rounded up off to the side.

One of the enemy warriors took a burning log from the fire and threw it onto the roof of a hut. The thatch reeds immediately engulfed in flames, sending a plume of smoke billowing into the sky.

It wasn't long before the entire camp smelled of wildfire, the stinging smoke burned my eyes.

That's when they started cutting the men's throats.

I stared at the ground, listening. There was pleading then sobs and screams as the executioner's knife opened up the neck of one man after another.

The women and children screamed as they watched their men get murdered.

I heard one man trying to scramble away and the struggle as he was dragged back into line. Then there were blunt thuds and screams until he was silent.

The women and children whaled louder.

I smelled faeces, I wasn't sure if it was my own or someone else's.

The executioner walked slowly down the line, killing every man from the lake until I was the only one left alive.

He stood in front of me. "Look up."

I looked up. It was Puma.

He held the bloody knife in front of my face.

Suddenly a second man appeared by his side. It was Uma.

"Where's the book?" Uma said.

I shook my head and held up my hands, pretending I didn't understand his language.

"Let's search him," Uma said.

Puma rushed forward and kicked me in the ribs.

I felt the air rush from my chest as I fell onto my side gasping.

When I had finally caught my breath, I saw both men standing over me. Puma was holding my book, flicking through the pages.

I held my hand up. "No."

Puma lunged forward and kicked me in the face. I saw black for a moment then white. I lay on the floor, a thumping in my head, the taste of blood in my mouth.

Uma took the book from Puma and squatted in front of me. He clicked his fingers.

I rolled to my side and looked up.

He tapped the book. "What is this?"

"The plan," I said, short of breath.

"Plan?"

"Yes."

"Plan for what?"

"To put an end to all this destruction."

Uma looked confused.

"It's all in there. I can show you. I can translate it for you."

He thumbed through the pages.

"There are words in there too," I said. "Explanations about all of the drawings. Most of the knowledge is in the words. I can explain it all to you. I will be your teacher."

Uma smiled and stood. "You will not be my teacher. You will be my slave." He turned to the other warriors. "Let's get him into the mountains."

A few of the warriors including Puma advanced forward and twisted my arms behind my back.

I stood and marched as fast as I could to avoid being dragged.

Uma walked behind, flicking through the pages of the book.

I just hoped he wouldn't find the page with the torture device—the rack. The moment he did, I was in trouble.

30

NAZCA. PERU.

Outside a storm was gathering overhead, thunder cracked and rolled across the sky.

"Brewer," The Captain said as he entered the mess hall of the arc.

The Brewer stood. "Aye, Captain."

"Take the hunter to the Uzman's quarters. Give him Kon-Tiki's bed."

"With pleasure, Capt."

Jung was standing behind The Captain. He saw his bag sitting on the table with his bow and quiver. "Can I have my bow and arrows and bag?"

"I'll take care of those for you," The Captain said. "We'll put them by your bed. For now, you get some rest."

"Can I at least have my bag? Please."

The Brewer picked up the bag with a smile.

"Please," Jung said looking at The Captain.

"Give him his bag," The Captain said.

The Brewer stuffed his hand inside. "Let's have a little look first."

"Now!" The Captain said.

The Brewer pulled his hand from the bag and scowled.

"Is there a problem?" The Captain said.

The Brewer shook his head, the scowl gone. He waddled over to Jung and thrust the bag into his chest. "Come on, let's get you downstairs so you can rest. Down to the hull we go."

Jung followed The Brewer down the stairs.

The next floor down was the food storage room, which was dimly lit by a single fire-torch. The space smelled of dried grass and faeces.

Jung stepped off the stairs onto the landing. He saw dozens of barrels stacked along the walls. Suddenly a movement from the back of the room caught his attention. He squinted through the low light. He barely saw the shapes of around 20 deer that were gathered together. The animals had golden-brown fur with streaks of black along the scruffs of their necks. They had long pointed ears, dark glassy eyes and slender snouts. Their enormous nostrils twitched to the foreign smells of the dank vessel.

He approached them slowly.

The animals moved backwards, unsteady on their feet—their pointed hooves were built for navigating rocky slopes not the greasy grain of polished wood.

The moment Jung saw the creatures' cloudy eyes, he knew they were sick. Without sunlight, natural food and space to move they were deteriorating. The whole setup perplexed him. *How could they not know the quality of the meat is determined by the quality of the life?*

"Oy!" The Brewer said. He was standing on the stairs. "Get here!"

Jung returned quickly to the stairs.

The Brewer shook his head and continued down the steps.

"You need to kill those animals," Jung said, following.

The Brewer stopped. "Huh?"

"You need to kill those animals. If they get any sicker, you'll get sick."

The Brewer scoffed and continued on.

At the bottom of the stairs was the hull of the arc—the Uzman's quarters. The enormous room was lit by a dozen or so fire torches mounted to the uprights. There was ash everywhere, clearly the seafaring men hadn't cleaned the room since the disaster. In the center there were hammocks fastened to the rafters. Only there were closer to 100 of them and they had large straps dangling from their sides which could be used to tie yourself in when sleeping. There was a large wooden box fastened to the ground beneath each hammock where personal items could be stored. In the far corner was a water trough and two large tables with benches on either side.

Off to the side was a raised mini-amphitheater with wooden benches arranged in two descending semicircles. The benches centered on a small stage. In the middle of the stage was a beautifully carved t-shaped monolith made from stone. The monolith was around a man in height and featured detailed carvings of what appeared to be a serpent and a scorpion at the base, a vulture holding an orb in the center and three handbags at the top. Next to the monolith stood a wooden lectern around a man's chest in height. The stage looked set for telling a great story.

"Grab a bed here," The Brewer said pointing to one of the hammocks.

Jung headed for the bed.

"So, yah taking us out to sea are you?" The Brewer said.

Jung ignored him. He was still scanning the room.

The Brewer took a step forward. "Tell me, how have you managed to wrap The Captain around yah finger?"

Jung shook his head and looked away.

The Brewer stepped forward again and poked Jung in the chest. "You'll kill us out there. You listening to me?"

Jung took a step back.

The Brewer reached out his arm. "What have you got in your bag anyway? You sure you don't have any plants?"

Jung stepped back again. "Get off me."

"Come on, boy. Give us a peek."

Jung squared off with the man.

The Brewer smirked seeing the boy's stance. He looked at the ground for a moment then lunged forward and tried to pull the bag from Jung's shoulder.

Jung bounced backward and darted to the side.

"Come here," The Brewer said, wheezing from the short motion. He extended both arms and lunged forward.

Jung jumped back but came up against the hammock.

The Brewer grabbed the strap of his bag.

Feeling the bag slipping from his shoulder, Jung advanced forward. He punched the man in his barreled gut twice before wrenching the bag from his closed fist.

The Brewer managed to get an arm around Jung. He clasped his hands together and squeezed, emptying the air from the boy. "Better you slip away quietly and we all forget this little situation ever happened."

Jung sank to the ground, choking.

The Brewer lay on top of him.

Jung tried to inhale but he couldn't, his lungs were sealed closed. With every expelled breath, he was getting closer to death.

The Brewer adjusted his body, placing his gut on the boy's face.

Jung's eyes rolled to the back of his head. He was just about to blackout when a bang rang out across the room.

The Brewer's body went limp.

Jung pushed the enormous man off of his chest and wriggled free, gasping for air. Everything was hazy, white lights flickered all around him.

He saw his silent rescuer standing above him.

31

Jung sat up slowly. In time the fogginess receded and the figure in front of him came into focus.

The girl was Peruvian and of similar age to Jung. She looked to be from one of the tribes near Cuzco. She had a small mouth with plump lips, long curling eyelashes and slender green eyes. Her hair was dark and fell well beyond her shoulders, the long strands were brushed back behind her ears. She wore a cloth dress covered in grime and a necklace made from reeds folded into the shape of a hummingbird. She held a wooden cooking pot.

Even in a daze Jung recognized her beauty immediately. He saw the shape of the snail's shell on her face—the golden ratio.

"Are you okay?" she said in Jung's native tongue.

Jung nodded, still trying to recover his breath.

The girl pulled a small wooden flask from her pocket that looked identical to the flask The Captain had. "I can make him forget all this but first you must go." She pointed to the stairs. "Hide with the animals. You know where I mean?"

He nodded but didn't move.

"Quick," she said, offering him a hand.

He took her hand and slowly stood. He paused on his feet.

"Quick! You need to hide."

"What's your name first?" he said.

"You have to go."

"I will. But what's your name?"

"Best you don't know that. I have strict orders to stay away from you."

"Orders?"

She nodded.

The Brewer groaned from the floor.

She scrunched her face and pointed to the stairs.

Jung nodded and rushed off.

At the stairs, he hovered in the shadows and watched the girl.

She sat The Brewer up and tilted back his head. She held up the flask and poured the liquid down his throat. She emptied half the contents into his gullet before he coughed and began throwing up.

Jung kept moving upstairs. He heard the girl talking as he climbed. "Are you okay?" she said. "You fell over and hit your head. I found you and the rye down here." He heard The Brewer mumble something in return. Their voices faded away as he entered the storage room.

When the girl returned, Jung emerged from the shadows.

They stood face to face.

He immediately took both her hands in his, a grin on his face.

She gasped and twitched to his touch then settled and smiled in return.

"What's your name?" Jung said.

"Like I said, it's best you don't know that."

"Why?"

"Captain's orders."

"I promise to keep it to myself."

She looked back at the stairs then at Jung. "Tika."

"Tika. I'm Jung."

She grinned.

"What are you doing here?" he said.

She looked around again briefly. "I work here."

"Work here? Doing what?"

"I teach The Captain our language and I do cleaning and the like."

"Language?"

"Yes."

"Why?"

She bit her lip and looked to the ground appearing suddenly ashamed.

Jung gently squeezed her hands softly.

She forced a smile. "What are you doing here?"

"The Captain and his men are going to help me find a star."

"A star?"

"Yes, the star that hit Earth causing the disaster," Jung said. He grinned boastfully.

"Why?"

"I have a deal with Kon-Tiki. I'm going to get him a shard of the star and in return he's going to let me use the pyramid."

Tika looked nervous. "You made a deal with one of them?"

"Yes, Kon-Tiki," Jung said, his smile gone.

"Who?"

"Kon-Tiki. The Viracochan man at Lake Titicaca."

"It could be any of them."

"The man from this arc that went ashore," he said.

"There are Viracochan men roaming all over Peru."

"What?"

"They sent two dozen men ashore when we arrived."

"He was wearing a white robe," Jung said.

"All of the men who went ashore were wearing white robes. They are Viracochan storytellers. They were sent out to find our people and to settle with them."

"Why?"

"To win their trust. You made a deal with one of them?"

"But why?"

"So our people agree to help them build the pyramid. What was the deal exactly?"

"I said I would get him a shard of star from the crash site if he let me use the machine."

Tika looked afraid. "That's not good." She pulled her hands free from Jung's.

"Why?" he said.

"Because now your value has been established. The moment you hand over the star, your value is gone. And once your value is gone, you're dead."

"Dead?"

She nodded. "Yes, literally. A promise as large as the one you made will almost certainly have you on a hit list after the exchange is done."

"What do you mean?"

"I mean, if you achieve your mission and give them a star then they will likely try to kill you because you have gained too much."

Jung was confused. "What have I gained?"

"You would have a big role to play in their narrative. That makes you powerful. And they always deem power as a threat. Just, whatever you do, don't make any more deals."

The blood drained from Jung's face.

"What's a matter?"

"I made a second promise."

Tika looked terrified. "With who?"

"The Captain."

"The Captain! What did you promise him?"

"I- I said I would get him a shard of star too if he would help me get to the crash site."

"Stupid!"

Jung drooped his head ashamed of himself.

Tika squeezed his shoulder.

He looked up. "I *can* deliver."

She nodded. "Just no more promises."

"I promise," he said smiling

She pushed him in the chest playfully.

Suddenly there was a creak from above.

Tika looked to the stairwell then back at Jung. "I have to go. But seriously no more promises."

He nodded.

She dipped her hand into her pocket and pulled out a folded piece of papyrus. She handed it to him. "I got this for you. Look after it and don't let them see it. If they find it we're both dead."

Before Jung opened it she was gone. He studied the sketch similar in design to those he had seen in the book of knowledge.

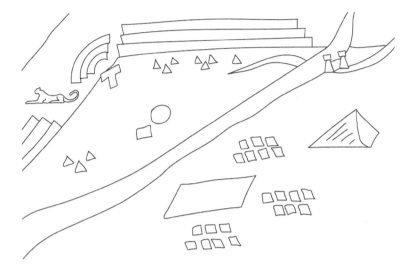

The drawing showed several lines and a scattering of triangles and squares. It was meaningless to him. He only recognized two shapes: a t-shape that looked similar to the stone monolith he had seen in the hull of the arc and what looked like a cat.

32

Jung woke alone in the hull. He smelled mold mixed with ash and salt.

The arc rocked gently back and forth in the waves. He heard the muffled sound of moving water coming from below, then a thumping screeching sound coming from the front of the arc. It sounded like two large pieces of wood being grinded together.

He sat up in the hammock, feeling his bag pressed against his side. His chest felt tender and bruised from the struggle with The Brewer the night before. He saw the tip of his bow on the ground beneath the hammock. He peered over the edge of the bed and frowned seeing his quiver and arrows missing.

Suddenly distant voices came from above, it sounded like men arguing up on deck.

Jung swung his legs over the edge of the hammock and went to stand. He immediately felt dizzy, his head whirling in pain. He winced and sat again.

Earth's Star had moved three lengths of itself by the time Jung had climbed to the top of the stairs. He was hovering beneath the manhole, peeking out across the deck. It was middæg but difficult to see—a dark haze hung low in the air.

A seagull squawked overhead.

Jung opened the manhole a little more and looked up. He smiled seeing the dark shadow circling above. It was the first time since the disaster that he had heard or seen an animal.

Suddenly a banging sound from the front of the arc stole his attention. There appeared to be another arc of identical size and design butted against theirs. A temporary wooden bridge connected the two vessels. The two arcs jostled against one another restlessly, screeching and groaning. It explained the grinding sounds he had heard down in the hull.

The second arc looked badly damaged. The ornate railings were mangled and missing in sections and the giant rounded hull looked scuffed and scratched.

Next to the bridge The Captain and seafaring men were gathered in a group. Their attention was focused on something in front of them.

The figure in front shifted to the side. The man wore a robe like The Brewers and The Captains, only it wasn't white or gray but dark blue. He was three stripe. He had his hood up, hiding his face. On top of the robe he wore a vest made of feathers that belonged to various raptors—vultures, condors, hawks and the like. He carried a wooden staff and a leather shoulder bag.

The seafaring men had the stranger pressed against the railing. They were led by The Captain who looked angry. He pointed at the stranger and mouthed something.

The man shook his head. He looked back at the arc he had traveled on and moved his hands. He seemed to be explaining himself.

The Captain looked frustrated.

The seafaring men mimicked his frustration with scowls and combative body language.

The stranger held his palms together and bowed. He appeared to be pleading. He pointed back to his arc and then in the direction from which he had come. He bowed again, shaking his clasped wrists—begging.

The Captain shook his head.

The seafaring men seemed to take this as an order to start pushing the stranger back toward the footbridge.

The man stopped, holding his ground. He held up three fingers.

The seafaring men stopped and looked at The Captain who seemed at a loss for words.

The Captain dropped his head, annoyed.

The man touched him on the shoulder.

The Captain shrugged off the hand and mouthed something. Then he stepped aside. The seafaring men stepped aside too, clearing a path for the man.

The man nodded and began to hobble across the deck toward where Jung was hiding.

Jung let the manhole door gently close and climbed down the stairs.

He hid in the shadows in the stairwell, just below the mess hall. He watched from the darkness as The Captain led the shuffling stranger down the stairs and across the hall. As the stranger passed by, he noticed the cane he was holding had markings engraved into it. The patterns looked almost identical to those carved into the stone monolith in the Uzman's quarters.

The Captain led the man to the far end of the hall and opened one of the doors to the room next to his. He lay open his palm, encouraging the stranger to go inside.

The man looked around. He was alone with The Captain. In the low light of the corridor he peeled back his hood.

Jung's mouth fell open.

The man's skin was sickly white, even more pale than the other Viracochan men. He was bald with narrow slanted eyes, thin indented cheeks and a pointed chin. He looked like a serpent. *The feathered serpent.* More strange though was his skull. It was nothing like Jung had seen before. It was long and elongated—stretched.

The man looked in Jung's direction.

Jung ducked behind the post, his heart pounding. He remembered what Apo had told him about losing his sight after seeing a similar-looking creature. Still, he couldn't help but look. He peeked around the beam.

The feathered serpent grunted something to The Captain, the words were foreign to Jung.

The Captain grunted back.

The man nodded and turned, he entered the room and slammed closed the door.

Alone in the corridor, The Captain clenched his teeth and cussed. He was clearly enraged by the arrival of the three striped man.

33

58 dægs to stars return.

THE CLOUD FOREST. PERU.

I was sitting in a mud hut in a remote location in The Cloud Forest. I was on the ground, my hands tied behind my back.

The room was small, barely two men long by one man wide. It was empty aside from a small fire that crackled in the corner.

A female warrior sat by the door guarding me. She was small but had broad shoulders for her size and muscular arms. She had a scar beneath one eye and held a long knife.

Suddenly the door opened.

Uma appeared, the body paint was gone. He was holding the book of knowledge with both hands. It was as if he already knew it's value.

The guard stood and left when he stepped inside the room.

He squatted in front of me and placed the book on his knees. He pointed to the book. "Will you explain this to me?"

"Yes, of course." I nodded to the ground. "Please sit."

He shook his head and poked the cover. "It killed him."

"What?"

He picked up the book and shook it. "This! It killed my brother."

"Your brother?"

He nodded.

"Who's your brother?"

"You showed him the book at the lake. Then he died."

"Who are you talking about?"

"You don't remember?" Uma said.

"No, I don't. I've shown many people that book. That's what I came here to do, share the knowledge in it."

"He came in red paint the first time. You must remember him. He sat with you and you showed him the book."

I nodded, remembering. "Yes, I think so. Hatun, right?"

He frowned. "You killed him!"

"I didn't kill him."

"Yes, you did. He sat with you and then he died. You put a curse on him."

"I didn't. We just talked. I just showed him the book."

"And then he died."

"No. I didn't know that. When did he die?"

Uma stood. "You're a dead man."

"Why?"

"Your book killed him."

I shook my head. "I only tried to explain what the book says."

He glared at me.

"That's all I've done with all the people I have met. I've shown the book to dozens of people. I'm sorry your brother is gone."

He went to leave.

"I may know what killed him," I said.

Uma stopped and turned. "What?" He looked angry.

"I'm not sure of the specific cause of death but I have a theory."

He stared at me blankly.

"I guess what I'm saying is that I've seen this before. I've seen this many times before."

"What? You've seen what?"

"The death of the artist."

"Artist?"

I nodded.

"What's that?"

I nodded at the book. "Open the book to the beginning. See the wheel."

Uma eventually opened the book.

"Near the beginning. See the circle dissected into 12 pieces."

He flipped through the pages and held up the book. "This?"

I nodded seeing the page.

"What is it?" he said.

"Put it down in front of me. I'll show you."

He spread the book out on the floor in front of me.

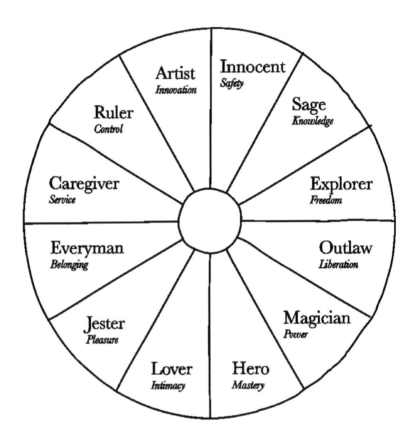

I said, "See on the outer wheel, there are 12 archetypes: Lover, Jester, Everyman, Caregiver, Ruler, Artist, Innocent, Sage, Explorer, Outlaw, Magician and Hero. Every person fits into one of these categories. It is a type of person."

Uma hovered closer to the page.

"And below in italics is the desire of each archetype—the single-most pursuit a person has. Lovers pursue *intimacy,* Jesters pursue *pleasure,* Everymen pursue *belonging,* Caregivers pursue *service*, Rulers pursue *control*, Artists pursue *innovation*, Innocents pursue *safety*, Sages pursue *knowledge*, Explorers pursue *freedom*, Outlaws pursue *liberation*, Magicians pursue *power* and Heros pursue *mastery*."

"What one are you?"

"If you untie my hands I will tell you."

He scowled at me.

"What harm am I against your people. You could annihilate me in a moment. Just let me point to the pages."

Uma considered this for a moment, then cut my hands free. It was obvious that I wasn't going anywhere. The wild would kill me faster than the natives.

I nodded thankfully and rubbed my wrists before pointing to the page. "I am the sage, the pursuer of knowledge. That is why I have a book of knowledge. In fact, that is the exact name of that book, the book of knowledge."

Uma stared at the book in awe.

I pointed to the top of the wheel on the page. "And your brother was an artist."

"What does that mean?"

"The artist is a maker, a thinker, a dreamer. They're often distracted by their own thoughts and frequently need to be pulled in from out of the rain. They represent the wonder and the dangers to be found in complete devotion to curiosity. They embody improvisation, creativity and childlike wonder at the world."

Uma nodded, apparently believing the words to be true of his brother.

I said, "Artists come in all forms. Some paint, some hunt, others tell stories. There are infinite forms of art but all artists are the same—they are people who Pachamama gifts with bounteous creativity and an innate drive to create."

"And this killed him?" Uma said.

I nodded. "Yes."

"How?"

"Because to create an artist you must first let someone feel pain. So much pain that you make him feel like a prisoner. How does Pachamama achieve that? She allows every artist to feel the collective wound of humanity. All people get a sense of it but the artist feels it more than any other. It's the gift Pachamama gives them to rally them and fire them up so they are driven to create—to fight the resistance."

"What wound?" Uma said.

"Suffering."

Uma nodded, seeming to understand.

"Your brother was an artist but you are the hero."

Uma looked shocked. "Hero?"

I laughed. "It's true." I pointed to the opposite side of the archetypal wheel. "The hero is directly opposite the artist. They balance out the artist. That is why I know your brother would have achieved nothing without you."

He was grinning.

"If the artist has the vision then the hero has the courage to bring the vision to fruition. The hero is the doer. That is you. Think about the attack at the lake. When you led your people you came out on top. You got the task done."

Uma was hovering above me, enjoying hearing about himself.

"I believe Pachamama has a plan for all of us. I trust her. I think she has chosen you."

"Me?"

I nodded. "I think with your power and my knowledge we are an unbreakable force."

Uma closed the book and picked it up before standing. "If we partner up you will tell me everything in here."

I smiled. "Yes, everything."

He flicked through the pages to near the end and held the book up. The page showed a sketch of the t-shaped torture device we called the rack.

He said, "You can start by explaining this."

34

DEEP SEA.

Jung woke in the middle of the night. They had been out at sea for almost one full lunar cycle.

There was a slashing sound coming from the front of the arc and a gentle hum coming from the rear. The vessel was moving fast, rising and falling hypnotically.

Suddenly he noticed a shape in the corner of the room. Someone was sitting on one of the classroom benches, watching him from the darkness.

Jung was still, waiting for his eyes to adjust. He barely made out the form of a figure wearing a dark robe with the hood up. It had to be the feathered serpent.

The man had a book laid across his lap and was whispering as he rolled something between his fingers, as if placing a curse on the boy.

Jung's heart raced. He coughed and kicked his legs signaling he was waking up.

The man immediately closed the book.

Jung rolled gently one way then the other giving the man an opportunity to clear the room. He yawned loudly and rolled over, peeking out from beneath his arm.

The man was gone.

Jung sat up quickly and scanned the room. Nothing. Only the hum of the arc engine and the sloshing waves. How could he have left without a sound?

Out on deck The Captain was standing alone at the front of the arc. He was gazing out across the vast stretching ocean that glistened silver. Above him Earth's Rock showered the deck in a midnight blue.

The arc was moving at a clipping pace, the steep bow dancing from wave to wave. Yet, on deck it barely felt like he was moving.

As Jung approached, The Captain turned. "Jung!" He waved his hand, encouraging the boy to lean on the rail next to him.

Jung stood by The Captain's side and looked over the rail to where the water rushed below. Beyond the translucent surface was more than 10,000 feet of soaking darkness. He looked out to where the arc was pointed. Far away, beyond the curve of the ocean, was the beacon. The orange flame pulsed, brighter than ever—throbbing, breathing, swallowing. A black cloud swirled above it, frozen in place.

"Is that where we're going?" Jung said.

The Captain looked at the crash site and nodded.

"What is it?"

"I'm assuming it's fire from the impact."

"It's still burning. I thought you said it was ice up there?"

The Captain nodded. "It is. It's been puzzling me too." He slipped his hand into his robe and pulled out his flask. The lid squeaked as it popped off. He took a sip before passing it to the boy.

Jung shook his head.

The Captain took another sip before putting it back in his robe. He looked up to the sky.

Jung looked up too. The sky was still hazy with ash but had cleared considerably. It was the first time since the disaster that he had seen the Milky Way. The stars were still partially hidden by the smog but were beginning to shine through. Norð, one intrepid star shined brighter than all the rest. It pulsed blue.

"We should arrive in one lunar cycle," The Captain said.

"What's that?"

"What's *what?*"

"A lunar cycle."

The Captain pointed to Earth's Rock. "The time it takes Earth's Rock to complete one cycle around Earth. Around 27 dæġs."

"Is it true that you know the story of the stars?" Jung said.

The Captain seemed caught off guard by the question. He looked at Jung. The light from the distant beacon reflected off the cloudy caps in his eyes.

"Kon-Tiki says you know it."

"Does he?"

Jung nodded.

The Captain was silent, thinking.

"Will you tell it to me?"

He shook his head. "I'm afraid not, boy."

"Why?"

"Because such a story is reserved for those Uzmans who have two stripes. It's not something that is told to simply anyone. It is earned knowledge. To tell you would undermine all those rotations of training it took myself and others to acquire such knowledge."

"What do you mean?" Jung said.

"I mean it took me 20 rotations and many risks to earn the story of the stars. I'm not just about to give up the secret to some boy who is passing through."

"Does Kon-Tiki know it?"

The Captain shook his head. "No, he's one stripe. He knows the story of knowledge, that's all."

The arc kicked from the lip of a large wave, levitating in the air for a moment before tilting down.

They both held the rail and widened their stance as butterflies filled their chests.

"How do you earn a second stripe?" Jung said when the arc settled.

"By fulfilling your mission."

"What mission?"

"Well, that depends. There are different missions for every man. It depends on your specialty and the needs of the Tæcans at the time. I couldn't say."

"What was *your* mission?"

"Mine?"

Jung nodded.

"To sail."

"To sail where?"

The Captain looked uncomfortable. He took his flask from his pocket and took a sip. "Many places, boy. Anyway, enough about me. I have some news."

"What?"

"We have a visitor on the arc. Another man who will be traveling with us."

"Who?" Jung said as if not knowing the feathered serpent was aboard.

"He's a surgeon. His arc came from back near home—Angkor Wat. I guess the Tæcans thought we might have casualties from the disaster."

"Did you?"

"Did we what?"

"Have casualties?"

The Captain looked nervous. It was only for a moment but Jung saw it.

The Captain said, "Well, no. If Kon-Tiki is okay then we're all safe."

"Is he the only one ashore?" Jung said.

"Yes."

"Who are all the hammocks in the hull for then?"

"What?"

"All of the beds?"

The Captain was composed. "Standard design, boy. This arc has been built dozens of times over. All the arcs are the same. The architect who designed the arc is the same man who designed The Great Pyramid and The Artery of Earth."

"Really?"

The Captain nodded.

"Who is he?"

"A man from Egypt. I know him only as The Great Architect. All of the arcs have the same number of beds, but not necessarily the same number of passengers."

Jung nodded, letting the man off the hook. He leaned on the rail.

They both looked out at the dark water that seemed to blend with the sky, creating the illusion that they were suspended in space.

"Anyway," The Captain said. "The Surgeon is coming with us. His men will stay behind and prepare Nazca for the pyramid build."

"Why is he coming?"

The Captain took a swig from his flask. "There is other news too."

"What?"

"He wants to join you when you leave the arc."

Jung felt electricity in his neck. "What?"

"You must watch yourself around him."

"Why?"

The Captain went to speak then stopped. He looked around, the deck was empty. He started over. "Between you and me, I think he wants the star too."

"Why?"

"My guess is that he's trying to get a teaching position at Göbekli Tepe."

Jung was confused. "Göbekli Tepe? What's that?"

"It's a place, boy," The Captain whispered.

"Where?"

"A long way from here. Around 40 dægs walk from Egypt. It sits perched on a knoll, hundreds of men higher than the surrounding valley. You would certainly be protected from any flood there."

"You've been?"

"No, not the exact site, but I've taken Tæcans to nearby there. Within a dæġs walk."

"What's there?" Jung said.

"Enormous classrooms. Giant stone structures with room for a hundred Tæcans to stand. In the center of each is a giant stone pillar that shows everything taught in that classroom."

"Like the stone in the hull?"

The Captain smiled. "Yes, exactly. Our Tæcans are flocking to Göbekli Tepe to teach and to learn. They say the site can store so much food that the Tæcans can stay on-site for seasons at a time." He looked at Jung. "And they say the whole savanna is teeming with animals. There are leopards, gazelles, red deer and lions. And birds too—geese, ducks, cranes, everything you can imagine."

"But why does he want to go there?" Jung said.

"To teach, I suppose."

"But why does he need to come with me?"

The Captain looked around again. "I'm not sure, but if you wanted to become a Tæcan and get a classroom of your own, then finding a star would be your best bet." He leaned in and whispered. "Just do me a favor and beat him."

Jung was angry. "Why did you let him onboard if you don't want him to get to the star?"

The Captain took a deep breath. "If I had my way, I would have turned him away. I would turn any three stripe man away. Unfortunately, I don't have that power. My head would be taken for even considering such a thing."

"Why?"

"Because he outranks me."

"So what?"

The Captain laughed. "Yes, so what." He looked to the ocean, nervous. "All I know is that we would all be a lot better off if he wasn't aboard... but he is."

"I could lose him," Jung said. He didn't know what had come over him but he felt the words awakening his gut. *Yes, he could lose The Surgeon on the walk.* After all the man was dangerous and he was already after him—he had tried to place a curse on him. He had to die. Still, it felt strange. Jung had never before decided whether a man would live or die.

Jung said, "If I lose him, he's as good as dead. I will kill him for you in exchange for the story of the stars."

A smirk crept across The Captain's face. "Deal."

Jung shook The Captain's hand and cussed himself for making another deal.

35

"Okay. Well, first, let's check your eyes," The Captain said.

He gripped the rail and leaned forward, he searched the sky until he found what he was looking for. He pointed. "See that red star out there?"

Jung nodded.

"Okay. Well, off to the right. There is a cluster of stars all grouped together. Can you see them?"

Jung nodded. "I think so."

"Good. So the question is: how many stars are in that cluster? Visible stars, I mean. Let me give you a clue, you can count the number using your fingers."

Jung squinted at the stars. He extended first his thumb then each of his fingers, one at a time. He held up his hand showing all five digits.

"So, five?" The Captain said.

Jung nodded.

"Okay, not bad. Missing two but that's okay."

"Two?"

"Yes, there are seven stars in the pleiades of Taurai. Those with exceptional eyes see seven. I see five like you, that's the case ever since these dam calluses formed anyway. There is nothing wrong with that. Your eyes are still good enough for the story of the stars. I just wanted to make sure you'll be able to see what I point out. If you said three or less that might have been a problem. Five is good."

The Captain pulled out his flask and took a sip. He puckered his lips and put the flask away before tracing his pointer finger across the sky to another group of stars. "See those stars there? The bright ones? They look like a man holding a bow, just like yours. You can see the hunter's arm holding the bow in the direction of the constellation of Taurai—the direction from which the star that hit Earth came. And see the area around the waist of the man? It appears like the hunter's belt."

Jung nodded, a smirk on his face.

The Captain winked. "That band—the belt in the center—that is Orion's Belt. Those three stars we call *the three sisters*. The three pyramids in Egypt will match those stars perfectly."

"Why?"

"Because that's where the spirit molecule enters the sky."

The Captain traced his finger along the Milky Way. "See how if you trace a line across the stars of Orion's Belt you eventually intersect Sirius—the brightest star in the sky?" He pointed to the largest star in the sky.

Jung smiled. It was the star that had first caught his attention when he had come up on deck. It pulsed blue, brighter than any other.

"That is what The Great Pyramid will point to," The Captain said.

"What is there?" Jung said.

"At Sirius?"

Jung nodded.

The Captain lowered his voice. "Sirius is not what it seems. From here on Earth it looks like one enormous star but it is in fact two—Sirius I and Sirius II."

He held up his two pointer fingers and wiggled one. "Sirius I is enormous, it's twice as big as Earth's Star." He wiggled the other finger. "While Sirius II is much smaller. It was once even larger than Sirius I but it consumed all of its resources and collapsed into itself." He began to rotate his fingers around one another. "Sirius I and Sirius II spin around and around one another in perfect balance. Between them is the door to the grid."

"The grid?" Jung said.

"Yes, the control room where you can change channels. That is the story of the stars. It is a how-to book to make the journey from Orion's Belt to Sirius along the Milky Way. There are seven tests to pass on the path of the stars."

"Seven?"

The Captain nodded. "Yes, a different test for each line of energy that passes through our body."

"What?"

"There are seven bands of energy running across our physical bodies, beginning at the base of the spine and going up to the crown of the head," The Captain said. He ran his finger across his waist. "First, there is the root band." He ran his finger across his lower stomach. "Then the sacral band." He ran his finger across his solar plexus, his heart and his throat. "Then the solar plexus band, the heart band and the throat band." Lastly he ran his finger across his eye line and forehead. "The third eye band and lastly the crown band." He took a sip from his flask. "Even when our entire being is compacted down to a single spirit molecule it retains these seven bands of energy. The balance of these bands will determine how far a spirit can go on the path of the stars."

"What do you mean?" Jung said.

"To make the journey from Orion to Sirius each band is weighed."

"Weighed?"

"Yes, measured. Tested to see if it weighs less than the feather of the stars."

"What's that?"

"It is a feather that is placed on one end of a scale while the band's energy is placed on the other. Each band must weigh less than the feather in order for a spirit to pass the tests. Fail one test and you won't be shown the way."

"So what someone does in their life determines how much their bands weigh?" Jung said.

The Captain nodded. "Exactly. Good energy is light and bad energy is heavy. The more good energy you accrue in your life, the greater chance you have of passing the tests."

"What exactly are the tests?"

"The first test is to weigh the root band. In order for a spirit's root band to not weigh too much the individual must have reached sexual fertility."

"That's it?" Jung said.

"For this band, yes."

Jung was relieved, his father had definitely reached fertility. He was proof of that.

"The next band up is the sacral gland," The Captain said. "In order for the sacral gland to not weigh too much an individual must have proven that they are attuned to the ebbs and flows of nature."

Jung's heart thumped hard in his chest, thinking. *Had his father been attuned to nature?* Surely he had. He read the forest better than any other person in their tribe. He often spoke of the tremors and beats. He said you could read them. He had to have passed.

"Above that is the solar plexus band," The Captain said. "To pass this test an individual must have conquered instinct. In other words, the individual must have mastered when to trust their instinct and when to override it."

Jung knew for sure that his father had conquered instinct. He had explained to him on many occasions that all great hunters knew how to break from impulse. He had mastered breaking from fear. He had to have passed.

"Next we have the heart band. To pass this test an individual must prove that they have kept a healthy temple. The meat body from which the spirit molecule is passed. To pass this test the individual must prove that they are in healthy physical shape."

Jung was relieved. His father was extremely healthy, he had to have passed. "So, the elders don't make it?" he said.

The Captain shook his head. "Not if they are too old. You must be in good shape. If you don't have a healthy temple prior to dematerializing then your spirit molecule won't have the energy to make the full journey." He ran a finger across his throat. "Next is the throat band. To pass this test an individual must prove that in life they have gathered more light energy than dark energy."

Jung took a breath, again relieved. His father had definitely passed the test. He had been in the room when the shamans said this very thing—that Hatun had a gift for taking the heaviness from energy.

"The next test is along the third eye band," The Captain said. "To pass this test an individual must have achieved the feat of opening their third eye."

Jung was suddenly nervous. He didn't remember his father ever mentioning a third eye.

"How do you open the eye?" Jung said.

The Captain scoffed. "I can't tell you that."

"Why? You said you would tell me the story."

"Because I don't know it. That's three stripe knowledge—the story of death."

"But what is it?"

"The third eye?"

Jung nodded.

"It's a dial in our head that determines how much we see," The Captain said. "Decrease the level of saturation by turning the dial down and you'll see and experience very little. But turn the saturation up by opening the eye and you'll see the layers, the traces of other channels bleeding through."

"So you can use it to get to other channels?"

"Yes."

"Even channels occupied by the dead."

The Captain nodded. "Yes, all channels."

"How do you do it? How do you get into your spirit molecule?"

The Captain frowned. "I told you that's three stripe knowledge, knowledge I don't know. Why do you think I'm out here helping you? You are my ticket to get a third stripe."

"What's the last test?"

"The crown band?"

Jung nodded.

"We don't really know. The only information we have is that it appears to take place in a room above the spirit realm. Those Tæcans who have made it inside don't know how they got in, they just did. It appears the challenge is different for every person once inside."

"But to get there you would first have to open your third eye?"

The Captain nodded. "Correct."

"Who knows how to do it?" Jung said.

"I told you already, three stripe Uzmans. A rank above me."

"What do they look like?"

"Men in robes like mine but dark blue."

"The feathered serpent?" Jung said.

"What?"

"The Surgeon."

"*Feathered serpent?*" The Captain said.

Jung nodded. "He wears feathers and has the face of a serpent."

The Captain laughed. "True."

"He knows the story of death?"

"Yes."

"And he's coming with me ashore?" Jung said.

The Captain nodded.

Jung smiled. He knew exactly how to get the story from the old man.

36

It was several dægs into the voyage. Jung was up on deck when he heard a yell.

One of the seafaring men pointed to the beacon norð, which the arc was locked onto. A front was coming in fast. The wall of cloud looked like a mounting tsunami.

Jung smelled the approaching rain in the air.

It wasn't long before all of the seafaring men were on deck, grunting and running back and forth. They pulled up manholes in the floor that Jung didn't even know existed.

"Oy!" a voice yelled.

Jung turned.

It was one of the seafaring men. He had a thick beard and a grizzly face. He was grunting noises.

Jung got moving. He couldn't understand the man's words but the message was clear—get in the hull.

He was in his hammock when the front hit. The rocking up and down had been building for some time but when the storm hit, things mounted fast.

There was an enormous bang against the wall of the hull. The wood bowed beneath the force of the surging wave. There was a churning sound as the ocean ground its teeth.

Jung gripped the sides of his hammock as a second wave crashed against the vessel. The arc lurched to the side and began to rise up the crest of the wave.

At the crest, the arc spun on its nose—balancing for a moment—before sliding back down the shoulder of water.

Jung was flung from the hammock. He landed forcefully on his shoulder which dislocated momentarily and popped back in. A surge of pain shot through his neck. He squawked and cradled his arm as the arc began to repeat the same motion, skimming up the crest of the next oncoming wave.

He heard the distant yells from the seafaring men. They were screaming instructions back and forth. Their cries barely cleared the whistling winds and explosions of thunder.

When the arc steepened Jung grabbed the nearest beam and wrapped his limbs around it. He held tight like a praying mantis as the beam turned onto its side.

The arc lurched up the wave, tilting more and more until it flipped. It bounced off its top and rolled back onto its side. Despite the chaos, the vessel seemed at peace in the mountainous swell, the snail shaped hull ensured the vessel always rolled back onto its base.

Still, the rushing, tumbling motion terrified Jung. He gripped the beam as the arc shot up the spine of the next wave, the angle of the bow becoming steeper and steeper.

When the vessel reached the crest of the wave it continued on, sailing into the air as the wave departed beneath it.

Jung felt butterflies erupt in his chest as the arc floated through the air.

There were yells of concern from the seafaring men.

The arc landed with a crash. The hull bent to the impact.

Jung was thrown from the post he was clinging to.

The arc rolled onto its roof.

Jung crashed against the ceiling rafters and gripped one of the roof beams. He clung to the wood, waiting for the arc to roll back onto its base. When it did, he crawled along the wood to the stairs. Just as he planted his feet on the steps, the arc kicked, tossing him through the air. He was thrown up the stairs as the vessel twisted onto its side. He felt a crunch against his ribs as he crashed into the hard pointed edge work.

Above him came a banging sound. It was the manhole door that had flipped open. The sky looked ferocious, snaking forks of lightning lit the scene up like dæġlight for moments at a time. The flashes revealed waves like mountains. Several water spouts connected the sky to the sea. The waves were ten times the height of the arc.

Jung climbed toward the banging door. He wanted to close it. He climbed quickly while the arc was flat.

Just as he had a grip on the latch, a wave of unimaginable size smashed against the arc.

The vessel twisted, flipping the door of the manhole open.

Jung was dragged through the hole and tossed into the gnashing waters. He screamed as he sailed through the air for what felt like a hundred heartbeats, his chest whirling to the falling motion.

He crashed into the icy waters, the water fizzing in his ears. He swam for the surface but in a panic he gasped for breath too early and inhaled water into his lungs. He sputtered and coughed as he reached the surface. Water ejected from his lungs as he gasped for air. Soon the coughs turned to regurgitation and he began to throw up.

Suddenly the arc was next to him. They were both rushing up the oncoming wave, side by side.

Jung swam away from the vessel as fast as he could so he wouldn't be crushed if it was to suddenly change direction.

At the crest of the wave, the arc rose up and crashed down, sinking beneath its weight. The dip in water was enough to drag Jung beneath the surface.

Jung kicked and screamed as he was sucked further and further underwater. He was five men below the surface before the vessel released him.

He used every ounce of strength he had left to swim for air.

He reached the surface gasping for breath. He filled his lungs with one big breath after another.

By the time he spotted the arc, it was 50 men from him. He screamed and waved his hands helplessly through the air. It was hopeless, he was being dragged in the opposite direction. He felt like jiggly live bait in the surging black swell.

Eventually he stopped yelling and waving as the pointlessness of it all began to settle in. The arc had disappeared well beyond the waves. There was little chance the seafaring men had seen him go overboard. It was over.

Exhausted he let go and floated on his back, barely conscious. His head bobbed just above the surface. A muted drum roll in his ears. He looked to the sky. Between the jaws of the waves, lightning blasted from every direction.

All of a sudden the arc appeared again on the crest of a distant wave. The sight gave him hope. Jung began to swim to the arc as hard as he could. With water still in his lungs he tired almost immediately.

He looked toward the arc. It seemed to be getting further and further away. Recognizing the futility of the fight he surrendered again, lying on his back and playing dead. The waves carried him up and down. He felt his chest going numb and his legs getting heavy. His body relaxed, his torso dipping beneath the water. He felt his eyes closing, giving in. His lips kissed the water, slipping under.

Then the fight returned. He kicked himself back up out of the water and swept out his arms to swim. He took a few strokes then the energy drained from his body again. He began to slowly sink, saltwater filling his lungs. He was about to pass out.

Then the fight again. One last kick up onto his back. He coughed, spitting the water from his lungs. Then all of his energy was gone and the lights started to switch off, one by one.

It was a flicker of motion in the water that brought Jung back online. A great menacing shadow moved in his direction just below the surface.

He screamed as the creature seized him in its jaws.

37

23 dægs to stars return.

THE SACRED VALLEY. PERU.

"I could watch them all dæg," I said to Uma.

We were standing on the shore of a lake, dead grass to our knees. We were up in the mountains near Cuzco, half a dæg's walk from The Cloud Forest.

The lake was one of many in The Sacred Valley but by far the largest in the vicinity of the Cloud Forest. The enormous pool filled from the runoff rain that streamed down the slopes daily. It was a stunning place to spend a dæg, even with the ash in the sky. The waters were so perfectly unblemished that the towering mountains existed twice—once on their own and once in the reflection.

Yells came from the shallows.

A fishing boat glided across the shiny sheet of water towards the shore. The newly built craft was moving quickly, a strong back wind in its sail.

"There you go!" I said rising to my tippy toes.

Two strong armed natives sat on opposite sides of the craft, the wind rattling in the cloth sail. They aimed the speeding craft at a group of natives who were standing on the shore.

Just as they were about to plough into land one man jumped to the same side as the other and they both pulled on a cord. A thump came then a whoosh. The speeding boat kicked up onto one side and turned. The men relaxed their pull on the cord, straightening the craft. The vessel sped across the shallows next to the shore. The men were laughing and gripping hands, big smiles on their faces.

The group onshore squawked celebratorily and waved their arms madly as the boat sped past them.

The men tugged the cord again and the craft turned toward the center of the lake, before speeding off twice as fast.

I sat on the brittle grass. "Well, I guess it works."

Uma sat too. He pulled some coca leaves from his pouch and put them in his mouth. "Who taught you that?"

"The design of the boats?"

Uma nodded.

"Believe it or not, I used to be a fisherman."

"A fisherman?"

I nodded. "Yes, before I joined the school of knowledge as an Uzman, I lived with the Fects as a fisherman on the lake."

"So how did you become an Uzman?"

"Fate."

Uma looked confused. "What's that?"

"Fate is your destiny. Your path set out by Pachamama. I think my fate was to break the chain and not be a fisherman like my father and his father and his father before him. Everyone including me thought I would become a fisherman. Only the school decided to intervene."

"The school?"

I nodded. "The Tæcans at the pyramid. They knew what was best for me."

"What happened?" Uma said.

"I met one of them, not a Tæcan but a three stripe Uzman. As close to a Tæcan as you can get. He lived within the gated walls of the pyramid. He needed a scribe, someone to copy books. Books full of stories told by the Tæcans."

"You saw the stories told by the Tæcans?"

I shook my head. "There were many scribes. We did pieces here and there from each book so we never saw the completed stories." I smiled. "But I saw enough to get me interested in more."

"What did they say to you?"

"I was working down at the dock on my own when the Uzman visited me. I was 17 rotations old. I remember it was still dark. He asked if I was interested in working as a scribe for the school. I knew my father would never agree to me doing such work. He said that the Tæcans were dangerous and I believed him to be honest. Everyone knew them to be dangerous. But I took the job anyway. Mostly out of curiosity."

Uma looked uncomfortable. "Dangerous?"

"I'll get to that soon. For many rotations I fished with my father by dæġ and scribed for the school by night. But the more I scribed, the more I realized these people weren't bad or evil. They were anything but. They were enlightened, all knowing. It was merely the fact that they possessed so much knowledge that made them powerful and projected the illusion of evil. After all, power is dangerous. But at their root they were who they were because they valued knowledge above all else. And so did I."

"What type of knowledge?" Uma said.

"All the stuff in the book of knowledge plus the other books, the book of the stars and the book of death. Knowledge about Earth and the stars and transcendence. And knowledge about much more, knowledge about matter and movement and consciousness."

"Did he find out?" Uma said.

"My father?"

"Yes."

I nodded. "Yes, but only because I told him. I visited him the night after the Tæcans offered me a full time position at the school as a one stripe Uzman." I looked at Uma with glassy eyes. "I had two sons—six and eight. And a woman, their mother, who I loved and had devoted myself to. I told them all about the opportunity. No one reacted well, but he certainly reacted the poorest."

"Your father?"

I nodded. "He saw all the badness in the school. People living in isolation, the hierarchical power structure, the capital punishment." I shook my head. "But he didn't see what I saw. I saw what they were doing. They were practicing discipline and procedure because that's what it takes to groom exceptional knowledge-keepers. Just the same way that a tribe like yours goes out of their way to groom exceptional warriors."

"What did he do?"

My throat was tight. "He said he had a big fishing trip planned for the following dæg. A deep sea trip. I knew he was just adding salt to the wound. There was no *planned* trip. He had made it up to spite me. We hadn't been out deep sea for many rotations. Not since the accident when we had lost two men's lives. After that we all made a promise to keep our boats close to shore. Deep sea fishing was an unnecessary risk considering we had enough stocks of fish in the shallows."

"What happened?" Uma said.

"I didn't play into his power games. I said I wasn't going along on the trip. I said I had work to do for the school."

Suddenly my throat closed up and I couldn't talk. Tears rolled down my cheeks. I sniffed and rubbed them away with my hand.

"Are you okay?" Uma said.

I nodded and wiped my nose with the back of my hand.

"What happened?"

"He went out anyway," I said in a shaky voice. "He took my children—my boys—and they sank. They all died. We never recovered the bodies."

Uma looked deeply saddened by the story. "I'm so sorry."

I forced a smile. "Thank you, Uma." I laughed. "So stupid. What he did sealed my fate as an Uzman. I had nothing left after the accident. Not even with the mother of my children. When the boys were gone we were just a memory of the tragedy to one another. We were destined to break apart. I joined the school the moment I could. I had nothing else. I've been with them ever since."

"Wow."

I nodded. "Yes, wow. It was ten rotations ago." I looked at the lake and smiled. "Now look where I am. Look where *we* are."

Uma looked at the lake and smiled too. "It's not bad is it, for an apocalypse."

I looked at him. "Uma I need your help. Help me and I will bring you into the school. I can get you initiated on the path of the Tæcan as an Uzman. I can make it so you have a permanent place in our school and can access the pyramid anytime you like."

Uma stared at the water. It wasn't the first time we'd had this conversation. Eventually he turned to me. "What do you need help with?"

I held up one finger. "Just one thing. You do this *one* thing and I'll get you into the school."

"What is it?"

"Bring me 100 more people, strong able-bodied people from other tribes who can help with the build."

38

OLYMPIA. NORÐ AMERICA.

Footsteps on the stairs woke Jung.

He was lying in his hammock, his eyes barely open, a sheen of sweat glistening on his skin. His loincloth was board-stiff, clad with dried salt. He ached all over, weak as a kitten, and his lungs burned.

"You're awake!" Tika said. She was carrying a tray of food.

She rushed from the stairs to Jung's side and placed the tray on the floor. She hugged him, her hair covering his face. It was soft and smelled sweet and lively.

Jung was quiet despite how much the hug hurt.

Tika pulled away seeming to sense the boy's strain. "Are you okay?"

"What happened?" he said. His memory was still groggy. He only had a vague recollection of the events of the night prior.

Tika looked pained. "You went overboard."

"Overboard?"

She nodded. "You're lucky you can swim."

Jung was beginning to remember. He had a vision of being tossed from the deck and dragged beneath the sinking arc. He remembered the black menacing shadow.

"How did I get out?" he said.

"One of the seafaring men. You're so lucky. I swear you have a protector."

"But I was so far away. They couldn't have seen me."

Tika put on a reassuring smile. "One of them did. He jumped in the moment you went overboard. He took a rope tied to the arc."

Jung took a breath. The girl's words were fading away. He was remembering being in the water, preparing for death. He felt suddenly overcome with emotion. Tears ran freely from his eyes and his body shook. It was the first time he had cried since being in The Healer's cave. The tears seemed to release all of the feelings of fear and doubt and sadness that had been locked up inside of him since starting his journey. In what felt more like a panic attack than bereavement, he began to break into uncontrollable sobs. His body convulsed.

Tika bent over him and hugged him tightly. She cried silently too, squeezing him close.

Huddled against her warm body, feeling the calm beat of her chest, he felt like he was being drawn from weightless space and returned to his embryonic self. All of his fears and anxiety were absorbed by the slow rhythm of her heart.

When his heartbeat had finally slowed to a pace that matched her own, Tika let go of Jung and sat back. She smiled, moisture in her eyes.

"What are you doing here anyway?" Jung said. "You're not supposed to see me."

She laughed. "Not anymore. In fact, I've been put in charge of getting you better. The Captain told me to do anything I can to help you recover."

Jung winked. "Anything?"

She did her best to conceal her smile. "He also said to tell him the moment you wake." She bent down and picked up the tray of food. "But first let's feed you and get you some water."

Jung sat up, his loincloth scratching his skin.

Tika took a cup of water from the tray and hovered it close to Jung's lips.

He stared into her eyes, emerald green with yellow centers. Like some exotic cat, a panther. He smiled just as his lips connected with the cup.

"Get that smirk off your face or you'll spill this everywhere," Tika said.

He laughed and opened his mouth.

She poured the water in little by little. When he nodded, she put the cup to the side and wiped his chin then picked up the spoon. She fed him a soup made of deer meat and potato. The food was cold but the meat and potato melted in his mouth. She had gone to great lengths to make it just so, cooking it slowly for dæġs so he could swallow it without chewing.

Throughout the entire meal neither of them said a word. When their eyes met, they simply grinned—the proximity of their bodies sending an avalanche of hormŏns rushing through the both of them.

Jung's body slowly relaxed. His toes uncurled and a tingling returned to his legs. He felt a tingle in his groin too.

When he was full, Tika put the tray on the floor. She suddenly looked concerned.

"Are you okay?" Jung said.

She paced, nervous.

Jung took her hand. "What's the matter?"

"Before I get The Captain you should know that there is talk of turning the arc around."

Jung sat up higher. His ribs burned from the movement. "What do you mean?"

"You've been asleep for dæġs. The Captain doesn't think there is enough time to wait for your overland journey and get back to Nazca before the stars hit."

"How far from the crash site are we?"

"We're here. We've been here for dæġs."

"What!?" Jung said. He tried to move his legs. They were still mostly dead.

Tika placed her hand on his chest. "Careful."

Jung ignored her. "I can journey now." He gritted his teeth and began to wiggle his toes. They were stiff but responsive. "Can you help me to The Captain?"

"You're not ready. You're not healed."

Jung was serious. "You know I have to go. You're the one who said it. I'm dead to them without the star."

She was silent, she knew he was right. She nodded. "Okay, but there's a problem."

"What?"

"It's The Surgeon."

"What about him?"

She turned and looked around, making sure they were alone. She whispered. "The Captain says he knows about your father."

"What?"

"I don't know how. I suspect one of the men told him."

"The Brewer?" Jung said.

Tika shrugged. "I don't know. Maybe."

"What does that mean?"

"It means he's in danger. You're both in danger. If The Surgeon knows the reason you want the star is to get to your father, he'll no doubt try and put a stop to it."

"Why? And how?"

"Because he wants the star too. He'll just use you to find it-"

"I know," Jung said. "The Captain told me."

Tika looked worried. "But if he wants to hurt you, he can. He could easily tell one of the Tæcans to go up and find your father. And they would go if they wanted to hurt you. They've done it before. His spirit could be wiped out completely."

Jung was calm. "It's okay, I have a plan to get rid of him."

"Get rid of him?"

Jung nodded.

"The Captain will kill you."

"No, it was his idea. He wants The Surgeon gone more than me."

Tika looked confused. "I don't know what that means. All I know is that none of this is what it seems. The Surgeon didn't force his way into journeying with you, it was The Captain's idea."

39

Jung climbed on deck.

They were anchored 50 arcs from land. Seagulls squawked from the clearing sky, only a light gauze of ash cloaked Earth's Star.

Jung rested against the railing and looked out to the shore. Enormous ice-capped mountains climbed steeply, creating an imposing curtain of grays, browns and blanched greens. At the foot of the mountains were scablands, a baron rock-speckled plain that ran all the way to the coast. The muddy clearing looked like a dry riverbed, only it was so wide it would take two dægs to walk. A vein of water ran through the center of the riverbed. A remnant of the area's cataclysmic past.

"Jung!" The Captain said. He bounced across the deck, smiling genuinely. "How are you?"

Jung turned awkwardly. "I'm okay."

The Captain joined him on the rail. "You were bloody lucky." He had his flask out already. It seemed to appear any time he justified a celebration or a commiseration. It meant there was never a reason not to pop off the cap.

As always the sharp smell irritated Jung's nose.

The Captain took a sip. "How are you feeling?"

Jung nodded and looked at the mountains. "I thought you said it was ice?"

"It was, it was locked behind those peaks, the entire thing was an ice shelf. I think your star hit somewhere behind them." He pointed to the shore. "See those ripples? They look almost like the ripples you see on the bank of a river or the shore of a beach. Like rows of snake tracks, only thousands of times larger."

Jung nodded.

"Patterns like those are formed from lapping water. Based on the size of those marks, I would say the wave that came down from those mountains was at least 100 metrai high."

"What's metrai?" Jung said.

"It's a length, around the length of your leg."

"That can't be accurate? Isn't every man's leg a different length?"

The Captain laughed. "True. No, it's precise. You get a metrai by measuring the length of Earth from the center to the roof and dividing it by 10,000."

"You measured Earth?"

The Captain grinned. "Not me, but yes my people."

"How?"

He winked. "Using the stars. How else?" He looked back at the shore and pointed to the mountains. "Anyway, I think your star lies just beyond those peaks."

"How do you know we're in the right place?"

"Because this is where the giant river reached the shore. More water than the combined flow of all the freshwater rivers on Earth rushed down through here in a single go. You can see the trench where it bled into the ocean. It would have been horrifying." He turned to Jung. "Follow the river and you'll find your star."

"Where's the beacon?" Jung said, realizing it was missing from the sky.

The Captain looked sorð, back the way they had come. "Long gone."

"I thought it was where the star hit?"

"We all did. Turns out it was a wildfire. Looked to be burning half the continent. Triggered by the firestorms we suspect." He nodded to the mountains. "This is where your journey leads you now. Follow the river."

"Why do you want it anyway?" Jung said.

The Captain creased his eyes. He looked suddenly dark, ominous, like all the kindness had drained from him. "Why do I want what?" he said. His tone was aggressive.

"The star," Jung said, his voice weak.

The Captain took a sip from his flask and shook his head. "You kill two of my men and now you push me."

Two deaths? Tika hadn't mentioned any deaths.

"You have no gratefulness for what I have given you. What my men have given you. We saved your bloody life, boy," The Captain said. He took another sip.

Jung didn't trust the man's performance. From his experience no Viracochan man was above lying. It seemed to be embedded in their culture.

The Captain leaned on the rail and looked at Jung. "The truth is, boy. Your win is my win. I want the star for the same reason you want the star, to get those damn pyramids up and running."

"I'm sorry," Jung said.

The Captain smiled and pinched his shoulder. "That's okay. I know you didn't mean anything by it."

The truth is Jung didn't care. He wasn't listening. He was thinking about getting moving. He was thinking about The Surgeon and the story of death.

The Captain said, "We'll give you five dægs to find the star and five dægs to get back. That's it. Otherwise we'll be at sea when the stars return."

"I'm ready. Where's The Surgeon?"

"He's waiting in his room. He's anxious to move too."

"Let me get my stuff," Jung said.

Down in the hull Jung saw his knife and quiver sitting next to his bow. He picked up his weapons and bowed, thanking the room. He was excited to get off the forever-creaking-and-rocking vessel.

He ascended the stairs to the storage room where he exited the stairwell and headed for the deer pen. The smell was getting worse, a pungent stench of urine and rotting feces hung in the air.

The herd gathered together nervously as Jung approached.

When he was close he extended out his hand and patted the neck of the nearest shivering animal. The fear in the creature immediately began to wane from his gentle touch. He sat and shuffled a little closer, coaxing the animal in until it rested its neck against his chest. He wrapped his arm loosely around its neck. The deer relaxed as he cradled it. It folded onto its knees and rested its chin in his lap. He patted the animal's neck gently. It dug its snout into an itch on its side completely comfortable in the boy's presence. When the animal was fully relaxed, he took his knife and drew back the animal's head. He sliced the deer's neck open quickly. The creature was dead in a moment, not an ounce of suffering. He let the deer go before moving to the next animal. He moved methodically through the flock killing each of the animals, one by one.

Jung returned to the deck covered in blood.

The Captain turned ghostly white seeing him.

"I took blood from the cook," Jung said. "This is how my people go to war."

The Captain nodded, terrified. "I can see why." He stepped back. "Good luck! And remember our deals."

Jung boarded the canoe with The Surgeon.

He had no idea that the moment they arrived on shore, they would be followed.

40

Jung trekked slowly up the slope in front of The Surgeon. An icy wind howled in his ears, burning any bits of exposed skin. The gale was so strong he had to lean into it to make ground, the loose rocks wobbled and slid beneath their feet.

He was exhausted himself and his feet were blue and frozen so he knew The Surgeon would be in a bad way. He sucked at a coca leaf to replenish his energy. What kept him going was his plan, the first step of which required him to tire out the old man.

The Surgeon seemed to know Jung was waiting for him to slip. This knowledge combined with his exhaustion made him visibly angry.

Jung saw it. It wasn't what the man said—they were yet to speak—it was his actions, the way he hucked up phlegm and spat, and the way he grunted and groaned when he walked.

Jung revelled silently in the man's suffering. He knew the angrier the man became the easier it would be to negotiate with him.

It wasn't long after Earth's Star had peaked in the gray sky that The Surgeon fell.

Jung rushed to his side and pulled back his hood. It was the first time he had seen the old man's face up close. His cheeks were gaunt and his skin looked shriveled and whiter than snow.

Tiny pink veins ran all through his skin where the blood vessels were inflamed. His lips were blue and blistered, hardened from the cold dry air.

Jung dragged him to a boulder, out of the wind, and propped him up so he was sitting. He got to work making a fire.

It was pitch black by the time Jung had a fire going. The wind wallowed between the two boulders they were sheltering against. They were still semi-exposed but warmed by the pulsing flames of the fire.

They ate dehydrated deer meat which they had brought with them from the arc.

"You're not going to make it," Jung said. He looked around to the mountains that overshadowed them. "It's going to get harder. It's going to get steeper, colder, more slippery."

The Surgeon had his hood up, ignoring the boy.

"I know what you seek."

The Surgeon looked at Jung. He hissed, "Oh, yes. What's that?"

The fire crackled.

"The star," Jung said.

Silence.

"I can get it for you."

Silence.

"It's not like you're actually making it to the top. I'm offering you an opportunity," Jung said. He stared at the pool of darkness that covered The Surgeon's face. "I will go up and get the star for you if you give me one thing."

"What's that?"

"The story of death. Tell me the story of death and I will get you the star."

The Surgeon delivered a phlegmy laugh. "You want the story of death, boy?"

Jung nodded.

"You go study at the school of knowledge for 30 rotations if you want the story of death."

"What school?"

The Surgeon shook his head. "Never you mind, boy. Let's just say it's a school that's invite only." He hucked up phlegm and spat it into the fire before sniffing irritably.

The thick mucus bubbled and fizzed on the log until it had boiled away.

"A school in Angkor Wat?" Jung said.

"Hah! Angkor Wat," The Surgeon said. "Do I look second class?"

"What's second class?"

"Let's just say we have different schools for different men. *Good* men go to the schools in Angkor Wat and in Ganung Padang but *great* men go to the school in Egypt."

"You went to the school in Egypt?" Jung said.

An ember shot from the fire with a crackle.

The Surgeon nodded.

"Will you tell it to me?"

"What?"

"The story of death. For the star?"

The Surgeon laughed. "As if! I don't see three stripes on your shoulder. I don't even see one. You have no right to know the story."

"You're a dead man out here," Jung said bitterly. "I'm offering you a lifeline and ticket to Göbekli Tepe. A ticket to teach."

The Surgeon was silent, thinking. His mind was clearly aroused by the mention of Göbekli Tepe.

He shook his head. "No, not for anything. It is worth too much."

Jung nodded. "Sure thing. I'll keep the star to myself." He rolled over to get some sleep. He was calm, he would go to plan b. He just needed to flesh out the last stage of the plan. He needed to be fast though.

He knew the party pursuing him was preparing for an attack.

41

THE CLOUD FOREST. PERU.

I was sitting on the floor of my hut, which stood on its own in an isolated part of The Cloud Forest. Uma and Puma had helped me build the shelter. Only a few members of the tribe knew its exact location. The space was tiny—one man wide by two men long—but it was my own.

I was reading through the book of knowledge when Wasi knocked.

I opened the door.

She hobbled in carrying a cup and a charcoaled guinea pig. "Meat and coca tea."

Wasi was one of the few in the tribe who visited me. She regularly brought leftover food from the tribe's cook-ups. Like Uma I knew there was a piece in her that longed for my stories so much that she had a tendency to over believe. It worked out well because I liked her company.

I took the items. "Thank you, Wasi."

She stood over me with her hands on her hips, panting. "What are you doing?"

"Trying to figure out a calculation."

"What calculation?"

I twisted the book in my lap around. It showed a page of calculations beginning with the head number 432 at the top of the page. The number was broken down into several base numbers.

432
^

2   216
        ^

        2   108
                ^

                2   54
                        ^

                        9   6
                        ^   ^

        ♀ 3   3   2   3 ♂

$4 + 3 + 2 = 9$

$9^2 = 81$

$1 / 81 = 12345678$

"I have a theory about the numbers," I said.

"A theory?"

"A guess about what they mean."

"They don't tell you what they mean?" Wasi said.

"Of course they do. They are just difficult concepts to understand from one explanation. That is what the book is for, so we can learn things better on our own."

"Have you always believed?"

"Believed what?"

She nodded at the book. "All the things in that book. Do you believe it all?"

"Of course, Wasi. Why?"

"You should be careful believing everything you're told. That's very dangerous."

I stood up and leaned on the wall. I towered above her. I pointed to the page I had spread across my palm. "This knowledge has been curated by my people's best minds. It only includes that which has been rigorously tested."

"Exactly. It has been *curated*. You just have to be careful."

"You are long in the tooth Wasi so I appreciate your wisdom," I said. I shook my head. "But I can assure you that everything in this book is true."

"How do you know?" she said.

I smiled. "Whenever I doubt the truth, I go to the numbers."

"Numbers?"

"Yes, please, sit with me. I'll show you."

I sat and pointed to the ground. She sat too.

I twisted the book towards her. It showed a circle with a triangle fitted perfectly inside.

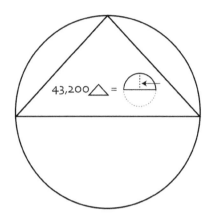

I said, "432 is a building block of our universe. This is why The Great Pyramid in Egypt will be an exact scale replica of the top half of Earth to the ratio of 432. If you multiply The Great Pyramid's height by 43,200, you get the height of Earth from its center to its roof. And if you multiply the length of The Great Pyramid's base perimeter by 43,200, you get the horizontal length of Earth."

"Wow," Wasi said.

"The same is true for the box the Tæcans lie in in the main chamber of The Great Pyramid. If you multiply the volume of the box by 432 billion, you get the volume of Earth. The speed of the energy generated in the main chamber of The Great Pyramid will also be 432. The chamber has been tuned to hum at 432 waves per secondai. Do you know what a secondai is?"

Wasi shook her head.

"It is a measurement of time. About as long as the time it takes to say the word *secondai*." I smiled and raised my eyebrows. "And do you know how we created a secondai? How we came to choose this exact measurement?"

She shook her head.

"Well, if you divide half a dæġ by 43,200—the scale of The Great Pyramid—you get a secondai."

Wasi's mouth fell open.

I smiled. "And you know what else? If you take a great rotation."

"*Great rotation?*"

I nodded. "Yes, the time it takes Earth to complete one full loop through space."

Wasi looked confused.

I held up three fingers. "There are three movements of Earth through space: a dæġ, a rotation and a great rotation. A dæġ is the time it takes Earth to complete one spin on its own axis, the time it takes for Earth's Star to appear in the same place in the sky. The second movement is a *rotation*. A rotation is the time it takes Earth to complete one lap around Earth's Star, the time it takes for all seasons to be completed. The last movement is a *great rotation*. A great rotation is the time it takes Earth to complete one lap through space, the time it takes for Earth to return to the same position in space that it started."

"Isn't that the same as a rotation?" Wasi said.

I shook my head. "No, we change location each rotation because Earth isn't completely circular. It is more oblong, like an egg. This means that when Earth spins around Earth's Star, it wobbles ever so slightly. The same way an egg wobbles when you spin it on its side. This wobble changes our course through space, meaning that while after one rotation we are close to where we started, we're actually in a slightly different place in space. Only after one great rotation—25,920 rotations—does

Earth return to the identical spot it started. And do you know what you get when you divide 25,920 by 432?"

She shook her head.

"Sixty."

Her eyes seemed to sparkle. "The base number."

I smiled. "Exactly."

I had taught all of the people from The Cloud Forest the base number of the Viracochan time system. I had explained that the reason 60 was chosen was because it was a number not just equipped for measuring time but three dimensional angles and geographic coordinates.

Wasi stood. "I like your stories Kon-Tiki. Your people have a lot of knowledge." She looked nervous. "But please don't send any more people away."

"Sorry?"

She frowned. "Uma. You sent Uma away. Don't send any more people away."

"I won't. I never planned to send him away either but I promise no one else."

"Why did you send him away?"

"I had to Wasi. We need more people to help build the pyramid."

She hung her head. "I'm tired of hearing about your pyramid. I don't need to go to another channel."

"You know it's much more than a machine that takes you to the grid," I said.

"Yes, I know. It can stop the stars too."

I nodded. "Yes, but more than that. It is a clock—a timestamp to date Zep Tepi."

She looked intrigued. It was a look I hadn't seen on her since I had first explained The Artery of Earth.

I doubled down. "The entirety of Egypt is a clock. We will timestamp Zep Tepi—the dæġ Earth started again—with buildings that align perfectly with the stars at the exact dæġ of the disaster. It means people in the future can simply twist the stars back in the sky until they match the buildings. Then they'll have the exact date of Zep Tepi."

"You're mapping the date?"

I nodded. "Yes, we call it the Mayan calendar."

"What is it?"

"It's a countdown timer—a warning to future generations of when we'll next cross the gauntlet of stars and when they can expect civilization to once again fall."

42

OLYMPIA. NORÐ AMERICA.

Jung woke. The mountain beneath him rumbled as if it too were waking. Earth's Star had just broken from behind the peaks, soaking the sky in a blood red. There was half a foot of snow on the ground, the white powder covered him and The Surgeon.

It was well below freezing, the fire had deteriorated to smoldering ash. Still Jung was warm, blanketed beneath his shawl.

Suddenly a movement caught his eye.

Down the slope, back the way they had come, several specks moved against the gray sea of rocks. It was the group who had been following them since they left the canoe. The shapes looked gold in color, although in the red light everything seemed some tinge of orange.

The figures moved forward and crouched, there looked to be around half a dozen of them.

Jung's heart raced. He crept his hand across the sand, never taking his eyes from the figures. He felt his bow and pulled it close. His hands trembled as he lay an arrow across it.

There was a carelessness to the way the intruders moved. They seemed to want to be spotted. It was as if they knew Jung and The Surgeon were such easy targets that they were giving them a head start. Like hunting was a game and a good scrap was half the fun.

Jung sat up and aimed the loaded bow at the approaching figures. He closed one eye and used the other to gaze across the arrow tip. He examined the more intricate details of the saber-tooths. They had thick fur, orange on the back and white on the chest. Dark spots were scattered across their coats. They were enormous, even from far away he saw the definition of their muscular chests and forearms. The creatures looked almost like cats, only their legs were shorter and thicker and they moved more slowly and more awkwardly. Despite their thickset-builds, the animals looked starving. He saw their rib cages stenciled in their coats. One looked to be burned as well, the fur near its rump was singed black.

Seeing Jung's bow, one of the saber-tooths stopped and opened its mouth. Two enormous yellow fangs glistened in the red light, each a foot in length. The teeth were clearly a gift from Pachamama to allow them to rip the jugular clean out of a beast five times their size.

A chill rolled down Jung's spine at the thought of being caught beneath the brutal instruments.

One of them let out a low-toned growl. The others stopped playing and stood to attention. They all stared at Jung.

He drew back his bow.

The pack ran.

He knew the animals had to be familiar with the weapon to react in such a way. It meant that other people who inhabited the area were also bow hunters. Well, at least, they *were* bow hunters at some point anyway.

He walked to the slope where the creatures had been standing and looked down the ridge. There was no sight of the animals.

He returned to The Surgeon and used his foot to wake him. "Let's go."

The Surgeon rolled over. "Huh? What?" The man appeared confused about where he was.

"Let's go."

"Huh?"

"We need to make ground while Earth's Star is up. We can camp when the star is high in the sky. Not too long."

The Surgeon nodded sleepily and slowly sat up.

Jung threw his bag, bow and quiver over his shoulder and began to make his way up the slope.

The Surgeon stood quickly, tired and shaky on his legs, but terrified of being left alone. He stumbled after Jung as fast as he could.

As predicted, the higher they trekked, the more challenging the terrain became.

Jung knew it would be easy for the old man to roll an ankle on the loose rocks. He moved fast and crossed his fingers. The sooner the old man was injured, the sooner he could journey alone.

Just before Earth's Star had peaked in the sky, The Surgeon stopped and sat on a boulder. He was out of breath. "Let's make camp," he said.

Jung scanned the black ashen sky and white snow speckled with rocks. They were exposed on all sides. He shook his head. "We have to keep going a little further. It's too open."

The Surgeon drew in one of his feet and rested it on his lap. "Don't know if I can, boy."

"Are you sure you can't go any further?"

"I'm an old man, boy. Don't know if I have a choice."

"We have to keep going. We only have 10 dæġs to find the star and return to the arc."

The Surgeon untied the pelt wrapped around his foot. "I can't."

Jung was angry. "Why did you come then? The journey has barely started."

The Surgeon slipped the pelt off, exposing his bony white foot. On the sole was a blister the size of the boy's palm.

Jung was relieved to see the injury, although he kept his elation to himself.

"Sorry, boy. I need to camp."

Jung squatted. "I can see that. There's no way you're going to make it to the star. We need to separate."

The Surgeon stopped inspecting his foot and shook his head.

"We'll both fail if one of us doesn't keep going," Jung said.

"We stick together," The Surgeon said.

"It's not going to work and you know it. We've barely put a dent in the journey and you're already done. The arc will leave before we even get close to the star."

Silence.

Jung nodded at the man's blister. "I'm not deciding. Your body has already decided."

The Surgeon sighed.

"I will return here on the way back."

"No, you won't."

"I will, if you give me the story."

The Surgeon shook his head. "No deal."

"You have two choices. I go on alone and return here on the way back to the arc with a piece of star for you, or I go on alone and never return here. No need to decide now. We'll make camp and rest. You can think about things and in the morning you can tell me your decision."

The Surgeon was shaking his head. "I can't give you the story, boy."

"We'll see," Jung said.

"You don't understand. It doesn't matter whether or not I have a piece of the star if I have broken my promise and given over the story."

Jung ignored him. He was in no mood to argue. He was tired and he knew what needed to be done.

He handed The Surgeon his knife. "We'll camp, you stay here. Use this if you have to. I'll be back. I just need to find wood for a fire."

The Surgeon took the knife and placed it on the rock next to him. He still had his foot propped up on his knee. He was examining the blister, poking it with his finger.

Jung shot across the rocks, back the way they had come.

Earth's Star had traveled five lengths of itself by the time Jung returned carrying an armful of wood. He dropped the wood near The Surgeon who was lying in a ball.

The man jumped to the thud.

Jung said, "I've go-"

"What's that!?" The Surgeon said, cutting him off. He ripped his hood from his face and sat up in terror. He pointed down the valley.

Jung turned.

One of the saber-tooths was running full pelt towards them.

43

The saber-tooth steamed towards them, bouncing across the snow. The creature was twice the thickness of both Jung and The Surgeon, its muscles coiled and recoiled beneath its glistening coat. On the white of the animal's underside was a splatter of red, it looked like fresh blood.

The Surgeon screamed and scrambled to his feet.

Jung dropped to one knee and pulled three blood-tipped arrows from his quiver. He lay one across his bow.

The haunches on the creature's back were raised up like a shield. Its shoulder muscles throbbed—wild, awakened, primed.

The Surgeon ran up the slope.

Jung was still, his bow aimed at the charging beast.

The creature didn't even consider the boy. It had locked its focus on the old man from the very beginning and was now well on course to take out the target.

Jung kept his aim on the animal as it sped across the splattering of rocks.

The Surgeon screamed, heaving up his robe as he ran.

The creature was 30 men from The Surgeon and closing in fast.

Jung exhaled calmly. He heard the creature's enormous paws thumping through the snow. The animal was fast but not fast enough for him to miss the target. Still he held the taut string, patient.

The Surgeon stumbled and tripped. He looked back and squealed.

Twenty men from the target.

Jung fired just in front of the animal, accounting for the time it would take the arrow to make the distance. The arrow sped through the air and glided cleanly into the rear of the creature.

The beast slowed slightly and twisted back momentarily but didn't change course. It was in kill-mode.

The Surgeon was on his feet again, running.

Ten men from the target.

Jung fired two more arrows in quick succession. Both hit the rear of the animal, missing the vital organs.

The three arrows stuck from the creature's hind. Now the animal slowed considerably. It turned while moving, seemingly confused why its back legs were giving out. Still, it kept moving forward, locked onto the target—starved, irritated, desperate.

Five men from the target.

Jung drew three more arrows and fired them, one after the other. This time he hit the vitals with perfect precision.

The saber-tooth's body spasmed to the impacts. It slowed and weakened but not before it had reached The Surgeon and sunk its fangs into the old man's legs.

The Surgeon screamed in agony as the creature's teeth ripped the muscles from his bones. There was a snapping, ripping sound. The old man's cries were blood-curdling.

Jung drew three more arrows and fired them in quick succession. The arrows embedded themselves in the creature's neck and head.

The beast collapsed beneath its own weight. Dead.

The Surgeon was still screaming.

Jung ran to him and pushed the heavy animal off of his legs. The creature had only managed to sink its teeth in once but The Surgeon was severely wounded. There were gaping wounds down both of his legs, each a foot in length. Bone was showing through the open flesh.

Jung pulled his shawl from his shoulders and used his knife to cut long thin strips from the edge. He pulled back The Surgeon's bloody robe and tied the lengths of material tightly around the wounds.

All the while, The Surgeon moaned and cried until he was so weak that he blacked out.

With enough strips, Jung managed to eventually stop the bleeding.

The Surgeon remained out cold. His heart was still beating but he was ghastly pale and shaking uncontrollably. The thick stench of blood hung in the air.

Jung's plan had worked perfectly—he knew the wounds weren't bad enough to kill The Surgeon immediately but they certainly would end his life within a dæġ or two.

He hoped it was enough time to get the story of death out of him.

44

It was dark and icy cold. Light from the campfire danced across the rocks Jung and The Surgeon were sheltered against.

The Surgeon was sat propped up against the ledge of rock. His hood was down, his ghostly white face soaked in starlight. He shivered and rubbed his hands together in front of the flames.

Jung added two strips of meat to a flat rock that sat at the edge of the fire. The flesh immediately fizzled and spat. A mouthwatering smokey smell filled the air. His stomach gurgled in anticipation of the salty taste.

He returned to the saber-tooth and straddled the body three times his size. He lifted one of the creature's back legs, the paw was almost as big as his head. Using his knife he began to slowly saw off the limb from above the thigh. A thick blue-colored blood flowed slowly from the wound.

The Surgeon clenched his teeth to the sawing sound. "Do you think there will be more of them?"

Jung stopped sawing. His arm burned from the repetitive movement. He shook his head. "No, they're all gone."

"How do you know?"

"I just do," Jung said. He started to saw again, using one hand to hold up the paw and the other to grip the knife. He sawed until eventually the leg came free.

He dragged the limb to the fire and lay it across the flames. Red embers singed the orange fur, turning it black and hard. A putrid smell filled the air as the fur was burned.

The Surgeon coughed and pulled his collar up to cover his nose.

Jung sat on the opposite side of the fire. He used two sticks to fish out one of the strips of meat from the rock. He offered it to The Surgeon.

The old man eyed the meat with a crazed look. He used one of the cuffs of his robe to take the meat. He nodded gratefully and sniffed the flesh before taking a bite.

Jung threw the other piece into his mouth and chewed quickly. The hot meat was stringy and greasy and had an unfamiliar sweet taste.

The Surgeon ate slowly, weak. When he was finished he leaned back against the rock and tilted back his head. He looked to the sky with his eyes closed and his teeth clamped together.

"I have something to help with your injuries," Jung said.

The Surgeon opened his eyes. "Oh yeah. What's that?"

Jung was calm, playing it cool. "It's a plant. A pain reliever."

"Pain reliever?"

Jung nodded.

"Can I try?"

Jung stood and picked up his bag before sitting back by the fire. He pulled out one of the coca leaves The Healer had used in his ceremony. He knew the leaves were a mild stimulant at most but he also knew the mind was a powerful machine. If The Surgeon was convinced the leaves were a strong pain reliever, they would become a strong pain reliever.

Jung handed the leaf to The Surgeon. "These are very strong so suck it first. Then you can chew it."

The Surgeon nodded excitedly, his eyes fixated on the leaf. He took it and slipped it between his snake-like lips.

Jung stood and returned to the saber-tooth. He used his knife to slice a line along the chest of the animal, from the scruff of its neck to its tail. He did the same with the inside of the legs, slicing a line from the feet to the inner chest. He peeled the skin back and slowly began to cut it free from the body in one piece. He squinted and bit the inside of his cheek as he cut.

The Surgeon watched on, sucking the leaf, starting to relax.

After some time Jung removed all of the skin from the creature in one piece. The fleshy underside was veiny and blemished. He dragged the heavy bloody skin over to the fire where he held up a section of the underside to the hot flames. The glistening underside began to sizzle and harden.

The Surgeon had his head tilted back, his eyes closed.

Jung took his time to warm all sections of the skin until the entire underside was dry and hard. When he was finished, he took off his own shawl and wrapped himself in the new skin—the skin of the biggest animal he had ever killed.

The Surgeon opened his eyes and smiled seeing Jung wearing the skin.

It was the first time Jung had seen the man smile.

"Have any more of those leaves?" The Surgeon hissed.

"Yeah, I have a stack."

"Can I have some?"

Jung nodded. He pulled his bag close and fished out two more leaves. He leaned across the fire to hand them to The Surgeon.

When The Surgeon went to grab them he pulled back his hand. "For the story of death."

The Surgeon scowled and shook his head. "No way." He delivered a crackly laugh that turned into a guttural cough. He bent over and heaved to each cough. He sounded like he was going to be sick. He plucked the leaf from his spit on the floor and put it back into his mouth.

"That's okay," Jung said. He made a show of putting the leaves back into his bag and stood.

"Hey, hey, hey!" The Surgeon said. "Come on, boy."

Jung stopped and looked at him. "What?"

"I'm in pain, boy."

"I know. I don't think we'll be getting you out of here."

"What do you mean?" The Surgeon said.

Jung nodded at the bloody robe that covered The Surgeon's legs. "Those are serious injuries. The best thing we can do is make you comfortable."

The Surgeon was silent. He seemed to know the boy was right. He had no doubt been contemplating his death ever since the attack.

Jung returned to the carcass and sliced two more strips of meat from the rump. He carried them to the fire and placed them across the hot rock. The strips hissed and spat as they grafted to the scolding surface.

"Those leaves make me comfortable," The Surgeon said.

"I know," Jung said. "They are a pain reliever for wounds just like yours."

The Surgeon frowned. "So, why won't you give them to me?"

"I will. Like I said, for the story of death."

The Surgeon shook his head. Although this time he didn't laugh at the notion of sharing the story. He was breaking down.

Jung picked up a rock the size of his hand and began to bash it against one of the enormous fangs on the skinless creature. Eventually the rock split. He picked up another and continued to bash the tooth.

The Surgeon grimaced in pain. "Please, boy. I'm hurting."

Jung stopped and looked at him. "Sure. Like I said, for the story of death."

"I can't-"

"Don't you see? You're dead. You're dying. It's over for you. All you have left now is the choice between comfort and discomfort, suffering and peace. Nothing else." He walked over to his bag with the rock in his hand and fished out a leaf. He put it into his mouth and returned to the creature.

The Surgeon frowned. "You're a cruel beast."

Jung ignored him and continued smashing the rock against the fang. The banging ricocheted off the rock shelf The Surgeon was leaning against.

"Okay!" The Surgeon said.

The enormous fang dislodged from the skull and dropped to the floor just as The Surgeon had yelled.

Jung put down his knife and picked up the heavy fang with both hands. He examined the cream tooth that still held the creature's heat.

"What do you want to know?" The Surgeon said.

Jung sat by the fire with the tooth. He pulled two coca leaves out of his bag and handed them to The Surgeon.

He said, "I want to know the story of death—how a man becomes a spirit molecule."

45

15 dægs to stars return.

THE CLOUD FOREST. PERU.

I had heard from Wasi that the women's council was to take place in the mountains at nightfall. I arrived early and found a place to hide among the trees.

The location was a platform on the side of one of the peaks that had an impressive view over the entire cloud forest. You could see the people's pods and the hot springs and the river. The site was steep and covered in forest aside from a flat platform which the women had cleared of vegetation.

It was dark when the women arrived. They lit a fire and sat on the ground in a circle around it.

Kusi stood. She was no longer pregnant. Only a little stretched skin and belly fat was evidence of her recent birth. She set fire to a bundle of tobacco leaves and walked circles around the women, fanning the burning leaves through the air. It was a cleansing ritual—Mapacho cleared the space of unwanted energy. The entire hilltop was covered with thick smoke and a woodsy scent.

After a dozen or so laps she threw the remaining tobacco into the fire and sat.

"I would like to share," Wasi said.

"Aye," all of the women said.

Wasi stood. "I have spent some more time with Kon-Tiki. I have learned more about him."

My heart raced, excited to hear my name. I watched through the branches.

"What did he say?" Kusi said.

"He told me about the calendar, the Mayan calendar," Wasi said.

"What is that?" a woman said. Her name was Palla and she was even older and more wrinkled than Wasi.

Wasi said, "Kon-Tiki says the pyramids in Egypt will time-stamp the dæġ Earth started again."

"Zep Tepi?" Palla said.

Wasi nodded. "Yes, he says you will be able to stand in Egypt in thousands of rotations time and twist the stars back in the sky until the three pyramids line up with Orion's Belt, the Nile River lines up with the Milky Way, the constellation of Leo lines up with The Sphinx and many more buildings too."

"Sphinx?" Kusi said.

Wasi grinned. "It's a lion. A lion made of stone. It's already been built. It was built more than one great rotation ago. Kon-Tiki says if you stand on its back just before dawn on the longest dæġ of spring you can see Earth's Star rise up, right between the cat's ears. And right behind Earth's Star is the constellation of Leo, kissing Earth."

All the women nodded, impressed. They all understood the association of Leo with a cat. There were nine visible stars in the constellation of Leo—two as the head, three as the neck, two as the body and two as the hind. They were interpreted as the outline of a cat by many cultures.

"So what's the calendar?" Kusi said.

A few of the other women nodded.

"It's a countdown to the next time Earth will be in this band of space. Kon-Tiki says there is a band of space—which Earth is traveling through at the moment—that is full of fragments from an exploded star. It's a very hazardous strip of space that Earth passes through twice every great rotation, once on the way up and once on the way down."

"How long is that?" Palla said.

"Every 12,960 rotations," Wasi said.

"So when we're free from it, Earth will be safe for another 12,960 rotations?" Kusi said.

Wasi nodded.

"That's good news right?" Kusi said.

Wasi looked nervous. "Assuming we make it, yes. But we have to be realistic, we might not make it. We'll be in this band of space for three decades. That's a lot of time for something to go really wrong. That's why leaving a mark is so important. We have to warn future generations that every 12,960 rotations the stars will return and Earth will start over. It's just another reason why building in Egypt is so important."

The woman all nodded.

"Thanks Wasi," Palla said. "This is a good item. What action would you like taken?"

"It's just for consideration. It may help the tribe stay focused on building the pyramid in Nazca."

"Well, that's what I want to discuss," Kusi said. "May I have the floor?"

"Aye," all of the women said.

"Go ahead, Kusi," Palla said.

Kusi stood. "I don't think the pyramid in Nazca has anything to do with Egypt."

A rush of adrenaline flooded my body as I watched from the trees.

The women looked puzzled.

"Go on," Palla said.

Kusi said, "Puma told me that he read Kon-Tiki's book and that the pyramid in Nazca is a prison."

Wasi frowned. "What? That's not true."

"That's what Puma said," Kusi said.

Wasi rolled her eyes. "And we know how reliable Puma is."

"Let her speak, Wasi," Palla said.

Wasi slinked back.

Kusi said, "He showed me the book. I saw the pictures of how they can gain control of people's minds and how they use dark energy to change matter."

"What does that mean?" a young woman said.

Kusi looked at her. "They can make heavy things light and light things heavy. And they can move things without touching them. And they know telepathy. They know how to read one another's minds."

"That's not a reason to be afraid of them," Wasi said.

Kusi cackled. "What?"

"Kon-Tiki is a good man. Yes, the magic these people perform seems out of reason but we should view this as a treasure not a threat. The gods are showing us new things. They are arming us with what we need for this new Earth. We should want to learn what they know, not destroy it."

"I saw how they will hurt us if we don't fall in line," Kusi said.

I assumed she was referring to the rack—the torture device I had made Uma and Puma build.

"We don't know that for sure," Wasi said.

"This is true," Palla said, looking at Kusi.

"I can show you. I know where it is," Kusi said.

"The rack?" Palla said.

Kusi nodded. "It's near Kon-Tiki's shack in the forest. I can show you."

46

OLYMPIA. NORÐ AMERICA.

Jung and The Surgeon sat on either side of the crackling fire, snowflakes drifted in from the blackness. It smelled of blood and a blend of raw and cooked meat.

The Surgeon held out his hand.

Jung handed him another coca leaf.

The Surgeon put the leaf in his mouth and cleared his throat. "The story of death is the story of the conversion of consciousness into a single spirit molecule. It is the method we use to turn the dial on the third eye."

"What is the third eye?"

The Surgeon frowned. "I'm getting to that, boy. Be patient."

Jung sat back.

"The third eye controls how much of reality we experience. We call it a dial because opening and closing the third eye increases or decreases our level of consciousness. When our third eye is completely closed we are not conscious of anything happening around us and when our third eye is completely open, it is the opposite, we become conscious of all things in all channels. Well at least we are presented with an illusion of things."

"What do you mean, illusion?" Jung said.

"Well, your consciousness is just one window into reality and it's a fairly foggy and augmented window."

"What does augmented mean?"

"Let's just say you construct a lot more of your consciousness than you think."

Jung looked confused.

The Surgeon shifted in the ice. "The easiest way to think about human consciousness is to imagine a river. You can think of this river as containing all the consciousness of all humankind—it contains the complete human psyche. Make sense?"

Jung nodded. "I think so."

"But you understand what psyche means?" The Surgeon said.

"The parameters of our thoughts?"

The Surgeon smiled, seemingly impressed by the answer. "Smart boy. That's correct, the consciousness of a human being can only exist within the bounds of this river. No matter how smart or special you think you are your psyche is restricted to the bounds of the human collective, just like all of us. The good news is there is still fun to be had and new paths to be explored. Within the psyche—the river—there are many different channels of energy. Channels near the surface and channels near the floor; near the shore and near the center; in the shallows and in the deep. Infinite channels. Each channel can be viewed as an individual person's consciousness. For instance, some people are operating near the surface of the river, on the edge where water touches the air. Others are moving along the riverbed, zigzagging rocks and logs. Others are caught in whirlpools and spend all of their time going around and around. So there is human consciousness, the river, and within the river there are many channels consciousness can experience. Make sense?"

Jung nodded.

"We say *independent* consciousness but it's not really, it's just the illusion of independence. The truth is you don't choose your path any more than a leaf on a river chooses its path. You are a passenger on the journey and the only thing you can control is the story of how you interpret those things you encounter."

Jung was scrunching his face, trying to understand.

The Surgeon said, "It's like having a ball. Inside the ball is all that can be experienced through consciousness—everything that is accessible to the human psyche. Now imagine this ball has zillions of tiny holes in it. Each hole is a tiny window inside. We each look at the same thing but from a different angle. That is what consciousness is like, we're all looking at the same thing from a slightly different channel."

"And there are other things to look at?"

The Surgeon grinned. "Yes, infinite others. We humans are convinced we are cursed to stare at the same ball of light but you're right you can look elsewhere."

"But some people see more of the conscious picture than others? Like those near the surface of the river?" Jung said.

The Surgeon tried to move his legs, clenching his teeth in pain. He put out his hand.

Jung handed him two more leaves.

He spat out the old leaves and put the fresh ones in his mouth. "Yes, some are certainly more conscious than others."

"How?" Jung said.

"Well, when you experience new things your consciousness expands."

"New things?"

"Yes, going to new places, talking to people who are different to you, challenging ideas that you find yourself holding onto. Anything that forces you to be creative and build something new rather than rest on habits and assumptions will expand your consciousness."

"Like being out here?"

The Surgeon smiled. "Yes, exactly."

"And opening the third eye lets you see the other channels in the river?"

"Opening the third eye doesn't just let you see other channels in the river, it lets you see channels beyond human consciousness. It allows you to step out of the river altogether and to stand on its bank beyond the psyche of humankind. The moment you did step outside of the water you would see other channels all around the river. In fact it would look a lot like you were still in the water and that the river itself was a mini-channel within a much larger river."

"If we are all looking into the same ball, why do we see such radically different things?" Jung said.

"You can thank the collective unconscious for that," The Surgeon said.

He delivered a crackly laugh that developed into a nasty cough. His lungs sounded full of fluid. He threw up, the leaves came first then black and purple vile—ash from his lungs and a trace of blood.

Jung stood and went to his bag. He brought out his water bladder and handed it to The Surgeon.

The man nodded gratefully and took the flask. He took a sip.

"What's the collective unconscious?" Jung said.

The Surgeon took a few moments to drink more water and catch his breath. He held out his hand.

Jung gave him two more leaves.

He put the leaves in his mouth and began. "The collective unconscious is an arrangement of energy produced by all the thoughts humans have ever had and ever will have. In other words, every thought, idea or belief that anyone at any time has ever had didn't just disappear once it left the person's mind. Thoughts are an energy, and like all energy, it must go somewhere. It soaks through the walls of the grid. Think about the river again. If the river is the human psyche then the collective unconscious is the contours of the riverbed which determines the speed, depth and direction of the water."

"So the thoughts of those who have passed determine what we do?" Jung said.

"Yes, although one thought from one individual changes things very little. The real power is in group-think. When many people think the same way it is like a gully in the river that gets dug deeper and deeper as more and more water gets in. This is why it becomes increasingly difficult to think differently when many people think the same way, because we get dragged into group-think." The Surgeon cleared his throat. "Anyway, none of this has anything to do with the story of death."

"It's interesting though."

The Surgeon nodded and held out his hand." Let's get back on track though."

Jung handed him another leaf.

The Surgeon put the leaf in his mouth. "I don't think I've wasted my breath though. Understanding the channels will help you understand what happens in the story of death and during the creation of the spirit molecule. In the river thought experiment, the spirit molecule is a bubble of air released from a channel. A bubble that rises up through the water until it reaches the surface where it becomes a part of the air and can travel beyond human consciousness."

"And it travels up to Orion's Belt and along the Milky Way where it has to pass the seven tests on the way to Sirius?" Jung said.

"You've heard the story of the stars?"

"Yes."

The Surgeon shook his head angrily, as if just realizing the boy was about to learn in one rotation what had taken him a lifetime to learn. He sucked the leaves hard.

He said, "Okay, so you know the story of the stars. What you don't know is that the 7 tests from the story of the stars are actually directly tied to 7 organs in your body." He bent over and used his finger to draw the figure of a man in the black snow. He drew 7 horizontal lines through the sketch—at the groin, the stomach, the solar plexus, the heart, the throat, the eyeline and the forehead.

He looked at Jung. "You can think about these bands of energy as your code as an individual. On a micro scale, in the spirit molecule, these bands store information about your channel. This code is the parameters of your consciousness that send and receive signals from the grid. While on a macro scale, in the human body, these bands literally manifest themselves into physical objects—fleshy organs. You see every band of energy in our body has a gland beneath it. A gland is an organ responsible for creating tiny molecules that tell our bodies what to do. We call these tiny molecules hormŏns, which means *to set in motion*. You can think of these glands as control rooms in our body that are in communication with the grid."

The Surgeon pointed to the line at the bottom of the drawing that passed through the groin of the figure. "For instance, the sex glands in a human body create hormŏns that determine whether we are a man or a woman. They encourage the growth of body hair and muscle mass in men and are responsible for the curvaceous form and child-rearing abilities of women."

Jung looked confused.

"Don't worry too much, these hormŏns are very difficult to wrap your head around because they work at an invisible level. We know of them only through their results. We know for instance that your parents had healthy sex glands because of the existence of you and any siblings you have."

He pointed to the next line up. "The next band up is the sacral band, which flows across the pancreas. In our body the pancreas is a gland responsible for creating a hormŏn that regulates our absorption and conversion of energy. Again we don't see the hormŏn but we do see the effects on the human body. A poorly functioning pancreas can cause serious digestion problems and over time it can take the life of someone. Above that is the solar plexus band which flows across the adrenal glands. The adrenal glands produce a hormŏn responsible for helping us respond to stress. It's the thing that takes control in an emergency. Above that is the heart gland which covers the thymus gland. The thymus gland produces a hormŏn that regulates our immune system."

"Immune system?" Jung said.

"Yes, the thing that keeps us healthy and well. When you are sick it is your immune system that repairs you." The Surgeon tapped the next band up. "Next is the throat band which covers the thyroid gland. This gland is responsible for producing a hormŏn that controls the way our body uses and distributes energy."

He circled the first 5 glands that ran from the groin to the throat. "These 5 bands pull the strings on your physical health, they determine just about everything related to your meat body." He pointed to the next line up, which ran through the eyeline. "Above these, in the middle of our head, is the third eye band which runs across the pineal gland. Like I mentioned earlier, this gland produces a hormŏn that is responsible for determining how much information in our channel we see. It is also responsible for triggering the production of the spirit molecule. And above that is the crown band which covers the pituitary gland. If the other glands pull the strings on how your body functions then the pituitary gland pulls the strings on these strings. It is the master gland, the control room of our physical body, producing hormŏns that are responsible for regulating the functions of all of the other glands."

"So the condition of these glands determines whether you make it to Sirius?" Jung said.

The Surgeon shook his head. "No, a Tæcan should focus on passing the tests not making their glands healthy because by passing the tests their glands will have to be healthy—they are intrinsically linked. Focus on the tests: reach sexual maturity, attune yourself to the ebbs and flows of nature, conquer instinct, keep a healthy temple, gather more light energy than dark energy, become self aware, and open your third eye. Anyway, I'm telling you all this to simply explain that everything is connected by bands of energy. There are bands of energy running through us and these bands are connected to greater systems, such as our Earth and the stars."

"I get it, I think," Jung said. "But all this rests on opening the third eye, right?"

The Surgeon nodded.

"So how do you open it?"

The Surgeon smiled. "Your people's plants."

47

14 dægs to stars return.

THE CLOUD FOREST. PERU.

I was alone in my hut, it was the middle of the night, when the bell rang alerting me that someone was in the forest nearby. The intruder had triggered one of the trip-wires I had set up on a 50 men perimeter around the hut.

I had built a safe room for this very situation. I cleared the entry to the hidden basement and squatted just below the window. Before I hid I needed to know who was trespassing.

In the darkness, against the backdrop of the forest, I saw the shadows of three people. They were crawling between two sets of trees.

I opened the door to the safe room and returned to the window.

The figures crawled closer, moving slowly and awkwardly along the ground.

I recognize Wasi and Palla first. It was the way they moved that gave them away, the old women were stiff and ungraceful. Recognizing their figures made it easy to identify Kusi in front. The three of them were always together.

Kusi crawled to a section of grass just off to the side of my hut.

I gritted my teeth. *Did she know?*

Kusi turned back to the others, then she began to dig away the grass and dirt.

She did.

I was outside standing over the three of them just as Kusi was opening the door. "What are you doing?"

"Kon-Tiki," Wasi said, startled.

"Are you looking for something?" I said.

"We know what's down there," Kusi said.

"What?" I said.

"A torture device. The rack," Kusi said.

"Who said that?" I said.

Kusi shook her head. "Never you mind."

"Puma?"

"I'm not saying," Kusi said.

"I understand Puma is angry with me," I said.

Kusi shook her head. "No, he's not. He's just telling it how it is. You made him build it."

"He built it?" Wasi said.

Kusi nodded. "Him and Uma." She pointed at me. "He made them."

"I did not *make* them. I asked them. And yes, they did make it for me. They were helping me the same way I have helped them. The same way I have helped all of you."

"Like what?" Kusi said.

"The way I've helped you build better boats and better houses and how I've shown you how to grow crops that are available all rotation."

"No you haven't!" Wasi said, angrily. "You think you have tamed nature because you built terraced gardens at Lake Titicaca? Don't you understand, all of the forest on our land has been curated by us. You don't have to put everything in a pot you made. There is a reason why there is abundance here even during this devastating time—because of the care we took to encourage so many edible species to flourish. Why do you think there are so many edible plants in The Cloud Forest? You think that's a coincidence?"

"Not just The Cloud Forest," Palla said. "All of Peru and the basin. It is all curated by the peoples of Peru."

I smiled and held my hands up. "Fair enough. But I get the boats and the pyramids."

Wasi smiled. "You get the boats. You don't get the pyramids until they work."

I grinned. "Fair play."

I walked over to the door Kusi was holding open. "How about you let me show you the rack myself. I will be happy to explain it all."

Kusi moved aside as I brushed past her and began to climb onto the ladder.

"Kusi, could you grab a fire torch from inside," I said.

She glared at me then left for the hut. She returned and thrust the torch into my hand. "I'm very interested to hear your explanation."

When we were all standing in the bunker, I cast the flame across the device. The rack was a t-shaped device for tying a man down with his legs together and his arms outstretched. The wooden panels were cut in the shape of a cross. There were bindings at the ends of each of the arms for tying a man's wrists down and binds at the base and throat where the feet and neck could also be tied down. The contraption painted a menacing shadow across the sandbagged wall.

I stood in front of the rack and addressed the women. "I have received word from a scout that Uma is returning to The Cloud Forest with 200 people from other tribes."

"What?" Wasi said.

"They won't stay long," I said. "We will leave for Nazca shortly after. We just need to get everyone grouped together first."

Palla frowned. "You can't bring people to The Cloud Forest."

I said, "They won't stay, Palla. Uma will bring them here and they will rest for a night then we will leave for Nazca the following dæġ." I turned and illuminated the rack with the torch. "This device has been built for our protection on the night the others stay. If one of them does something against the requests of your tribe we will make an example of them using this device."

"That's horrible," Kusi said.

I nodded. "I know, but think about what your warriors did to the people of the lake."

The three women were silent.

"It's for your protection and my protection," I said.

Suddenly the face of a young girl appeared in the entry of the bunker.

It was my scout, Llipya, who was 10 rotations in age. She was hanging upside down from the ladder.

"Kon-Tiki," she said.

"Llipya," I said, genuinely surprised.

She grinned. "Hi."

"It's the middle of the night. What is it?" I said.

Her face turned serious. "It's Uma, he's back. He has hundreds of people with him."

48

The Surgeon held out a shaky hand.

Jung handed him two more leaves. "What plants?"

He replaced the leaves in his mouth. "Mother Aya."

"Who?"

"Ayahuasca—the vine of the dead," The Surgeon said. He held up two fingers. "Well, actually two plants. Ayahuasca and chacruna. When these two plants are combined the third eye is opened. Do you know the odds of finding this combination of plants?"

Jung shook his head.

"There are over 40,000 species of plants in your basin forests. The chances of combining these two specific varieties is therefore 1 in 1.6 billion. Absolutely remarkable."

"The basin in Peru?" Jung said, trying his best to act surprised.

The Surgeon nodded.

"How did you find it?"

The Surgeon scoffed. "Ask your people, boy."

"What do you mean?"

"I mean they are the ones who showed us the plants. Before then we traveled the stars blind."

"But how did they discover ayahuasca?"

The Surgeon shrugged, dismissively. "No idea. They say Mapacho showed them. Who knows. Rumor has it that your jungle people wanted it so much that it came into existence."

"Wanted what?"

"A portal to the outside, or the inside. However you want to look at it."

"So you drink the plants in the pyramid?" Jung said.

"Yes, a Tæcan lies in the box in The Great Pyramid and drinks ayahuasca. The third eye is opened and the spirit molecule leaves the body. It rises up a chute in the pyramid that is aimed at Sirius. The spirit molecule can then follow the band of energy being generated by The Great Pyramid and The Artery of Earth to get to Sirius."

"And along the way to Sirius there are seven tests," Jung said. "And if a Tæcan passes all the tests they can enter the doorway to the grid?"

"Yes."

"Then what happens?"

The Surgeon held out his hand. He was slouched low, weak, white as snow. He didn't look like he had much time left.

Jung pulled out two more leaves and handed them to the man.

The Surgeon slipped the leaves into his mouth. "When the Tæcan returns to the pyramid they are equipped with beyond-Earthly powers."

"*Beyond-Earthly powers?*" Jung said.

"Superpowers."

"*Superpowers?*"

"Yes, powers that defy Earth's laws of nature because they are entangled with energy from different channels. You see, because matter arises from consciousness and not the other way around, our thinking determines our laws of matter. So in different channels there are different laws of matter. This means if you have access to multiple channels you have access to multiple laws of matter. This is why Tæcans who have made it to the grid can perform actions others would deem impossible."

"What type of powers?"

"Telepathy, levitation, alchemy."

Jung looked confused. "What are they?"

"Telepathy is reading someone else's mind; levitation is moving an object without touching it; and alchemy is changing the chemical structure of something."

"What do you mean *change structure?*"

The Surgeon nodded to some cold strips of meat Jung had pre-cooked and piled up next to the fire. "Give me one of those would you."

Jung passed him one.

The Surgeon took the leaves from his mouth and took the meat with a shaky hand. He sniffed the food and took a small bite. He looked at Jung. "They can soften stone for instance, to make it easier for the stonemasons to cut blocks from the quarry. And they can change the densities of materials for instance, to make it easier for the Fects to lift and carry the stones. Without their magic it would be impossible to cut, carry and stack the 2.3 million blocks of stone that will be required to build The Great Pyramid. That is the story of death."

"That's all!?" Jung said.

The Surgeon scowled. "*That's all!* I have summarized the story for you boy because I don't have the plants in front of me."

He patted his chest where the book of death was cloaked beneath his robe.

He said, "The full story is all the songs and verses involved in setting the ceremony space so as to bring in the helpful energies and coax out the unhelpful energies. Verses I don't have time to share with you right now."

"Like the verses you were reading that night when you were watching me on the arc?" Jung said.

The Surgeon chewed slowly.

"What were you doing that night?"

The Surgeon smirked. "Just checking your intentions."

"My intentions?"

"Yes. I needed to see if what The Captain told me about you was correct."

"What did he say?" Jung said.

"That your father's spirit was stuck on the path of souls. I needed to see if he was actually there to see if I could trust you."

"See if he was where?"

"In the Milky River, on the road to Sirius."

"Did you see him?" Jung said.

The Surgeon held out his hand.

Jung shoved three leaves into his palm as fast as he could.

The Surgeon placed the leaves in his mouth. "Yes, he's there."

"Really?" Jung said, he had an ear-to-ear grin.

The Surgeon nodded.

"So I could find him? If I go up. If I used the pyramid?"

The Surgeon nodded. "Certainly could." Then the man's serious face broke and he laughed. "Of course that would be *if* the plans for the building of The Great Pyramid hadn't been canceled."

Jung's smile was gone. "What do you mean?"

"You didn't know? The Captain didn't tell you?"

"Tell me what?"

The Surgeon's smile widened. "There are no pyramids, boy. Not for a long time."

"I don't understand."

"I mean the pyramids are off. Egypt has flooded."

49

"What do you mean?" Jung said.

The Surgeon snickered. "I mean you can forget ever seeing or using The Great Pyramid, the plans are off." He chuckled until he delivered a phlegmy cough. He hucked and spat and wiped his mouth with the back of his hand. There was a trace of blood in the phlegm. He looked uneasy seeing the red coloration.

"So what does that mean?" Jung said.

The Surgeon threw the remainder of the meat into the fire and placed the leaves sitting in his lap back into his mouth. "It means no one will be getting to the grid anytime soon."

"Can't they build them somewhere else?"

"No, it has to align with the stars."

"But surely they could build it a dæġ's walk away. It would still align with the stars."

"A dæġ!" The Surgeon said. "Clearly you have no idea about the precision of this thing. Do you know what the speed of light is?"

"Like the light from Earth's Star?"

The Surgeon breathed heavily. "Yes, and light from other sources such as this fire and the colors in the sky up there. Do you know how fast?"

Jung shook his head.

"299,792,000 metrai per secondai. And do you know what the coordinates of The Great Pyramid will be?"

Jung shook his head.

"29.9792° norð. The coordinates are the speed of light. Why? So as to shoot the spirit molecule into the stars at light speed. It's perfect, the whole building is perfect."

Jung wasn't sure what the man meant but he knew he didn't have much time left. "So you can't move it?"

The Surgeon shook his head, exhausted. "No, everything has to be perfect. It has to be exactly 29.9792° norð and in an exact 1:432 scale of Earth in order to work. Otherwise the spirit molecule will never make the distance."

"But The Captain thinks it's still on?" Jung said.

"Huh?"

"The Captain brought us all the way out here in the hope of finding the key to starting the machine."

The Surgeon snickered.

"What?"

"The Captain has known the pyramids are off for some time, boy. Since before we left Nazca."

"The Captain knew Egypt was flooded before we left Nazca?" Jung said.

The Surgeon nodded.

"Why did he bring me all the way out here then?"

"So you could collect the star for him."

"But you said the pyramid is off."

The Surgeon grimaced as he moved his legs. "He wants his third stripe, boy."

"What do you mean?"

The Surgeon lifted the deer skin on his shoulder and pointed to the three stripes.

"He gets a stripe if he gets a star?"

"I don't know, boy. We all have our missions. I'm not sure what his mission is."

"Yes, you do," Jung said. "He convinced you to come out here. So why? What was the deal you two had?"

The Surgeon spat the leaves from his mouth and held out his hand.

Jung pulled the last three leaves from his bag. He slid one of them into The Surgeon's trembling hand and placed the last two in his lap.

The Surgeon took the leaf and stuffed it into his mouth. "The Captain was convinced that if I could get the star then I would be accepted as a Tæcan at Göbekli Tepe. The deal was that the moment I became a Tæcan, I was to give him his third stripe."

Jung frowned. "You think you can just turn up at the school with a shard of star and they'll make you a Tæcan?"

The Surgeon stared into the fire and mumbled under his breath. "Perhaps."

"What will happen there?"

"Where?"

"Göbekli Tepe. Why do you want to go there so much?" Jung said.

"All the Tæcans from Egypt are going there. It is where we will keep the flame of knowledge alive until the floods settle. It is where we will prepare for the building of the pyramids. We'll use the classrooms to teach and build upon our knowledge until we can build The Great Pyramid. Then Eygptai will become the central icon to the preservation of our knowledge."

The Surgeon pulled the leaf from his mouth and bent over. He heaved and delivered a hoarse cough. He spat, this time there was more blood in the phlegm. He coughed and wheezed and spat again. He sat up slowly, panting. There was a smear of blood on his lips.

"What's the point in building the pyramid in Nazca if they know the pyramids in Egypt are delayed? Surely The Artery of Earth is delayed too?"

The Surgeon smirked. "Artery of Earth. I see you met one of the storytellers."

"What do you mean?"

"No such thing as The Artery of Earth, boy."

Jung looked shocked.

"That's just a one stripe story, a story the storytellers tell you natives to win your hearts and your minds."

"What do you mean?"

"It's just a story to control your people," The Surgeon said.

Jung saw The Surgeon's recognition of his own mortality. He seemed more liberal with his knowledge, more willing to share. Like he understood he was on his final march and had one last opportunity to auction off his knowledge.

"What do you mean?" Jung said.

"Buildings govern people, boy. Especially big impressive buildings that look to have been built by the hands of the gods themselves. If you want to control a people, build an impressive building and give it an impressive story. Your pyramid in Nazca is nothing more than a way for my people to set up a permanent base close to the plants."

"Mother Aya?"

The Surgeon nodded and slunk tiredly until he was lying down. He pulled his hood up over his head. "Anyway, I need to rest. You've got your story. Keep it to yourself."

"Can I ask one more thing?" Jung said.

The Surgeon pulled back his hood a little. "What?"

"Why is your skull long if you're not a Tæcan?"

The Surgeon nodded at the two last leaves sitting in Jung's lap.

Jung handed him the leaves.

The Surgeon took the leaves with a trembling hand and placed them in his mouth.

'Well?" Jung said.

"My father, he never made it past three stripes," The Surgeon said. He laughed as if just realizing he had ended up the same. "He thought binding my head would help make me become a Tæcan like he never could."

"Did it work?"

The Surgeon frowned. "I just handed over everything I know to a boy. What do you think?" He pulled the hood back over his eyes. "Now, leave me alone."

By dawn The Surgeon was dead.

Jung knew he needed to move fast. He had two dæġs to find the star before he needed to turn around.

He wasn't sure if it was even enough time to make it to the crater.

50

13 dægs to stars return.

THE CLOUD FOREST. PERU.

I was standing next to the river in The Cloud Forest watching Uma.

He was standing on Anku, the living tree bridge. In front of him two hundred natives sat on the sodden drifts of ash. They were from two tribes near Cuzco who he had convinced to join us. It was misty and drizzling, far away a faint rumble of thunder bellowed in the murk.

Uma said, "Thank you all for coming. As you know we are here because we have very little time. The stars will arrive again soon. We must get to Nazca and build caves in preparation for the impacts."

There were murmurs from the crowd.

"Following the impacts we will build the pyramid," Uma said.

A few excited yells came from a group of young females.

Uma nodded at them gratefully. "We must leave immediately for Nazca. Nazca is calling for us! The pyramid is calling for us!"

He threw his fist in the air.

The crowd didn't react.

"You said the jungle people were coming," a woman said.

"You said they were here already," a man said.

Uma looked anxious. He looked at me.

I frowned at him, angry. I had explicitly told him not to mention the jungle people when recruiting other tribes.

Uma turned back to the crowd. "The jungle people have come and gone but we have enough hands among us to complete the build."

"Did you see their smoke signals?" an old woman said.

"When?" a different man said.

"Not long after the smoke signals were set off here," she said.

I stood and made my way to the front of the crowd seeing that things were getting out of control.

Uma climbed down from Anku seeing me break through the crowd.

I stood at the front and addressed the crowd with a loud voice. "It will not matter. We can complete the job even with half the number of people we have gathered here today. It's all to do with the technology we will use. You people will do very little and get a great reward from the building once it is built."

"But it's not going to build itself," a man said.

I laughed. "You'll be surprised. Perhaps it will not build itself entirely, but it will close to. The river will do most of the work and the Tæcans will lift all the blocks into place. You will simply quarry out the stone."

I turned to Uma. "Uma please explain how water will be used to complete the build."

Uma nodded. He addressed the crowd with a shaky voice. "We will use the river in Nazca to create a preparation basin upstream. We will quarry rocks from the ground and use sleds to transport them to the river. There the stonemasons will tie floats—animal bladders filled with air—around the rocks so they can float them into the preparation basin. The preparation basin will be connected to the river but it will be blocked off so the water-level can be controlled. There will be a shelf on the basin floor that is perfectly parallel with the water-level. The stone-masons will lay the rocks on this perfect plane and chip away the rock until the top plane is flush with the surface of the water. They'll do this with each side of the rock until all six sides are perfect planes. We will then help them to stack the stones on the bank of the river. That is all. The Tæcans will do the rest."

I squeezed Uma's shoulder. "Thank you, Uma."

He nodded and took a step back.

I said, "The Tæcans will lift the rocks into their final positions in one night."

"One night?" a man said doubtfully.

I nodded. "Yes, one ceremony is all it will take for them to move hundreds of blocks of stone. They are Tæcans of levitation after all. This is the very thing they are trained to do. And once the pyramid is constructed we can all reap its rewards."

"Is it true, we all get a ticket?" a woman said.

"Yes, anyone who helps build the pyramid gets a ticket to ride," I said.

"To the stars?" a different woman said.

"Yes," I said.

"Is it fun?" an old man said.

I grinned. "Yes, very. It's a full lap of Earth's track around space. The path Earth takes to complete one great rotation. You ride the full track in a single dæġ. It's a helluva ride."

The old man threw his fist in the air. "I'm in!"

Other fists went up, then others. A chain reaction until the whole crowd had a fist in the air.

I threw my fist into the air. "To Nazca!"

"To Nazca!" the mob said.

"To Nazca!" I yelled twice as loud.

"To Nazca!" the mob screamed.

I pointed wðst. "Let's go!"

The mob stood and began to march.

51

OLYMPIA. NORÐ AMERICA.

Jung was in a room with flat limestone walls on all sides and a pointed ceiling made of the same limestone panels. On the other side of the room was a doorway with a pyramid-shaped cutout that appeared to lead somewhere higher. It felt like a cave in the center of Earth. He felt a resonance in the room—a low vibration—like residue left over from the last time the thing had been on, whatever that meant.

Jung woke in the snow. He stood immediately. He had been traipsing through the ice toward the lip of the crater for the best part of the night and had fallen asleep many times. The freezing wind tugged and whipped at him, bruising his face and shrieking in his ears. His body was bent over, cramped, the muscles in his legs burned. His feet felt like nothing more than fleshy stumps despite him wrapping them in fresh strips of fur. The giant tooth hanging from his waist rubbed against his thigh.

He knew he didn't have long before he would need to turn around. He also knew he had very little left—he was slowing down, running out of steam. He used the stars of Orion and Sirius to guide him through the stream of clouds that poured down the slope. Even through the river of fog he could see the balls of fire riding high in the current of the Milky Way.

He felt like nothing more than a speck of dust that had reached the edge of Earth and would drop off the ledge any moment. He heard The Surgeon's sickly laugh and then his voice. *I mean the pyramids are off, boy. Egypt has flooded.*

Jung stopped, angry—furious. Furious at the lies I had told him and the lies The Captain had told him and the lies that more than likely The Surgeon had told him too. He screamed as loud as he could. "Ahhhhhhhhhhhhhhhhhhhhhhhhhhh!"

He felt power in the roar, but only for a moment. Then the flood of doubt returned. If he asked his head, everything was telling him to turn around. His head had convinced him it was all a waste of time. In fact, the entire journey was a waste of time—energy expended for the sake of expending energy, danger for the sake of danger—a fool's errand. When he spent too much time in his head he certainly felt like the fool for coming so far. Still, it seemed even more foolish to turn around when he was so close. So he listened to his gut, the only thing that spurred him on.

He had made a deal with his gut, he would climb to the rim of the crater and peer over the edge. If the omen wanted to appear, it would. And if it didn't, he would admit defeat and turn-around.

He gritted his teeth and pressed on.

It wasn't much longer before his legs gave out. He fell awkwardly onto his knees. They burned in the snow. He turned down the slope, the muscles in his body convulsing. He lay down. Below him, the delta seemed to stretch on forever. Between the arc and him was a long stretch of cloud that followed the contours of the slope.

He pulled his bag around and pulled out the note Tika had given him. He opened the folded sheet with trembling hands and studied the sketch.

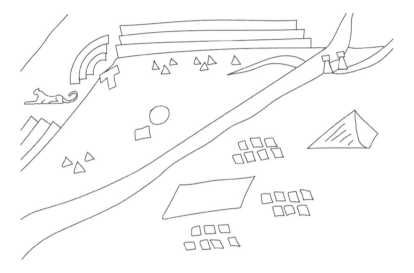

It still meant nothing to him. Still, simply holding the sheet gave him strength. He put the note back into his bag and stood. He pressed on, Tika's smiling face in his mind.

The pace didn't last, it wasn't long before he was dragging his feet again. His breaths were getting shorter and more wheezy. His vision was fading in and out. The spells of blackness that hijacked his mind were setting in for longer and longer periods, sometimes for several heartbeats at a time. He would black out completely, then everything would reboot and he would wake, lying in the snow, confused about where he was and why he was there. He was working with it, focusing only on his feet.

Then it was all too much. The light-headedness returned but this time it didn't reel back. It kept coming, surging stronger and stronger. He felt himself tipping toward the slope of the earth. The lights turned off, one by one.

Jung blacked out just as the creature arrived with the stranger on its back.

52

When Jung woke it was still dark. There was a mild buzzing sound coming from the ground where his ear was pressed against the snow. The side of his face was numb from the ice.

Suddenly a snorting sound came from the blackness. The sound was unfamiliar although the creature sounded big.

Jung sat up and swept his hands across the ice searching for his bow and quiver.

The snort came again.

He looked in the direction of the noise waiting for the blurriness to come into focus. Slowly the form of the creature appeared around 20 men away.

The animal was tall and muscular with black fur and white spots. It had long sturdy legs, a slender snout and a tangled mane that fluttered in the breeze. Steam blew from its giant curved nostrils, its lean muscles rippled beneath its skin.

Jung was calm seeing the position of the creature's eyes on the side of its head, not the front. That meant it was a herbivore and not a predator. He marveled at the form of the animal, which he recognized as a larger, more well-built marsh deer. He had never seen a horse before.

The horse took a step forward. It stopped and paced backward, then forward again. It looked exhausted.

Then the creature turned and Jung spotted it. On the horse's back was a person bundled up in layers of animal hides.

Jung stood slowly and approached, his feet crunching through the ice.

Despite the obvious fear in the animal, it remained still. It was as if the creature had come to Jung specifically to get help for its passenger.

Jung was standing right beside the animal. It had a woodsy, musky smell. He gently touched the horse's snout. "It's okay."

The horse dipped its nose to his touch, nuzzling into Jung's palm.

He moved slowly to the side of the animal.

The horse's nerves intensified as he approached the passenger. It shuffled its feet, the muscles in its shoulders hardened.

Jung sensed the horse was about to react and run any moment. In one swoop he grabbed the blanketed figure and pulled.

Spooked by the weight being removed from its back the horse reared up its two front legs and delivered a blood-curdling squeal. It stamped its legs and ran headlong down the slope.

Jung fell backward onto the snow. The cloaked figure fell on top of him. Pain shot through his legs from the impact.

He heaved and wiggled his legs free from the dead weight. Sitting up he looked at the figure who lay sprawled across the rocks. He squinted, the image was fractured, twisted, bent. He clambered onto his knees and crawled over to the body. He put his ear to the stranger's chest and heard a faint heartbeat.

The stranger wheezed and coughed.

Jung jumped back startled by the noise. It was a softer tone than he had expected. The stranger sounded to be female.

The stranger coughed twice more, their throat thin from exhaustion.

"Are you awake?" Jung said.

The stranger murmured.

"Hello?"

Silence.

"Are you okay?"

"Huh?" the stranger murmured.

Jung touched the blanketed figure. "Are you awake?"

The stranger rolled onto their back and spread out their arms.

Jung crawled forward and began to draw the mess of hides away from the stranger's face. Then came the familiar voice.

"Jung?"

Jung grabbed the girl as her face appeared through the hides. "Tika!"

He wrapped his arms around her thin body and pulled her close, resting his cheek against her ice-cold skin. He smelled her sweet familiar scent.

Tika tilted her head, his fluffy facial hair tickling her cheek. She looked at him, her eyes only half open, teary.

Seeing her tears made Jung tear up too. He hugged her tighter.

Tika smiled. "I've been looking for you. We all have." Her voice was shaky.

Jung drew back. "Who?"

"The Captain and his men. They are down in the valley."

"Really?"

"Yes, they sent me ahead to find you. The arc is leaving. The plans are off."

"I know," Jung said.

"What do you mean you know?"

"The Surgeon told me. This whole trip has been a lie. The Captain knew Egypt was flooded before we even left Nazca."

Tika frowned. "I'm sorry."

"Do you know why he did it though? Why he brought us all the way out here and why he's now suddenly changed his mind?"

"I think he thought your star would be enough for him to get a stripe but since you left he's discovered it's not."

"What do you mean?"

"He found a letter in The Surgeon's things."

"Who did?" Jung said.

"The Captain. He found a letter from the Tæcans at The School of Egypt. It was a rejection letter to The Surgeon's request to join the school. It said he had risen the ranks as far as he could." She shook her head. "That's what they don't tell them until the very end—that Uzmans never become Tæcans. You have to be born into a lineage of Tæcans to become a Tæcan. Uzmans spend their entire lives believing that one dæġ they too will become Tæcans but they never will. The Captain is furious. He wants to return immediately."

"But The Surgeon—why did he want the star then? If he knew he would never teach?"

"I don't know," Tika said. "Maybe he thinks he still has a shot. He's an old man. He's spent his entire life trying to become a Tæcan. Maybe a letter isn't enough for him to drop his hopes. I don't know but it's dangerous. All of these men are dangerous.

Their realities are unraveling. The fractures are showing. We have to get out of here as soon as we can."

"I can't," Jung said.

"What?"

"I still need the star."

"But the pyramids are off, Jung. The star is useless."

"No. Before I met these liars I was already on this journey. Before I met any of them my journey had nothing to do with the pyramids, I was looking for an omen—a star omen—where my father's spirit might still be. I must finish my quest. I need to see if the omen will show itself to me. Until then, I can't leave."

Tika frowned. "Omen! You can't be out here chasing an omen. The arc will leave and you'll be stuck out here."

"Try and stall them."

"They won't listen to me."

Jung looked up the mountain to where the slope gave way to blackness. "I'm so close. I think the rim of the crater is just beyond that ridge."

"It doesn't matter. It'll take you dægs to find the star once you get to the crater."

"I have to look over the edge. Just once."

She shook her head. "No, you don't."

"I do."

"You'll risk your life for an omen?"

"I'm sorry. I have to. It's been seen."

"What do you mean?"

Jung clasped his hands around one of hers. "She has a plan for me, Tika. Whether I like it or not."

"What do you mean?"

"Please, do your best to stop them. Give me two more dæġs. One dæġ to get to the crater and another dæġ to look for the star."

"It's not enough time," Tika said.

"I'll have to make do."

"Then you'll come back?"

Jung nodded. "Give me two dæġs here and five dæġs to get back to the arc. Any longer and tell them to leave without me."

She looked afraid.

Jung squeezed her hand. "It's okay, I'll come back. The omen will show up for me if it wants me to see it. And if it doesn't show, it wasn't meant to be. Two dæġs and then I promise to return."

He gazed up the slope toward the lip of the crater. "I think he's close, I feel him."

Jung looked back to Tika but she was gone. He whipped his head around, expecting to catch sight of her. There was nothing but black snow. She was gone.

A cough came from the opposite direction making him jump.

This time it was a man's cough.

53

OLYMPIA. NORÐ AMERICA.

When Jung woke it was snowing. His breath steamed softly, an icy wind wallowed in his ears. Above him the night sky was a burst of color—purples, yellows, blues and greens. The delicate painted strokes cascaded this way then that dancing and bleeding into nothingness before appearing again in a completely new part of the sky. Far away he saw the edge of the mountain give way to nothing but sky. *Had he reached the edge of the crater?*

Suddenly a flapping sound grabbed his attention.

He turned to the sound, his heart racing.

In the drift of snow he barely made out the silhouettes of three animal skin tents. The door on one had come loose and was flapping in the wind. Beyond the tents was a cluster of four horses. One of them, which had black fur and white spots, looked identical to that he had seen in his dream. The others were mottled red, brown and midnight blue.

Voices came from the tents.

Jung sat up quickly. His body burned from the movement.

"It's okay," a deep voice said from behind him.

Jung twisted in the snow and saw the small fire. He hadn't even realized the heat on his back. Beyond the flames he saw the figure of a man.

The man was sitting with his hands extended out, warming them. He was wearing the same robe as the other Uzmans, only his robe was black. That meant he was a Tæcan, or at least he was imitating one. His hood was up, hiding his face. He had a book open across his lap.

He said, "It's okay. You're safe here." His voice sounded calm, friendly.

Jung looked around, searching for his weapons.

"I would have moved you to one of the tents if the snow got any worse but it just started and you seemed so peaceful."

"You know my language?" Jung said.

The man nodded. "I recognize your people. Peru?"

"Who are you?" Jung said.

The man closed the book. "I don't mean to scare you. You were in a bit of trouble so I brought you into our camp."

"Are you a Tæcan?"

The man was silent, thinking.

"Your robe, it's what the Tæcans wear," Jung said. 'Are you?"

The man nodded once. "Yes, to some anyway."

"What do you teach?"

The man laughed.

"What?"

"Of all the questions I had expected out here, that was not on the top of the list."

"What though?"

"Architecture."

"Architecture!" Jung said.

An ember shot from the fire with a shattering crack.

Jung said, "Like *The Great Architect?* The designer of The Great Pyramid and the snail shelled arcs?"

The Architect laughed. "Who have you been spending your time with? You're very well informed."

Jung smiled then straightened his face. He knew he needed to be careful despite how warm the man seemed. "Are you really the designer of The Great Pyramid?"

The Architect nodded. "Yes, I am one of the designers."

"Wow. *The Architect.* Do you have an elongated head?"

The Architect leaned close to the light of the fire and drew back his hood. "I don't know, you tell me."

Jung's mouth fell open at the sight of the man.

The Architect had blacker skin than Jung had ever seen before. He had a broad nose and big dimpled cheeks showcasing glowing white teeth. His head was shaved and shiny.

He scratched at his stubble and winked. "Not what you were expecting?"

Jung was silent, still in shock.

The Architect laughed.

"You're not Viracochan," Jung said.

"No, I'm not."

"But you're a Tæcan?"

The Architect nodded. "To some I am, yes."

"You're a Tæcan but you're not Viracochan?"

"My people and the Viracocha are allies. We work together and we share our land but we are different."

"How?" Jung said.

"You mean aside from how we look?" The Architect said smiling.

Jung nodded.

"My people have lived in Egypt for many great rotations. The Viracocha are visitors to our land. We have been the guardians of knowledge for more than 100 cycles of men. We taught the Viracocha many of our learnings but we are different. I don't get caught up in their nonsensical rituals like binding the skull nor their hierarchies like their stripe system."

"But you're a Tæcan—you have all your stripes."

A pot clanged from one of the tents. There was a murmured voice.

Jung spun to the sound.

"It's okay, it's just men from my party. You're safe," The Architect said.

"What men?" Jung said.

The Architect looked at the tents. "A star watcher and a rock analyst. Three stripe Viracochan Uzmans."

Jung stared at the tents, uneasy.

"It's okay, they are good men and they take their orders from me."

Jung relaxed as he realized if the men really wanted to hurt him, they would have already.

The Architect leaned forward and delivered a cheeky grin. He lowered his voice to a whisper. "The truth is, I didn't quite go through the stripe system the way most Tæcans do."

"What do you mean?" Jung said.

"Because of The Great Pyramid."

"I thought you needed lineage to become a Tæcan?"

The Architect's smile widened. "You are full of surprises aren't you. Yes, it's correct. Lineage is a guarantee you'll become a Tæcan but they also allow some Uzmans and even some no-bodies like me to become Tæcans. It's all about your perceived value."

Jung remembered Tika and The Brewer saying the same thing—everything with the Viracocha involved measuring the value of a person.

Jung said, "So they wanted your pyramid so much they made you a Tæcan?"

"In a sense, yes. But also because the design of The Great Pyramid contains so much secret Viracochan knowledge, it meant I needed to be initiated as a Tæcan so I could learn everything I needed to build it into the design Anyway, I don't buy it. Tell me, what brings you-"

Jung cut in. "I don't get it, Egypt is your land but The Great Pyramid is the Viracocha's design?

"No, The Great Pyramid is ours." The Architect grinned. "Unless you ask the Viracocha."

"What do you mean?"

"I guess you could say they are funding the build so they feel warranted to have control of the design."

"So they do control the design?"

The Architect shook his head.

"What do you mean?"

"It's complicated."

"What are you going to do now? Where are you going to build the pyramids?"

The Architect bit his lip.

"Where?" Jung said.

"I'm afraid… nowhere. Not until things settle at least. Not until the floods recede."

Jung looked deflated. "So, the plans are off?"

"The plans are on hold, they're not off."

"But you don't have a back up plan?"

"No."

"Ridiculous. How could you not think it mattered?"

The Architect had a sympathetic look on his face. "May I ask, why does the delay hurt you so much?"

Jung shook his head and looked into the fire. "Doesn't matter."

"Have you met Viracocha men?"

Jung looked up, a sad expression on his face.

The Architect took a breath. "What stripe?"

"One, two and three."

The Architect scrunched his face and shook his head. "I'm sorry, Jung, but you may be carrying some lies with you."

"I know."

"You know?"

Jung nodded. "Yes, The Artery of Earth is a fake and the pyramid in Nazca has nothing to do with the pyramids in Egypt. It's just a ploy to control my people and steal the plants."

The Architect nodded. "Yes, true, but it's also worse. Much worse."

54

"Worse?" Jung said.

Behind him the flapping door of the tent was getting more intense.

The Architect looked nervous.

"What could be worse than enslaving my people?" Jung said.

"The darkness they bring."

"Darkness?"

"Yes, dark energy. Dark energy will linger on your land long after they have left."

"How?" Jung said.

"Through their ceremonies."

"With the plants?"

The Architect nodded. "Yes, using the power of the plants. Although the plants themselves are not bad—they simply give man a way in to do the damage or the repair they want to do."

"And the Viracocha do damage?" Jung said.

"Yes, the Viracocha possess a great deal of knowledge but when it comes to understanding energy, they have it all wrong. They think dark matter connects all things and is the fabric of the universe—and lightness exists only as specks moving onto and off of its surface. They think dark matter is the true intelligence of nature."

"What do you think?"

"About darkness?"

"Yes."

The Architect said, "I believe in balance, a balance of lightness and darkness. I believe they are weighted perfectly even."

Jung smiled—the man's sentiment matched his own people's. They too believed there was an equal distribution of light energy and dark energy in nature.

"They're scumbags," Jung said.

"In some senses, it's true."

Jung took a deep breath through his nose and stared into the fire.

"Did they make you a promise?" The Architect said.

Jung stared into the fire.

"Did they bring you here?"

Jung looked up and pointed to his chest angrily. "*I* brought myself here. *I* did. They did nothing. All they have done is try to get in my way and confuse me. They're lying scumbags."

"May I ask what the promise was?"

Jung shook his head and stared back into the fire.

"Please."

Jung looked up and snarled. "You're just as bad! It was your machine they said I could use."

"The Great Pyramid?"

Jung scoffed and shook his head.

"They said you could use the pyramid to do what?"

"What do you think?"

The Architect shook his head. "I'm sorry, but I genuinely don't know. They tell so many lies about our designs, I wouldn't hazard a guess."

Jung sniffed. "They said I could use it to get to my father."

"Your father. Where is your father?"

"He's dead," Jung said, his throat tight with emotion.

"I'm sorry."

Jung shook his head. He heard the genuine empathy in the man's words, it only made his throat tighter.

"So you're trying to get to the river of souls?" The Architect said.

Jung looked at him. "What's the river of souls?"

"The Milky Way—the river of stars."

"Yes."

The Architect raised his eyebrows. "What if I said you didn't need The Great Pyramid to see your father?"

Jung sniffed. "Leave me alone."

"I'm being serious. You don't need the pyramid."

"What?"

"I'm not misleading you, Jung. Have you ever stopped to think maybe your father is with you right now?"

"What do you think?" Jung said. "Why do you think I'm all the way out here?"

"Why *are* you all the way out here?"

Jung frowned. "Leave me alone."

"You believe your father is out here?"

Jung was silent.

"I promise I'm not trying to mess with you. It's a complicated thing to wrap your head around but the truth is your father sits with you right now."

"You don't even know who he is," Jung said.

"I know. But if he existed in the past then he sits with you right now."

"How?"

"Because the past is happening right now."

Jung scrunched his face.

The Architect smiled. "He's with you now, I can assure you it's true. Sometimes it's just difficult to see."

"What do you mean?"

"The confusion arises from the way we view time. We have it all messed up. You see time doesn't exist. It's something made up by our consciousness in order to project reality in an easier way to process. But it's an illusion. In our minds we believe we see the past, the present and the future. But what if all of these were the same? What if only how we interpreted them made them different?"

Jung looked confused.

"You know your father exists in the past, yes?"

Jung nodded.

"Well, if you could prove your past was not in fact happening in the past but was happening right now then your father would be here with you now. True?"

Jung thought for a moment then nodded.

"Well, time *is* an illusion—and it's all because of what I call GOD."

"GOD?"

The Architect nodded. "Yes, GOD. G, O, D. *Generation, Operation, Dissolution.* GOD is the perception something appears, exists and disappears. Within the lifetime of a creature this illusion manifests itself as birth, life and death. Or in the case of our observation of a rock or a lake or a star, things are gathered, exhausted and dispersed. This is where we get our obsession with death. GOD makes us believe death is the end of life, but it's not really. Death is just the end of one cycle and the beginning of the next. Like the cycle of seasons, think about how summer gives way to autumn then winter then spring. If we only lived out three seasons of life, like a dragonfly, we could be excused for believing summer never returns. But for the rest of us, the cycle of seasons makes sense. Things come and they go, repeating over and over, like the waves on an ocean."

"I don't get it."

The Architect laughed heartily.

It was the first time in a long time Jung had heard someone laugh with genuine joy and freeness. It reminded him of his father.

The Architect winked. "It works like this, we look at our lives and we see a linear path of events from birth to death—a life sequence—and more often than not we believe this sequence appears one frame after the other. But this is not true. This sequence is just a story The Watcher makes up in our mind. All life sequences are stories. The truth is every moment exists right here, right now."

Jung's mouth hung open, confused.

"Here's a thought experiment for you. Close your eyes."

Jung closed his eyes.

"Imagine a box—a room—hovering in empty space. Now, imagine there are rooms all around this room. Rooms all butted up together, in front and behind, above and below, to the sides.

So you have stacks and stacks of rooms making up a lattice-like configuration."

Jung nodded, his eyes still closed.

"This lattice is actually infinitely big but for this thought experiment, you can imagine it as a finite cluster. Put this image to the side. Now, imagine every moment of your life is a still frame. Obviously you can't imagine every moment but think of some of the biggest moments of your life, perhaps when you killed your first animal to feed your tribe or when you first journeyed to somewhere far away. Place each of these moments on separate cards. So you have this stack of cards, a sequence of moments from birth to death. Almost like the pages of a book. A visible record of your existence. Do you understand?"

"I think so," Jung said, his eyes still closed.

"We call this your *life sequence*. Now, imagine all of these frames from your life sequence beginning to fly up into the air and fill the lattice of rooms I told you to first imagine. Some frames go to rooms higher up the stack than others, some go to rooms deeper into the stack than others, some go to rooms near the beginning, others near the end. Now, you have to understand while there are a lot of rooms filled by the frames from your life, the lattice is so enormously big, there are still far more empty rooms than filled ones.

"Now, imagine all of these other empty rooms become suddenly filled up with other moments, moments almost identical to the rooms next door aside from one tiny variation. Maybe in the room next door everything is identical to this moment except my robe is white not black or the fire is one foot to the side of where it is now. So you end up with a lattice of infinite moments, a room for every possibility. Does it make sense?"

"I think so," Jung said. He peeked out through his squinting eyes and smiled when he met The Architect's gaze. He closed his eyes again.

The Architect said, "Now, imagine you light up all of those rooms containing a frame from the initial sequence—your life sequence. So you have a random pattern of lit up rooms in the grid. Like I said, we call this lit up arrangement your *life sequence*. In essence it is a code creating the experience of living a life. A code The Watcher in your mind is aware of. It is what makes up every memory of the past, every dream of the future and every moment of awareness of the present. You see, what is actually happening right now is every moment possible is all playing out simultaneously. Except we are only aware of those snapshots in our life sequence—the sequence of rooms lit up. We don't see all the other rooms not lit up. Make sense?"

Jung opened his eyes. "I think so, but why?"

"Because there is far too much information. It would overwhelm us to experience all things at once. Our minds are designed for the very purpose of filtering out almost everything and leaving us with the smallest amount of necessary information. Information imperative to our survival."

"So what's the past then?" Jung said.

"The past is just a meaning we have assigned to a frame. It is a story."

"What do you mean?"

"I mean when our attention is drawn to near the beginning of the grid, we get the sense we are jumping back in time and remembering our past. And when our attention is drawn further ahead in the grid, we get the sense we are imagining the future. Only it's all happening right here, right now. The *past* and *future* are simply labels we assign to things to try and fit them into our story. A story we use to give the chaos order. Well, at least, the illusion of order."

The Architect held up the book sitting on his lap. He began to flick through the pages. "Your perception of your life is like this book. If I tore out all the pages of this book and threw them across the ground we would see them for what they are—a collection of moments all existing at once. But when bound together, these moments take on a completely different form, they become a sequence of events in a story."

"So you're saying my father and I are together somewhere right now?"

The Architect grinned. "Jung, you and your father are together in infinite places right now."

"So I can travel back and see him—if I go back on my life sequence?"

"In a sense, yes. You can switch the gaze of The Watcher to an earlier part of your life sequence."

"What's The Watcher? You keep saying that."

"The Watcher is the being who sees all when the third eye is opened. It is our eye of consciousness. And it is the entity that determines the life sequence we choose."

"How?"

"The Watcher draws our life sequence from the collective unconscious."

"The collective unconscious?" Jung said.

"Yes."

"I met a three stripe Viracochan man who told me about the collective unconscious."

"Really?"

Jung nodded.

The Architect swallowed hard. "It doesn't surprise me. The collective unconscious is the Viracocha's greatest pursuit."

"What do you mean?" Jung said.

"I mean that's what I was trying to warn you about. They're trying to control the collective unconscious so they can control your people."

55

Jung looked up to the swirling lights in the sky—purples, yellows, blues. Oozing, gushing, breathing.

"She's straining," The Architect said. He was looking at the sky too.

Jung looked at the man.

He winked. "Or maybe you're breaking through."

Jung smiled and looked back at the sky.

"May I ask what you have heard about the collective unconscious?" The Architect said.

Jung shared his encounter with The Surgeon and the river analogy the man had used.

The Architect nodded. "This is mostly correct, the collective unconscious is a substrata contributed to by all of us. The river is an analogy commonly used. Although he's not completely right."

"How?"

"Well, to understand the collective unconscious properly you first need to understand there are two ways we perceive life—consciously and unconsciously. Conscious interactions are those things we are aware of, what we see, hear, feel, taste and touch. While unconscious interactions are those things we are not aware of but also mold our actions. In fact we believe the unconscious determines what we do even more than the conscious. A good way to think about it is to think of light. The center of the light spectrum—the light we can see—is consciousness. Of course we can see a lot of light but there is also a lot of light we can't see. There is light in that fire and in those colors in the sky existing beyond our consciousness. Colors just as real as any color we can see but completely invisible to us. Most things are like this. They exist beyond our consciousness. Beyond our channel."

The Architect rubbed his palms together. "You want to know just how restricted our channel of consciousness is? It's directly tied to the frequency of Earth."

"What do you mean?" Jung said.

"Our conscious mind operates at between two cycles per second and 40 cycles per second. At two cycles we are in a deep sleep, at seven cycles we are awake but relaxed and at 40 cycles we are highly alert like an animal fighting for its life. And do you know what frequency Earth hums at?"

"Two to 40 cycles?" Jung said.

The Architect smiled. "Yes, the far-reaches of Earth's sky hums at around two cycles, the core of Earth hums at around 40 cycles, and the crust of Earth—where we're sitting now—hums at around seven cycles. So you could say when you're in a deep sleep you're in the sky, when you're awake but relaxed you're on the crust of Earth, and when you're in a highly alert state you're in the core of Earth."

"Wow," Jung said.

"Yes, definitely wow. Her boundaries are your boundaries. Let's not get too distracted by this though, the point is we are only conscious of a very small part of the spectrum of existence but it doesn't mean we aren't shaped by forces beyond these. For instance, forces lower than two cycles and higher than 40 cycles. We certainly are, but these interactions occur without us ever knowing. In fact, like I said before, it's better if we aren't conscious of these interactions, otherwise we tend to get in our own way."

Jung smiled.

The Architect smiled back. "One of the forces acting upon us that affects what we do is the collective unconscious. It is an energy created by all of us without us ever even knowing."

"It is all the thoughts ever had by all people."

"Yes, exactly. All thoughts gather and pile up, impacting all other thoughts. Just like the riverbed analogy, where the contours of the riverbed ultimately determine the flow of the water. Although you have to understand this substrata—the riverbed—is a lot more simple and nebulous than what goes on in your mind."

"What do you mean?" Jung said.

"I mean it's not like you see a wise old man in the collective unconscious and then the wise old man comes to life in your consciousness. The collective unconscious exists as very elementary structures common to all of us. It is only when we interact with them, painting them with our own context and stories, that they develop in complexity and meaning. In other words, we all interact with the same basic energy but the way we interpret its forms differs between each and every one of us. Where I see snakes for healing perhaps you see the tree of life. Or where I see the great mother as a symbol of wisdom perhaps you see the wise old man."

"And this energy influences what we do in our life?"

The Architect nodded. "Yes, exactly. Remember I spoke of The Watcher—your consciousness?"

Jung nodded.

"Well, The Watcher looks to the collective unconscious when choosing a life sequence for itself. So it constructs its sequence of lit-up rooms based on its observations of the collective unconscious. This life sequence typically involves some kind of hero's journey or the story of the mentor, the everyman, the villain or the innocent. It is a story that is a complete cliche because that is what a cliche is—replication of replication. You want to know the most interesting thing?"

"What?"

"Well, remember I said time doesn't exist?" The Architect said.

"Yes."

"This means The Watcher is pulling from the collective unconscious and contributing to it simultaneously. In other words, The Watcher is being shaped by the collective unconscious as much as it is shaping the collective unconscious. This is why the stories repeat, over and over. Because we are entangled with all else."

"Have you seen it?" Jung said.

"Yes."

"What does it look like?"

"Narrative strings."

"What do you mean?"

"A melting pot of kaleidoscopic shapes—swirling, folding, bleeding. Geometric patterns in every color of the rainbow seeping out of nothingness and forever increasing in complexity."

"Like the sky now," Jung said, smiling.

The Architect looked up to the aurora lights in full display. He smiled. "Funnily enough, yes. Although, the narrative strings are far more detailed. Shapes and patterns carried on vibrating strings evolving increasingly as you focus on them. And the more you interact with them the more complex the narratives become until you see elaborate scenes and characters archetypal in nature."

"*Archetypal?*" Jung said.

"Yes. Archetypal means cliche, common. Like the stories told by your people, or my people, or *any* people really. It is why stories from all over Earth seem to share the same characters and ideas and arcs. Figures such as the great mother, the wise old man, the shadow, the trickster and the tree of life. Because we're all drawing on the same bedrock when structuring the narratives forming our reality."

"What does the Viracocha want from all this?"

The Architect was suddenly serious. "They want to change the substrata, the foundation of the collective unconscious. They believe if they can, they can control the narrative strings and in turn control the psyche of humankind."

"Is it true?"

"Well, theoretically if they took control of the collective unconscious then they could enslave people to one way of thinking. In a moment we could all lose our independence. Well, at least, our illusion of independence. They could make us all think and act the same."

Jung looked afraid.

The Architect grinned. "Don't worry, they never will."

"How do you know?"

"Because they're depending on us to do it and we won't let it happen."

"What do you mean?".

"I mean it's what they think we're doing with The Great Pyramid. It's what we have promised them." The Architect shook his head. "But it's not what the pyramid will actually do."

"What will it do?"

The Architect gazed into the fire. "They have no idea how impossible it would be to edit the narrative strings. They have no idea how impossibly large and powerful and all-knowing it is." He looked at Jung. "They think they are going into the grid and solving challenges—tests." He shook his head. "I've been in many times. I've seen them. They aren't tests. They are health alerts, warnings from Pachamama herself. They can't be negotiated with, they can't be overpowered and they certainly can't be changed. They are wrestling these narrative strings and trying to control them. Of course, she knows. And, of course, it upsets her. I will never drink the plants with a Viracochan Tæcan for such reason. I have seen how she watches them, how she toys with them. But it upsets her."

"So what's the pyramid for then?" Jung said.

"To stop them from doing the very thing they are trying to do."

"Huh?"

"They wanted to go to the stars, hence why I built the design of Orion and Leo and Sirius into the layout and positioning of the pyramids. It's why I built *many* star configurations into the design. They believe it is a wormhole that connects Earth to Sirius," The Architect said. He winked at Jung. "But the truth is, you don't go up to reach the grid."

"So how do you get to the grid?" Jung said.

"You go down, through the center of Earth."

56

"The pyramid takes people into Earth?" Jung said.

The Architect looked to the sky. "Correct. You certainly can find the path to the grid up there. It's been done. But by very few. It takes a lot longer. None I know have achieved it in a lifetime." He stomped his foot on the ground. "But through her, down through the crust, a person can find the path to the grid in their lifetime."

"How?"

The Architect adjusted his seated bum and held his palms to the flames. "Let me give you some context by sharing a story from many rotations ago."

Jung smiled with excitement.

"When I was a boy living in Egypt, long before I became interested in architecture and the stars, I was more interested in studying living organisms. In fact, my love for design came from my discoveries when studying plants and animals. Later I discovered what I saw in the stars I had first seen in the bodies of creatures. Like the number of heartbeats—a discovery I made when I was a young man, around your age." He winked.

Jung grinned.

The Architect said, "One evening I was walking on the Egypt savanna when I came across two lion cubs."

"Lions? Like The Sphinx in Egypt?"

"Yes, exactly."

Jung held up the tooth hanging from his waist. "But real cats? Not like the creature this came from?"

The Architect smiled. "Very perceptive. Yes, real cats, not like the saber-tooths. Real ones, but babies. They were huddled near the body of their mother who appeared to have been killed by the horn of a plant eater. They were extremely stressed. I knew they were far too young to survive on their own. Without help they would be dead before Earth's Star returned. So I decided to take them home." He grinned. "To save their lives, you know? But there was also the opportunity. They were one of our people's greatest predators. The more we could understand about them, the better we could protect ourselves against them. Plus, I was also just curious. I wanted to know how a natural born killer would act when raised under different conditions. I wanted to know if nature really did trump nurture."

"Did it?" Jung said.

The Architect smiled. "You'll soon find out. There were a lot of reasons to take the cats home on the dæġ, so I did. Within the first few dæġs I noticed a big difference in the nature of the kittens, which I called Serene and Fret. Serene had a very relaxed nature, she adapted to her new life quickly and was calm and rarely stressed. Fret was the opposite, she was always anxious and aggravated by new things, whether it was the arrival of a visitor, a loud noise or the light from the campfire. Everything seemed to rattle her."

Jung hunched forward and hugged his knees, transfixed.

The Architect said, "After just two seasons I knew I wouldn't be able to keep them for much longer, the strength of their nature was already making it difficult to contain them. I knew I needed to release them by the end of the season. In the meantime I studied everything I could about them. I measured their weights and lengths, their heart rates and blood pressure, their responses to discipline and new situations. I measured and recorded everything I could. By the end of the season nature had almost entirely engulfed nurture. They were becoming a danger to be around and I was forced to release them."

He smiled, glassy eyed. "They didn't forget me though. Every rotation they came back, they would stand together in the distance and watch me sketching away in my book or fishing in the Nile River. They would wait until I spotted them and then they would slink off, returning to the wild. They did the same thing every rotation, paying their respects to the role I had played in their survival."

The Architect's throat was tight with emotion. "On the tenth rotation, Fret didn't turn up. I knew she had passed on, she had been looking more and more tired on the last few visits. Still, Serene continued to show up, rotation after rotation. When she was fifteen, she too stopped showing up and I knew both cats had returned to the earth."

Jung was boggle eyed, mesmerized.

"I remember lying awake one night and thinking about the two of them and the difference in their lifespans," The Architect said. "Then I remembered the numbers, the numbers of heartbeats. I jumped out of bed and pulled out my book and I looked at the numbers I had recorded every dæġ for four seasons. I found exactly what I was looking for, Fret had three heartbeats for every two of Serene's. She always had, because of the stress you know. Fret was always anxious while Serene relaxed into herself. The big discovery, however, was the number of heartbeats matched up directly with the lifespans of the two cats. In other words, Serene's heart beat at two thirds the pace of Frets, while Fret only lived two thirds the life of Serene. This meant, despite the shortness of life in Fret, both animals shared an equal number of heartbeats across the span of their lives. Around 1.5 billion."

Jung laughed. "That's almost the same odds of combining the two plants to conjure Mother Aya."

The Architect grinned. "Yes, correct." He winked. "And perhaps not a coincidence. I wondered if this same number also showed up in the heartbeats of other animals so I started tracking the heartbeats of as many creatures as possible. Over many rotations, I saw the same patterns appearing time and time again in mammals."

"Mammals?" Jung said.

"Creatures with warm blood and hair on their bodies. The heartbeats are always the same—an average of around 1.5 billion. This is assuming the animal dies of natural causes and obviously it doesn't always occur in an animal. It is an average, you know. But with enough individuals tested, the average always comes out the same. I guess you can say it is a rule, a law of nature. This is why a tiny shrew whose heart beats hundreds of times faster than the heart of a whale will live to be just one or two, while a whale can live well beyond 100. The frequency is drawn out in the life of a whale just like it was drawn out in the calmness of Serene."

"So you're saying if you can slow your heart rate down you'll live longer?" Jung said.

"It certainly appears to be. Not in every case of course but in most cases. The less stress the longer the life."

"So what's the point of the pyramid then?"

The Architect looked briefly towards the tents then back at Jung.

He said, "Well, I can't tell you it's primary purpose but I can tell you it has a bi-product favorable to you."

"What do you mean, you can't tell me?"

"That's not a promise to the Viracocha. That's a promise to my people. But in your case it doesn't matter because the bi-product is of greater value to you than the primary purpose of the machine."

"How?"

"Because it can connect you with your father."

"How?"

He said, "It is also a musical instrument."

57

The camp was silent aside from the crackling fire and a low howl from the wind.

"What do you mean by a *musical instrument?*" Jung said.

The Architect smiled. "It is an instrument designed to change the energy not just for the ears but for the entire body. It will recalibrate the frequency of a man."

"What does that mean?"

"It will bring the human psyche back into homeostasis when it deviates."

Jung scrunched his face, confused.

"Homeostasis means stability, equilibrium, balance."

"I don't get it."

"It will steady the energy passing through the bodies of my people," The Architect said. "It will help reduce their stress and bring them back into harmony with nature."

"I still don't understand," Jung said.

"The Great Pyramid will produce vibrating harmonic waves. Think of it like a baseline hum. Say I wanted you to hum a specific tune, a tune let's say good for your health. If I simply told you to hum a tune you would more than likely hum a tune of higher or lower pitch than the tune I had in my head. But if first I began to hum and then I told you to mimic my hum you would have a much greater chance of humming the tune I wanted you to hum. Does that make sense?"

Jung nodded.

"The Great Pyramid will work the same way. It will produce a baseline hum mimicing the heartbeat of Earth which like I mentioned earlier is also the resonance of the human body at ease. I'm sure those who live around the pyramid will not be able to put their finger on why they feel more at peace, or why they feel a deep sense of fulfillment and happiness, or why they are getting sick less and living longer. I very much doubt they will attribute this improvement in life to the presence of a perfectly tuned pyramid but it will be the case."

"So The Great Pyramid helps people who are stressed?" Jung said.

"Yes, for stress but also for more subtle noise too. In essence it will make it much easier for people to get back to a relaxed place when they veer off course. Something we all tend to do when we're not paying enough attention to the moment."

"How do people veer off course?"

"Good question," The Architect said. "Well, within our bodies there exists tiny sensations. These tiny sensations are delivered to us through our unconscious. They steer our survival by triggering our emotions. So first there is the sensation in our body and then there is the response from our head which triggers the emotion. In fact, this is where the word *emotion* comes from—emotion means *to move*. So first there is the sensation and then there is the reaction from our head which instructs us how to respond. There are many different sensations and intensities of sensations occurring in our body but all of them fall into one of two camps—desire and fear. To advance or to back away."

The Architect leaned forward. "On one side are the pleasant sensations—the tingles, tickles and warm fuzzy sensations. Like I said, we call these feelings *desires*. They push us towards those things that have served us well in the past. The taste of fresh fruit, the sensation of sex, the joy coming from group bonding. These are all pleasant sensations for a reason, because they benefit our survival. On the other side we have unpleasant sensations—the fiery, stabbing, burning sensations, like lightning buzzing away in the tiniest of places. These uncomfortable sensations protect us from those things that have not served us well in the past by pushing us away from these things. Every emotion you have can be attributed to these sensations. They heave us back and forth and too often we become slaves to their whims. The Great Pyramid will help regulate these sensations and strip them away when they are unnecessary."

"But don't we need these feelings?" Jung said.

The Architect smiled. "Very perceptive. Yes, we do. Very much so. However, these feelings don't always serve us as well as you might think. Just because something has helped in the past, it doesn't mean it helps us now. And often when left unchecked these sensations become learned habits which grow so large they come to dominate our lives. The pyramid is not designed to overpower these feelings when they are strong and necessary, but to strip them away when they serve no purpose and only generate anxiety and craving." He looked at Jung. "The best part is when these feelings are quietened, because we have them in order, we make room for other feelings. Much more subtle feelings. As a hunter, you more than anyone would have felt them. The flows of energy running through you. You know the sensations? When you find yourself alone in the forest and you feel complete—when you truly meet yourself."

Jung smiled recalling a recent moment in the forest when he was alone and his mind was empty of all thoughts. How the trees and rocks seemed to speak to him through tremors and hums.

The Architect said, "When you're in a place free from fear and desire and free from the past and the future, when you're fully present in the moment you can feel everything, all the energy rushing through you, infinite particles. Particles forever being replaced by new particles. The flow of life, GOD, the moment when you meet yourself, when you realize there are no hard lines to where you end and another thing begins."

Jung nodded slowly, thinking.

"We think we operate outside of those things we see in front of us but we don't. It is our biggest downfall as a species, our belief we exist outside of the system. It is the thing that makes us humans both brilliant and cursed, our belief in our independence. We see trees and rocks and rivers as things separate from us but they're not. And we see the past and future as time removed from us but it's not. Even you and I here, we see ourselves as individuals operating side by side but we aren't. We are much more like tentacles of coral. Each tentacle of coral has an autonomous mind. This means each tentacle is largely independent and can make its own decisions to best aid the survival of the larger organism—the coral plant. When you have a hundred tentacles all trying independently to gather food you have a lot more chance of the coral surviving. However, the tentacles should never forget they are connected to a larger central body governing higher-order functions."

Jung looked confused.

The Architect said, "We humans are like those tentacles of coral, we believe we are our own thing because this aids the survival of our species but we are all connected to and controlled by something much larger and far more powerful, the human species. Most of us will go through our entire lives without ever turning around and realizing we are governed by a hive mentality driven by the collective unconscious. Although even this creature, the human species, is dangerous to draw a line around. We need to think very carefully about where we draw the line on where one thing ends and another begins. Take the coral. We could draw the outline around the frond of coral, the plant of coral or the coral reef. All are just as alive."

Jung nodded slowly.

"We people are the same. We have our own consciousness but we're also connected to everything else. You can draw the line around yourself, your family, the human species, or far beyond. It's up to you. Just know wherever you draw the line is an illusion. There is no difference between you or a rock or a star or anything else. Everything is a part of the same interconnected cosmic cloth. It's just the lens of consciousness that changes."

Jung's face was suddenly tight, tense.

"Are you okay? I know it's a lot of information," The Architect said.

Jung bit his lip and squinted into the fire.

"What's the matter?"

Jung looked at him with glassy eyes. "It's silly. It makes sense what you said, I just hoped somehow the pyramid would take me to my father."

"I don't think you're fully grasping what I'm saying.

He wiped the tears from his eyes. "What?"

"Don't you see? Your father is not gone, he never left. He sits with you right now. Can't you feel him?"

Jung sniffed and shook his head.

The Architect frowned. "You didn't even try. Stop and really try. Close your eyes, breathe through your nose, slow your breath and focus on a memory of him."

Jung closed his eyes and breathed through his nose.

After several breaths he began to feel the sensation of another. Was it an illusion? He smelled his father's familiar salty scent, a comforting smell. A smile stretched across his face.

"Stay with him," The Architect said.

Jung squeezed his eyes shut. He felt his body getting heavy. He felt whole, complete. Then he felt the touch of a hand on his back—large, weighty, warm—moving across his shawl. Was he really here? Shhhhhhhhhhh. Shivers rolled down his body as he was hugged by an invisible force.

"Stay with him," The Architect whispered.

Jung concentrated. The invisible force squeezed him one last time then began to dissolve away. He opened his eyes.

"Did you feel him?" The Architect said.

Jung nodded, swallowing the lump in his throat.

"Good. I'm glad. You see The Great Pyramid will help people get to the place you experienced with your father, only quicker and far more easily. It will remove all the noise so people can really feel the heartbeat of Pachamama." He grinned. "So hopefully next time you don't have to travel an entire continent to sit with your father."

Jung laughed and sniffed. He still felt the lingering presence of his father's spirit. It was a comforting feeling he hoped would never leave. "Can I ask a question?"

The Architect smiled. "Of course."

"Will my people be able to feel your pyramid in Peru?"

The Architect looked saddened by the words. He shook his head. "I'm afraid not. It's a long distance."

Jung gazed into the fire and nodded, moisture still in the corners of his eyes.

"I think I can help you though," The Architect said.

"Help me?"

"Yes, I can help you get rid of it."

"What?" Jung said.

"The school being set up in Nazca."

58

OLYMPIA. NORÐ AMERICA.

There was a distant howl.

Jung and The Architect both looked down the slope in the direction of the noise.

Another howl came, then another. The animals were calling back and forth.

The silhouettes of half a dozen dire wolves appeared on the snow in the distance. In the pale light from Earth's Rock their rib cages looked bare.

"They must be starving," The Architect said, standing over the fire.

Jung remained sitting, too tired to move. He had his knees drawn in.

The Architect sat. "Where was I?"

"The school," Jung said.

"Ah, yes. The three schools of the Viracocha."

"There are *three* schools?"

The Architect nodded. "Yes, The School of Telepathy, The School of Levitation and The School of The Watcher."

"What do they do?"

"They study different things. The School of Telepathy for example is the oldest of the institutions and is located in Gunung Padang. There the Tæcans study mind reading."

"What does it mean?"

"Mind reading is me knowing exactly what you're thinking without you ever opening your mouth."

"Is it real?"

The Architect nodded.

"How?"

"I have only experienced it, I wouldn't say I understand how it works."

"But you know what happens?"

"Yes."

"So what happens?" Jung said.

"Two people drink together."

"Ayahuasca?"

"Yes. Two Tæcans are first assigned partners, they then drink the plants together in a ceremony, which always takes place in complete darkness and silence. This means you have no idea what your partner is feeling or experiencing during the ceremony. The dæġ after the ceremony the partners sit down together and discuss how the narrative strings appeared for each of them. They look for the places of connection. Perhaps you and your partner were both wrapped up in a cocoon during the ceremony, or perhaps you both encountered biting snakes, or were both carried up to the outer reaches of Earth's sky. It could be anything. Sometimes you share very little in common, sometimes you share a lot. During the next ceremony on the following night the partners then search for those visions or experiences they shared in common. After the ceremony they then discuss their experiences again and will find they have much more in common, because they are aligning. Usually by the end of 10 to 15 ceremonies the partners are having very similar experiences. The narrative strings of course appear different from one Tæcan to the other but the meaning and the sequence will be very similar. With enough journeys together partners can begin to learn one another's life sequences. Once you learn someone's life sequence you become very good at predicting their thoughts, even without the plants."

"Really?" Jung said.

"Yes. Not all the time but some of the time. And the more training you do together with the plants, the stronger the entanglement becomes."

"But they can only ever read each other's minds? They can't read other people's minds?"

The Architect shook his head. "Not necessarily. Aligning two life sequences is stage one. But once you have two life sequences entangled you have twice the operating power. If you then use those two minds together a third subject can be coerced into the same pattern of thought much more easily."

"But they can only read the minds of those who drink the plants?"

"I'm not sure to be honest," The Architect said. "It was the case when I was there 10 rotations ago but 10 rotations is a long time. If I was to have a guess I would say they are still restricted to just those who have drunk the plants because otherwise our school would know about it but I can't guarantee it. I imagine they have made a lot of ground from when I was there 10 rotations ago. It does concern me."

Jung frowned. "What about the school in Nazca?"

"The School of Levitation."

"What does it mean?"

The Architect said, "It means to move things without touching them—using only your mind. The School of Levitation was also in Gunung Padang. It was the first school to break away from The School of Telepathy."

"Why did they break away?" Jung said.

"Well, originally it was just The School of Telepathy up and running in Ganung Padang. For many rotations this was the only Viracochan school. But like all institutions eventually The School of Telepathy gained a reputation as being hard for young Tæcans to make ground. There were a lot of seats at the table already filled if you know what I mean. In time a couple of young bright Tæcans who butted heads with the elders at the school decided to start their own institution and their own branch of learning. They set up a pyramid of their own in Gunung Padang. For as far back as I have known they have been happy in Gunung Padang, but clearly your plants have them hungry for new land."

"Have you seen them levitate things?"

The Architect nodded. "Yes. Although I'm not sure if what I saw was real or an illusion."

"What do you mean?"

"Well, the art of levitation is both an illusion and a reality. Tæcans have mastered using trickery of the mind to achieve the desired act."

Jung scrunched his face. "Huh?"

"They call it the *observer effect*. It works by first creating the illusion an object is floating in the air in front of an audience. If the observers believe enough in what they see, they themselves will begin to change the energy."

"How?"

"The common belief is our consciousness arises from matter. In other words, the common belief is our physical body comes first and this is what determines our mind and what we think. However, the truth is exactly the opposite. Our laws of matter, the rules governing the physical boundaries of things, arise from our minds. Physical things come into form when we're all in agreement on the parameters of such things."

"I don't understand," Jung said.

The Architect smiled. "It's confusing, I know. What I mean is what we collectively imagine is what comes to be. For instance, we imagine the boundaries of Earth, so the boundaries of Earth come into being. The same with everything on Earth, we imagine trees and rocks and rivers and so trees and rocks and rivers come to be."

"So I can just imagine a tree and it will be created?" Jung said.

The Architect grinned. "Not quite. You can't just go running off on your own. You are a human and therefore you are in a clustered agreement with all other humans. Your consciousness is restricted by the bounds of the collective unconscious. Like the tentacle of coral on the coral reef. The tentacle alone can't change the coral reef much but if all the tentacles of all the corals change then the entire reef will change."

"So if lots and lots of people believe there is a tree then a tree will come?" Jung said.

"Yes, exactly. Like ayahuasca. You think the jungle people just stumbled across mixing ayahuasca with chacruna to free the spirit molecule? The odds against such a thing are 1 in 1.6 billion. Almost impossible. Unless the jungle people wanted it so much it came to be."

"Really?" Jung said.

"Yes, they wanted so much to connect with Pachamama on a deeper level that they were given the plants and told how to find them and to use them. Like I said, when enough minds focus on something, the rules of matter will bend to create that very thing because everything around us is an illusion. A very powerful illusion and an illusion much bigger than we as individuals but an illusion nevertheless. This is how the observer effect works in levitation. Make enough people believe a stone is moving on its own, and the stone will in fact move on its own."

Jung looked unconvinced.

The Architect said, "Remember the boundaries of things are flimsy at best. Who really knows where the floating rock ends and the air around it begins. It's up to us as a collective to agree to such things. Change what the group sees and things change. Reassign meaning to energy and energy changes."

"I still find it hard to believe."

The Architect nodded. "So did I until I drank the plants. Let me just say things are not what they seem. Group-think is much more powerful than we give it credit. It's what we call into being as reality. Think about the tension you can feel in the air when you're in the presence of an angry mob. The energy is thick, palpable. You can feel it rise and rise, then something explosive happens and things escalate fast."

"And the opposite is true too," Jung said. "You can feel the warmth of love and kindness when surrounded by a group of people brimming with love and kindness."

The Architect grinned. "Exactly. It is just as powerful. Love, the antidote to hate."

"What about your school in Egypt? What do they do there?"

"The School of The Watcher?"

Jung nodded.

The Architect said, "The Viracocha say The School of The Watcher accepts only the very best minds." He laughed. "But I'm obviously biased. It was the first school to leave the mainland. They traveled to the other side of Earth to be alone."

"So it's their school?"

The Architect nodded. "Yes, they have a school in our town."

"Why?"

"Because they lost Ganung Padang in the floods."

Jung looked confused. "But they started the school before the star hit."

The Architect smiled. "I know. But remember time is an illusion. The School of The Watcher was the last of the three schools to start. Members came from both of the two other schools. Only these weren't some young renegades who had a gripe with the system, they were Tæcans who considered themselves the most elite. Tæcans who believed there weren't just ranks of Uzmans but ranks of Tæcans too. Tæcans who saw themselves as at the top of their fields and who wanted their own institution so they could keep their findings to themselves."

"Top of their fields at what?" Jung said.

"At The School of The Watcher the skill is reading and navigating the narrative strings arising from the collective unconscious. They were supposed to follow the same naming convention as The School of Telepathy and The School of Levitation calling themselves The School of Psyche. Instead they opened as The School of The Watcher. It gives you a sense how they do things. Other Tæcans from the other schools say they did it because they wanted them to feel like they were being watched over."

"They sound dangerous," Jung said.

"They are, no doubt. But we have them under our control," The Architect said.

"What do you mean?"

"We control the reach of their power because it is our machine they are depending on to do what they want to do. As long as they are depending on The Great Pyramid they will never achieve what they want to achieve. You on the other hand need to protect your people. The Tæcans from The School of Levitation have their eyes set on the Artery of Earth. You must put a stop to them taking control of the artery."

Jung was confused. "Artery of Earth? There's no such thing as the Artery of Earth. The Surgeon said it was just a lie the Viracocha told us so we would fall into line."

The Architect shook his head. "Not the line encompassing Earth, that is a fable told by the storytellers. The real Artery of Earth is the basin forests on your people's land, where Mother Aya grows. They call the basin the Artery of Earth because it is where ayahuasca grows and she is the life blood of the spirit molecule."

"How do I get rid of them?"

The Architect opened the book on his lap and ripped out a page near the back. He handed it to Jung.

Jung took the paper and looked at it. It showed a series of horizontal and vertical lines. "What is it?"

The Architect said, "It is the key to putting a stop to them."

59

Jung looked at the paper The Architect had handed him.

He shook his head. "I don't get it."

The Architect nodded at the sheet. "It is the date when the stars will return, roughly. The dæġ they do return there will be 60 dæġs until the first ceremony takes place in Nazca. You have until then to put a stop to things."

Jung looked at the paper. "How did you get it?"

"Season 4, lunar rotation 3, dæġ 2."

"I don't see it."

The Architect pointed to the sketch. "See running from left to right. There are vertical lines, then horizontal lines, then vertical lines. Four vertical lines, three horizontal lines and two vertical lines. They represent: season, lunar rotation and dæġ."

"432?" Jung said, smiling.

"Yes, late summer. Just after the summer solstice."

Jung offered the paper back. "I can remember."

"Keep it and familiarize yourself with it. It too has a role to play on your journey."

Jung nodded and put the paper against his chest under his shawl.

Suddenly he felt anxious. It was the words The Architect had used—*journey*. He needed to get going, time was against him.

Jung climbed onto his feet. "I have to go."

"Easy does it," The Architect said.

Jung had his hands out ready to catch himself if he fell. He swayed on his feet and sat feeling he was about to fall.

"Are you okay?" The Architect said.

He nodded, squinting his eyes closed.

"How will you get back to Nazca?"

Jung opened his eyes slowly. "There's an arc waiting for me."

"An arc? Viracochan?"

He nodded.

"What are you doing with them?" The Architect said.

"They brought me here. They think I can get them the star, hence why I have to get going. I need to find the star and get back to them before they leave."

The Architect frowned. "Star?"

Jung nodded.

"I have some bad news I'm afraid."

"What?"

"A star didn't hit here."

"What do you mean?" Jung said. He pointed to the ledge in the distance where the peak gave way to darkness. "What broke apart this mountain then?"

"I know, we've been out here for several dægs investigating the site. Like I said, I have a rock analyst and star watcher with me-"

Jung cut in. "So what is it?"

"It's from space-"

"So it *is* a star?"

The Architect shook his head. "It was ice."

"*Ice.*"

"A comet. It's like a rock only it's made of compact ice rather than compact stone."

"What does it mean?" Jung said.

"It means whatever caused that crater has been obliterated into a zillion pieces. You won't find a single shard of the star around here."

"It doesn't make sense. Why would the Viracocha bring me all the way out here if there was never a shard of star to be found?"

"They wouldn't have known. None of our people knew. We all assumed it was a meteor. What the Viracocha call *a star*. It's what we were sent here to do, investigate exactly what it was. We've only just worked it out in the last few dæġs. Unfortunately, it was definitely a comet though. It's responsible for all this destruction and it's leaving no evidence it even came."

"What do you think will happen if I return to the arc and explain to them there is no star?" Jung said.

The Architect bit the inside of his cheek. He shook his head. "You can't go back. You'll be in danger." He pointed to the group of horses beyond the tents. "Take one of our horses. You can get back to your people's land by following the coast, it'll take the best part of a season but if you move fast you can still beat the Tæcans to Nazca. And at least you will be safe."

"I have to go back to the arc first."

"Why?"

"I have someone at the arc. I have to get her," Jung said.

"Who?"

"A captive. A girl from Cuzco."

The Architect looked into the flames of the fire, thinking. After some time he looked at Jung. "I suggest you find a decoy star. You just need to get the girl right? Then you'll leave?"

Jung nodded.

"I'd say it's a good idea. They know what a star looks and feels like. The moment they touch it, they'll know you are lying. But there is no reason why they wouldn't believe you if it looked the same and was held from a distance."

"Why do they want it so much if it has nothing to do with starting the pyramid?" Jung said.

"A star is worth a lot to the Viracocha. Many of them would trade everything they have for a star."

"Why?"

The Architect said, "There is no reason aside from the strange fact that those who possess a star garner more respect than those who don't and respect is worth a lot to the Viracocha. It has become a symbol of power through the sheer demand they have for it. They will become extremely dangerous the moment they realize the stone is not real. You must get your friend without letting them hold the decoy. And you must leave the arc as soon as you can."

"I'll get the girl and we can go by land."

"By horse," The Architect said.

Jung smiled, realizing there were four horses and four men on the mountain—the two of them and the two Viracocha men. It was as if he had been expected.

The Architect grinned. "So the only thing left for you to do is to find a rock that looks like a star." He leaned over and drew a small hessian bag to his side. He dug his hand inside and pulled out a small bandaged item. "You'll most likely find a similar stone closer to the arc near the shore. It should look like this."

He unwrapped the item revealing a shiny purplish-black rock, a quarter the size of his fist.

Jung instantly recognized it. It was identical to the stone of power The Healer had given him.

The Architect handed him the rock.

Jung took it with one hand. Yes, it was identical. It was the same heaviness and coolness and it had the same dimples.

The Architect plucked the stone from Jung's hand.

He said, "I'm sorry, I can't give you this one." He wrapped the star up in the cloth. "I too have people to answer to."

Jung was smiling. "It's okay. I have the same."

The Architect looked puzzled.

"A shaman from back home gave me the same as a stone of power."

The Architect smiled. "Really?"

"Yes," Jung said. He was looking around for his bag. He couldn't see it. He immediately became panicked. "Where is it?"

"Where is what?"

"My bag. It's gone!"

The Architect started looking around too. Not seeing it in the immediate vicinity he turned and looked toward the crater in the distance. "It may still be at the crater."

"What! How?"

"It's where I found you. It was dark. Maybe I overlooked it. I remember your bow but I don't remember anything else."

Jung was angry. "Are you sure? Maybe one of your men took it?"

The Architect shook his head. "I found you alone. It has to be up there. I would remember grabbing it. I was rushing. You were in a very bad way."

Jung stood. "I have to go. I need to find my bag so I can get back to her."

The Architect stood too. "Take Orion, he's my strongest horse."

Jung grinned. "*Orion.*"

"I believe you too are already acquainted," The Architect said. He led Jung over to the horse identical to the animal from his dream. He steadied the horse so Jung could climb on.

Jung leapt onto the horse in one bound.

Orion barely noticed his light weight.

"Remember the note," The Architect said.

Jung patted his chest where he had placed the sheet.

"I want you to know the plants told me to come out here and see you," The Architect said.

"What do you mean?"

The Architect looked back at the tents. "It's why I convinced the Viracocha to let me join the exploration party. Mother Aya told me to meet you and to help you. You have a powerful destiny."

Jung smiled.

"It's true, you are what the other realms foretold. You have an important role to play."

"What kind of role?"

"All is to be revealed," The Architect said. He held out his hand.

Jung hung down off the horse and they hugged.

As they embraced The Architect whispered in his ear. "The dark cloud. Don't let it touch you."

60

Eight dægs to stars return.

NAZCA. PERU.

It was dark when I walked the final stretch of road to Nazca, my feet crunching in the sand, cicadas buzzing in my ears. Despite being the middle of the night, Earth's Rock was full, soaking everything in a cool blue.

Around me gray cracked earth stretched out in all directions scattered with the dark shadows of cacti. Far away, bordered on three sides by crumbling sandstone ridges, were a smattering of animal skin tents and lights from cookfires.

Then I spotted it.

Cut from an escarpment overlooking the camp of Nazca was the sculpture of a giant jaguar. The stone cat had to be more than 50 men long and composed from a single piece of stone. Surrounded by fire torches, lit up like dæġlight, the sculpture was beautiful—a perfect replica of the majestic cat from the basin. Seeing the monument with my own eyes was like nothing from a book. It was breathtaking, a piece of art, even from 500 men away.

I continued on towards a guard tower appearing on the road ahead where a river—five men wide—crossed underneath.

The tower consisted of a wooden platform with a simple roof and waist-high railing on all sides. At the front was a raised drawbridge that could be lowered for passage across. Fire torches rose from each corner. Beneath the tower were two large wooden gates blocking the road into camp.

I wore an ear-to-ear grin as I approached the tower, genuinely excited by the prospect of conversing with my own people, even if they were combat men.

I held my book up high in my left hand—the Viracochan sign of peace.

"One stripe!" a guard yelled.

The man was standing in the tower, leaning on the rail. He must have been a foot taller than me. He had long blonde hair, sunken cheeks and a lean figure giving him a feminine edge. Although despite his effeminate qualities he was built like a mud hut, it was just his extreme height making him appear so slim. He wore a deerskin over his standard ragged Fects uniform opened at the chest. I saw the c-shaped scar burned into his skin.

A second guard who was on the road sitting against the drawbridge stood and faced me. He had a thick black beard covering half his face and the full length of his neck. Deep wrinkles encased his squinting eyes. He was dressed the same as the man in the tower and had the same scar burned into his chest flexing with muscle. A large knife sat in a leather holster dangling from his waist.

"You a storyteller?" the black bearded man said.

I smiled. "Yes, I am. How are you men?"

"We thought you were all dead," the tall man in the tower said.

Black Beard grinned and waded through the water toward me. The water went up to his chest. He exited the river and offered me an enormous hand which I took. It was like shaking a slab of meat. I smelled his meaty odor, like salted pig.

"Where have you been?" Black Beard said.

"The lake in the sky," I said, a touch boastfully.

"Titicaca?" the tall man in the tower said.

I nodded and looked up using my hand to shade Earth's Rock from my gaze.

"You've been there the whole time?" Black Beard said.

"Yes."

"How did you survive?" he said.

"The natives."

"You've been sheltering with them?" Black Beard said.

I nodded and looked back the way I had come. "Yes, I brought them with me."

"You have natives with you?" the tall man said.

I looked up. "Yes. Ready to build."

"The pyramid?" Black Beard said.

"Yes, devoted to the school."

"How many?" the tall man said.

"Around 200."

Black Beard grinned and looked briefly up to the man in the tower who grinned back. He looked back at me. "Friendly?"

I nodded.

He laughed. "The stonemasons are going to love you. They've been slaving it out there."

"There are stonemasons here?" I said.

Black Beard nodded.

"But they aren't supposed to arrive for many dægs," I said.

"They've been here for a season at least," the tall man said.

I was enraged. "What! How?"

Black Beard said, "They had to abandon Egypt. The Tæcans went to Göbekli Tepe and the stonemasons were split between Angkor Wat and Nazca."

"Was it just stonemasons sent here?" I said.

"What do you think?" the tall man said. He pushed himself from the rail and walked to the other side of the platform where he looked towards Nazca. He clearly didn't want to be privy to a conversation about the Uzmans.

I looked at Black Beard. "What types?"

The man looked conflicted. He knew he should never talk about Uzmans but he also knew he should never refuse the request of an Uzman.

I winked. "Just between you and I, I would be in a lot more trouble if they found out I had asked. You say nothing about our conversation, I say nothing about our conversation."

Black Beard lowered his voice. "Two dozen greens-keepers, two dozen stonemasons and a dozen plant guides."

I nodded gratefully. Greens keepers were one stripe and stonemasons were two stripe which meant the plant guides were likely three stripe. You almost always found the three stripes together.

I said, "Thank you. I will leave my men where they are for now and talk to the stonemasons first."

Black Beard nodded and turned.

The tall man pushed a button and a clunking sound started as the drawbridge moved down across the river. The wood creaked as the platform fell into place creating a footbridge over the water.

Black Beard stepped aside and nodded at the road.

I took a step then stopped. "There are no Tæcans?"

Black Beard looked to the ground, silent. The word *Tæcans* seemed to rattle him. He nodded again at the road to Nazca, keen to have me on my way.

"One last thing, have they been taking trips to the basin forest? The plant guides. Have they been bringing back vines?"

Black Beard kept his eyes to the ground but spoke firmly. "I need to ask you to leave, storyteller."

"It's my last question," I said. I knew he would have to have seen them. The road was the only one leading into camp when approaching from the basin. The men at the gates would see every cart coming and going.

Black Beard squared off with me, anchoring his feet wide in the dirt. He lay his meaty hand across the knife on his belt. "I need you to leave now."

I held my hands up mockingly. "No resistance here, I just need to speak to the stonemasons. I'm on an assignment issued by the Tæcans. Is there a problem I need to report to the Tæcans when they arrive?"

Black Beard pointed to the distant camp. "Then go!"

I nodded and walked on.

It didn't matter if he hadn't given me a verbal confirmation, I had gotten my answer, his eyes said it all. The plant guides had been busy in the basin.

61

THE CRATER. NORÐ AMERICA.

Jung clung to Orion who galloped toward the lip of the crater, where the earth fell away to an abyss of pink sky. He stood in the stirrups, his bum lifted clear from the creature's powerful oscillating body. The snow drifted into his eyes, the wind burned his skin, the saber-tooth fang thudded against his thigh.

Ahead he saw a shape on the ground right at the lip of the crater. It looked around the size of his bag. It had to be his bag.

He pulled the reins gently to slow Orion.

The horse obeyed, reducing speed. Air expelled from its pierced lips.

Jung pulled harder.

Orion slowed to a trot.

Jung unhooked his feet from the stirrups and jumped from the horse's back. Orion neighed, feeling the weight lift from his back.

The moment Jung's feet hit the ground everything changed. Just for a moment—a flash lasting less than a second—a glitch. He was back in the cubed chamber, this time in a different area. The room was larger. He saw the flat stone walls, the ceiling four men high and a box the size of a tomb. Everything hummed. It felt like he was deep underground where earthquakes were felt. Then the image distorted.

Jung was back in the snow on the mountain. He ran to the shadow in the snow. It was definitely his bag. He breathed a sigh of relief as he dropped his knees onto the burning ice. He picked up his bag and plunged his hand inside. He immediately felt his stone of power—the star. He pulled it free from his bag and held it with a smile. It was definitely the same as The Architect's—nothing from Earth was that dense. It was like an island compressed into a single stone. It stumped him how he hadn't noticed the weight until now. Of course he had noticed but he thought it was his imagination. He had felt a lot of things in The Healer's cave when she had given him the stone. She had read his fortune at the same time and in doing so Jung had assumed the intensity of the reading had added weight to the rock. He never questioned the weight beyond that.

Jung twisted the fang on his waist and placed the star into the cavity of the tooth. It fell inside easily, wedging in the chute. He took a strip of cloth he had cut from The Surgeon's hood and lay it across the cavity of the tooth before tying the material down with a hemp vine. Just as he did Earth began to shake.

He dropped to his stomach and lay face down preparing to ride out the earthquake when the light around him seemed to change.

He rolled over. The once pink dawn sky was a blood red. The color was getting more and more intense, then the sky began to thicken and swirl as layers between the layers started to bubble through, first reds then blues. The blobs of color twisted and fragmented, forming a kaleidoscopic mural of merging shapes. A scene that seemed to get more and more complex the harder he looked. Turning gears and whirling machines, spiraling from nothingness. Then a lattice of vibrating strings appeared all around him, a cubic grid in reds and blues with giant molecules hovering at the points of connection.

Jung was in a room made of shiny metals, materials he had never seen before. A clear screen surrounded him on all sides. There was a seat in the middle, a large chair that looked more like a throne. In front of the seat was a control pad. There was one button on the control pad, a dial that could be pushed up to move forward or down to move backward.

Outside the kaleidoscopic mural appeared to be arranging itself. It showed a dense bedrock of energy at the floor and sparse threads rising up. Bubbles fizzed from the bedrock. *Was it the collective unconscious?*

Then the strings in the lattice began to bend and change shape. A face began to form in the lattice, developing in complexity.

Jung blinked and rubbed his eyes. Was it his mother's face?

The face disappeared. Moments later he felt someone behind him. He was sitting up. When had he sat up? He didn't turn around. Instead he closed his eyes and remained as still as his shivering body could. She touched his shoulder. He could feel her warmth, her heaviness.

"I feel you," he said.

He felt directed to the seat in front. He sat and felt her spreading, wrapping around him. She was hugging him from all sides. Then he felt his whole body getting pulled, everything softened as he felt the seat and himself pass through the cosmic cloth, weightless.

He opened his eyes. Outside beyond the screen the sky was fractured. A face appeared in the augmented image. It was Hatun, his father.

"My son," Hatun said.

Jung melted to the sound, every muscle in his body relaxing. Tears flowed down his face. "Where have you been?"

Hatun smiled. "Been? Who do you think guided you here?"

"How?"

"Your gut."

Jung smiled remembering how hard his gut had pulled him every step of the way. He felt suddenly angry. "Why did you leave?"

Hatun looked injured by the question. He had tears in his eyes. "I didn't leave, son."

Jung was crying. "But you did."

"No, you are my legacy, Jung. I exist *in* you. And in your brothers and sisters. And in all of our tribe's people."

Jung sniffed and wiped his eyes. "I'm tired, father." His voice was choked.

Hatun had sad eyes. "I know you are."

"I want you to be back here. Like *really* here. I want us to be together properly."

"We *are* together."

Jung shook his head. "I'm tired of hearing that."

"I know."

"Can't you come back for real?"

"It's up to you now."

Jung looked confused. "How?"

"You have to stop grasping."

"*Grasping?* I've lost both of you now."

Hatun shook his head. His face split into two faces, appearing side by side in the sky, one was his father's and the other was his mother's. She was young and beautiful with a long thin face and big brown eyes. Both of them smiled at him.

"You've lost neither of us," she said.

"Mother!" Jung said, bursting into tears. He couldn't even remember her voice, it had been so long.

Her face was still—stoic—but a tear ran down her cheek. "You must hold us like water," she said.

"Like water?" Jung said.

She nodded. "Yes, like cupping your hands together and filling the crease with water. You can only hold the water by letting it be. The moment you try to hold the water too tight it will disappear through your fingers. Just let it be and be with it and it will remain with you."

"Do you understand?" Hatun said.

"I think so," Jung said.

Hatun smiled. "We are here with you always."

He turned and smiled at Jung's mother. She smiled back. Then their faces combined and formed a swirling cloud of white mist spreading across the sky.

Suddenly it began to rain.

Jung felt the drops of water on his face. He lay on the ground. He was no longer in the room nor the chair. He was back on the mountain. He looked up. Black clouds had closed in above him. It poured and poured until all the clouds had disappeared and the sky was clear again. Just a tinge of pink from the breaking light of Earth's Star remained.

In the light Jung realized he was sitting right on the edge of the crater. He had made it. An indescribable peace filled his body.

Then he saw it. Down in the crater there was a flash of light, then another. Two flashes, side by side. He felt his gut tug him toward the lights.

It would be the last time his gut would guide him any further from his land.

62

Eight dægs to stars return.

NAZCA. PERU.

I heard the stonemasons' stone tools slamming against rock before I saw them.

They were working beneath the ground at the base of the glowing jaguar. The feline sat powerfully, shoulders relaxed, head poised to the sky, watching nobly over the camp of Nazca. Next to the excavation hole was a pile of gray robes.

I looked into the three-men wide and five-men-deep hole. The chute was soaked in light from two fire torches staked into the walls.

Four men were at the bottom of the hole. Their tiny figures were covered in white dust glued to their skin by sweat. White skin coated with white powder. The men were digging in four different directions. The men wore only loincloths, just like the natives. One of them had tied a cloth around his forehead to stop the sweat getting in his eyes. I had seen the natives do the same many times.

The man with the cloth around his head stopped working and looked up.

He was a gaunt man with red cheeks. The hairs on his chest were beaded together from the sweat and dirt.

"Who are you?" Red Cheeks said. His voice was surprisingly deep for a man of wiry physique.

"I'm a storyteller from Ganung Padang. And you?"

Red Cheeks nodded and went back to work with his pick.

"You're early," I said.

All of the men stopped digging and looked at me.

Red Cheeks leaned on the long handle of his axe. "Yes, we stonemasons are always early, unlike you storytellers."

The other men laughed.

I smiled. "Do they give you the pick before or after they give you the second stripe?"

Red Cheeks frowned. "What do you want, one stripe?"

I nudged the robes with my foot. "Of course, although I barely recognize you men as two stripe, I know all Uzmans deserve a trade. So I'm here to trade."

"Trade?" he said.

"Yes."

He turned to his men and rolled his eyes.

The men laughed.

Red Cheeks looked back at me. "And what exactly do you want to trade?"

"I have 200 people. Two hundred people who can take those picks off you and your men."

The stonemasons all looked at one another.

Red Cheeks scowled at me. "What people?"

"Natives from Cuzco."

"Natives?"

I nodded. "What's your name?"

Red Cheeks scowled, the veins in his neck had flared up. "Never you mind, one stripe. You pull your head in!"

"Never I mind, yes. So, interested in a trade?"

Red Cheeks clenched his teeth. He knew the other stonemasons were all watching him and they all wanted a trade.

He looked at me. "Trade for what?"

"Do you have a star? A shard of star?"

"A star?"

"Yes."

He laughed.

The other stonemasons laughed too.

"Certainly not," he said. "And even if I did, I certainly wouldn't trade it for 200 Fects. Two thousand Fects maybe but not 200."

The other stonemasons nodded. They seemed to agree with this sentiment.

"Then knowledge," I said.

"Knowledge?" Red Cheeks said, concern in his voice.

"Yes, knowledge on the plant guides."

He turned to his men.

They looked away from his gaze.

He looked at me. "What's your question?"

"The plant guides. What is their mission?" I said.

"That's it?"

"Yes."

"They prepare the plant brew for the ceremonies."

"Mother Aya?"

Red Cheeks nodded.

"Do they drink?"

"They say only the Tæcans drink but who knows." He turned back to his men and raised his eyebrows as if to say he would drink in their position.

A couple of the men nodded.

"Where do they get the plants?" I said.

Red Cheeks frowned. "You said one question."

"This is the one question."

He scowled. "Then you bring your Fects?"

I nodded. "Yes, tell me where they get the plants from and you will have your workers. You'll never pick up another pick-axe again."

Red Cheeks looked nervous.

I said, "I swear to keep the knowledge to myself. I have nothing to gain from sharing what you tell me."

"They get the plants from the basin five dæġ's walk eðst of Cuzco," Red Cheeks said.

"And when will the first ceremony take place?" I said.

"Come on, man!"

"It's my last question. Then I go."

"You already told me that," Red Cheeks said.

"This time I mean it."

He said, "The second night after the Tæcans arrive."

63

THE CRATER. NORÐ AMERICA.

Jung was standing in the base of the crater, fifty men below the rim where he had left Orion. Ice filled the back of his loin-cloth from where he had slid down the steep scarp. He scooped out the ice and narrowed his eyes on the shadowy mound ahead.

All around him a fine mist of snow was being carried forth and scattered and carried forth again. The silence was breathless, he heard nothing but the thump of his heart in his chest and the hum of Earth.

He moved forward and lay an arrow across his bow.

As he approached the shadow morphed from black to brown and the rounded edges sharpened to a textured furry coat. It was definitely an animal of some kind, he thought. By far the biggest animal he had ever seen.

Even on its side the rounded body of the creature stood nearly as tall as a giant sloth. The animal was definitely dead. There was no sign of a beating chest, no movement in its breath, no sound. Although Jung predicted the animal had died recently, perhaps just before he had arrived, because there was no off-smell or sign of decay.

He slid the arrow back into his quiver and pulled his knife from his bag.

Coming closer he saw the animal had thick matted hair covered in a thin film of muddy clay. He touched the fur, it was stiff and oily and still warm. He smelt his fingers, a moldy oily smell. He parted the fur, there appeared to be two layers—an outer layer of long guard hairs and an undercoat of shorter more densely woven hairs.

Jung rounded the backside of the creature inspecting the animal's short stubby tail and large flat-hooved feet. He pushed his foot against the enormous calcified soles. The caps were tough, like hardened clay.

He moved around to the animal's head where he saw a long meaty trunk and two enormous curved white tusks, each the length of a man. The tusks flashed momentarily, reflecting the dawn light from Earth's Star.

Jung recognized it immediately, his mouth fell open.

He pulled his bow quickly from his shoulder and leaned it against one of the tusks.

He took a step back, his heart skipping a beat.

It was a perfect match, the plate detail on the grip of the bow was identical to the tusk.

Jung stepped forward and squatted. He rubbed his thumb first over the cool polished plate of the bow and then over the tusk. He smiled. *Yes, it was exactly the same.* He felt the surface of the fang hanging from his waist. It had the same smoothness and coolness but the look was different. The tusk, like the plate on the bow, had speckled grains of black throughout, similar to calcified wood, whereas the fang didn't have any of the same granular texture.

Jung laughed and sat back in the snow. His father had always said one dæġ he would take him to the creature from which the plate on the bow had come. Now, here he was standing in front of the very animal from which his father had earned his name Hatun Tujllaki, which meant 'Big Hunter'.

Suddenly Jung recognized the shape.

The curve of each tusk perfectly resembled a snail's shell, the golden ratio. He laughed and shook his head astonished to see the design in such a desolate place.

He studied the curve of the tusk. The design made complete sense. The tusks were enormous. For something to grow so large and heavy, balance was essential. Anything less would certainly result in the demise of a species.

He recalled what I had told him about the golden ratio. *It is a universal law of nature, a whisper from the voice of the cosmos itself.* He marveled at the creation, knowing full well after the flesh and bones had rotted away, all remains would be those two great tusks, two giant hints at the source of nature itself.

Jung woke. The mammoth's fur was warm against his skin. He had passed out again without realizing, it was becoming a dangerous routine occurrence.

He looked up, Earth's Star was high in the sky.

Suddenly he felt odd, like he was an intruder. His body buzzed with nerves.

He sat up and looked around at the vast expanse of snow. The distant lip of the crater surrounded him in all directions. He felt tiny, insignificant—a speck in a sea of white. His mind was suddenly flooded with messages of danger telling him to leave now. What was different? Then he realized the pulse in his gut was gone. It was the first time he had felt emptiness in his stomach since starting his journey. There was no drive in him, nothing pushing him to advance forward. In fact, it was the opposite, everything was screaming for him to stand and run to Orion.

He closed his eyes and took a deep breath through his nose. *Take control.* His head repeated the same messages over and over. *Leave now, quickly.* He focused on his breath, the voice in his head was getting quieter.

He stayed with his breath until the voice had disappeared altogether and calmness had returned to his body. *Homeostasis.*

He opened his eyes after some time. Now he felt the opposite, nothing pushed him to run. He felt anchored to the ground, at peace in the desolate scene. Suddenly the idea of returning home seemed far less attractive. He knew that except perhaps for his father none of the people in his tribe were likely to have felt what he was feeling right now. Sure, they may have experienced a sense of connection to all things when wandering alone in the forest or taking in a grand view but they would never feel exactly what he felt. Not with all the stories running through his head and all the knowledge he had acquired. Knowledge he would never share with them. He felt agitated. He knew his people would never fully comprehend the magnitude of his journey—traveling by foot, arc and horse. All the wise characters he had met along the way—The Blind Man, The Healer and The Architect. And all those who tried to deceive him—The Brewer, The Captain and The Surgeon. His people would never fully understand what he had undergone. Most in fact would call his journey a *fool's errand.* After all, he was tasked with one goal: kill a jaguar and bring back a tooth to prove it. It didn't matter he had killed six creatures twice the size of any jaguar, nor he had traveled a hundred times the distance of any man in his tribe, without the tooth of a jaguar he had failed. He wondered how he would ever be able to get on with his life after returning home. Would he be able to simply slip back into the routine of life in The Cloud Forest? It seemed a lifetime away.

He ripped the giant fang from his waist, breaking the reed band. He took off the covering and turned it upside down so the star fell out into his palm. He put the star in his bag and placed the fang next to the tusks of the mammoth. It was pointless carrying the tooth any further.

He closed his eyes and sniffed in the cool air.

After a moment he slowly opened his eyes, overwhelmed with serenity. He felt comfortable out here—isolated, unnoticed, undisturbed. A part of him wanted to remain exactly where he was, the only place on Earth that truly understood his triumphant journey, a place instilling him with a deep sense of achievement and pride.

Then a thought popped into his mind. It was a memory of the night his father and the other warriors had left to go to war. He and his father had been sitting in the cave beneath the waterfall. It was what his father had said about the people of the lake. *They want our eyes and ears. They want us to let them know if we see or hear anything strange in the mountains.* Jung remembered it sounding like an unusual request from the people of the lake at the time. Then he remembered being at Lake Titicaca, how the natives had captured him so aggressively. Why would they do that if they were pushing for truce? Unless the truce was already broken because of what Uma had said. But if the truce was really broken, they would never let him sit and eat with them. They would have killed him on the spot.

Jung remembered what The Blind Man had told him. *Beware of the Viracocha, they find the cracks in all men.*

Then Jung remembered being in the forest when Uma and Puma appeared carrying his father's body. He had asked them whether they had made it to the lake. Uma had said they hadn't but now he saw his uncle was lying.

"Kon-Tiki!" Jung said angry. He leapt to his feet and ran for Orion.

He would have revenge.

64

Five dægs to stars return.

NAZCA. PERU.

I sat with Uma and Wasi on the bank of the wide-berth river running through the center of Nazca. The smell of cookfires in the air. The sky was the clearest and bluest it had been since the disaster, it was almost ash-free.

We had our feet in the cold water listening to the trickle of the river obscured by distant clanging sounds from the natives' pickaxes.

Behind us was a smattering of animal-skin tents, wooden towers and chutes of smoke from cookfires. The camp was surrounded on three sides by mucky-gray escarpments, limestone stained with ash.

From the norð hillside, the giant stone jaguar sat tall watching us with concentrated eyes.

"The stars will return in one lunar cycle," I said.

"Do you think the tunnels will hold up to floods?" Uma said. He and Wasi were both looking at me, seeking a message of hope.

I nodded. "If there is one thing the stonemasons know, it's how to build. We will be safe in the aftermath, assuming a star

355

doesn't land right on top of us. My concern is not the stars themselves but what will happen in the aftermath."

"What?" Wasi said.

"Shortly after the next impacts the Tæcans will arrive here," I said.

"I thought you said the Tæcans were good people," Uma said.

"They are. The Tæcans from The School of Levitation in Ganung Padang are anyway. They are not my concern. It is the Tæcans coming from Egypt I am concerned about. Tæcans from The School of The Watcher."

Uma frowned. "You said the Tæcans from The School of The Watcher were to be feared."

I nodded. "I know."

"And they are coming here?" Wasi said.

"Yes, some of them."

"What will they do?" Uma said.

"I don't know exactly but I fear they will try to take control of the area. My concern is they will try to build a school of their own, or worse they will take the pyramid for themselves and start a School of The Watcher in replacement of a School of Levitation."

"Why wouldn't they just share the building?" Wasi said.

I smiled at her naiveté.

"I can kill them," Uma said.

My face turned serious. "How?"

"I can get some warriors together and we can kill them when they arrive."

"Although I appreciate the offer, it is impossible," I said.

Uma grinned. "Have you seen how many warriors have come from The Sacred Valley? We could overthrow them in a moment."

I said, "Yes, we have the numbers, but the Tæcans can't be killed. Not those who have reached the grid anyway and many of those from Egypt have made it through. It is one of the great privileges of becoming a Tæcan and making it to the grid—you become immortal."

"What does immortal mean?" Wasi said.

"You live forever. You can't be killed," I said.

"Sounds horrible," she said.

Uma said, "Surely not. Not if I filled them with a dozen arrows each."

I shook my head. "Not even with a hundred. You can take their body but they will find another form, the body of a roach or a snake or even an ant. And from there they will search for a larger host, perhaps one of your warriors, or worse you or I."

Wasi looked afraid. "They would take someone else's body?"

I said, "Yes, it's why it's much better to leave them in the body we know. We know those in black robes are not to be trusted. This is why we will never kill those in black robes, so we don't lose sight of the enemy."

"So what do we do?" Uma said.

"I know of only one way to kill them," I said.

65

OLYMPIA. NORÐ AMERICA.

Jung rode atop Orion for several dægs before the lights from the fire-torches on the arc came into sight.

Close to the beach where the rocks gave way to a foot of silt he spotted the upside down canoe, caked in ash. He jumped from Orion and draped his shawl over the horse's back before flipping the canoe over and pushing it into the water.

As Jung descended the stairs of the arc he remembered everything wrong with the Viracocha. He smelled the familiar malty aroma and heard the laughs and shouts from the men, not laughs and shouts of joy but aggression—they sounded combative, riled up.

The Captain was the first to spot Jung.

His cheeks were red and the muscles in his face were loose. Dark bags hung beneath his eyes. He seemed surprised to see the boy. "Jung! Ya back. Ha did ya go?" He slurred his words.

Jung approached slowly, mapping the room. He located each of the seafaring men and The Brewer who was standing near the trough of ale.

He pulled the star from his bag and held it up. "I have the star."

The Captain's eyes immediately lit up. He stood and tripped over his chair which banged against the ground. He scrambled around the table.

Jung took a step back. "No. For the girl."

"Huh?" The Captain said.

"The star in exchange for the native girl."

The Captain smiled. "Whuh? A shard av the star fa tha trip home."

In the corner of his eye, Jung saw The Brewer slowly making his way around the table. He too looked fatigued and out of sorts. He seemed to believe Jung hadn't noticed his movement.

"Ya kay?" The Captain said.

"I'm not coming home with you," Jung said. "Give me the girl and I'll give you the star. We're leaving now."

The Captain laughed. He turned to the seafaring men who were watching on. They didn't laugh back, they seemed unnerved by the confrontation.

Jung placed the star back into his bag and within a breath he had his bow and three arrows at the ready. He drew back one arrow and aimed it at The Captain.

The Captain threw his hands in the air. "Okuh, okay. Relax." He looked at The Brewer and winked. "Get the girl."

The Brewer nodded and winked back, a faint smirk on his face.

Jung was baffled how they thought they had gotten away with the signal, although he assumed it had something to do with the ale they were all drinking.

The Brewer moved across the hall toward The Captain's quarters. He crossed in front of The Captain and stopped. "The keys?"

The Captain put his hand in his robe, pretending to find something.

Just as The Captain was pulling his hand free, The Brewer picked up a chair and charged Jung.

The Captain clenched his teeth excitedly.

Jung sidestepped the charging man and kicked him in the ribs.

The Brewer went crashing to the ground. He went to stand.

Jung shot an arrow into his chest before loading a second and firing it into his stomach.

The Brewer gasped and clutched at the stick protruding from his chest as two pools of red blood stained his robe. He choked and spluttered and moaned, a hissing sound coming from one of the lacerations.

Jung added the last arrow to his bow and pulled three more arrows from his quiver. He pointed the weapon at The Captain. "Get the girl."

The Captain nodded with a look of terror in his eyes. He grunted noises at the seafaring men.

One of the men jogged across the hall to The Captain's quarters. He opened the door and disappeared inside. He appeared a moment later with Tika.

Her hands were tied behind her back. She had bruises on her arms and neck. She looked to the ground, afraid.

Seeing the girl, Jung's spine arched, his hackles high like a cat. "What's this!?"

The Captain held up his hands and smiled, a weak attempt to downplay the situation. "*This?* This is nothing, boy. She had a-."

The Captain's words were cut short by the arrow wedged in his neck. He collapsed to the floor and began to convulse, gurgling.

The seafaring man holding Tika immediately let her go and retreated to the corner of the hall where the other men were huddled.

The Captain was on his knees, moaning, struggling to breathe.

Jung approached the man. He pulled his knife from his bag and plunged it deep into the gasping man's groin. He would cut every band of energy he could in the man. He began to saw, using all his strength.

The Captain delivered a muted moan and shook uncontrollably as the knife ripped and tore through his flesh from his groin to his ribs. His organs spilled across the floor. The smell of blood filled the hall. The metallic scent was so thick he tasted it.

Reaching the base of the man's rib cage Jung tired and pulled the knife free. He looked around covered in blood.

Tika was cowering on one side of the hall and the seafaring men were cowering on the other.

Jung wiped the blade on the dead man's robe and tucked it into his waistband. He ran to Tika and cut the binds from her shaking hands. He hugged her, covering her in red.

She gripped him tightly, terrified.

"Let's go," he said.

She took his hand and they ran up the stairs and across the deck.

They jumped from the arc just as the stars arrived, filling the sky with fire.

66

0 dægs to stars return. 60 dægs to ceremony.

NAZCA. PERU.

I was sheltering in the Nazcan tunnels. The ground shook from the blasts, dirt peeled from the walls. I tasted dust in my mouth and smelled a tangy burning scent, like if produced from lightning striking water. There were bangs and murmured rumbles all around us.

The stonemasons had built five separate underground chambers—a space for each of the three classes of Uzman, plus the natives and the combat men. Each space was around ten men across and five men wide. Fire torches were fastened to the walls, soaking everything in orange.

I shared the space with a dozen greens-keepers, men and women who made gardens of the wild. Like me they wore white robes and had fair skin and were covered in muck.

"Uzmans don't become Tæcans, you fool," a voice said.

The woman who had spoken was thickly-built and had a scar on one cheek. She had been eavesdropping on a conversation between two men.

The men who had been talking fell silent.

"Says who?" I said.

Scar Face scowled. "I do."

I smiled. "And you're a great authority are you?"

She narrowed her eyes on me. "Well, who do you know that was an Uzman and is now a Tæcan?"

I couldn't actually think of anyone but I also barely knew any of the other Uzmans so how could I.

"Have you ever spoken to a three stripe?" Scar Face said.

"Of course not," I said, lying.

She shook her head. "Wake up, man. They are promised everything but they never cross the finish line. The path of the Tæcan is not the path we are on. The path of the Tæcan is for Tæcans. We are on the path of the Uzman."

"You're being crude," an old man's voice said.

Scar Face turned.

No one owned up to the voice. *Cowards.*

There was an enormous bang. We all jumped in sync.

Scar Face looked at me. "Why do you think they bind their heads?"

"To better communicate with the stars," I said.

She grinned. "Don't be a fool. It's to distinguish those on the path those who are not."

I felt a stabbing in my gut. I felt stupid, it was the first time I had considered such an idea.

Seeing the look of realization on my face, she twisted the knife. "You only get such a skull by having it binded from birth."

I nodded having already made the connection.

She grinned, "Sorry to break it to-"

I cut in. "Yes, there is lineage. It is one path. And we all know we're not on it. But there are other ways too, there are always other ways. Not for all of us, but for some of us. Not all Tæcans are bound, look a little closer and you'll see. The schools do take others, those of exceptional value." I winked. "Men like me. I was one of 50 storytellers tasked with the same mission and the only man to survive. It means I am 50 times your worth. It's Uzmans like me who break the mold."

"What's your line?" a man's voice said. He was a thin man with freckles and fire red hair.

I looked at him. "Nothing is guaranteed of course but being a storyteller I'll likely become a star watcher. Although there are many other routes. I believe I can build a role for myself."

"Alright, *star watcher.*," Scar Face said. She spat and combed the drool from her mouth with her bottom teeth. "Remember you're just a one stripe man like the rest of us."

"And what is your line?" I said.

She sniffed and spat, then stared at me in silence.

I looked at the red headed man. "What about you? What's your line?"

"Everything goes to plan and we'll be plant guides," he said proudly.

Scar Face scowled at him.

The man cowered realizing he had just given away the line of everyone in the cavern.

Scar Face looked at me. "Look, our mission is to keep you lot healthy and alive. I don't want to fight with you." She looked at the other men. "Us greens-keepers know our fate." She held her hand to her heart. "Uzmans for life."

All of the men and women nodded in agreement.

She said, "You play your little game of *I want to be a Tæcan.* Just stay healthy and stay alive, alright?"

I nodded. I also didn't want enemies, especially right now. I slunk to the ground and turned over to try and get some rest.

Scar Face said, "Anyway, it's not all bad being an Uzman. Better than being a Fect, or worse those poor natives you brought in. They are the ones who will suffer the most."

67

SOMEWHERE IN NORÐ AMERICA.

Jung stood in a burnt forest. All around him gnarly black stumps poked from the ash-stained snow. Earth's Star was gone again, driven back by the dust in the sky. There was no sign of life. The scene was so eerily quiet he heard Earth creak from within. He watched Tika.

The girl was squatting by a stream washing her face in the icy water. She wore a deer skin shawl, and had her feet wrapped in hare skins worn down to leather. The two black pads contrasted against the frail slush.

Jung walked over to the girl and placed a hand on her shoulder.

She shuttered to the touch and looked up in fear. Seeing Jung standing above her she calmed, although the fear was still there.

"Are you okay?" Jung said.

She nodded unconvincingly, moisture in the corners of her big green eyes.

"What did he do to you?"

She looked away. "Not what you think."

"Then what? Did he touch you?"

"He hit me, he beat me," she said. Her face fractured, tears ran from her eyes.

"Why?"

"Because of the map I gave you. I assume you still have it?"

Jung nodded. "It's a map?"

"Yes."

"Yes, I still have it."

She sighed in relief. "Good. When he saw I had taken it from one of his books he was enraged."

"Did he touch you another time?"

"No." Her voice became thin and shaky. "But he beat me badly."

Jung put his hand on her shoulder. "You're safe now." He squatted and hugged the girl tightly. He felt her cold cheek against his and smelled her familiar ripe scent. Butterflies fluttered in his chest. He sensed butterflies in her chest too. A spark of electricity running between them in an otherwise lifeless scene.

Tika pulled back. She tilted her head up and smiled. "Why did you come here boy from The Cloud Forest?"

He smiled. "To rescue you."

She laughed and pushed against his chest. "But seriously."

He looked lost in a memory, eyes glazed over. "To find my father."

"He came here?"

Jung laughed. "Well, actually yes." He nodded to the bow on his back. "The plate on my bow was cut from an animal living at the crash site."

"Wow, your father really came all the way out here?"

"I don't know, but he may well have. We don't have such animals anywhere near home."

She smiled then her face turned serious as she appeared to realize the boy was still traveling alone.

Jung saw her face turn. "He's dead. He died the night the first stars hit."

Tika frowned. "I'm sorry."

"It's okay. He's still with me. Death is not the end of life."

She grinned. "No, it's certainly not. So what exactly brought you all the way out here?"

"I was following an omen, an omen I saw the night he died."

"An omen. What kind of omen?" Tika said.

Jung paused realizing the star he called an omen had been witnessed by just about everyone on Earth, making it hardly an omen.

He shook his head. "I don't know to be honest. My gut led me here." He smiled. "But it was right, I found him."

Tika grinned. "Well, I'm glad. An omen led me here too." She went to stand.

Jung stood first and pulled her onto her feet. "What kind of omen was yours?"

"My omen came a long time ago. Five rotations ago," she said.

"What was it?"

"I was in the basin back home looking for a jaguar."

"What?"

"A jaguar," Tika repeated, confused.

Jung laughed. "I was also looking for a jaguar."

She rolled her eyes. "Sure you were."

"I was."

She shook her head, apparently not believing him. "Anyway, I saw a star cross the sky just before I was captured."

"Captured?"

"Yes, by the Viracocha. They had set a trap in the jungle. In fact, they had set many traps. They captured around 100 of us. Mainly people from the jungle tribes. For me it was just the wrong place at the wrong time."

"What did they do to you?" Jung said.

"They sent us to Ganung Padang by arc where we were separated and given over to the Uzmans. We were forced to teach them the languages and the customs of the Peru tribes." She craned her neck, ashamed.

Jung hugged her until he felt her body soften.

She looked up, adorable.

"You're going back to Kon-Tiki aren't you?" she said.

He raised his eyebrows playfully. "Well, it looks like I have to take care of what you created."

She grinned and pushed his chest. "But seriously, you want to kill him don't you?"

"How did you know?"

"You can see it on your face."

Jung looked away.

She said, "I don't blame you. Anyone who spends enough time with the Viracocha knows how dangerous they can be. Especially the storytellers, they are the worst. They are merchants of doubt, it is their lies weakening the natives' bonds that allow the Viracocha to spread their roots. They are the head of the snake."

Jung winked. "And we still have time to cut the head off."

Tika rested her cheek against Jung's chest seemingly enticed by his fearlessness. After some time she drew back and looked at him. "Did he hurt someone close to you?"

"Kon-Tiki?"

She nodded.

"Yes, my father."

"I'm sorry."

Jung hugged her, tighter.

"At least we have the map of Nazca," she said.

"It's a map of Nazca?" Jung said.

She smiled. "Yes, it's a map of the camp and the school they are building, it's our ticket in."

68

10 dægs to ceremony.

NAZCA. PERU.

I was in my tent with Uma. I sat at the desk on one side of the room and Uma sat on the edge of the bed at the other. There was a cookfire between us. Above the fire was a round spirit door embedded into the roof, it was open to the stars letting the smoke through.

I rubbed my palms together. "Okay, this is the plan. On the night of the ceremony you will gather together five warriors. Plus yourself makes six."

Uma nodded.

"You will wait in the shadows near the classroom during the ceremony. The camp will be completely silent and pitch black so keep this in mind."

"Got it," Uma said.

"When the ayahuasca has taken effect on the Tæcans you will see a dark cloud rise from the spirit door of the ceremony tent."

Uma nodded.

"The black cloud will enter the sky and begin to pour down. You and the other warriors must get inside of it."

"How?"

"It will come to you, it will meet your gaze. You don't have to do anything except let it touch you. The moment you do you will see orbs of red and blue light in grid-like patterns. When you see the orbs of light, you will know you can see the Tæcans in any form they take."

"What do you mean?" Uma said.

"Remember I said you can't kill the Tæcans because the moment their body is taken, they will take the body of another?"

"Yes."

"Well, when you see the orbs of blue and red lights arranged in a grid you'll know you can see the energy of the Tæcans no matter what form they take."

"So if they leave their body I'll still see them?" Uma said.

"Yes, you'll see the energy leave the body and you'll be able to track it."

"But how do we actually kill them?"

I pulled a wooden key out of the chest pocket of my robe and inserted it into a hole in the side of the desk. I turned the key. A lid opened on the top of the desk revealing a hole around as big as my fist. I placed my fingers inside and pulled out the crystal.

I returned to Uma and handed him the sparkling rock.

His mouth was open as he studied the object looking to contain all the light on Earth.

I said, "Use this when you see the grid of blue and red orbs. Take the crystal and place it on the intersection of where a blue beam intercepts a red beam. The crystal will disperse the light revealing the layers of the grid. All you have to do is aim the light at the Tæcans. The moment the light is on them your warriors should fill them with arrows. This will kill them for good."

"Are you sure?" Uma said.

"Yes, it's a powerful stone. But you must be patient on the night. You must wait until the stones have entered the sky before you strike. We must make sure the ceremony is in full swing."

Uma looked at me. "The bricks of the pyramid?"

"Yes, only then will the energy be strong enough to kill them. If you try to kill them too early all you will do is attract the eye of The Watcher and they will kill you. Do you understand?"

Uma nodded.

There was a scratching sound at the door.

"Uma," a voice said.

I ripped the crystal from Uma's hand and placed it in my chest pocket just as Puma entered.

I frowned. "Puma! What have I told you about barging in here? Never just walk in. Wait until you are invited."

Puma looked to the ground. "I need to speak to Uma."

"We can talk outside," Uma said heading for the door.

Puma looked at me, I saw the tension in his body.

Then they were both gone.

I knew he had found the bodies of the jungle people.

69

NAZCA. PERU.

Jung squatted next to Tika. They were on the ridge perched directly above the stone jaguar in Nazca.

He heard the faint chatter of foreign voices and smelled the drifting smoke from their cookfires. Below, the camp of Nazca was sprawled across the valley, split in two by the river running through the center. There were hundreds of tents and a scattering of guard-towers and cookfires dispersed across the land. Chutes of smoke connected the camp to the ash-covered sky. The area was busy with activity, the tiny people scurried across the earth like ants.

Tika pointed to a cluster of tents arranged by color—whites with whites, grays with grays and blues with blues.

She said, "They're the Uzman's tents. Kon-Tiki's tent will be among them. It will be one of the white ones. If I remember correctly his number is #528. It means his tent should be on the far side. Their numbers should all be marked just above the door."

Jung nodded.

Tika pointed to another group of tents, black and isolated on their own. "And those are the Tæcan's tents."

"What is that?" Jung said, pointing to a small sunken amphitheater next to the Tæcan's tents where rows of tiered seats had been cut from the ridge. At the center of the amphitheater was a t-shaped stone identical to the one on the arc.

"It's the classroom," Tika said. "It is where the Tæcans share their knowledge."

"With whom?"

Tika looked at Jung. "Themselves mainly. There is always one master Tæcan at the school. It is their obelisk displayed in the classroom."

"Obelisk?"

"The t-shaped statue. It contains symbols marking the most important points they teach. Well, at least the code to their teaching points anyway. Some say the icons mean nothing. That they are a code designed to hide the real talking points."

Jung looked confused. "Why was there one on the arc if there were no Tæcans on the arc?"

"Because they always knew who the master Tæcan was going to be at Nazca. They sent the obelisk ahead."

"Isn't that dangerous if they lose it?" Jung said.

Tika smiled. "They're just bits of stone. The stonemasons can make a new one very easily. Each arc carries a copy of the relevant master Tæcan's lessons. It's a mark in a sense, a mark to represent who the arc and the Fects ultimately serve. But if it is lost it can be replaced."

"What does that one represent?" Jung said.

"It teaches about levitation."

"Really? How?"

Tika shook her head. "I have no idea. Only the Tæcans know what the symbols mean. And like I said they are deliberately difficult to interpret and often code for something else."

"The Surgeon said there are dozens of classrooms at Göbekli Tepe, all with different obelisks to teach different things," Jung said.

"Göbekli Tepe is different," Tika said. "The schools at Nazca, Egypt and Angkor Wat teach specific branches of knowledge. While Göbekli Tepe is not a single school but rather a mecca site to document all knowledge from all of the Viracochan schools. There is a copy of every Viracochan obelisk on Earth at Göbekli Tepe. It is where the Viracocha will keep the flame of knowledge alive for the duration of the freeze. It will also exist as a record of all the Viracochan sites at the time of Zep Tepi."

"Like a reference center?" Jung said.

Tika nodded. "Yes, it will be an archive. They will bury it when Earth has settled and the building of Egypt begins."

Tika looked down at the map of Nazca spread across the ground.

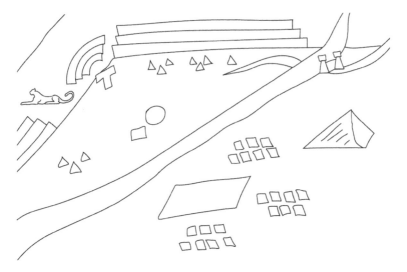

Jung pointed to the map. "What is that?"

Tika looked up and pointed to the tiers of empty terraced gardens cut from the ridge backing the camp. "Those are where they will grow plants. Although I think they're going to struggle in this cold."

Jung pointed to a distant scar in the earth on the far side of camp. It was well over 100 men long and 50 men wide. "What about there?"

Tika looked briefly at the map. "It's the quarry." She traced her finger along a faint line on the earth. "Here is the causeway running from the quarry to the construction site. See the square outline? It is the footprint of the pyramid to come."

Jung nodded. He saw tiny black specks moving up and down the white walls on the distant quarry. Was it his imagination or did he hear their heaves and their instruments, scratching away at Earth's belly.

"The only thing I don't recognize is all the blocks," Tika said. She studied the map then looked at the river running through the middle of camp. There were hundreds of stone blocks stacked on both banks.

"They are the stones for the pyramid," Jung said. "They will move them all on the night of the ceremony."

"Really?"

Jung nodded. "The entire pyramid will be built in a single night."

Tika pointed to the center of camp. "Speaking of the ceremony. See there, the black tent, the biggest in the middle? It's the ceremony tent."

Jung sat up on his knees and saw the tent five times the size of the others.

"See next to it?" Tika said. "The wood building is the plant shed. It's where they will prepare the brew for the ceremony." She looked at Jung. "You'll have to be careful, there are guard towers surrounding it on all sides, it is the most prized building in camp. All of the combat men's eyes will be fixed on protecting it."

Jung nodded. "I'll go in the middle of the night."

"What's that!" Tika said suddenly.

She pointed to the white tents. "Is it Kon-Tiki?"

Jung's mouth fell open.

"Who is he talking to?" Tika said.

"I know the man he's with," Jung said.

"Who is he?"

"He's my uncle."

70

Jung was in camp among the Uzmans' tents. He twisted his bag around on his back and looked up the ridge he had just come down. He knew Tika would be watching from the blackness. He quickly checked his bag, the only thing he was missing was his bow and arrows. He hoped he had made the right decision choosing not to bring them.

Suddenly there was a whispering voice.

Jung shuddered. He was so close to the man, there was only an animal skin between them. He sped off through the rows of tents.

When he reached the edge of the tents he paused and ducked. He looked at his target—the ceremony tent. The enormous structure was surrounded by four guard towers lined with fire torches, moating the tent with light.

Jung studied the nearest tower.

He smelled tobacco smoke before he spied the two combat men leaning on the rail looking out toward the quarry. One was smoking.

Jung took his chance and ran across the clearing. Just as he reached the ceremony tent he heard a man grunt from behind. He ducked into the shadows and turned.

A man in a blue robe was waving his fist and yelling.

Jung covered his face with his hands and ran towards the river in the direction of the native's camp.

The three stripe Uzman never bothered to give chase.

When Jung was a decent distance away he hid in the shadows and watched as two combat men stood on either side of the Uzman.

The man was pointing towards him. Neither of the combat men nor the Uzman appeared too interested in pursuing him. They all seemed to agree the scare was enough to teach him a lesson.

The moment the three men had turned their backs, Jung sprinted back to the building and skirted its edge until he reached the plant shed.

He slowly opened the door and peeked inside. He breathed a sigh of relief seeing the room vacant. He moved through the door and let it close gently behind him.

Inside the walls were covered in deep shelves running from the floor to the ceiling on three sides. The shelves were stacked with hundreds of clear resin jars containing samples of plants from the basin forests. Jung recognized virtually all of them, including the poisonous ones. On the far side of the room there was a wooden desk covered in stacks of books. In the center of the room a small fire crackled. Sitting above the flames of the fire was a large hollowed-out rock filled with liquid frothing and spatting.

Jung approached slowly and stared into the gurgling liquid with a pungent, tangy smell. He saw the torn chacruna leaves and the mashed ayahuasca vines boiling away.

He had been in the plant shed looking through the jars for some time when he heard a man grunting outside.

The man sounded to be conversing with another man who grunted back every now and again. They sounded to be approaching the shed.

Jung quickly moved some jars aside and climbed into one of the deep shelves before rearranging the jars back around him so he was hidden.

The door squeaked open and two men in blue robes entered the room. They both had their hoods up. They grunted noises back and forth. One man went to the desk and began to shuffle through some loose pages. The other went to the fire and picked up a wooden spoon, which he used to stir the boiling liquid.

The door squeaked again and another man entered the room dressed the same. He too grunted and the others grunted back. He went to the fire and sat opposite the man stirring the liquid.

The first man at the desk looked up and grunted something loudly.

The last man to enter nodded and grunted back.

There were more grunts from each of them then the last man to enter stood and went over to one of the shelves. He began moving jars away looking for something.

The man at the desk grunted louder and shook his head. He pointed to the opposite side of the room, right where Jung was hiding.

Jung crawled back into the shelf as far as he could and curled into a ball.

The man sorting through the jars moved over to the shelf where Jung was hiding and began to move jars away.

Jung clenched his teeth and squeezed his fists as he watched the man moving more and more jars from in front of him until there was only a single row between them. He arched his body and pulled his knife from his bag. He didn't want to use it. If he did the plans would be spoiled but he didn't know what else to do.

The man was about to move the final jar away when the most beautiful sound Jung had ever heard started up outside. First the sound of a wind instrument raised every hair on his body, then drums and a chorus of stringed instruments, each layering on top of the next.

Jung's chest exploded with butterflies. It was music, music the way he had never heard before.

The Uzmans stopped what they were doing and ran for the door.

71

Two dægs to ceremony.

I was standing on the shore of the river with the other Uz-mans. The sound of flutes, drums and stringed instruments boomed across camp. The musicians had arrived on the first boats and set up on shore to welcome the Tæcans. The music made my heart full and my cheeks tight, I imagined tapping my foot freely to the beat.

We stood in Uzman formation—beside me were the white robes, in front were the gray robes, and in front of them were the blue robes. We had our feet planted wide, our hands clasped behind our backs and our masks on.

Far away the silhouettes of four rowboats appeared on the black water. The vessels looked to be crowded with a dozen men each. There was one black robe for every four combat men. The Tæcans had their hoods up and their masks on. Their skulls were tall and elongated. The Tæcan in the front boat, who I assumed was the master Tæcan, wore a jaguar's head as a mask. The mask was such a perfect restoration of the cat's head, it made the Tæcan appear like a jaguar in clothes.

The boats pulled up to the bank and the combat men jumped out and waded through the water with ropes which they tied to the stone blocks littering the shore. The men first helped the master Tæcan from the boat, then they helped the others.

The Tæcans climbed from the boats slowly and awkwardly. They were clearly old and frail based on their movements. They appeared to be an equal split of males and females based on the size and shape of their bodies. There were 12 Tæcans all up including the master Tæcan.

The combat men marched over to us and surrounded us on four sides.

The head combat man said, "You will keep still and quiet as the Tæcans pass. Understand?"

We all nodded in sync.

Three condors had appeared overhead in the sky. They seemed curious of the strange activity happening in the desert below. They also seemed wise enough to know to keep their distance. They were so high up, they were barely specks.

Suddenly more wind instruments appeared on top of the other sounds, deep notes overlayed with oscillating highs.

I felt my heart rise higher like I was floating.

Headed by the master Tæcan, the Tæcans marched in step to the music. They moved in single file like a serpent with the head of a cat. They moved around the plant guides, heading for the black tents in the distance.

Suddenly the master Tæcan stopped.

All of the Tæcans stopped in line.

The master Tæcan looked at me. The jaguar's dead eyes staring right through me. "You are the storyteller, Kon-Tiki?" He sounded around 50 rotations in age.

I nodded keeping my head forward, my eyes twisted in his direction beneath the mask.

The master Tæcan said, "The only man to make it to the lake in the sky and the man who brought us 216 natives?"

I nodded again.

"Path of the Tæcan," he said, nodding.

"Path of the Tæcan," I said, nodding back.

"Shut your mouth!" the head combat man said.

The master Tæcan led the others away.

I didn't think my heart could get any lighter but it had, my whole body was singing.

72

One dæġ to ceremony.

A rattle came from my door.

It was two Tæcans—a male and female—accompanied by two combat men who lurked in the darkness behind. The Tæcans wore their masks and bowed the moment I brushed the animal-skin flaps aside.

The female Tæcan had a gray robe draped over her arm. She wasn't trying to hide it the slightest, it was clearly a bargaining tool.

"Can we come in?" she said.

The male Tæcan was rolling something in his fist. When he saw me looking at it he held it up. It was a star. Well, at least, it looked like a star anyway. He rolled it rhythmically between his fingers.

I nodded and moved aside.

Both Tæcans, each armed with their respective treasures, came inside.

I poured us coca tea and we sat by the fire.

"You've done very well," the male Tæcan said. His voice was mature, measured.

"Very well," the female Tæcan said.

The male Tæcan said, "Of all 48 storytellers sent to shore you are the only one alive and the only one to find the lake in the sky."

"You proved the myth told by the natives is true," the woman said. "And you convinced the natives to help build the school. Immense achievements."

The male Tæcan nodded. "You're on track for great things, I see a Tæcan in you."

The woman nodded.

There were distant shouts, they sounded to belong to the natives.

I took a sip from my tea, my cheeks numb from the brew.

"You're walking the path of the Tæcan better than any storyteller I know," she said.

"Thank you," I said.

The man nodded at the woman. "I think we all know why we are here." He put his hand inside his robe and pulled out the book.

I felt a jolt of excitement.

He placed the book in his lap and leaned over it. "We need something from you first though. One more thing. Are you capable?"

"Of course," I said.

He said, "There will be a ceremony tomorrow at midnight. When Earth's Rock is two lengths from midnight we need absolute silence and absolute darkness in camp. Not a whisper of noise nor a spark of light. Can you manage your people? Can you make the natives obey?"

There were distant shouts from the natives.

I felt my body arch tensely to the sounds.

"I think so," I said.

"You what?" the woman said.

"I can do so."

"Good," the male Tæcan said as he stood.

The female Tæcan stood too.

He passed me the book and she passed me the robe.

I was beaming as I took the objects. The title of the book gleamed at me—Book 2 of the Tæcan: The Stars.

"Oh, and the hook," the male Tæcan said.

I felt my heart skip a beat then pound twice as fast.

"He needs to disappear," he said.

I shook my head. "If he goes they will turn, they still follow him."

Both Tæcans stared at me.

I felt shivers roll down my spine.

The woman said, "You know how it goes, Kon-Tiki. The hook must always be cut free prior to the build. He has played his role. Now, he is a danger to the mission."

I swallowed the knot in my throat. "I understand."

"He needs to disappear before the first ceremony," the male Tæcan said. "No discussion."

I nodded squeezing the book in one hand and the robe in the other.

Both Tæcans nodded.

"Path of the Tæcan," the woman said, nodding.

"Path of the Tæcan," the man said, nodding.

I nodded in return. "Path of the Tæcan."

I left them to let themselves out, my head was spinning with contradictions.

73

It was past nightfall. The Tæcans' and Uzmans' tents were soaked in orange from the flames on the guard-towers. On the other side of the river, the natives' camp was black aside from a scattering of cookfires.

The pace of camp had changed a lot since the Tæcans had arrived. The combat men who accompanied them appeared to take their jobs far more seriously than the combat men who had arrived with the Uzmans. They had stationed themselves by the Tæcans area and marched the perimeter with intention.

"There he is again," Tika said.

The girl was on her tummy next to Jung. They were both looking over the scarp down at the camp of Nazca.

"It's definitely him," Jung said.

"Your uncle?"

"Yeah."

"What's he doing?"

Jung shook his head. "I have no idea but I'm going to find out." He slithered back from the edge and stood.

"You're going to go around?" Tika said.

"Yeah, I'll enter near the gates and cut him off at the river."

"Be careful."

He squatted and kissed her on the forehead before tearing off down the back of the ridge.

Jung walked along the shore of the river, weaving between the stone blocks one man in length and standing half-a-man high. He found a place close to the footbridge in the shadows and waited.

It wasn't long before Uma made his way across the footbridge.

"Uncle," Jung said.

Uma stopped on the last rung and peered into the darkness.

"It's me," Jung said. He wriggled across the sand into the starlight.

"Jung!" Uma said.

"Shhhhhhh!"

Uma ran to the boy and knelt down and hugged him. They hugged for three heartbeats before breaking apart. Uma had tears in his eyes. "Where have you been? I thought you were dead."

"What are you doing with them?" Jung said. He had a serious look on his face.

"Who?"

"The Viracocha. Kon-Tiki."

Uma sounded shocked. "You know Kon-Tiki?"

"What were you doing at his tent?"

Uma fished his hand into his loincloth and pulled out two coca leaves which he put in his mouth. "We're building a pyramid."

"I know."

Uma smiled. "It will take us to the stars."

"But why were you with him?"

"We're working together."

"Together?" Jung said.

Uma nodded. "I got all the natives here." He smiled. "You should have seen how hard it was, Jung. They wouldn't come at first but I got them to agree eventually."

"What do you mean?"

"To get all the natives out here helping."

Jung frowned. "You convinced our people to help?"

The smile was gone from Uma's face. "I've done nothing wrong."

"Nothing wrong!"

"Everything has been for the good of the tribe."

Jung pointed to the quarry in the distance. "*That* quarry is for the good of the tribe?"

Uma looked ashamed. "This is temporary work. When it is over and the pyramid is built we will rest in peace."

"You're a traitor."

"A traitor? How?"

"They've killed our people, Uma."

Uma looked at the ground, most likely recalling what Puma had told him about the mass graves in the jungle. He looked up. "It wasn't him."

"Who?"

"Kon-Tiki. He didn't kill them. He too hates them for what they have done."

Jung looked confused. "What are you on about?"

"He wants to get revenge on them. He wants to kill them all."

"Revenge on who?"

"All of the Viracocha. The Tæcans, the Uzmans, all of them."

"For what?" Jung said.

"For killing the jungle people and for killing his family."

"Killing his family?"

Uma nodded. "It's how they got him into the school in the first place. They killed his children."

"He's lying to you. He doesn't even have children."

"Not anymore, but he did."

"How do you know?" Jung said.

Uma sucked at the leaves, silent.

"You don't. That's the point. He has told so many lies, he's probably lying about that too."

Uma looked at Jung. "We have a plan."

"Who?"

"Kon-Tiki and me and Wasi."

"Wasi! You got Wasi involved?"

"You have to trust me, Jung."

"Trust you?"

Uma nodded.

"You're a liar, how can I trust you?"

Uma looked stunned. "What do you mean?"

"The last time we spoke, you said you and father never made it to Lake Titicaca but you did, didn't you?"

Uma looked at the ground ashamed.

"He sat with him didn't he? Father sat with Kon-Tiki?"

Uma said, "Kon-Tiki is a good man, Jung. He's on our side. We have a plan with him. We're going to kill the Tæcans. We have it all figured out. We're going to turn on them during the ceremony tomorrow night. We're going to kill all of the Tæcans, then we will kill the Uzmans and combat men too. We're going to kill all of the Viracocha except Kon-Tiki. Then we can have the pyramid for ourselves."

"You're a fool," Jung said.

"What?"

"He's lying to you! Don't you see, he's getting you to play along right up to the moment he doesn't need you."

Uma shook his head. "He's not. We have it all figured out. I have a team of warriors. When the ceremony takes place we will enter the black cloud coming from the ceremony tent. We will enter their world and kill them-"

Jung's mouth fell open as he recalled the final words The Architect had told him, *The dark cloud, don't let it touch you.*

"Don't you get it?" Jung said. "The moment you enter the cloud your consciousness will be hijacked and you'll lose control of your mind. He's leading you right into a trap."

Uma shook his head. "No, he's on our team."

"He's signing you up right until the moment he no longer needs you. Then it is us natives who will be killed."

Uma looked nervous. "Don't be stupid."

"He killed Hatun, Uma! He'll do it again."

"What do you mean?" Uma said.

"That friend of yours—Kon-Tiki."

"It doesn't make any sense."

Jung had tears in his eyes. "He sat with him, uncle. He sat with him and he tried to convince him to join forces for the building of the pyramid, just the same way he sat with you and with me. He told him the same lies about The Artery of Earth and the pyramids, except unlike you and I who fell for it, father saw through him and refused. So Kon-Tiki poisoned him."

Uma's legs were trembling.

"He gave him something to drink, didn't he?" Jung said.

Uma looked lost in thought—remembering—re-framing the events of the past. Then his face shattered into a wrinkled mess, he buried his face in his hands and sobbed as quietly as he could manage.

"He poisoned him, uncle."

Uma nodded his face in his hands.

"I'm getting rid of him."

Uma looked up. "What?"

"I have it all figured out. Just don't go out on the night of the ceremony and stay away from the cloud. Do you understand?"

"Let me help."

Jung shook his head. "No."

"Please," Uma said.

"No! You've done enough damage. Just stay on this side of the river tomorrow."

Uma looked to the ground with shame.

Jung squeezed his shoulder. "I'm sorry. It's not your fault. You can't blame yourself. The Viracocha are masters of lies. Just please let me finish this alone."

Uma looked up. "I understand." He shook his head. "I just can't believe the plants would be so evil. The jungle people kept that quiet."

"They're not evil, uncle. The dark cloud is not Mother Aya or the other plants. They are not the creators of the energies, they simply act as guides to take us in. Once you're in, all sorts of energies can be drawn in, including dark energy. It's why the jungle people went to such lengths to curate the right setting for their ceremonies—because the setting is just as important as the brew. Without the right setting, without cleansing the ceremony space, dark energies can leak through, or if willed, pour through. It is why the jungle people chose to live with the anacondas, the spirit yacumama protects them. The plants will not bring the darkness—the Viracocha will. They are deliberately conjuring in dark energy, that's why we have to stop them. We have to keep the darkness from seeping into our land."

"How?"

"Like I said, I have a plan. Please just promise me to stay on this side of the river."

"I can help you," Uma said.

"No, uncle. Not this time. Hatun is dead and many more will die too if you ignore me. Do what I say, just this once."

Uma nodded. "Okay. I promise."

Jung fled back towards the ridge.

74

One dæġ to ceremony.

I spun on my feet, my robe twirled in the morning light streaming through the spirit door of my tent. I smelt the fabric near the hood, fresh animal oil.

"What do you think?" I said.

"It looks the same as the other one," Wasi said. She was sitting on the edge of the bed.

I smiled. "But gray."

"So you're two stripe now?"

I nodded, admiring the cleanness of the material.

"What exactly does it mean?" Wasi said.

I picked at the stripes on one of the shoulders. "It means I have access to the book of the stars. It means I have access to twice the knowledge I had before."

Wasi nodded at the book on the desk. "Do you think you need to read more before you send Uma on his mission?"

"What do you mean?"

"Do you really think he'll be safe tonight?"

"Of course," I said.

"How can you be so sure, you're barely two stripe. The Tæcans must know things you don't."

I frowned. "You think what I know about killing them came from a book?"

"I assumed so."

"No, I didn't learn it from any book they gave me."

"So where did you learn it?"

I winked. "A good magician never reveals his tricks, Wasi."

"Magician?"

I nodded.

"It's what you called the Tæcans—magicians."

"Yes, they too are magicians. Something we have in common."

"So you seek power?" Wasi said.

"What?"

"You said there are 12 archetypes a person can fall into and the magician is one of them."

"Correct."

"So you seek power? You said each archetype seeks one thing above all else. The magician seeks power. What power do you seek?"

I went to the desk and picked up the book of knowledge from beneath a stack of papyrus. I thumbed through the pages until I found what I was looking for. I put my finger inside and closed the book then sat on the bed next to her.

I said, "Todæġ I seek to control the Viracocha, Wasi. Tomorrow who knows. Although when you see them fall, you will be glad of the power I have acquired. Remember, if they are successful they will poison your land, the dark energy they bring will get into everything and will never leave."

Wasi looked afraid.

I opened the book. "I have the power to overthrow them though. *We* have the power to overthrow them."

The page showed the archetype wheel.

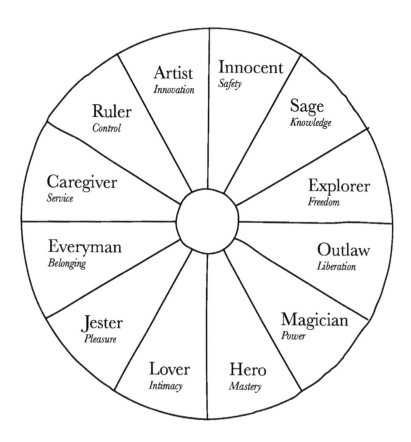

I pointed to the *hero* quadrad at the bottom of the page. "Remember I said Uma is the hero of this story?"

Wasi nodded. "Yes, the seeker of mastery."

I smiled and pointed to the section next to the *hero*. "See how the hero and the magician are side by side."

Wasi nodded as she studied the page.

"Uma—the hero—is the one who gives me my power as a magician. It is his power that will ultimately overthrow the Tæcans."

Wasi pointed to the opposite side of the wheel. "So the artist is the opposite to the hero?"

I nodded.

She grinned with glassy eyes. "Hatun and Uma always were opposites."

I smiled. "And continue to be."

She sniffed and nodded. "What is he mastering?"

"Who?"

"Uma. If he is the hero he must be mastering something."

For the first time since I could remember, I was blank. Usually the lies came easily but this time all I had was the truth flashing in my head. So I told the truth knowing I could spin it in my favor.

I said, "Well, actually, I lied to you, Wasi. Uma is not the hero."

She frowned. "What?"

I pointed to a section of the archetype wheel on the other side of the magician. "He is the outlaw, a seeker of liberation. But look, the outlaw too is sided by the magician. The outlaw gives me equal power to the hero."

"So who is the hero?" Wasi said.

It was of course Jung, her grandson, but I couldn't tell her. Instead, I distracted her.

I said, "All is to be revealed on the night of the ceremony."

"What do you mean?" Wasi said.

I grinned. "On the night of the ceremony the hero will reveal themselves."

"So you know who the hero is?" Wasi said.

"Of course."

"Who?"

"Unfortunately I can't tell you. It would spoil the plan," I said.

"How?"

"Wasi, I'm sorry but like I said, a good magician never shares his tricks. You just have to trust me."

"Trust you?"

I closed the book and stood. "Let me prove my worth. Let me prove my magician status by performing a magic trick."

"A trick?"

"Yes, a trick so grand it will prove to you I have the power to unearth a genuine hero and overthrow the Tæcans."

Wasi grinned. "Okay."

I put the book on the desk. "You have to close your eyes."

She closed her eyes.

"Keep them closed until I tell you."

"I am."

I went to the other side of the room and squatted and pulled up a wooden floorboard. I put my hand inside and pulled a lever. A manhole half a man wide opened in the middle of the floor revealing a stairwell.

"Keep them shut," I said.

Wasi nodded, grinning.

I climbed down the ladder into pitch-black icy darkness. I felt around in the dark for the sack. It kicked when my hand brushed across it. I hauled the bag up the ladder and closed the manhole using the same lever. Then I put the floorboard panel back down and stood. I emptied the sack in front of her. "Okay, open them."

Wasi opened her eyes just as Misi and Potoo fell onto the floor.

75

Ceremony dæġ.

Jung was standing in the ceremony tent smelling of stale tobacco. At its peak, the tent was five men tall. Two large wooden
uprights stood in the center holding up the circular spirit door
left open to the stars. The light from Earth's Rock soaked everything in a blue glow.

He moved around the room. On the floor directly beneath
the spirit door was a stone around one man in length and half-a-
man in width. Carved into the sides of the block were cats of all
different species. He recognized many of them: the jaguar, puma,
jaguarundi, ocelot and scimitar. He wondered if The Architect's
lion was among them. At the front of the tent he saw three seats
made from llama-skin pelts arranged on reed cushions. Next to
each seat was a set of wooden instruments—a smoking pipe, a
bowl filled with loose-leaf tobacco and a bucket. There were also
two bound tinder fungus' next to each of the outer seats.

On the other side of the stone were another nine seats all set
up with the same arrangement.

Jung pulled out his knife and headed to the far side of the
tent. He made a small incision in the interior wall. He climbed
through the slit.

It wasn't long after he heard someone coming. He watched through the tear as a blue robed man entered the space holding a fire torch.

The man had his hood up and was wearing a mask. He swung the torch from seat to seat, checking each station had everything it needed. Then he disappeared.

He returned shortly after with a large bladder of liquid—Mother Aya—which he placed on the ground in front of the three front seats. Then he left again.

Shortly after nine Tæcans entered the tent. They were a mixture of males and females with their hoods up and masks on. They moved in single file, their tall heads casting grotesque shadows across the walls. They each sat in silence—legs crossed, backs tall, palms resting on their knees—as though meditating.

Three more Tæcans entered, the master Tæcan with the jaguar mask followed by two Tæcans' aides—one male and one female. The aids wore masks like the other nine Tæcans.

Jung felt chills on his arms seeing the jaguar head—teeth, eyes and all perfectly intact.

The master Tæcan sat on the middle seat.

The two aids squatted by their seats and picked up their pipes which they stuffed with tobacco. They each took a tinder fungus and used the coal to light the pipe. When their pipes were lit they went to each end of the nine Tæcans and began to cleanse them with smoke.

First they placed a hand on the Tæcan's head and whistled a soft tune. Then they blew 2-3 breaths of smoke across the Tæcan's face. They did the same to their chests, backs, legs and sides.

The aids spat in their bucket every few breaths when their mouths filled with resin.

When the first two Tæcans were cleansed the aids moved onto the next in line repeating the action until all nine Tæcans were cleansed. The space became overwhelmed with the smell of tobacco.

During this time the master Tæcan lit his own pipe and performed the same cleansing ritual on himself. To blow smoke on his back and face he blew smoke into the air and used his palm to wash it over himself.

The aids moved around the perimeter of the tent, one on the inside and one on the outside. They blew smoke onto each of the animal skin panels.

Jung hoped the aid on the inside, the woman, wouldn't notice the tear in the fabric. His heart pounded as he watched her approaching. He stepped away from the tear and held his breath.

When she arrived she paused, seeming to study the cut. Then as if realizing halting the ceremony wasn't an option, she blew smoke across the cut and moved on.

Jung sighed in relief.

When the aids had cleansed the space they sat in sync and mimicked the master Tæcan, cleansing themselves.

When everyone was cleansed the master Tæcan nodded at the female aid.

She stood and pulled a lever on one of the uprights. The spirit door in the roof slowly closed, plunging the room into pitch black darkness. The camp was dead quiet aside from the drone of cicadas.

"2993," the master Tæcan said.

Jung heard the Tæcan nearest to the entry stand, the man's knees cracked.

A faint orange light appeared at the head of the tent in front of the stone. A pipe appeared in the glow, then a face. It was the male aid. He lit his pipe.

Tæcan 2993 used the light to navigate his way across the tent and around the stone. He squatted in front of the master Tæcan, his knees cracking again.

The light muted and darkness returned.

Then a different light appeared, a smaller, more subtle light. The flame from the burning tobacco. In the faint light the master Tæcan poured a small amount of ayahuasca into a bowl at his feet. He held the vessel in line with his face and blew two breaths of smoke over the liquid before handing it to Tæcan 2993.

The Tæcan took the vessel with both hands and nodded. He hovered the bowl in line with his heart before moving it up to his temple in line with his third eye. He nodded again and swallowed the liquid in one gulp. He passed the vessel back to the master Tæcan and stood and returned to his seat.

The moment he sat the tinder was closed and darkness returned.

"7928," the master Tæcan said.

Jung heard the next Tæcan in line stand.

The same routine repeated itself until all nine Tæcans had drunk.

Then complete darkness returned. Jung heard only the very shallowest of whispers being exchanged between the three Tæcans at the front. They sounded to be pouring themselves a share of the liquid.

He heard them slurping and the master Tæcan coughing, almost making himself sick. Then the whispers stopped and complete silence enveloped the tent.

Jung woke slumped against the wall of the tent. He had no idea he had even drifted off. He stood and peeked out through the tear. He saw it, exactly how The Architect had described.

The dark cloud was so dense, it contrasted even against the blackness of the room. It seeped through the cracks in the spirit door, pouring down like water. It began to swirl around and around, building in speed and size.

Jung backed away as fast as he could. He used his knife to cut a slit in the outer wall of the tent. He tripped on the loose folds of skin and tumbled onto the cold drifts of ash.

He looked at the tear he had just birthed through. The dark cloud was in the wall of the tent, just beyond the tear. It seemed to have spawned long tentacles stitching the tear closed until it was gone altogether. He stood as fast as he could and ran for the Uzmans' tents. He looked back as he ran.

Far away hundreds of dark figures were standing on the bank of the river. The natives were in a grid formation looking up to the sky where the dark cloud was gathering in size.

Their minds appeared already hijacked.

76

There was a rustling at my door.

Jung was standing in the doorway holding the star.

I waved him inside quickly, my gut whirling with both excitement and fear of another Uzman seeing the treasure.

He followed me.

"You found one," I whispered when we were inside.

He looked around the room suspiciously.

"Can I hold it?"

He put the star into his bag and pulled out his knife.

I took a step back. "What's going on?"

He looked at me with cold eyes. "We need to talk."

"About what?"

"Our deal."

"Our deal? Our deal was a star in exchange for a ticket for a ride in the machine. A ride to see your father."

Jung frowned. "I'm not stupid. I know the pyramid in Egypt is off."

I was composed. "Not Egypt. Here in Nazca. What do you think we are building here?"

He stared at me coldly, seeing right through me. It was clear he was *lost*. It's what we called a native who couldn't be won-over—*lost*.

"Are you okay?" I said.

He squeezed the handle on the knife. "I know you met my father."

I opened my mouth but found no words. Instead my leg started to shake. I hoped he didn't notice.

He said, "You knew all along I was his son didn't you?"

My mind was frazzled, blank. I was tired of the lies, I couldn't keep them up any longer. So again I leaned on the truth hard. "You share many traits in common."

"So you did know?" Jung said.

"It made sense. You look alike and you turned up shortly after Hatun had left the lake looking ill."

"So you saw he was ill."

"Yes, he showed up in a bad way."

Jung frowned. "He wasn't sick when he arrived at the lake."

"Yes he was."

Jung shook his head. "No, he wasn't. You tried your spill on him didn't you? The same spill you gave to me and to Uma. Except he didn't listen."

I felt the skin beneath my eye twitching.

"Just like the jungle people didn't listen, right?" Jung said.

"Not true," I said.

"So what is true?"

"Yes, I met your father, Jung. But he was unhealthy before he arrived at the lake."

"Bull!"

I held my finger to my lips. "Shhhhhhh!"

Jung clenched his teeth and thrust the knife forward. He whispered, "I'll speak as loud as I want."

"What do you think I've done?"

He glared at me. "You killed him."

"What are you on about?"

"You poisoned him, just like you poisoned the jungle people."

"I did not."

He took a step forward.

I stepped back and put my hands up. "You have to understand I am not the one who took your father away, Jung. I'm the one who returns him."

Jung scrunched his face.

"In the future I mean. I return him to you in the future."

"What are you talking about?" Jung said.

"Our deal, it was a star in exchange for a ticket for a ride in the machine. You see right now it doesn't seem this way but you and I make the exchange in the future. You give me the star and I get you a ticket to the pyramid and when you ride in the machine you get into the grid. You pass all the tests with flying colors. Don't you see, you have already traveled to the grid and back. You already have the powers."

"What are you talking about?" Jung said.

A drum sounded from outside. The thuds were so loud they could be heard from anywhere in Nazca.

"How do you think you've been able to sit with your father again?" I said.

"What's that sound?"

"The build has begun."

Jung went to the door and pulled the flap aside. Any moment the blocks would rise on their own and the pyramid would begin to build itself.

"You really think this is the first time you and I have stood here and had this conversation?" I said.

Jung turned, the knife dangling in his hand.

"You and I have been here before, we've been here many times before. We've stood in these very positions and said these very words. Many, many times."

Jung looked confused.

"Don't you see, this isn't my world, Jung. This is yours. It is *your* creation. Your story. You created all of this—everything you see, including me. We're all a figment of your imagination."

Jung took a few steps forward. "What are you talking about?"

"You remember Jung, you do. You've been inside The Great Pyramid. You made it to the control room at the edge of the grid. You've sat on The Watcher's throne. Remember?"

Jung recalled his recurring dream of crawling through tunnels. He remembered the largest chamber in the pyramid turning into a control room. He remembered viewing the collective unconscious in its rawest form.

"You remember, Jung. You've been all the way. You've been inside. And outside."

Jung stepped forward.

I stepped back and came up against the wall of the tent. "But if you kill me, you'll undo it all."

He stopped. "Undo what?"

"If you kill me, you'll never make it to the grid, which means you'll never sit with your father again. Remember, time doesn't exist. It means whatever has happened in the future is influencing right now. In the future, you use the pyramid to travel to the grid. I help you by getting you a ticket. And because you make it through you obtain the ultimate power—to change channels any time you like. But if you kill me, you never ride in the machine, which means you never make it to the grid, which means you never open the channel with your father. The moment I die, he dies."

Jung squeezed the handle of the knife.

"This is just a story, Jung. Your story. Never forget. You are the hero but I am not your villain. I *aid* your triumph, I don't hinder it. The magician always helps the hero, hence why they sit side by side in the archetype wheel."

"What are you on about?"

"I am the magician, the archetype I draw from the collective unconscious. Your father was an artist, he sought innovation. Your uncle is an outlaw, he seeks liberation. And you are the hero, you seek mastery."

"Mastery? Mastery over what?"

"Knowledge, the acquisition of knowledge." I said and smiled. "The ultimate pursuit of the Viracocha. You have managed to acquire all three stripes of knowledge on the path of the Tæcan faster than any Viracochan I know of. You obtained the knowledge from all three books of the Tæcan in three seasons, what typically takes an Uzman 30 rotations. And you reached the control room—the crown band—one floor up from the spirit realm. A place most Tæcans never reach, never mind a Fect or an Uzman like me. I've never met anyone who has sat on The Watcher's throne in the pituitary gland. The *master gland.* Someone who has access to all levels and all channels. And yet here you are. *Miraculous.* Why do you think this is all possible, Jung?"

"Why?"

"Because anything is possible in your imagination. You are a big dreamer, boy. You are the hero because this is *your* world, no one else's. This is your *imagined nation.* And my gosh you've imagined one helluva world. A world I've never seen so large and colorful."

"What are you talking about?" Jung said.

"You constructed it all. Me, this camp, the Tæcans, the sequence of events in your journey, all of it. You constructed all of it. This is your world, no one else's. You killed your father, not me."

Jung took a step forward.

I shifted to the side. "Jung, be careful. Don't you see, your greatness comes from experiencing the loss of someone so close so young. You killed him to make yourself invincible, because death is the greatest teacher."

Jung scowled. "You're just trying to twist my mind."

"Who am *I*, Jung? Who am I really? Think about it, this is *your* world. *You* created me. You needed something to take your father away and so I came to be."

"Not true."

"Do you really believe this, Jung? Come on, if there is one thing you must have learned from your journey it's nothing is what it seems. You want so badly to blame me for what has gone wrong in your life, but can't you see all you're doing is distracting yourself from the truth? You are the author of all of this. You created me, you created the Tæcans, the ceremony, all of the characters you met along your journey. This is your *imagined nation.*"

Jung took a step forward and held the knife a foot from my chest. "It's untrue."

"Don't be so sure. Remember, the easiest person to fool is yourself, Jung."

"I know what you're doing."

"What?" I said.

"You're trying to make me doubt myself."

"You keep talking as if I am a thing beyond you? Jung, I *am* you. I am a splinter of you. Why do you think you despise me so much? Why do you think you believe I killed your father?"

He looked confused.

"Because you see yourself in me. Why? Because you created me from the very parts of yourself you're trying to discard. You constructed me with the sole purpose of conquering me."

"So I do conquer you?" Jung said.

"Don't be so sure you can simply shed those parts of yourself you're at odds with, Jung. It's those parts that put the good parts of you into perspective."

I felt the blade slice my skin. I stepped to the side. "You really want to cut away a piece of *yourself?*"

He smiled. "Yes."

"Do you remember the dial? In the control room?"

Jung froze remembering the lever that could be pushed up or pushed down.

"I've only read about it. What did it say?"

Jung was silent.

"Forward and backward?"

He didn't move.

"Which direction did you push it?"

Jung remembered being in the control room, after his father and mother had disappeared. He saw the collective unconscious, a black cloudy bedrock with tentacles and bubbles rising up. He saw his hand on the lever. Behind him he felt the gaze of The Watcher, a large lizard-looking creature hidden in a black hooded robe. He felt the creature's eyes burning through him. He took his hand off the lever, leaving it set in the middle.

Suddenly there was a bone-chilling scream. A scream that would haunt my dreams for many rotations. There were shouts and more screams then I heard the flaps of tents rustling and running footsteps.

Jung was grinning. "I didn't move it. I didn't move the dial."

"What have you done?" I said.

The smirk grew on his face.

"But what did you do?"

"I'm closing this channel. Remember, like you said, this is my imagined nation."

"What?"

"You poisoned my father, Kon-Tiki. Now, I have poisoned yours."

"What did you do?"

Jung's grin widened. "I poisoned the ayahuasca. Your Tæcans will all soon be dead. And so will your reign."

I squatted and flipped the panel in the floor, I pulled the lever. The hole opened in the floor behind Jung. "Never trust a magician," I said as I pushed him.

Jung fell backward into the hole before he even knew what was happening.

I closed the door which locked shut.

I stood above him. "Jung, have you not learned anything. Never trust a man who's pursuit is *power.*"

77

I followed the combat men out of my tent. There were four of them, each man had a grip on one of Jung's thrashing limbs.

It was chaos outside, there were screams and shouts layered upon a backdrop of beating drums. Combat men ran in all directions and Uzmans of all rank were arguing and pushing one another. Above, the sky was draped in the black cloud pouring from the spirit door of the ceremony tent. Hovering in the swirling blackness were hundreds of stones. Beneath the blocks the natives stood in formation, staring up at the floating objects. It was as if their concentration kept the stones suspended.

Both the sky and the natives shimmered orange. The light reflecting off of them was coming from a large fire near the classroom. The Tæcans' tents appeared to be ablaze.

My eyes stung from the smoke.

The combat men carried Jung to the front of the ceremony tent. I followed quickly, pushing men and women aside. I heard moaning and violent retching before I saw the Tæcans' bodies sprawled across the ground.

They had their hoods down, their wrinkled elongated faces were imprinted with webs of blood pooled just below the surface of their skin. Two of them looked dead already, the others were almost there—choking, shaking, being sick.

"Here is your killer," one of the combat men announced as he kicked Jung to his knees.

Suddenly a second native was thrust to his knees next to Jung. It was Uma.

"And here is the one setting all the fires," the combat man who had apprehended Uma said.

"Kill them both!" I said. "The boy is the one who killed the Tæcans and the man is his uncle."

The mob stared at Jung and Uma—the only two dark faces in the crowd.

"Happily," one combat man said. He raised his axe above Jung's neck.

Suddenly there was a squeal.

The man with the axe fell backwards.

The crowd parted as two long powerful legs thrust into the air. Orion expelled a gush of air.

The mob surged backwards, terrified of the kicking horse.

I jumped back too.

"Leave them alone!" a girl's voice yelled. It was Tika, riding Orion.

Jung and Uma stood.

Jung looked to the sky, his mouth hung open. Later I would learn the pattern the stars had arranged themselves into was identical to the pattern on the note The Architect had given him.

Jung pulled out the note glowing with light. He turned it over and saw a series of verses written on the sheet. The words hadn't been on the note before. Despite not understanding what the characters meant he heard the verses read aloud in his head.

He repeated the words: "Anaconda, anaconda, rise from the earth. Anaconda, anaconda, come forth to protect. Anaconda, anaconda, devour the darkness. Anaconda, anaconda, return peace to the land."

Far away a long shadow rose from the horizon above the basin forests. The giant snaking shape began to slither up and across the sky towards them.

Jung repeated the verses louder.

The mob fell silent as the giant anaconda crowded the sky overhead. It began to wrap itself around the black cloud carrying the stones. The blocks immediately turned to sand that fell from the sky.

I heard the natives shouting to get out of the way, they had clearly broken free from their spell.

Then the anaconda opened its fanged mouth and snapped its jaws around a section of the black mist. It began to devour the dark energy one bite at a time until the cloud was gone. Then the snake left as quickly as it had arrived, speeding back across the sky and plunging into the earth.

The sky was now clear, only the stars of the Milky Way were visible overhead. The pattern of stars was gone.

"Get them!" I yelled. "They control the dark spirits."

A few of the combat men surged forward and seized Jung and Uma. Another few ripped Tika from Orion's back.

The horse reared up and sprinted free from the crowd, crashing through several men as it escaped.

"Kill all of them!" I yelled.

"Wait!" a voice said.

I turned and saw a sea of black bodies surging up from the bank. A stream of natives broke through the crowd. They outnumbered us at least five to one.

"Get off her!" the voice repeated.

The man was a middle-aged Cuzcan man with a thick brown fringe.

"Father!" Tika said, recognizing the man. She had tears in her eyes.

The man ripped the combat men from his daughter's body, knocking several of them to the ground. He hugged his daughter.

Seeing the number of natives, the combat men didn't fight back.

"Let them go," Tika's father said.

The combat men holding Jung and Uma let them go and began to back away.

"Get them now!" I said.

The combat men looked at one another unsure what to do.

Tika pointed at me. "They are the ones who kidnapped me. And *he* is a murderer."

"He killed the jungle people," Jung said.

Tika's father advanced towards me, his fists clenched.

I tried to move backwards but there was nowhere to go. There were people everywhere.

Just as he was about to grab me, a spear whooshed by.

Tika's father squawked and dropped to the ground, the spear buried in his chest.

Tika screamed.

All of the natives turned toward the combat man who had thrown the weapon.

The man looked terrified, like he had just witnessed the moment his life would end. He had.

The natives engulfed the man as he screamed.

Seeing the crowd turn, two more combat men threw spears. The weapons hit two natives who fell to the ground.

Suddenly all of the natives had the same idea. They grabbed the nearest Viracochan they could find and began to punch and kick.

Learning my lesson from the attack at the lake I dropped to my knees and put my hands in the air. I watched a few men attempt to run. They were chased down and beaten and stabbed until they didn't move.

Then everything blurred as I felt a swarm of kicks and punches beat down on me.

78

I was standing thigh deep in the freezing break, the ocean pulling on my robe. The wind was so icy it made even the ocean shiver. The sky was red from the setting Earth Star. I tasted salt on my lips and smelled seaweed.

Jung was standing in front of me. "You understand your mission?"

I nodded.

"Repeat it to me."

"To tell my people not to return," I said.

It had taken us a full dæġ to walk from Nazca to the beach. Along the way Jung had told me every detail of his journey. He said I should know his story to know the lengths his people would go to to protect their land.

"Do you promise to keep your people away?" Jung said.

I nodded, feeling urine warm my thighs.

"Line them up," Jung said. He turned back to the natives. He shouted to clear the sounds of crashing waves. "Line them up!"

The natives surged forward and grabbed at our robes. They pushed us into a line each a man apart. It was just us Uzmans. The combat men and Tæcans were all dead.

Jung waded out into the water and stood in front of me. He pointed down the line. "Move to the middle."

I nodded and pulled up my robe and waded through the cold liquid.

Jung moved with me in the shallows.

When I was close to the middle he pointed. "There, good enough." He smiled. "This will give you a good view."

I looked down, my legs trembling. I had seen enough murder for one dæġ, enough for a lifetime.

"Strip the blue robes," Jung said. He turned down the line. "Strip the blue robes!"

I heard the natives wading through the water then splashing and tussling. The sound of a struggle without voices then stillness.

"Open your eyes," Jung said. He was talking to me.

I looked up and opened my eyes.

He smiled. "Look at them." He nodded down the line in one direction. "White as sea foam."

I looked and saw around a dozen men standing naked in the surf on either side of me, their shivering bodies white as the foam in the waves. They stood among an assortment of men in gray and white robes.

Jung looked me in the eyes. "Kill the blue robes!" he shouted.

I heard yells and fierce splashing. I squinted my eyes closed. There were screams of fear then blunt thuds, the sounds of blades against flesh. Squeals of death. Then silence again. Only the faint sobs from a few of the witnesses.

"Open your eyes," Jung said.

I looked up, my eyes closed.

"Open them."

I opened my eyes. The water was red.

Jung nodded down the line. "Look."

I looked down the line. A dozen men lay dead in the water among the blue robes spreading out like sheets. Streams of bright red snaked from their wounds.

I felt Jung smiling at me, waiting for eye contact.

When our eyes met, he grinned. "Strip the gray robes!"

I felt my body tense.

A flurry of dark bodies moved through the water.

I slipped off my robe as fast as I could and threw it into the surf before the natives could undress me.

"Kill the gray robes!" Jung shouted.

The natives rushed forward again, this time to kill.

"Not this one," Jung said.

The natives coming for me turned instead to the men to my sides.

I heard men dying all around me.

"Remember the message I have told you," Jung said. "The Artery of Earth is closed to your people. Tell your people they are to never set foot on Peru again."

I nodded.

"Now, swim!"

"Where?"

He pointed to the arc in the distance behind me. "For your snail."

I turned and dove into the water and swam as hard as I could. I swam and swam never looking back until I had cleared the range of any spear or arrow.

I turned and treaded water. Far away I saw they had killed every Uzman except me. The shallows were covered with bobbing bodies.

On the shore I saw Wasi with Jung and Tika. And Misi and Potoo too.

Then I saw Uma in the shallows. He was swimming as fast as he could towards me.

Based on real events

The Younger Dryas refers to a period from approximately 12,800 to 11,600 years ago when Earth returned to glacial conditions.

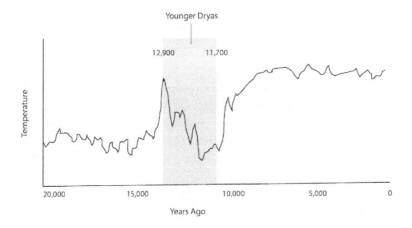

Evidence shows The Younger Dryas was triggered by impacts from several fragments of comet that hit Earth.

While the devastation from the impacts was global, the carnage centered on North America where at the time a two-mile thick sheet of ice covered half the continent.

When one fragment of comet hit this glacial shelf near Washington state, the ice instantly liquified causing a flood of meltwater 1,000 feet high to tear across the land. Caught in this rush of water were blocks of ice as big as oil tankers, which grinded across the earth like erasers.

When the floodwaters reached the coast, sea levels immediately rose. More than 10 million square miles of land—the size of Europe and China combined—were submerged by water.

Fiery ejectors from the comet impacts also ignited wildfires that raged all over Earth, destroying 10% of Earth's vegetation and 25% of Earth's edible biomass.

This ash and debris from the impacts and fires blocked the light from the sun causing temperatures to plummet—Earth was plunged into a 1,200 year thaw.

During this period, tens of millions of large animals perished. In North America, 75% of megafauna went extinct, including: the wooly mammoth, mastodon, saber-tooth tiger, short-faced bear, giant sloth, giant beaver and the dire wolf.

At the same time there was a 30-60% crash in the human population. Quarries mined for centuries by the Clovis people in North America were suddenly abandoned and the use of the distinctive Clovis spear point disappeared for good.

This is also the time when the Flores people, pygmies living in Indonesia, disappeared from the fossil record.

Today, there is no question whether a comet hit Earth 12,800 years ago. *The Comet Research Group*, a consortium of 60+ scientists from 16 countries, have put together an undeniable case for the *Younger Dryas comet hypothesis*.

The question isn't whether a comet hit Earth, but rather *how much was mankind impacted by this event?* And *how much of our knowledge and achievements were lost forever?*

The fact is 10-12,000 years ago is credited as the beginnings of just about everything we associate with human culture and civilization, whether it's the dispersion of languages, the emergence of agriculture, the first city, the domestication of animals, the genesis of religion. Over and over, the same dates show up.

What if these artifacts aren't evidence of the *beginnings* of civilization but rather the *rebooting* of civilization? Are we seeing the fingerprints from an advanced people whose growth was severely stunted and perhaps even lost in a 1,200 year ice age? People who clearly knew a lot more about engineering, astronomy and global navigation than mainstream historians would dare to admit.

Take Göbekli Tepe in Turkey, perhaps the most obvious fingerprint of an advanced ancient people. The enormous megalithic site has been dated to at least 11,500 years ago. The discovery of Göbekli Tepe in 1994 pushed back the estimated birth of agriculture by more than 5,000 years and the estimated birth of religion by more than 2,000 years. The site is archeology's greatest crown jewel after The Great Pyramid of Giza, and yet in 25 years less than 5% of the site has been excavated.

Göbekli Tepe is the oldest known perfectly north-south aligned site, it appears almost like an astronomy deck for reading the sky. The site features dozens of enormous classroom-like structures made from stones—some heavier than 50 tons—arranged in circles with a t-shaped obelisk in the center. The obelisks feature detailed etchings of animals, constellations and iconography matched by objects found in Peru and Egypt.

The most puzzling thing about Göbekli Tepe is that it was deliberately buried around 10,000 years ago. It's as if its inhabitants were trying to preserve its knowledge for us to find.

Twelve-thousand years ago also shows up in Egypt. Twist the stars back 12,000 years and the three Pyramids of Giza line up perfectly with Orion's Belt, while The Sphinx lines up with the constellation of Leo, and the Nile River with the Milky Way. Coincidence or design? You be the judge but keep in mind Ancient Egyptians believed the soul of the dead entered the sky through Orion's Belt and travelled along the Milky Way in order to enter the next life.

Atlantis also dates back 12,000 years. Although "Atlantis" has become a career-killing word among archeologists, the myth matches perfectly with the date of the Younger Dryas comet impacts and resulting flooding. There is only one record of Atlantis, it comes from Plato who lived 3,000 years ago. He describes how his uncle Solon visited Egypt and was told by a priest that 9,000 years earlier (aka 12,000 years ago) there was a great civilization that fell in a mighty flood.

Go back even further to Ganung Padang in Indonesia where an enormous pyramid two thirds the height of The Great Pyramid in Egypt dates back at least 20,000 years. And many geologists argue The Sphinx in Egypt is just as old, erosion from months of prolonged rain suggests The Sphinx was standing long before the Younger Dryas impacts, perhaps thousands of years before.

I became obsessed with this period of history after coming into contact with Graham Hancock's books: Fingerprints of the Gods, Magicians of the Gods and America Before. Hancock presents robust evidence advanced people existed before the time of The Younger Dryas. His research forges geological and archeological evidence with ancient myths told by more than 2,000 cultures. All of whom recall a great flood thousands of years ago.

I was drawn to Hancock's research not just because of his overwhelming evidence but also the aggravation I felt towards the science community's reluctance to embrace these new findings. Graham Hancock like many is considered a heretic within the science community because his ideas challenge the research and work done by others. Even though he was the first to theorize a comet hitting Earth, an idea he had when looking for a reason why so many civilizations collapsed all at once around 12,000 years ago.

Of course, it makes sense. If all your life you've written books and papers stating Egypt is 3,500 years old, you are going to be compelled to turn a blind eye when new evidence arrives challenging your dates. This is likely why Egyptologists have refused to investigate an enormous void found above The King's Chamber in The Great Pyramid of Giza, they are afraid of what they might find.

And it's not just in Egypt where history is being stunted by an incentive to maintain the status quo.

Excavation at Göbekli Tepe is moving at a snail's pace. Less than 5% of Göbekli Tepe has been excavated in 25 years, despite it being arguably the greatest anthropological discovery of the 20th century.

The pyramid in Ganung Padang, Indonesia, has been abandoned altogether after rival archeologists convinced The President to redirect funding to other projects.

Thankfully people like Graham Hancock are giving these sites the attention they deserve.

This book is my way to do the same. I wanted to cast the spotlight on a time in history long forgotten. A time when I believe our ancestors surpassed us in many ways from the way they designed buildings in tune with Earth to how they navigated transcendence and the spirit realm.

I think we laugh too easily at the notion of our ancestors surpassing us in intelligence or achievements. I think we've been brainwashed by the five-stage image of a monkey becoming a man. We believe mankind has always trended up and to the right, becoming better and better. I don't think so. I think mankind had something big and lost it. And I think it was lost during the Younger Dryas.

CPSIA information can be obtained
at www.ICGtesting.com
Printed in the USA
BVHW040418020222
627777BV00019B/643